LEGEND UNDONE

LEGEND UNDONE

ANGIE DAY

RAHNE
PRESS

Rahne Press is a publisher in the United States. The city of publication is Cedar City, Utah.

www.angiedayauthor.com

Library of Congress Control Number: 2019908391
Cataloging-in-Publication Data is available upon request.

ISBN: 978-1-7338144-0-9 (hardcover)
ISBN: 978-1-7338144-2-3 (paperback)
ISBN: 978-1-7338144-1-6 (e-book)

Edited by Suzanne Johnson
Cover Design by Sarah Hansen at www.okaycreations.com
Interior Formatting by Chris Lucas at www.eightlittlepages.com

First printed in the United States of America.
10 9 8 7 6 5 4 3 2 1

For my first child.
I wrote this book while waiting for you.

CHAPTER
ONE

Two Decades Ago

My hand gripped her fragile human arm. Her warm energy waited just beneath her skin. I stared down at her wide eyes and quivering lip. My desire coaxed her energy out as it eagerly left her cells and fused into mine.

My body instantly recognized the warm flood rushing into me. Power charged through me as she faded. My vision sharpened with fresh intensity as chills spread across my back. I loved that feeling.

The sound of a giggle came from behind me, pulling at my attention. I rolled my eyes and focused back on the human dangling from my grip. I siphoned enough energy to slow her heart rate, now almost too faint to hear.

I released her arm, and she thudded to the ground. I looked down at the human, her little heart pattering on. The familiar guilt swept in, threatening to drown out the roaring energy in my body.

"Done," I called as I turned my back on the human.

"Already?" Nikki asked.

She wrapped her hand around the arm of a man. The

dazed human stood helpless as Nikki pulled his energy into her body. Her free hand pushed her long, black braid over her bare shoulder.

Nikki only tied up her hair during a fight or a hunt. It was convenient, and it let people see the series of diamond studs that went up her left ear.

"Not all of us like to play with our food." I stared at her, crossing my arms in front of me.

Nikki smiled and glared at the same time as the man's knees buckled. His eyes closed as her hand pulled away from him. I couldn't hear a heartbeat. Nikki stepped over his body and walked toward me.

"Hey, don't mock." She grabbed my right arm and twisted it to show the underside.

We both looked at the embedded mark on my arm, centered perfectly between my elbow and my wrist. The black dagger pointing toward my hand shimmered brilliantly.

The mark of the Shadows.

"These pretty marks don't come cheap." Nikki grinned as she looked at her own arm with the same dagger.

She was the one responsible for giving all the new Shadows their marks. She had mastered destroying cells so beautifully that it was almost a form of art watching her work.

We were what the humans called Legends. Our abilities were inherited from an experiment done generations back. Brilliant but irrational scientists created a set of serums targeting five areas of the brain to enhance and extend human ability on a cellular level.

Despite the era, the experiment worked. The result was us, the creation that the majority of the human race never wanted to admit actually existed, the Legends.

"Takes a lot of energy to make these, and our fearless

leader is bringing in more Shadows lately." Nikki dropped my arm.

Nikki didn't just use her power for the Shadows. Black, curved lines spread across the brown skin on her back like wings. The markings reached over her shoulders and down her arms, almost reaching her elbows.

The enhancements from the original creation of Legends affected the way our minds react with or control individual cells. We called these the Five Levels. The abilities allowed us to create, change, read, and destroy cells. The rarest ability was to extract energy from other Legends.

The actual order of the powers was irrelevant. Each Legend had his or her own talent, and it only mattered how many each possessed.

Nikki peered down at the woman lying near my feet. She stared, probably trying to gauge whether or not the woman was still breathing. A nervous lump formed in my throat.

"Speaking of Alec," I said in a rush. "Let's head back."

"You miss your boyfriend so much that you can't finish off this one's energy?" Nikki raised an eyebrow at me as she bent down.

She grabbed the human's wrist, yanking it up as she stood.

I looked at the woman stirring with the movement. My stomach twisted. A thought nagged in the back of my mind. *This wasn't right.*

My gaze flicked back up to Nikki's cutting brown eyes. She stared at me, a smile playing on her lips.

"Come on, Mara," she said. "You know the last bit is the best. Don't you want it?"

Being ruthless was a requirement to be a Shadow. Even after a lifetime with them, I wasn't sure if I had it. But I had gone too far to turn back now. I was a member of the council and had been a Shadow for as long as I could remember.

I listened to the sound of the woman's heart. My hand reached forward, sensing the warmth of her energy. Nikki was right. The final burst of life was always the sweetest, enough to make my toes curl.

"We could leave her alive," I muttered.

The guilt reverberating through my body silenced as my mind focused on how much I wanted the energy. My mouth watered.

"Why? She's just a human. You're a Shadow. This is what we're made for." Nikki narrowed her eyes as she moved the woman's wrist closer to me.

I touched the woman's hand, sliding my fingers under Nikki's to take hold of her wrist. Nikki let go and watched me. The energy swirled through my palm. The woman took her final breath, and her energy gave one last cry as it left her body. A gust of sweet release caressed any worry away.

My breathing sped as the power mixed with the rest. I dropped the woman's hand, and her body fell to the ground again.

My fingers twitched with the new energy. I caught Nikki looking at me. Her eyes stared a little too long.

"You're right. You should head back to the mansion." Nikki nodded toward me.

"I can help cover this up." I shook my head.

"No, I've got this." Nikki stopped my hand.

"What's going on? I mean, I know it'd be easier for you with all that destroying talent, but you never get stuck with cleanup." I pulled my eyebrows together, pausing to look at her again.

Her eyes looked at my face a little too deeply. The longer she gazed, the louder the voice in the back of my head spoke up to tell me something was off.

"Go see Alec," she said, and my questions vanished.

At the sound of his name, I forgot the humans lying around us. I didn't care about making their deaths look like accidents, or the fact that Nikki never offered to do cleanup duty. Each of my concerns died instantly.

I turned toward home and ran. I crossed over the grassy expanse that became more isolated the closer I got.

The mansion was hidden away in the forgotten parts of the American Midwest. The only things that surrounded the building were scraggly trees and dry grass that always waited for rain.

When I arrived at the mansion, I gazed at the familiar, towering pillars and the resilient stone walls. It may not look like home to most people—it was too lavish and cold for that—but it had everything I needed. I had been brought into the Shadows when I was little, and they were the only family I had known.

As I descended into the valley that concealed the mansion, bigger trees became denser but not enough to block out the sun. Dead leaves covered the bare dirt. Nothing could grow in the path where the Shadows walked in and out daily.

The heavy, metal doors to the mansion rose just ahead. I concentrated on the air molecules in front of them and created more, rapidly multiplying the density of the air. A few steps away from the door, my body hit the denser air. I coaxed the cells to move enough to shove the doors open, revealing the Shadow guards standing just inside.

My steps didn't falter as the energy dissipated from my body to perform the act of opening the doors. So much energy remained that the loss barely mattered.

I wandered down the grand hall studded with golden wall sconces and ornate molding near the ceiling. I needed to find Alec and report to him about the trip, but really just to see him. The unsettled feeling in my stomach didn't go away. I still thought about Nikki, about the woman.

I turned the corner and almost ran into Thayer leaning against the wall. His brown hair and olive skin reflected the incandescent light from the wall sconces in the hallway. He was the type of person who was so attractive he didn't have a sense of personal space.

"Bright smile, no personal bubble, and waiting in dark corners." I smiled at him. "It must be Thayer Cade."

He laughed as he put an arm around my shoulders, pulling me even closer. I stood a few inches shorter than Thayer's height. He had his classic five o'clock shadow that he sported no matter the time of day, but that was only to distract from his bright, caramel-colored eyes.

"Sharp blue eyes, shiny blond hair," he said as he stroked a hand through my hair. I turned my head and snapped my teeth at his fingers. "And a little feisty. It must be Mara."

"Did you ever doubt it?" I raised an eyebrow at him.

Thayer shrugged easily. "I don't know, with your talent for changing, you could fool any of us here."

As a Level Three, I could create, change, and destroy cells. Changing had always come easily to me, far more than any other Shadow here. I still envied Alec and Thayer for being Level Fours, though. Even between the two of them, Alec was stronger, or at least willing to go further to get what he wanted.

"So, where's Nikki?" Thayer asked, running a finger along my arm.

"She stayed to clean up." I stepped around him and kept moving farther into the mansion.

"Hold on, hold on. Nikki Cortez actually volunteered?" Thayer scoffed as he followed me, a little too close for comfort.

"Yup. Thought it was weird too." I slowed my walk when I heard Thayer mutter under his breath.

He didn't say anything else, and the silence made me even more disconcerted than before. I stopped walking and turned around to look at him.

He had a strange expression on his face that I couldn't quite identify. I focused on his eyes and tried to study them. The deeper I bored into his brown irises, the more I wanted to see. The energy in my body blazed and pushed me beyond my normal abilities.

A peculiar feeling came over me. The longer I looked, the more I understood him.

In a flash, a series of images played in my mind.

A room filled with boxes and old furniture. The dust scattered into the dank air. The stone floor matched the style that ran through the entire mansion.

In the back corner, a wooden cabinet stood tall. The shining finish hadn't seen the sun in ages. The door to the cabinet opened, revealing a hidden safe. A small metal box with a number pad.

A hand typed in the code. Five numbers in a row. The lights flashed green. The metal door to the safe popped open, cracked enough to make me want to look inside.

Just as the door to the safe was about to open, the image faded.

I was still looking at Thayer's eyes but had to force myself to focus back on them, instead of the images. I shuddered at the lingering feeling.

It wasn't real. It was like watching a daydream.

Thayer narrowed his eyes and kept looking at me. He wasn't just concentrating. He was questioning. I shook my head. This didn't make sense.

"What just…" I turned around to leave again.

Thoughts spun in my head faster than I could breathe. I had never felt anything like that before. *What was it?* I needed an answer. I needed Alec.

"Wait, wait…" Thayer grabbed my arm and pulled me around to face him.

I snatched his arm and twisted his wrist backward until I heard the satisfying pop that told me the bone had broken.

"Stop me again and I'll do more than snap your wrist." I released his hand when I finished talking.

Thayer twisted his arm back into place and smoothed his shirt. The immense amount of energy racing through his body would heal the break in a matter of minutes. As Shadows, we consumed and spent energy freely because it cost us nothing.

"Understood." Thayer flashed his sexy grin.

A flurry of butterflies sputtered inside of me at the sight of his brilliant smile set in contrast to his dark-toned skin. Thayer excelled at changing emotions, just like I excelled at changing my own appearance. It was a huge part of what made him deadly. No one wanted to hurt him, and he made sure of that.

Any thoughts I had were silenced again. I stared at his eyes, and all I wanted was to just stand here, breathing with my mouth open.

"Why aren't you ever this excited to see me?" Thayer huffed.

That comment snapped me back to the present moment. I shoved Thayer away with both hands.

"Because I love him. You, I simply tolerate." I smiled and raised my effortlessly arched eyebrow at him, waiting for his response.

"Tolerate, huh?" Thayer taunted as a smile played on his lips.

He stepped close enough to throw off my balance. As soon as my concentration lapsed, he took over. I didn't have time to close my eyes before the connection between us solidified.

My tense muscles relaxed enough to melt me into the stone floor. My heartbeat raced faster. All I could think about was the person standing in front of me. I wanted him closer. I wanted to do anything just to make him smile.

Love was the strongest thing he could make anyone feel. My smile grew as I recognized exactly what he was doing. The emotions had come on too suddenly and were too out of place to be genuine.

They weren't mine.

Knowing that, I was able to separate my actions from my emotions. I stepped forward and tried to keep my breathing steady, focusing on that instead of what my body and mind told me to feel.

"I take it back," I whispered and smiled up at him.

He held a steady gaze on me, concentrating all of his attention to keep the illusion going. I could tell he wanted to say something, but he couldn't talk and take me down at the same time.

"I shouldn't even tolerate you," I said as my smile fell.

Thayer was surprised enough to lose his connection. The heavy emotions vanished instantly. I dropped to the floor and swung my leg around to knock Thayer off his feet. As I stood back up, Thayer pulled me with him. We both crashed to the floor, laughing all the way down.

As we sat up with easy smiles on our faces, my eyes caught something just past Thayer. He had distracted me enough to nearly miss the other council members leaving a room barely within my view. I glanced at Thayer, who pretended not to notice anything. My mind tried to understand how there could have been a council meeting without Alec or me present. I searched until my eyes found what they needed.

The last person to exit the room was Alec Stone, leader of the Shadows. His deep blue eyes locked on mine, and my mind ignited at the sight of him. I stood as he caught sight of me. I gazed at his dark blond hair and sharply beautiful features. I had seen the humans' version of a male model. Alec blew every single one of them out of the atmosphere. His smile broke through the empty air in front of us.

"Finally," I breathed and stepped around Thayer to the person I wanted most.

The vast amount of human energy charged through my body, making my fingertips tingle. We rushed into each other's arms. Neither of us bothered with a greeting. Alec reached down and kissed me deeply. His hands touched either side of my head, pulling me closer like I was his prize possession. My already-racing heart soared even faster.

"Welcome back, Mara." Alec's soft lips moved against my mouth.

My body lit up. I leaned away from him and brushed my hair behind my ear.

"Was there a council meeting?" I asked, not fooled by Alec's sorry distraction attempt. "Without Nikki and me?"

I may still have been riddled with leftover emotion from Thayer, but I wasn't about to miss the fact that as the leader, Alec was the only one with the authority to organize the council.

"Yes," Alec answered and didn't even flinch about not informing me. "It was last-minute and nothing you need to concern yourself with, sweetheart."

His calm voice smoothed over my anger. I leaned into him and held him closer. He was the kid I had grown up with and the man I had fallen in love with, all at the same time. I glanced at Thayer. He stared at Alec's eyes just above my head long enough that Alec could be reading his mind. The look on Thayer's face changed as he broke his gaze and looked at me. I pulled away to say something, but before I could, Alec cleared his throat.

"Let's get out of here. I'm starving." He grinned and nodded toward the front doorway.

"No, I just got back..." I protested before Alec bent down and snaked his arms around my legs. In one motion, he lifted me up and over his shoulder.

"Aw, come on, baby. It's not like you to say no," he taunted as he walked with me slung over his shoulder.

"Put me down." I laughed and smacked his back.

His easy steps proved that my weight was inconsequential to his strength. As he faced the door I had just entered, my hands clamped on his shoulder and I tossed my body weight forward. I held on as I spun over him and landed with my feet on the ground.

I turned and crouched into a defensive stance, ready for Alec's countermove. He had stooped just as low as me. He inched closer, moving away from the tall candle holders that framed the doorway, and I smiled.

"Don't you want to be with me?" he asked playfully, his words dripping with sweetness.

I lunged forward as if I was going to barrel into him. He crouched instantly, his arms shooting out to stop me. At the last second, I jumped off my final step and flipped over his lowered body instead. My feet landed silently on the floor behind him. His arms caught empty air as he stumbled forward. He stood slowly and turned around to face me.

"Clever, as always," he said, smiling with what looked like admiration in his eyes. I shrugged my shoulders and looked back at him.

"I tend to get what I want." I smiled too.

"What is it that you want?" He stepped close enough for me to feel his chest rising with each breath.

The color of his eyes seemed cool, but the intensity they held was hot enough to start a fire. I loved the way his eyes could hold my gaze longer than anyone else's could. When I looked at him, I never wanted to look away.

"You." I smiled and ran my hand up his chest.

His body heat radiated against my hand. My fingers dragged across his muscles, over his heart, and up to the collar of his shirt. When my hand finally reached the skin of his neck, Alec grabbed it and laced my fingers in his.

"Right answer." He smiled, and his dark blue eyes gleamed.

The sound of someone clearing his throat from around the corner interrupted. I sighed as I turned around. I already knew who would be eavesdropping.

"You coming, Thayer?" Alec called back and waited for Thayer to step around the corner.

"Thought you'd never ask," he said as he cracked his knuckles.

Alec looked at the doors in front of us. I didn't even see him concentrate before light split up the middle of the doors. They swung out of our way as we walked through. The daylight lightened Alec's dark blond hair as he stepped out onto the loose dirt of the path.

Energy pounded in my body, exciting my every nerve. The empty grass fields and dead leaves sprawled out in front of me.

As soon as my black tennis shoes hit the ground, I ran.

CHAPTER
TWO

Small, tangled trees whipped by us as our feet pounded the earth.

Legends ran much faster than normal humans could. Not fast enough that they couldn't see us, but certainly fast enough that they couldn't catch us.

It must be annoying to move so slowly all the time. I thought.

Alec turned around to look back at me instead of ahead. His eyes glimmered with excitement the way they always did when he looked at me. A smile broke across my mouth. Just a second later, I realized that he should have paid attention to where he was going.

"Alec!" I warned just before he collided into a person.

We were far enough from the mansion that the dried grass had turned to baked dirt. Thayer and I skidded to a stop when we heard Alec and the man tumble to the ground.

"Hey, watch where you're going." The man lifted himself up and glowered at the rest of us. The woman behind him looked at all three of us. Her eyebrows shot up.

"Shadows," she breathed as her eyes froze on our arms.

She grabbed the man next to her and dug her nails into him with one hand. With the other hand, she grabbed the leather strap to the bag slung over her shoulder. The leather flap covering the bag had a peace symbol burned into it.

Ironic. I smiled.

Matching black marks in the shape of a dagger adorned each of our right forearms. If the couple recognized it and knew we were Shadows, it meant they were either Legends or well-educated humans. Judging by the defined level of their beauty and the careful way they held themselves, I knew exactly what they were.

"Well, if it isn't two Legends out for a stroll," Alec taunted as he brushed off the dirt from his jeans and maroon plaid shirt rolled up to his elbows to emphasize the dagger marked on his arm.

"Sorry, we didn't mean to…" the woman groveled and backed up.

Her brown, bushy hair framed her concerned face. She swiped at the man, trying to pull him away with her.

"Relax." I put my hands in the air. "We have no quarrel with you. We're just out hunting."

I smiled and flicked my eyebrows up. Alec smiled back at me before he turned his attention back to the on-looking Legends.

"Rogues," Thayer scoffed at the couple.

His eyes were glib and malicious in a way that shouldn't work together, but they somehow did on Thayer. For someone so involved in other people's emotions, he was excellent at turning off his own when he needed to, or when Alec asked him to.

Most Legends took small amounts of energy from many people to coexist peacefully. The humans didn't notice, and those Legends lived long, happy lives. Thayer called them

Rogues because in his mind we were the real Legends. To a Rogue, the humans were in charge. As Shadows, we hated everything about that life.

Living on too little energy, lying to everyone they met. The life of a Rogue was quiet, simple, and nothing like life at the mansion. I couldn't even imagine it all the way. It was like the thoughts didn't fit together in my mind, as if the pathway had been broken.

"Hunting? You honestly call it that?" the man snarled at me.

My eyes darted back to the sound of defiance and scanned him up and down. Jeans and a brightly colored shirt, just like all the humans wore. This Legend couldn't look more pathetic if he tried.

"Excuse me?" I asked as I detected the threat in his voice and stepped forward defensively in front of Alec.

Someone as powerful as Alec didn't need my protection, but I wasn't about to let anyone close to him if I could stop it.

"It's not just an animal you're killing, it's a human," the man countered aggressively.

All Legends needed human energy to survive. However, as Shadows, we took far more than was necessary. We didn't just survive. We actually enjoyed living and using our powers. That idea didn't always sit well with the other Legends.

"Aren't they the same thing?" Alec sneered playfully. I relaxed slightly when I saw the banter was a mere game to him.

"That kind of reckless behavior is the reason we have to hide. Humans won't accept us because they believe we're too dangerous," the woman reprimanded, now as fired up as her partner.

I saw the direction this conversation pointed and for one fleeting moment, I felt bad for them. Usually, no Legend was stupid enough to confront any Shadow, let alone a group of them. They were trying to be brave, and Alec loved crushing misplaced bravery.

"Who said we need their acceptance?" Thayer growled as he finally stepped into the argument. His muscles tightened with his fists balled at his side. He was an intense sight to behold, especially when he was angry.

"Don't you want to live without hiding?" The woman begged but kept her eyes firmly locked on the ground.

"We're not hiding." I glared at her. "You are."

"We all are," the woman said, barely above a whisper, and finally ventured a look up. "If we all just coexisted peacefully, they wouldn't have a reason to hate us."

It was odd that she honestly wanted us to pity their situation. I hadn't seen a true relationship with a human and a Legend before. I watched her carefully, waiting to see her motivation and, in part, to understand her.

"Yeah, that's not how that works. 'Hi, I'm a Legend who could kill you at any moment. If you don't attack me, I won't attack you. Let me know if you need a cup of sugar.' Your idea of coexisting isn't an option," Thayer mocked, stalking toward the woman.

She stiffened the closer he got to her. The man eyed Thayer nervously. The woman didn't even budge. Thayer was threatening, to say the least, but when his intriguing brown eyes locked on someone, the person never moved.

I looked the woman up and down. Slacked-jawed and wearing a nervous gaze, she was caught.

Charles, Alec's father and founder of the Shadows, had discovered Thayer when Alec and I were teenagers. He always said the three of us were a perfect combination. Alec could change the mind, I could change the physical body, and Thayer could change the heart.

I crossed my arms, drumming my fingers against my bare skin, and turned back to Alec.

"Not all of us are looking for a picket fence and a porch. We don't want to live with limited energy and pretend we're one of them when we're so clearly not. We are better than them." Alec smiled at the woman when her eyes darted to look at him.

He nodded slowly, as if she was too simpleminded to understand that living like the humans was a definite step down. If we did, we couldn't take all of their energy. We would have to give up all of our power.

"You can't beat them," the man challenged.

"You're afraid of a human?" Thayer scoffed.

"Humans. Plural. They have labs with weapons designed specifically for us. There are far too many people for any of us to overpower," the man explained, as if he could make us agree with him.

Legends, both Rogue and Shadows, hated living under the humans' oppression. We just had different ways of how to remedy that.

"Two labs that I have never heard anything interesting from are hardly a concern. And anyway, shouldn't you be happy about us hunting them? We're just evening the odds." Alec smiled and glanced over at me.

He saw the flecks of emotion in my eyes and winked at me. It reminded me that we were in this together. I took a breath and remembered that he was the one I swore to side with, no matter what.

"What's your plan? To kill all of them?" The man snorted, knowing that was both impossible and would eliminate our main power source.

"Look, all of us are Legends. All of us need human energy. All of us want to live—" Alec started.

"Not all of us need to live like you," the woman interrupted him, finally showing a fraction of a spine in this conversation.

"Because you're so noble?" Alec challenged back to her. "Tell me you wouldn't want to have all the energy you could consume. Tell me you don't fantasize about being able to flaunt your superior abilities to the world. You may think it's wrong, but can you tell me that you don't wish it?"

The couple went silent.

The man looked at the ground while the woman still glanced nervously between Alec and Thayer. Humans posed a threat to us, but in truth, we needed them. We needed their energy to survive. None of the Shadows wanted all the humans dead. We wanted them to be submissive.

"Why don't we call a truce, and we'll let you keep walking?" Alec offered.

He looked over at me and watched my shoulders relax. I didn't want Alec to hurt them. Despite the torture I rained down on the humans, Legends were part of us, even the Rogues.

Alec's eyes flashed the slightest hint of worry. This was the one point on which we always disagreed.

"You don't control us." The man raised his arms and looked directly at Alec.

It wasn't a statement. It was a challenge. One that the man would lose.

"You need to stop talking," Thayer warned and looked over at his leader.

"Give me one good reason," the man said, turning the threat to Thayer.

"You know, I think Mara may have misspoken earlier." Alec reached down and picked up a thin stick, twirling it in his hand.

Looking at it spinning around his fingers, it seemed harmless. My stomach fluttered at the sight of Alec's smirk lifting his mouth.

Alec looked down at the stick, and it slowly rose into the air. While hovering a few inches above his hand, the wood changed into a sleek metal. The very cells of the object altered to match what Alec coached them to be.

After a few seconds, the object became a mirror image of the dagger marked into his skin.

Without a word, the blade shot forward, obeying the changing air around it. Alec's eyes focused on the flying object, and my eyes followed. It halted before reaching the man's chest. He had his hands held up in protection, but he must have had just enough energy to force the air to stop the dagger. He looked up and smiled.

"And they say you guys are dangerous," he laughed.

The sound reached my ears first. The slick thunk of the dagger piercing through skin echoed in the air. My eyes flashed up to Thayer standing behind the man with one hand pressed into the guy's back and his other hand grabbing his shoulder.

I hadn't even seen Thayer move because I was too focused on the flying dagger. I wasn't the only one who'd made that mistake.

"Our quarrel is with you," Alec answered as the man sunk to his knees.

Excess human energy could have healed his wound faster than normal, maybe even allowing him to live. Most Legends didn't keep enough in their bodies for a feat like that, and this man had just used his energy to stop the first assault. Alec knew exactly what he was doing.

The woman shot forward. Within seconds, I had created a dagger in my own hand, barely even noticing the energy it took to do it. I ran forward until I stood a few inches in front of her, the tip of the blade pointing directly toward her heart. She froze but didn't look away from her partner.

The hilt of the dagger protruding from the center of the man's back as he fell forward. Thayer looked at his hand until the blood changed to a clear liquid—water. Then he wiped his hand off and stepped over the man.

I focused on the woman standing in front of me.

"Please don't," she whimpered as she finally looked up at me.

I didn't see her as a threat the way Alec did. I saw a fellow Legend. I saw the fear in her eyes and her trembling lip. She was just a woman, scared for her life.

"Alec?" I called quietly.

When I turned my head, he was standing by my side. My hand shook slightly. I didn't want to hurt this woman. I couldn't see a reason why I should. I looked into his dark eyes to give me a way out.

"We tried to show mercy," Alec whispered and brushed his finger along my defined cheekbone.

Hate filled my body. It penetrated every bone, every muscle, and every nerve. The intense feeling made my hands shake and my breath short.

We did try to take the high road, I agreed in my mind.

I squared my shoulders and took in another breath. My vision sharpened as I stared into his eyes, and my senses alerted. The handle of the blade was stiff in my hand, the cloth covering the woman's shoulder was soft, and Alec's hand on me was warm and strong.

"They threatened us," Alec emphasized, and his hand brushed my hair behind my ear.

My eyes turned back to the woman, and anger flooded through me. I tensed my muscles and tightened my grip on the blade. I forced it forward, just slightly. The woman sucked in a breath, rapidly shaking her head.

The anger in me seemed out of place now. Before I felt or thought anything else, Alec's voice cut in.

"They want to force us into groveling to the humans. We want to thrive," his calm voice tinged with excitement as he watched my eyes harden. I glanced over to Thayer, who had his stare trained on me, not saying a word.

Why was he concentrating so har—the thought hadn't finished before the next words reached my ears.

"Who is stopping us?" Alec asked loud enough to interrupt my internal debate.

His voice sent chills down my spine. He knew the answer to the question. It had been trained into both of our minds for most of our lives.

My eyes snapped back to the cowering woman in my arms. The only reason humans thought they could keep us down was weak Legends like this couple. They wanted to live with the humans and actually befriend them. That was never the Shadows' intention. We wanted to dominate.

Pride infused every cell of my body. The striking mark on my arm gleamed in the sunlight. The physical dagger in my hand fit what I wanted to do.

We were doing the right thing.

We were helping future generations of Legends.

More than anything, we needed to show the humans that we were something of which to be terrified. The need for dominance crashed through me.

I had a choice to make. I could listen to that annoying reminder in my stomach that this woman had done nothing wrong and that, especially being a fellow Legend, I should let her live. On the other hand, I could listen to the voice ringing in my mind and the emotions racing through my veins.

One choice was far more alluring than the other. I already knew what I would choose. It was what I always chose.

I plunged the dagger forward into her chest. Not a shred of guilt infected me before I switched my grip on the handle and yanked downward, opening the deadly wound farther.

"That's my girl." Alec smiled and lowered his hand to wrap around my waist.

As she fell from my grip, Alec pulled me close to him. His body replaced hers. One less person to get in the way of us living the life we deserved.

Relief washed into my heart as I looked at Alec's proud eyes and Thayer's relaxed shoulders.

"So, I heard there was going to be something to eat..." Thayer reminded us both. Alec lifted his head and looked at his best friend.

"First, take care of this." Alec gestured to the bodies on the ground. "Wolves roam in this area. Make sure it looks like our friends ran into a few of them. You can follow along when you're done."

"Whatever you say, boss." Thayer sighed and bent down to grab the ankle of the man, starting the job Alec had given him.

"After you." I smiled and patted Alec on the shoulder.

I grinned at Thayer. He shrugged it off with a faint smile and walked away. He always did. I spun on my heels and raced after Alec toward the nearest town.

I shook off the weight of the deaths that lay behind me. My feet carried me forward, and my mind focused on the two things that made me happy.

Alec and energy.

CHAPTER
THREE

When we returned, the night went on as usual.

I walked into two Shadows trying to create something strong enough that not even Nikki could destroy it. She was at home, so her lengthy black hair lay loose around her brown shoulders. About fifteen Shadows filled the courtyard to watch the others face her.

To her, it was an easy game because she always won.

We all challenged each other to push the limits of our abilities. The more we used them, the less energy we needed in our bodies to fuel our power. One human's entire energy reserve was enough to live on for a few days, if we didn't waste it too much on our powers. It was a normal evening with the Shadows, a life I was accustomed to loving.

Despite the ample distraction, I could not shake the images of the room and the safe from Thayer's mind replaying in my head.

A flicker of Thayer's brown eyes forced the memory to flare into my mind. A flash of his smile, and I could touch the feeling. When I looked at him, all I could see was the room and the locked safe I had imagined in his eyes.

After failing at trying to overlook the recurring flashes, I finally heeded my instinct. I slipped away from the crowd and walked off to find this room stuck in my head. If it even existed. I found the wooden door tucked at the end of a hallway that I never bothered to go down.

Dust coated the lights on the walls of the hall. The only rooms here were for storage. I put my hand against the warm wood and pushed the door open.

I knew where to look already. I had never snooped around here before, but I could clearly see the target in my mind. In the back of the room stood the object of my recent obsession—a tall, wooden armoire. I walked past the dusty boxes and covered furniture.

I opened the door to the cabinet and saw the safe that I knew would be sitting there. I moved my fingers over the numbers and typed in the code as my mind showed a picture of someone typing in the same code.

The lights above the numbers flashed green just as they had in the image.

My heart throbbed in my chest. Questions churned through my mind. I turned the knob and the safe door popped open. I had not been able to see what was inside from the earlier images. The memory or thought had stopped just before.

It wasn't a daydream. It was real.

I'm not sure what I was expecting to find. Maybe I was hoping it would be nothing. Inside, I saw a picture of a locket lying along the front of the safe. An ornate oval attached to a simple chain.

Behind that was an old book. It had nothing written on the blue cover or the binding. I could see the tops of the yellowed pages. Just as I was about to reach out for the book, I heard a voice.

"How did you find this place?" Alec's voice penetrated the once-silent air. I spun around, caught off guard. My focus on the book meant I hadn't noticed him and Thayer walk in.

"I didn't. I mean, I just came in here and found this safe," I tried to explain, but was unsure how. I spoke freely, knowing Alec would never keep something from me.

"How did you open the safe?" Alec pushed harder. I noticed now he did not seem just mundanely interested. He almost seemed worried.

"I saw the code in my head," I started again, this time watching his expression. "Well not in my head, I guess. It was more like pictures I was looking at." I stopped, not knowing where to continue from there.

"You read my mind?" Alec seemed to be accusing me and shocked at the same time.

"Alec, I'm a Three. Not everyone can read minds like you can." I dismissed him with a wave of my hand.

The highest Level in existence was a Four, and the strongest Level Fours were recruited into the Shadows. A little over twenty Legends called this mansion home.

The first Legend ever created escaped, too powerful for any of the scientists to stop her. She was a normal human until that first successful trial turned her into a Level Five Legend. The unexpected side effect of Legends being able to steal human energy had thrown them all off.

They never combined all Five Levels into another subject again. The possibility of Level Five power died when she was killed centuries ago.

"What you just described was mind-reading," Alec said. He seemed to be running through ways to explain this.

"Which means you're not a Three," Thayer huffed, like it wasn't the first time he said that aloud.

"I'm a Four?" I smiled and stood tall. Already being a Three and in the Shadows was proof of my skill but being a Four was even better.

"How could you have gotten into my mind? I would have noticed," Alec reassured himself. He was the most powerful Legend I knew. Even as a Level Four, his skill of changing and reading minds was unparalleled.

It was my turn to interrupt him.

"It wasn't your mind the pictures came from." I finished my explanation and waited for Alec to relax.

"The only other person who knew..." Alec looked at Thayer, his trusted number two. I looked at Thayer as well.

"It was his." I pointed at Thayer gently.

Thayer's eyebrows shot up. His eyes darted toward Alec. "I thought she didn't know how to do that." He raised his hands in surrender to be spared from Alec's disappointment.

"I just figured it out." I shrugged my shoulders and smiled at my achievement. I assumed they would be proud of me too. This new ability made me stronger and more lethal than I already was.

When I looked into their eyes, however, it was not pride looking back. Alec and Thayer both eyed me cautiously as I reviewed the contents of the safe.

"It's so strange. It almost feels like I recognize these. The little blue book. Although I don't think it's a book, is it? This locket, I know I must have seen this before," I mused.

I went to pick up the picture of the necklace and Alec rushed forward.

"Do you remember them?" Alec asked. He was still wearing that worried look.

"No, but I feel like I should. How could that be possible? It's like the memory is just...gone." I looked up at Alec.

He was standing close to me now. He reached up gently and put his hands on either side of my face. I waited for him to explain. His eyes just softened and looked deeply into mine.

"There is an explanation for all of this. Baby, calm down." His voice was steady, but his eyes seemed to be holding back.

I focused on the locket and the book, waiting for him to answer. As I did, the images slowly faded from my vision. The corners blackened, and the blackness traveled to the center of the image.

They were being destroyed. *Alec*.

"What are you doing?" I jerked my head away from his touch.

"I need Nikki," Alec snapped to Thayer.

"Don't move," I threatened, and Thayer froze near the doorway.

I stepped back, and Alec lowered his hands. I could see him thinking frantically behind his stoic expression. I looked at Thayer, who was staring with wide eyes between Alec and me.

"You're trying to take this memory away? Why am I not allowed to remember this?" I thought about the objects and continued to feel as though I had seen them before this time, but there was no memory...

"This isn't the first time you've changed my memory," I accused him. Alec's eyes were as wide as Thayer's now. He was caught.

"No," he answered and casually placed his hands in his pockets.

His tensed muscles told me he was faking the calm demeanor.

"What else don't I know?" I pushed harder.

He stared at me and shook his head as he walked toward me. He brushed his hand along my blond hair.

"I can see how confusing this is for you," he whispered as he pulled me close to him.

He guided my body to lean against his. I was so shocked that I didn't know what to do. He was the person who always made everything better. He was the person I had always trusted. A thought slithered through my racing mind.

What if that was a mistake?

"Let me change that," Alec whispered again as his hand brushed my hair down my shoulders.

I felt him nod slightly, and I wasn't sure why until I felt an uninvited emotion filling my body.

A creeping, calm feeling came over me. Slowly, I relaxed and realized everything was going to work out. Alec's clean scent and strong arms meant that I was safe. My muscles released automatically.

But something was wrong. Even the feelings couldn't make me ignore my thoughts any longer. It felt the same way that it had when I held that Legend's life in my hands. I recalled all the emotions I thought I was feeling.

Hate, pride, anger. Some of the strongest emotions. All of them came in so quickly, one after the other.

That's because they were not mine.

"The forest," I breathed, finally putting another piece together. I looked up at Thayer and watched as his eyes filled with fear while I filled with a burning rage.

I stepped forward but was stopped by Alec's arms still holding me. That didn't stop Thayer from flinching anyway.

"That woman. You forced me to…" I stopped talking and clenched my teeth together. My hands yanked Alec's arms off me.

"He didn't force you to do anything," Alec said.

"No, you're right. It was you. You're the one who calls the shots, right? He was just following your orders." I accused him instead.

"We're not the ones who ripped the dagger through her chest." Alec's stare turned cold. Guilt washed in, reaching even my fingertips.

"I..." I started and dropped my stare to the floor as my mind replayed what I had done.

"Hey, you have no reason to be ashamed. You're a Shadow. It's who you are." Alec reached forward and dared to touch me. As the warmth of his touch seeped through me, I looked back into his eyes.

"Is it?" I asked. The answer I really wanted was to know what he was keeping from me. Something deep inside told me that I was never meant for this life.

Once again, that same calm feeling edged its way inside. It took me less time to recognize its origin. I froze and snapped my gaze up to the inviting brown eyes that I knew would be waiting. Thayer.

"I warned you about trying to stop me." I slowly turned my head to glare at him. The calm feeling instantly left.

They weren't helping. They were manipulating. They combined against me as if I was an enemy with too much information. If they used their talents to attack me, the least I could do was repay the favor.

My adept ability to alter the physical nature of cells had its rewards, especially in times like this. I focused on Thayer. I honed in on the oxygen cells that filled his lungs and the air that surrounded him.

Under my influence, the oxygen slowly changed. The air thinned around him in a matter of seconds, leaving no oxygen for him to breathe. He gasped to find more air, and failed. He sank to his knees and clutched his chest.

"Mara, stop," Thayer choked out, using the remaining oxygen in his lungs. His mistake.

"You wanted a ruthless Shadow. You got one. I don't want to hurt him, but I will." I waited for a few more seconds. I slowly looked between Alec and Thayer, who was staring at Alec intently, waiting for his command.

"Baby, don't do this." Alec looked back at me as if he wanted me to stop but could not give me what I was asking. I met his lack of action with my flaming anger.

"Tell me what you know," I glared back, unwavering.

"I can't," he grimaced. He wasn't just worried anymore. He was panicked.

"You would let him die instead?" I questioned, not believing my own words.

Thayer's hands clawed at the stone, gasping for air. The anger filled me until I could feel it shaking my body. I stared at Alec's concerned eyes and willed him to tell me what was going on. For a moment, that was all I saw, just his eyes.

Alec was distracted enough by his struggling sidekick that I did something I was sure no one had done before.

I entered Alec Stone's mind.

The shock made me release my hold on Thayer, who finally drew his first breath in sixty-three seconds.

Pictures flashed across my vision. They were pictures I had not seen, at least not through my point of view.

A small, white house in the middle of a desert. I saw myself walk through the door. I stood in the back room. A little girl hid in the corner. I looked closer at her face. She almost looked like...

Me.

Alec shut his eyes to break the connection and shook his head. He took a calming breath and looked at me.

"Mara, don't peek around in places you don't belong," he gently chided me as if I had stolen a cookie and not just invaded his private thoughts.

He looked back at me, seeming both impressed and slightly angry. I tried to see more, but I could not get in again. All I knew was the secrets had something to do with my memories, and it all somehow came together with this book and necklace.

"How long have you been lying to me?" I commanded an answer from him. In truth, my heart was shattering. He was my person to rely on. Now I couldn't sort out what was real.

What if none of it was?

My thoughts betrayed me again by jumping to the worst scenario. I didn't want to entertain the thought that I was the only one who had fallen, the only one that cared. When I looked into his deep blue eyes, I saw how much he cared for me. I just didn't know if I could believe it.

"I never lied to you. I just couldn't tell you everything," he said in a low voice.

He didn't want me to worry, but it was too late for that. Alec had nothing to say that could soothe me now.

"Who else knew what you were doing to me?" I asked, stepping away from him.

Alec kept his mouth closed, his eyes begging me to stop asking questions. Instead, I turned to Thayer.

"The entire council." Thayer hung his head.

"Why?" I glared.

Thayer stood up, watching Alec warily. I focused back on his dark blue eyes, waiting for any answer that would make sense.

"Listen to me." Alec reached forward and clutched both

of my shoulders. "Every other time, you've always chosen for me to change your memories. Just trust me, I know this. It's easier..."

"Every. Other. Time?" I enunciated for him to hear how wrong that sounded.

"The last time you figured it out was only a few months ago," Thayer finally commented. Alec shot his gaze over to him. "Something is changing in her. We don't even know how long it will hold this time."

"Do you actually hear yourselves?" I looked at both of them.

Alec looked at me straight in the eyes. No shame. No guilt.

"If I stay, I'm not keeping my memories, am I?" I raised my eyebrow at him.

He glanced at Thayer as he took a step to stand between the doorway and me. Alec returned his gaze to me with eyes full of fake sympathy.

"No," he answered and dropped his hands from holding me.

I could see that he wasn't as concerned as he should be. After all, he was relying on changing my memories and going back to the way things were. In his mind, he had nothing to lose.

"But if I try to leave, you'll kill me?" I asked.

His mouth dropped open for a moment as he realized I was actually considering that option. Finally, real concern flickered in his gaze.

If I chose to leave, he would have to kill me to maintain his authority. Otherwise, there would be no merit to his threats.

"Mara, that's not...I can't do that. Not to you." Once he had time to think, he hung his head.

Betrayal or not, I could see that he really cared for me. Walking out would challenge those feelings. I hoped that Alec cared enough to let me leave. I had never seen him offer the same grace to anyone before. I took a breath and looked him dead in the eyes.

"Well if you can't tell me, and I refuse to forget, then we are at an impasse." I crossed my arms over my chest.

"I won't lose you. It will be easier once you've forgotten. Everything will go back to the way it was." He reached out and touched my arm softly. His eyes coated the romantic gesture in threat.

"I don't know if I want that anymore," I threatened and spun on my heel.

"I can fix that. Just stay." Alec raced forward and grabbed me by both arms.

His hands moved to either side of my face. His eyes flashed back and forth from each of mine. He was looking for any kind of approval. He knew he would need my consent or my weakness to gain access to my mind. If I was unwilling, he couldn't do it.

The only other way would be if I didn't have enough energy to fight him off. Unfortunately, for him, I was always high.

"I can't stay," I answered.

My decision was finally spoken aloud. The words didn't fit in my mouth the way they should. My mind didn't want to believe the sounds it just heard.

I should want to leave but I couldn't picture it. I looked at Thayer for a brief moment, wondering if he was altering my emotions again.

That was the problem. That was the reason I couldn't stay. I had no idea what decisions were mine and which they influenced. That anyone influenced.

I wasn't free here. Between Alec, Thayer, Nikki, and everyone else, I wasn't even close.

"I can't just watch you walk out of here," Alec growled and tightened his grip on my shoulders. I raised my hands to his slowly. As soon as my skin touched his, Alec yanked his hands back.

"Then don't watch," I said, looking directly into his eyes.

In a second, I watched Alec's expression change from scared, to angry, and then to what seemed like sadness. I looked up at Thayer and he stepped aside.

My heart dropped as I realized what I was leaving behind. This was my home, and these were my people. Without them, I would be facing the world of humans and Legends all alone, with the mark on my arm serving as a target on my back. No one dared take on the Shadows as a whole, but one on her own...

"Mara." Thayer reached out but didn't touch me. "We are your family."

When I looked into Thayer's eyes, I searched for a reason to stay. A reason that I could trust any of them. There wasn't one. This place wasn't my home. It was my prison. It kept me safe, but it kept me captive all the same.

"You *were* my family," I corrected him.

With a deep breath and a clenched jaw, I ran out of the room and toward the front entrance, past all of the Shadows who had overheard the argument.

Alec followed close behind as I rushed to the exit and shoved the heavy doors open. I heard his footsteps follow still.

"Wherever you go, we will find you," Alec challenged.

He knew what I was giving up and he understood how much that scared me. His mistake was thinking that was threatening enough to keep me here. I turned around and looked at him, trying to find a reason that I could stay. One reason.

His indigo eyes were blank and unburdened as they stared back at me. Thayer stood behind him, hoping I would step back inside. Nikki walked around the corner, her eyes filled with confusion.

My eyes flicked back to the person who had molded me into a monster.

"Please. Catch me if you can," I taunted Alec.

I whipped around, turning my back on them and the mansion of Shadows. Without hesitation, I took my first step away. Nobody had ever left the Shadows alive. I paused for a moment, waiting for an attack. Nothing happened. Alec was letting me go.

I took another step forward. Then I heard Thayer take a step forward. I paused again.

"Let her go." Alec's words stopped Thayer. "She'll be back," he promised.

Too bad it was one he couldn't keep.

I ran. I kept running until I could no longer see Alec's face in my mind. I ran until the tears dried on my cheeks. I ran until the waves of the West Coast finally broke my thoughts. I looked at the new sky in front of me. For the first time in my life, I was truly alone.

They would never find me here. Or anywhere. But they were welcome to try.

CHAPTER
FOUR

Present Day

She pressed the cold key into my hand.

"The windows just got fitted with new locks, ya know, crime in the area and all," the owner prattled. "The carpet is brand new, and it better look brand new when you leave. Anything else, you have my email."

I wanted a place that was nestled in the middle of as many humans as possible. Alec would expect me to be far away from them. Having just moved here, I had at least a year before Alec caught wind of me being in Portland. It had become my routine.

If I erased any evidence of me being here, that bought even more time. I stared ahead at the evidence in front of me in the form of a stressed apartment manager.

"Just another Saturday for you, huh?" I asked, stalling her until the people behind us went inside the house.

"It's not every Saturday that a tenant offers a year's worth of rent up front, but yeah, I guess." She shrugged, tapping her fingers against her arms while she waited. The door to the apartment next to us clicked closed, and the parking lot was empty.

I shot my hand forward, not wasting another second. My grip locked on her right arm as her energy burst from her body into mine.

"W-what are you doing?" She gasped as fear immediately paralyzed her. Heat surged up my arm and into my chest, overpowering the sound of her voice.

I needed her to forget ever seeing me, and in order to do that I needed energy, far more energy than I had in my body.

The warmth and excitement melded into each of my cells. My body awoke, reacting to the stimulating energy that it craved. I never wanted to stop, even when I looked in her sagging eyes and felt her body sink closer to the ground.

"Please..." she breathed as her eyes fluttered.

My fingers still tingled with the sensation of her energy. I concentrated on her face, trying to think of the fact that a death would draw attention to me. At this point, when I was so intoxicated with her energy, that was the only thing that saved her life.

I released her, and she stumbled forward into me. I grabbed her weak shoulders where her shirt covered her skin and pulled her up to face me. I looked in her exhausted eyes and connected my mind with hers.

"You can't remember what I look like," I said softly enough for only her to hear.

I found the parts of her memory that had any images of me. They disintegrated, leaving behind only the transactions between us that didn't show a physical appearance.

Her face changed, confused. I kept my eyes focused on hers.

"You're tired because you spent all day helping someone move in," I added.

I reached into her mind again and created new memories in place of meeting with me. Lifting boxes, holding doors open, and moving couches filled her mind, enough for the entire day.

Satisfied, I released her and turned toward the apartment door. She plodded down the metal stairs, shaking her head as she meandered to her car.

I twisted the newly cut key in the lock and pushed the door open.

I breathed in the scent of the new carpet and stepped across the metal threshold. Immediately, I shut the door behind me and turned the lock again.

I set my bags on the floor and pulled open the curtains of the front windows. A small parking lot lay in front of the apartment building. Behind that was undeveloped space covered in trees.

Alone. That was how I needed it.

In my experience, being alone was best. I continued walking through my new home. Eventually, I made it to the bathroom, where I caught a reflection of myself in the mirror.

I saw a woman with striking blue eyes staring back at me. Too bad these eyes were mine forever. They were the one thing on my body that would never change. After all, the eyes are the window to the soul, and nothing could change the soul.

My gaze moved to the temporary olive skin and freckles that surrounded my constant eyes. My face was framed by short, dark waves that still smelled like pine trees. The woman in the mirror was named Tylee and had been an outdoor extraordinaire.

I had started my journey by following the original workmanship style of the necklace. Between the years, I had followed lead after lead until I finally heard rumors about Portland, Oregon, of all places.

When I swept through the town, I found a few Shadows there. I recognized the twins, Fiona and Marshall, almost immediately by their matching black curls. Alec must have heard about my lead to Portland and sent them on their own search for me.

That was how he kept track of me. Whatever clue I found only made it easier for Alec to find me. Everything got back to him. I raced out of the city and watched carefully for them to leave.

The search was on hold for the next six years. I did everything I could to distract myself from the time passing. None of it worked. I felt every single second of the years that ticked by. It was easy during the day, but at night was when the loneliness descended.

Those years had taught me that I didn't just want to be free, I didn't just want to figure out what Alec had hidden. I wanted connection, a reason to live each day. I wanted to be around people, even if they were humans.

This next place was going to be very different.

I glanced down at my hands and admired the dirt that tirelessly clung to the underside of my nails. I watched as the brown bits fell away from my fingers and the callouses smoothed. My rough hands softened and lightened in color.

I looked back up in the mirror and kept my gaze on those everlastingly blue eyes. Around them, the skin began to lighten. The freckles faded away to leave only unblemished skin. My eyelashes lengthened. My hair grew to reach the middle of my back. The dark waves lightened to chocolaty-brown, loose curls.

I looked at the woman now.

She was drastically different from the one who had been there only a few moments ago. The dark skin before had hidden the structure of her cheekbones. Without the freckles, the eyes were more noticeable and unique. The longer hair covered more of her upper body.

The change felt good, even if it did take more of my energy. I took a deep breath and said goodbye to Tylee, the rough, dark-skinned, short-haired woman who had loved the outdoors. Now I looked at Kate, the sweet, long-haired, new woman who existed as my reflection now.

Changing my appearance had always come easily to me. The ability was quite rare to coach my own cells to alter their DNA without much effort. It was my talent, the Level at which I was most adept. The basic colors and shapes could be changed just by focusing my mind on them.

Major changes of height or weight took too much energy to be able to undergo as easily. Being able to change my appearance just by concentrating on it was only the beginning of what I could do as a Legend.

Every new city, every change in appearance, every second spent hunting a clue to the secret that Alec kept, all of it was worth it. The thought of seeing Alec's eyes looking into mine chilled me to the core.

I knew he allowed me to leave only because he didn't have the will to kill me. I also knew how that would have threatened his power among the Shadows. When I didn't return, he would have lost his credibility.

The only way to get it back would be to bring me back. Searching for me was the one thing that kept his status as a strong leader. Alec couldn't lead until he could make good on his promise to find me.

That night, in the place where I knew the Shadows had already been looking, I checked the lock on the front door. I locked all the windows again. I set the motion sensors at the entrances. If anyone did come in, at least it would wake me up. The few seconds of a head start would give me enough time to outrun a Shadow, even one completely high on human energy.

I never tied myself to anyone or anything. I tucked a small, leather suitcase in the bottom of the closet. Any sentimental thing was kept there, so I could leave at a second's notice. The one thing that kept me free was the fact that I was alone.

As my body fell onto the bed, I listened for any errant sounds. When I lay down, I took a few deep breaths. It had been over twenty years since I left the Shadows.

Due to our slow aging, Legends had a lifespan of about ten times that of a human. A few years passing felt like a few months. Even after all these years, the memories were still real enough to haunt my dreams. I tried not to think about him, about any of them, especially as I drifted off to sleep. It hardly ever worked.

This time, my dreams took me back to a memory of eight years ago when I had been living in Denmark. I worked at an ancient library and spent most of my time reading every theory I could on Legends. I wanted to know everything about what the humans thought of us. I also wanted to dig up anything I could regarding the necklace etched into my memory.

I was left alone, I didn't socialize with more humans than I needed to keep myself fed, and I had an ample amount of time to plan my next move.

I thought it was the perfect place. Until one day, it wasn't.

A shudder crept up my spine, telling me something was wrong. I had always listened, but this time I tried to chalk it up to paranoia.

The window in the front of the store caught my eye. I saw a woman with a long, black braid down her back.

I froze, unable to tear my eyes away.

I had a clear picture in my mind of whom I thought I was

seeing. She was also one of the people I had never planned to see again.

Nikki.

She was a member of the council. Alec trusted her and Thayer with everything.

I looked behind her and noticed a man on the other side of the street. He had each arm wrapped around a beautiful woman. I recognized his gorgeous face and gleaming brown eyes in the crowd of people.

My heart iced over as I stared at what I thought was impossible.

The Shadows were here. They had found me.

I should have listened to my intuition.

The second Nikki's eyes landed on me, I shook my head to her, pleading for her to keep her mouth shut. A cruel smile spread across her mouth.

She shouted a word that I hadn't seen or heard in a long time. A word that I could still recognize its exact sound.

"Alec!" Nikki's voice almost shattered the glass.

Thayer's eyes snapped up as he heard the sound from the short distance away.

In the next second, Nikki left the window, and the door burst open. I had already bolted behind the bookcases. My heart pumped adrenaline through every part of my body. I ran as quietly as I could to the back room. I rushed to the spiral staircase in the corner which led to the attic. There, I stopped just before opening the door to the roof.

My ears burned as I strained to listen for any hint of a sound. If I was going to escape without being seen, I needed to know exactly where they were.

"It was her," Nikki's voice confirmed.

"Are you sure?" Thayer's voice asked skeptically. "She could look like anyone."

"She has the same eyes," Nikki accused. "She stabbed us all in

the back the day she left. I couldn't forget if I tried."

I heard the pain in her voice. To her, I hadn't said goodbye. I'd just abandoned her. The same thing that her parents had done when they found out she was only a Three. To spite them she became powerful enough to attract the attention of the Shadows.

My departure was a reminder that no matter how strong she was, people always decided to leave.

"Well, she's gone, and if she saw you coming, we won't catch her now." Thayer's voice gave up. I listened for the sincerity, still suspecting that he might be trying to lure me out.

My hand latched onto the doorknob, and just as I was about to turn it, I heard another familiar sound.

"No!" Alec screamed. The sound of wood breaking and pages fluttering echoed into the dark corner where I stood.

His voice shook through the air. My body reacted to the sound of his voice. Something buzzed inside me at the victory of keeping Alec from something he wanted. I had never seen anyone accomplish it before now.

Despite this loss, his voice didn't hint at total defeat. The fight was far from over. Alec was nothing if not committed and driven. Unfortunately, the object of his obsession was me.

The familiar chills crept up my spine.

My body yanked itself back into reality as I sucked in a breath. I checked everything in the room. The early morning light passed easily through the curtains, showing me that the room was empty. I clutched the blanket to my chest and took in another deep breath.

The aching silence in the room left the raw sound of my soft sobs to linger in the air. No matter how long it had been, I could feel his breath chilling my neck and see his eyes.

My nightmares always felt too real. The problem was

that most of them had really happened. I hated the gamble of falling asleep.

When I looked up, I was still alone.

I was always alone.

After decades of avoiding people and never having another soul to talk to, I had become desperate. I needed some kind of interaction.

This new place was going to be different from all the others. I was done with waking up from nightmares alone. I was done with never saying more than a few words to another person. I was absolutely done with living my life in such fear that I never actually lived.

But after so many years, I had started to come to the conclusions that I might never find that locket. The only thing I may end up with is a picture I had sketched from memory.

"Today will be different," I said.

No one else was around to hear and my voice sounded louder against the empty walls. I had grown to hate the silence.

It was the riskiest choice yet. I knew the Shadows had already been prowling around Portland. I had to plant myself in a place where Alec would never think to look. I was going to be in a job bursting with humans, and in a place that put me in danger.

If the Shadows didn't find me, the humans might figure out who I was and cause a ruckus loud enough to draw too much attention.

As long as neither of them figured it out, I would be safe. Until then, I was walking a tightrope between my destruction and my salvation. It was the cost of hiding in plain sight.

Alec's fatal flaw was that he always underestimated me. That's what made this place a possibility.

He wouldn't think I had it in me.

At that thought, I wiped the still-hot tears from my eyes

and counted my breaths until the sun broke over the cloudy horizon.

Today will be different.

CHAPTER
FIVE

My heart thumped at the idea of surrounding myself with humans.

In the mirror, I watched as I pulled my curls from hanging down my back to a neat bun. My eyelashes darkened and lengthened as if I had applied mascara. My complexion was already even, and my eyelids darkened in a perfectly contoured fashion. A nice perk of my talent.

Once I was satisfied, I walked to my closet. The color of my jacket was a blue that was a few shades too light. I clutched the soft material and closed my eyes. I took a breath in and concentrated my mind on the cells of the fabric. The lighter blue darkened a few shades to the perfect color for the rest of the outfit.

I opened my eyes and took a deep breath, now feeling the loss of energy. I shook my hand, annoyed at how little energy I had. Altering inanimate cells took more effort than changing my own. A dull ache spread through my body as I adjusted to the lost energy.

A Legend's altered genes made our bodies stronger,

faster, and more efficient than a human's. But to sustain life, we needed human energy. To use our abilities at all, we needed even more.

My car tires squeaked on the shining parking garage floor. I pulled into the company parking spaces. The office was near the top of the building, and I opted to take the elevator, knowing I would catch other people there.

Humans were incredibly predictable, and I had to follow along with exactness if I was going to blend in.

On my way up to the office, I shook hands and brushed people's shoulders. When my skin touched theirs, I took a little energy from their bodies. Each time, I had to force myself to stop. The rush of energy came in, my body relaxed, and all I felt was utter bliss.

That's when I knew I needed to stop. Hanging on to the enticement any longer than that, and I would have a much harder time convincing myself to break the connection.

As the elevator rose higher, my adrenaline flared. I wiggled my toes in my ballet flats. It was one thing being in a stuffy elevator with a few other people, ones I could easily take out on my own. It was another thing to be in an enclosed office with all of them swarming around me.

By the time I arrived, I was energized and nervous enough to keep my mind alert.

I stepped out onto the light gray carpet and gazed around at the sleek lines and plain colors of the office. The place was crawling with humans. Some sat at cubicles. Others walked around with papers in their hands.

They should be harmless. I swallowed my fear, trying to see them as irrelevant to me.

"Hello, Ms. Martin. We have been expecting you," the receptionist greeted me.

My blood froze when I thought of what to say back to

her. I was trying so hard to be normal that I couldn't even find what that looked like. I started to turn, hoping words would come to me soon.

The CEO heard my name and turned around. The lights glinted off his balding head. Glasses adorned his long nose. He wore a dress shirt and a vest, all varying shades of gray and purple. He smiled and approached me with a hand to shake.

"Ms. Martin, what a pleasure it is to finally meet you," he spoke confidently. I shook his hand and smiled.

I was completely outnumbered. I breathed and reassured myself that I still had the upper hand. No one knew who I was, and surrounded by humans was the last place Alec would think to look for me. Although it scared me, ironically, it was the safest place to be.

"Thank you, Mr. Lyle. I am excited to be here," I said. The careful words flowed from my mouth easily.

A falsified application to the job and a video interview had landed me a job that most humans who looked my age could never get. According to my resume, I had graduated early and had already been working full time for longer than I should have.

To make my transition a little easier, humans were easily impressed, especially when they believed my lies.

All the eyes in the room fell on me, the new person. I noticed the stares and the elbow jabs between friends to get their attention. I knew the effect I had on humans, especially males.

I appeared to be in my young twenties, so I should be roughly the same age as most of them, but to me, they all looked like children. I politely ignored the giddy energy that had just made their Monday morning interesting.

Another side effect of the original experiment enhanced all of our senses, bodily functions, and DNA makeup. Our perfectly balanced hormones made each gender exquisitely defined. Legends were beautiful to look at. Every female was gorgeously feminine, and every male was intensely masculine.

I focused back on the CEO, Mr. Lyle, who had not lost his chipper smile.

"Oh, call me Robert," he said, waving his hand at the formality.

I glanced at the receptionist, who was shaking her head as if to tell me to ignore that request. A quick scan of her expression showed that she already liked me.

I relaxed a little, knowing I had already convinced two humans that I was normal.

The consulting company had a few chronic problems that had been taking a toll on the profits. I had signed on to work with them for the next year at least. They had offered me an office in their building so I could spend time there as I needed. I liked the option of being around people.

"Well, good. We have your office right at the end of this hall here. Let me show you." Mr. Lyle led the way and explained each of the offices we passed.

"This is John's office. He's the head of the accounting team here. The rest work either in the main-room cubicles or on the floor beneath us. But we like to keep him close."

I peeked in and saw a middle-aged man in the room with a perfectly straightened bookcase covering the entire back wall. He didn't look up from his computer.

"This is Linda. She is my assistant and right-hand gal," Mr. Lyle pointed, continuing on without me.

We walked past her leaning over a desk reviewing papers, a letter in her hand. She looked at me with inquisitive eyes, questions flying through her mind.

My sympathetic nervous system fired, and my muscles tensed.

Questions were never a good thing. The only thing that made me safe in a horde of humans was that they all thought I was one of them.

Then I looked a little longer, and slowly I relaxed.

She seemed like a bright, young person with more dreams than busywork. Her brown eyes were soft and warm. Her tight brown curls lightened to blond at the end—all of them pulled back into a barely controlled bun at the base of her neck. Her timid personality was evident by her constant eye contact with the ground and her tame wardrobe.

She had all the makings of a striking presence, but muted colors and her hairstyle prevented her from shining.

She was pretty, for a human.

As we walked by, I decided it was worth expending my recently gathered energy to make sure all her concerns about me were innocent. I concentrated on her mind and looked into her soft eyes. After a few seconds, I'd made the connection to be able to read her thoughts. I could not hear coherent words, mostly emotions.

She was stressed already, and it was only 9:00 a.m. I looked through her eyes as she saw me. She was intimidated just from seeing me. I smiled kindly and listened as her thoughts changed.

Maybe she won't be so bad, I read.

I blinked, and the energy drained from me. I focused on my steps so I didn't stumble as my body adjusted. Part of blending in meant I didn't have access to as much energy as a Shadow. I had to be discreet and carefully choose when to use my power or when to feed on humans.

I always monitored everything I did to make sure nothing would give me away. I took a breath and half-heartedly concentrated again on what or who Mr. Lyle was introducing next.

Over the years away from the Shadows, I had been mastering the skill of reading minds. It took a lot of trial and error to be where I am today. What little skills I started with, I had enhanced by remembering Alec in action.

It was unfair how talented Alec was at reading thoughts and manipulating minds. He could see anything he wanted to and about anyone. Everyone trusted him, and that had been my biggest error.

The tour continued as my thoughts maneuvered back to the task at hand. Mr. Lyle and I had arrived at the end of the hallway, where it opened up into a small foyer and then divided into more offices and a few conference rooms.

"My office is here on the end, yours is right on the other side of this conference room." Mr. Lyle's voice boomed over the chatter from the cubicles.

He walked past the conference room and stopped at a glass door with my name on the side. I walked in and saw what was to be my office for the next little while.

It had a large glass desk with bookcases on the opposite side and a window in the back. It was far more space than I needed, but that only spoke to the respect Mr. Lyle had placed on me.

"This shared wall is soundproofed and can be converted into a one-way mirror." He pressed a button under the desk and the sleek wall parted in slats to reveal a large rectangle in the center of it. I could see perfectly into the other room, where a mirror sat on the other side.

"Interesting setup," I commented. "I like the idea, though."

"Yes, at least we know how to do one thing—monitor our people." His hearty laugh shook the glasses down his nose a centimeter. I kindly laughed along and remembered there was one more office he hadn't shown me.

"Whose office is at this end of the hall?" I asked.

"Oh, yes! That is Kylan's office. He is the director of HR. You will be working with him the most. Come, I will take you to meet him," he said as he left and headed down the hall.

As he neared the space, he gave a light knock on the open door and called the man's name. He stepped around the corner and waited for me to follow.

"Kylan, this is the new analyst I've told you about. Her name is Kate Martin," he said and gestured for me to come around him into the office.

I stepped through the door and looked up to meet the HR director's eyes. They were a welcoming shade of green. His light brown hair was slightly long, but groomed back. He had a toned and strong frame vaguely hidden by his sharply tailored suit. He stood up behind his desk, holding a file of papers.

For a second, he just looked at me. Then he slightly tilted his head, a small smile playing on his mouth. The light shifted how it glanced off his eyes. The shade of green lightened from this new angle.

"Hello, I'm Kylan Beck," he said as he stepped out from behind his desk and set the papers down. He walked past his boss and stretched out his hand.

I cleared my throat. "Hello."

"It's nice to meet you. Kate?"

"Yes, thank you," I said and shook his hand firmly, then dropped it.

Mr. Lyle piped up and discussed the schedule of what the upcoming week would look like.

I focused on the boss, while Kylan focused on me. It was odd the way he calmly looked at me as if staring was still socially acceptable. I fought back the urge to squirm.

I hadn't been this nervous in a long while.

Mr. Lyle chatted on and on about problems he wanted to improve in his company. Within the first few minutes, I knew more about him than he would want to admit.

He prided himself on efficiency and sometimes forgot to care about his employees. He'd had the same assistant for three years and still called her Linda when her name was actually Lisa, as I'd learned from studying her thoughts. She was too sweet and timid to correct him.

I was the person to step in and study the interaction between employees and clients and improve it. That was my job on paper.

It was the perfect situation. I wanted to be surrounded by humans. I wanted to study them. I wanted to analyze what they did and why they did it. So many things about Legends and humans were the same, but all of the important things were opposites. I wanted to find out why.

Starting with Lisa.

I walked into Mr. Lyle's office and asked to borrow her for a few moments. We went into the conference room, and I closed the door behind me.

"So, Lisa, I wanted to sit down and talk with you first because, between you and me, you probably know more about this company than even Mr. Lyle. Am I right?" I started off nicely.

She just stared at me for a moment. Her eyes were wide with surprise.

"You know my name? I mean my real name...I'm..." she stammered, knowing it was a silly question, but not even Mr. Lyle knew it.

"I noticed the name signed at the bottom of the letter you were holding earlier. Lisa Moreno, right?" I confirmed with her.

"Yes," she said with a smile and relief. She sat a little

taller in her chair. "It's just, everyone calls me Linda. I haven't really ever corrected anyone, especially Mr. Lyle. I mean I tried to when I first started, but he never remembered," she admitted.

"Well, that is one of the first things to change." I smiled to let her know she finally had someone looking out for her. She smiled back, sitting with a straight back and her head held high. She had been slouched in hiding for too long.

"So, Lisa," I paused on her name, "tell me about Mr. Lyle."

She talked about the man she had diligently served for years. Her brain was a gold mine for company operations. This woman knew everything there was to know about the business. Most of the major deals and contracts had been written by her and just signed by Mr. Lyle. I needed her as my friend to help the others come around to me.

After talking with Lisa for over an hour, I noted how many times Mr. Lyle walked by, checking to see if we were done because he needed Lisa to do something. I would politely wave at him, and he would head back to his office.

Once we were through, we walked out together. Not a second later, Mr. Lyle came out of his office.

"Linda, do you know where those documents are I told you about this morning? I thought I left them on my desk," he said in one breath.

"I think you mean Lisa," I called out.

He stopped. She dropped her gaze to the floor and as if waiting for a rebuke or at least for him to brush my comment off.

"Pardon?" Mr. Lyle responded, leaning his ear toward me, as he clearly must have misheard.

"Her name is Lisa," I clarified and smiled at her.

Lisa looked nervously at Mr. Lyle and then back to me. He turned back to her and looked shocked. She nodded slowly.

"Lisa. Um, okay." He processed it. "Lisa, do you know where those documents are?"

Lisa smiled and told him where she filed the documents. This time, he listened and went to retrieve them himself after he asked her to show him where.

She mouthed *thank you* to me as she walked around the corner, leading Mr. Lyle to the documents. I turned around and headed back to my office with a smile on my face.

At the end of the workday, I was still typing on my computer. The lights in the surrounding offices shut off one by one. Mr. Lyle stopped by before he left.

"Nice work, Ms. Martin. It's only the first day and you already told me something that I didn't know." He smiled sheepishly now.

"That is my job," I replied. "I've seen plenty of leaders make similar mistakes. I'm just here to find and suggest how to fix them."

I thought of Alec leading the Shadows. He cared about the council members, and everyone else was irrelevant until they could serve a purpose. Thayer was in charge of knowing everyone's names, and Nikki kept them all scared enough to follow anything Alec said.

"Keep up the good work," he encouraged as he turned and left for the day.

I turned back to my computer as I finished taking down today's notes. I kept my eyes on my screen as someone else walked in and leaned against the doorframe.

"You know there isn't a bonus for the person who works the most hours, right?" Kylan remarked. I shifted my focus to him and smiled politely.

"Oh, I thought I saw a sign out front that said there was. My mistake," I joked, surprised at how easily the words flowed out.

"You know, I think you and I are going to get along." Kylan laughed and nodded.

"It's possible. Goodnight, Mr. Beck," I responded.

"Kylan," he corrected me.

"Kylan." I nodded.

"See you tomorrow, Kate," he finished politely, but his eyes seemed to hold something back.

He walked out, and my eyes followed. Something about his voice, his stare. As soon as he left the room, his absence felt like something was missing.

CHAPTER
SIX

Kylan's intense gaze mulled through my thoughts as I drove, forcing my attention back to his green eyes.

I shook off the lingering flutter and focused my stare on the road lined with high-rise buildings. I reminded myself of one of the reasons I came to Portland in the first place—to follow a lead about my past.

I was trying to track down any clue to tell me more about Legend history. Specifically, mine.

The history that had been hidden from me.

It was hard to picture a betrayal from a childhood friend, but the sting was still quite potent for me. Alec and I had been best friends as we grew up together. He and his dad were my whole world.

Alec's father had created the Shadows to put up a fight against the reviving labs and oppression from the humans. The labs wanted to give Legend power to any human they chose. But neither had recreated the serum from the original experiment.

The current Legends saw that as a threat. Making sure

no one could turn was also the safest way for the Shadows to ensure a constant human food supply. A charge that Alec had taken over after his father's death as the new leader. He was adamant about making his father proud.

He desperately wanted to be free from having to keep his identity and power secret from the humans. It hurt him that he could be so superior and yet still have to hide. To him, his goals were enough of a reason to keep my past from me.

In my mind, I couldn't see how anything was worth taking my memories and lying.

Unfortunately, those memories had still not returned. They had been buried for so long, they might never resurface. He and his father had hidden my story, along with answers about what my future was supposed to be.

That night, I drove to an old museum on the outskirts of the city. The businesses around had peeling paint and moss growing through the cracks in the concrete. After parking the car in front, I walked through the glass door under the old stone arches.

The stale smell hit my nose as soon as I walked in. It was nearly deserted except for the cranky receptionist and a few old-time patrons that were probably the only business this place saw during the weekdays.

My lead told me the locket used to be in this museum. It was my only solid clue in years.

As I pored over the exhibits and photos, my memory calmly recalled the day I first laid eyes on a picture of the necklace.

That was a memory forever burned into my mind. I could not forget that day if I tried. I could see Alec's dark eyes willing me to come back. I could hear him call me "baby" and feel him wrap his arms around me. That memory was nearly tangible.

Those images and feelings haunted my dreams at night and stole into my days. Those were the reminders that made me take careful steps down the aisles in the museum.

Wherever I hunted down a new lead, I always braced for the fact that he might be standing just around the corner. Experience had taught me that anytime I got closer to the necklace, he got closer to me.

I walked warily through the rows of dimly lit glass cases that held sad pieces of pottery and relics. My hope fell when I realized I had been searching for almost an hour. Discouraged, my eyes wandered around the old museum.

Across the red armchairs and smudged glass cases, my eyes yearned for anything close to that necklace. I stopped when I saw a photo collage of the museum when it was first built in 1893. The local folks all donated historic pieces to the opening-day collection.

I smiled as I thought back to that time. Lightbulbs had just become available to those who could afford them. I was so young, only about 120 human years old, back then. Despite the lack of modern technology, it was an exciting time to be alive.

Most of the pieces were exquisite compared to the ones that remained. My eyes flicked from one photo to the next. Nothing kept my attention long.

Finally, my eyes narrowed in on a small photo of a man's hands holding an open jewelry case. In the velvet-lined case was a single, small, and seemingly insignificant necklace. The thin chain wrapped around the mold of the case. The single pendant, lying on the bottom of the chain, instantly jumped out at me.

It was the necklace from the safe.

Immediately, I wanted to ask someone for information about the necklace. Before I moved my feet, a second thought came rushing in. Marching up and asking questions about that necklace would give Alec a source to find me.

Alec had two things to work with—anyone who had seen me and anyone who had seen someone asking about the necklace. My appearance was different every time I changed locations, so the first option was not as helpful.

The necklace always stayed the same, however, and whenever I asked too many questions about it, Alec was not far behind.

I could try to change her memories, but I had only done it a few times successfully. The landlord to my apartment had seemed like the change worked on her, but I didn't really know. I knew for sure I did not have enough energy for that kind of feat tonight.

To do it, I would have to go in and redirect every emotion and thought tied to this moment, or the memories could be brought back. The mind was incredibly resilient that way. I also couldn't destroy the places where the memories were stored or Alec would notice the gap and take that as confirmation I was here as well.

I stood there, looking at the necklace and fighting between both options. When I looked at the crisp image, despite its age, the goal in front of me was too enticing. My breathing sped, and my eyes narrowed. I had not seen a picture like this since the first time I laid eyes on the picture in the safe.

I could wait until I had more information, but I was never good at being patient.

Like every other time, I made the choice to dig further.

I rushed to the front desk and beckoned the receptionist. I caught her look of contempt but ignored it. She wasn't happy by my being there, but she followed me down the rows anyway.

"What is this photo?" I asked, pointing toward the simple

frame. She leaned forward and adjusted her glasses. She slowly read the nameplate underneath the photo.

"It says here, *Man Holding Gold Necklace on Opening Day*," she calmly spoke as she leaned back, uninterested.

"Do you know who was holding the necklace?" I rushed, counting the seconds that I kept her talking.

The longer I talked to her, the more she would remember my face. Every second added to memories that I might need to change.

"The owner," she curtly responded.

I struggled to keep my anger from flaring up. We were wasting precious moments. I needed her to not recall my face or anything about this interaction. Her annoyance was only solidifying this memory in her mind.

"Do you have any record of a name?" I prodded further as I purposely softened my tone.

It took a few more moments for her to think and decide how much she actually wanted to help me. To her, I was probably nothing more than a young annoyance.

"There might be something in the back," she said, not moving toward the back at all.

Instead, she just stared at me. My temper built again, but this time I didn't stop it from seeping out of my fake smile. I would have to waste my energy just to get her to talk to me at all.

"Could you please go check and brighten your attitude a bit?" I said through clenched teeth.

I focused on her eyes and accessed her mind. I manipulated her current thought process into a more obedient and cheery pathway. I released the dopamine in her brain, and the effects were immediate. I watched my work as her mouth turned up in a polite smile.

If she associated the memory of me with just another good day at work where she was being helpful, then she wouldn't have a reason to think anything was off. It was a stretch, but it was all I had energy for tonight.

"Of course, follow me," she said with her new, cheery tone, wandering to the back room.

My body ached as the energy left my cells. I blinked and took a breath to steady myself. My eyes looked up to the gray-haired receptionist disappearing behind the cases. I forced my body to walk forward as smoothly as I could fake it.

She stepped behind the desk and pulled out a couple of large books that took up almost her entire arm. She brought them out to the table.

"Here are the inventory books around that day," she explained, kindly now. She lifted the first book and brushed off the thick coating of dust.

Both of these books looked like they had not been touched in decades. She looked through one, and I scanned through the other. I immediately recognized the beautiful cursive writing filling the pages. Handwriting used to be like artwork. I missed that.

After a few minutes of searching, she found the description of the donated necklace on display. I closed my book and walked over to read from hers instead.

The listed name of the owner read *Anonymous*, of course.

"Were there any other events like this one? A place this necklace might show again?" I asked.

"Darling, this was a century ago. Are you sure this is what you're looking for?" She pulled her silver eyebrows together and looked at me.

"I'm absolutely sure," I said and stared back into her aging eyes.

"Well..." She eyed a tall stack of books nervously and then looked at the clock.

It was just past closing time.

"Could I check these out to review them on my own?" I asked kindly.

"We don't normally loan them out…" The woman shifted her feet.

"I'll bring them back. I promise," I answered.

Her face scrunched, highlighting the wrinkles on her forehead. She still didn't look convinced. I could tell her newfound mood was fighting against her logic. I reached my hand forward and laid it on hers. Humans thrived on skin contact. Ironically, so did we, just in a completely different sense.

"You can trust me." I smiled at her and watched her shoulders relax.

She nodded quickly and pulled out the books that I could review. I loaded up my arms as the dust flew all over me. Once I had as many cumbersome books as I could gracefully carry, I turned toward the door.

"Sorry I couldn't be of more help." The receptionist politely walked me to the main door. "I don't know if you will find anything in there, but good luck."

"Thank you. I'll bring these back in a couple of weeks," I said as she allowed the door to shut.

Now that my influence was gone, her normal personality was restored. I took one last glance back to see the scowl had returned to her face, and she hunched back over the front desk, right where she was when I entered. To her, it was just another night at the museum.

Perfect. I smiled. She may still have her memories, but at her age, she may not actually recall them because nothing important happened tonight.

For now, I was safe. At least, I had to convince myself that I was.

I looked at the books in my arms. My fingers tingled with anticipation at what they might hold.

CHAPTER
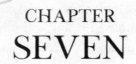
SEVEN

The books landed softly in the passenger seat of my car, and I pulled one out to keep with me.

I stood, and the damp breeze brushed across my face. The streetlights lit the tiny piece of the world around me. People drifted through the streets. Their swirling energy was only a touch away. I smiled and picked up one of the books and shut the door. My feet carried me out into the stream of people.

My fingers turned through the pages as I wandered through the crowded streets. I brushed as many people as I could while scanning through the second part of the book. Energy vibrated through my body, clearing my head.

The other donors were mostly local or within walking distance of Portland. I wondered if the necklace could still be in the area, maybe an inherited heirloom that never left home.

Directly in front of me, two men bumped into each other. Rather than apologizing, they had decided to blow the incident up. One man pushed the other, and he stumbled back into a little girl, almost toppling her over.

He didn't even notice before he stomped back to the man who had pushed him. I looked at the little girl to make sure she was out of the way. The woman beside her grabbed her hand, pulling her away from the fight.

Strangely, the little girl did not look at the man who had pushed her over. Instead, she looked at me.

She must have been about ten years old. It reminded me of the last little girl with whom I had a significant encounter.

Her name was Raven.

It was just a quaint little brick house with a large front window. But what was inside made my skin crawl.

I looked inside and saw a little girl, laughing. She was sitting at a table with her family, her shiny black hair falling around her shoulders. I could see the love in their eyes for each other. They were a picture-perfect family.

The father of the house began to dish up the food for his little girl.

As I looked, a deep anger came over me. I never had that. I looked at Alec with eyes ready to kill.

We walked up to the house and right through the unlocked front door onto the hardwood floor. The dim lights in the house barely showed the dark wood paneling on the walls or the color of the velvet furniture.

"Can I help you?" the father asked.

The rest of them looked at us with shock and confusion. I gazed back at them and didn't see people. All I saw were vessels holding the energy that they didn't deserve.

"Yes, I believe you can." I moved quickly, straight for the mom.

Alec went for the little boy. I'm sure he had his own reasons for that choice. I grabbed the mom's wrist as she stood to try to defend herself. The fear built in her eyes the longer I held her. The energy pulsed through her skin. Her adrenaline skyrocketed.

I took her energy. The racing, pulsing energy surged into my hand and through my body. My vision sharpened. My breath stopped. She fell to the floor, and the flow of energy halted. She lay in a pile on the floor, dead.

A deep breath allowed me to revel in the warmth flowing through me.

The dad shouted and lunged in my direction. The little boy dropped to the floor and Alec shot in front of me. He held the dad by his neck as the human struggled to push him off. Alec didn't budge. Misty, yellow light passed from the dad's skin to Alec's.

The human slowly stopped fighting, and once he was completely still, Alec released his hold. The body crashed against the floor. Alec turned to the girl.

"No," I told him, and he stopped moving. "She lives."

Alec's eyes questioned. The little girl's tears clung to her face. She scanned back and forth from me to Alec until I walked toward her. She stayed in her chair, knowing there was no place she could run. At her age, most humans would have still tried to escape. She looked around at her family lying on the floor before her eyes finally ventured up to mine.

"Why?" the little girl asked as her black hair stuck to her tear-streaked cheeks.

I walked over to her and dried her tears, brushing back loose strands of hair. My knee hit the warm wooden floor as I knelt down in front of her chair.

"What's your name?" I asked in the same sweet voice I had heard her mother use. I saw her eyes fill with fear and confusion. My smile didn't make sense to her.

"Raven Lancaster," the girl replied, confused as to why I would care about her name.

"Well, Raven, we will leave tonight, and you won't be able to tell anyone what actually happened. See, no one would believe you if you did. You would be deemed crazy and ignored. You will live on

with the guilt, knowing you watched your family die tonight and you walked away without a scratch," I whispered close to her face.

The fear in her eyes turned darker. She looked at me differently, beginning to understand just how cruel I was.

"Then, in seventy years or so, when you have lived your pathetic life and are waiting for death to come, then I will see you one last time. When you beg me to give you the same fate your family suffered here tonight, then I will grant your wish. Until then, goodbye, Raven," I finished.

She was so young, but she already understood the fate I had just condemned her to.

We left the house without looking back. Energy, pain, guilt, and anger spun through my head.

I had every intention of keeping my promise to her. In seventy years, I would tell her why, and I could tell myself why, I needed to project my fate onto a harmless human girl.

That night was the lowest I had ever sunk. Killing that little girl's family.

After that, I questioned the choices I had been making as a member of the Shadows. Alec's lies were the final tipping point.

I snapped back to the moment I was in now. I stood on the sidewalk staring at the impending fight. My eyes stayed connected with this little girl before me, and her eyes stayed with me until she disappeared down the road. I turned back to the humans about to throw punches at one another. I jumped forward and stood between the two of them. They both backed off, not wanting to hurt me. The guy who was pushed grabbed my arm.

"You better move, little girl," he growled at me.

I used the skin of his hand touching my wrist to pull enough energy from his body to calm him down. The other guy had grabbed my shoulder to throw me out of the way as well. I reached my hand up and touched his fingers. Both of their raging-fast energies poured into me.

They each began to droop and by the look on their faces, they were exhausted. I let go just before they were about to fall asleep.

As long as the humans didn't know I was a Legend, I always held the upper hand.

"Both of you, go home and get some sleep," I said firmly. "This fight isn't worth it."

I finished and watched as both of them were confused or just drunk enough to turn around and walk away. My heart thumped as the threat of being exposed by taking so much energy faded with them. The reward of the new energy spread throughout my body.

I took in a deep breath, enjoying the warm energy filling my system. Once the men were gone, I continued walking, right into another person.

I bumped into his chest and looked up to apologize before I realized it was him. I stopped and looked at him for a moment while the energy buzzed through me.

"Oh, I'm sorry, I didn't see you there," I blurted.

"No, you're fine." Kylan chuckled.

Silence radiated between the two of us. He looked past me at the scene that had just happened as if he was trying to watch it over again in his mind.

"What are you doing here?" I asked. This was pretty far out of town, and he was not someone I expected to be here.

"I live just on the outside of this area," he replied and asked his next questions without a breath. "What are you doing here? How did you do that?"

"How much did you see?" I tensed and asked, trying to joke away the scene.

"Those guys were pretty heated and you just stepped in between. How did you get them to calm down?" he asked, this time staring at me.

His eyes looked me up and down like they knew what they were searching for and just needed to find something to make it fit. I could see wheels turning in his head. I just didn't look any further for the specifics.

"Would you buy it if I said I appealed to their logical side?" I responded and shrugged my shoulders, waiting for him to laugh.

He did. The tension lifted as his chuckle calmed my edge.

"Okay," he said, still chuckling.

At this point, I had noticed his hand still lingering on my arm from when we ran into each other. Before I could look down at it, he patted my arm and removed his hand.

"What are you doing out here?" he asked, putting his hands back in his pockets.

He was probably the most inquisitive human I had ever met. I studied his expression to make sure I understood where his questions could lead. I didn't have enough energy in me to read his mind, so I could only rely on facial cues.

"Looking for a book at this old library," I replied and gently moved my curls off my shoulder. It was almost the truth.

"You came all this way for a book?" he scoffed and glanced down at the book in my arms.

"Yes." I stood my ground. He squinted, not believing my reason was good enough.

"What book?" He pressed a little harder and leaned over to see the cover. I pulled the book tighter to my chest to hide the title. Kylan looked up at me with curious eyes.

"*The History and Influence of the Armadillo*," I lied.

Kylan nodded his head and backed off.

"Fine, you don't have to tell me." He looked at me for a moment, deciding if he believed me or not.

"Can I walk you back to your car? This part of town is not exactly the safest."

I tried not to smile, knowing the only thing I would need protection from was the humans, and that was something he couldn't exactly help me with.

It was a chivalrous, human gesture, just unnecessary in my case.

"Thank you, but I think I will be just fine," I said as I walked backward, nodding to the spot behind him where I had just stopped a street fight.

I pivoted on my heel and continued walking away, not waiting for another response from Kylan. I almost completely forgot about the book I held.

"See you tomorrow, Kylan," I called over my shoulder, knowing he was still watching me. Now that he couldn't see my face, I smiled.

CHAPTER
EIGHT

Living here for a few months gave me something I had not expected. It gave me hope that maybe one day I could build lasting relationships, even with humans.

I knew it was risky, with either humans or Legends, but sometimes it seemed like it might be worth it. And those times were happening more often than not.

I walked into the office and greeted a few employees on the way to my desk. One of them stopped me before I was halfway there.

"Can we move our interview to this afternoon?" Chase asked excitedly. "I am leaving around that time to meet with the Grimaldi brothers."

I recognized the names as two wealthy brothers, renowned for their investments. Chase had been bold enough to bring up the idea to them, and now they wanted to buy up stock here.

Chase had been learning self-confidence and boldness, but his blond hair and soft skin made him appear younger. Most people took one look at him and chose not to take him seriously.

"The Grimaldi brothers? Wow, Chase, that's amazing!" I said, and he beamed proudly. "We can absolutely meet later. Good luck with your meeting."

He was bursting with happiness and immediately stepped forward for a hug. At the last second, he stopped and just settled for shaking my hand vigorously. His energy exploded from his body. I didn't even have to try to pull it from his hand.

My skin lit up as his energy raced through every nerve. I wanted to close my eyes and enjoy the power rejuvenating my body. I forced myself to keep my eyes open and focused on what I was doing.

I held the connection until his excitement dimmed down to calm happiness. When it did, I knew I should stop, but I wanted to keep going. I finally forced myself to take my hand away from his vulnerable skin.

The connection broke, and I could think clearly again.

I had to be careful. There was no limit to what my body could hold. Taking a small burst of energy only requires momentary contact.

The flow continues the longer we hold on, and it takes less than a minute for the entire reserve of energy to be stolen. In that case, the human dies a slow, but peaceful, death.

Chase pivoted on his foot and paused before continuing. My heartbeat stalled as he turned around and looked down at his hand.

His sharp eyes flicked back up to mine for a fraction of a second.

My mind raced through everything he could be thinking while my own thoughts flew into the mix.

What if he recognized the energy leaving?

What if I took too much?

I didn't move, and I definitely couldn't think to breathe.

Soon, he shook his head as if discarding whatever notion he imagined. He brushed his hand off on his pants and walked back to his fellow employees. Once there, they all slapped him on the back and shouted their congratulations.

My breath returned as my body relaxed. Living so closely with humans was proving to be much harder than I had anticipated, but strangely fulfilling. I wiped my hand on my white silk blouse and I smiled at a job well done.

"Job well done." Kylan finished my thought from behind me.

I turned, startled that I hadn't heard him approach. I could focus my attention really well, in one place. Once it was there, the other things around me fell away.

"Excuse me?" I asked him to clarify as my mind finished settling. I needed to know which part he was referring to.

"Chase," he pointed toward the employee at the center of admiration, "I would have never pegged him as the person to take down the Grimaldi brothers, but here he is." Kylan placed his hands in his pockets. "Thanks to you," he added, looking at me.

"Well, he hasn't closed the deal yet," I reminded him. "But he will. Thank you," I accepted. Kylan nodded.

"Well, now that your schedule is clear, would you like to have lunch with me?" He pivoted the conversation.

"Oh, thank you for the invitation, but I am..." I tried to decline, and he interrupted me.

"It wasn't an invitation," he said. "Mr. Lyle is heading out early today and wants us to have our weekly meeting earlier. So, lunch?"

He was more assertive than I gave him credit for. I was unsure if he was joking or if this was more than just a meeting. I opened my mouth to talk but couldn't before he cut in.

"Great! We have reservations at one o'clock. Be ready to

leave just before then," he instructed and winked just before he turned back to his office.

I was a little offended at how I didn't get a word in. His confidence was surprising. I shook it off and tried to continue on with my day. I grabbed the reports from the printer and headed toward Mr. Lyle's office. I walked in and noted Lisa no longer sat in the corner but stood over his desk, explaining the documents he was holding.

I smiled at yet another achievement of mine.

Lunchtime rolled around, and I wasn't remotely hungry. Chase's energy this morning was more than enough to keep me alert for an entire day.

I had taken more than I should have, but that kid needed to be knocked down a peg or two if he wanted a chance at reasoning with the Grimaldi brothers.

A knock came at my door right on time.

"Are you ready?" Kylan asked as he promptly walked straight into my office and behind my desk. "What are you working on now?"

He leaned over me and began reading aloud my notes. I stood to block his view of the screen. I waited for him to apologize for invading my personal space or privacy.

Nothing. I squinted at his arrogance, and he smiled.

"Yes, I'm ready." I reached past him and grabbed my bag to leave. I clicked off my computer screen to avoid more of his snooping.

"Good." He nodded as he led the way out. "The restaurant's not a far walk from here."

We rode the elevator down to the lobby in silence and rounded the corner to walk outside. He turned and strolled onto the sidewalk while I scanned for signs of restaurants, trying to guess where we were going.

"Where are you from, Kate?" Kylan asked me.

"Maine," I lied and tried to divert his attention. "Are you from here?"

"Sort of. I used to live here a long time ago but moved away. It feels good to be back, though," he said, taking in a deep breath of fresh air.

The tall buildings cluttered the edges of the cement sidewalks. Tall trees had been planted in between many of them, which served as the only green within sight.

"So, Maine. Is that where your family lives?"

"No," I answered, even quicker this time.

"Where do they live?"

"Is there a reason for the questions?" I said, ignoring the spark of irritation in my already-knotted stomach.

I was always suspicious of people looking too deeply into my past. I had trained myself to be cautious and aware of my surroundings. Him asking this many questions raised a huge red flag.

I searched around us to make sure I didn't recognize anyone from the Shadows. He didn't look like a Shadow, but on this little amount of energy, I couldn't distinguish between a Legend and a human anyway. The difference would be too subtle.

I narrowed my eyes and focused back on Kylan.

"Well, I figure all of us have to answer these prying questions when we talk with you. So, maybe you should get to see what it's like to answer them," he explained with a mischievous smile.

My irritation almost fizzled out.

"I asked those prying questions because it's part of my job. You're asking them to be nosy," I countered. "Am I wrong?"

"No," he answered. He still held his head high, but his answer showed signs of humility lying deep down. Enough to make me wonder if I should trust him. "I'm just trying to get to know you is all."

"We have been working together for months, and this conversation hasn't come up before," I noted.

"True, and for that, I apologize. But to be fair, I never had the opportunity to take you out to lunch before." He gloated.

"Mr. Lyle isn't leaving early today, is he?" I stopped walking.

"Well, Mr. Lyle always leaves a little early on Tuesdays. So, yes, but that may not be the reason I asked you to have lunch with me," he admitted easily.

He worked with Mr. Lyle more often and knew his schedule better than I did. He was still smiling because it had taken me this long to see through his plan.

"And what is that reason?" I asked, moving forward again.

He stopped walking and looked at me with the same deep look he had when we met. He looked at me like he was trying to figure something out and if he stared long enough, he might find it.

"To get to know you, Ms. Martin. As you put it, we have been working together for months, and this conversation hasn't happened." He smiled playfully and continued on walking.

At this point, we had turned the corner and walked almost to the end of the block when I saw what his eyes had fixed on.

Among the businesses and high-rises stood this little taco bar with a shabby apartment building above it.

An older couple stood behind the bar, cooking up meat and throwing it into homemade tortilla shells for their customers. A few tables stood on the wide sidewalk in front of the shop.

The worn sign had green letters on a wood background. The red awning came out from under the sign. The wooden, faded menu hung on the right side of the bar. The last person in line received his taco and happily paid the man in cash, telling him to keep the change.

"What is this place?" I leaned toward Kylan.

"This is the best lunch place around," he responded with arms open wide.

The couple had noticed Kylan at this point and walked around the bar and out of the shop to greet him with a fervent handshake.

"Mr. Kylan! So nice to see you again. Who is the lovely young lady?" the older man asked, nodding to me and reaching out his greasy hand toward mine. The man's eyes were framed by years of smile lines.

"Well, sir, this is Kate. She is the brightest new employee I've seen," he said, like I was a hero to be admired.

"Nice to meet you." I took his hand and gave it a firm shake.

"Wow, excellent handshake," he remarked to me and then leaned to Kylan. "I like this one, Mr. Kylan." He put his hand in front of his mouth, though he still spoke plenty loud for me to hear.

"Me too." Kylan nodded, patted the man's shoulder, and looked at me.

There it was, that same deep look. He tilted his head to the side again, and it gave me the same knotted feeling in my stomach.

"What will it be today?" The man hurried back behind the bar.

"The usual," Kylan said easily.

The man nodded, and his wife eagerly prepared the meal with her worn hands. Then the man looked at me. I tried to glance at the menu before he noticed I had no idea what to order.

"Would you like a suggestion?" Kylan whispered a little too closely, and it sent shivers up my spine. I elbowed him away and he laughed.

"I would like a number three, please," I said before Kylan could interject his opinion.

The man raised his eyebrows in surprise at my fast decision and started on it himself. Once we had our tacos, I reached for my wallet, but before I could pull out the cash, Kylan had already paid. We continued walking down the street, as there was nowhere to sit near the shop.

"I thought you said we had reservations," I said, looking at the full tables.

"We do," Kylan confirmed. "Just not here."

We walked down to a small park—really a glorified patch of grass—just a block over and made it to a bench underneath a large tree. It was among many other benches, but this one was the only one with shade.

Sitting on the surface was a folded card that had reserved written in cursive.

"Bench for two?" Kylan gestured toward that bench.

I smiled at the surprise and smoothed my skirt behind me before I sat.

"So, Kate, how do you like it here so far?" he asked as he took a huge bite of his taco, indicating that he wouldn't be talking for a while.

"I enjoy it," I said politely and waited.

Kylan waited too.

Finally, he moved his hand in a circle telling me to continue.

"I like the job. The city is beautiful. Being here isn't as bad as I worried it would be," I said.

Kylan was done eating, but he still waited for me to talk. I took my first bite instead.

Our digestion system could process food, but we needed more energy in our systems to live. Instead, we skipped a step in the digestion process and fed off energy we did not create ourselves—energy from humans.

"Even the food here is good," I added with a smile as the burst of flavor lingered on my tongue.

"So, what else?" he asked.

I squinted. "What do you mean?"

"You've mentioned all the basic, boring stuff. What about your family? Boyfriend? What brought you here? Your reasons are all nice, but they aren't exactly normal reasons to move across the country." Kylan shrugged, not looking at me.

His lack of eye contact gave me a sense of privacy, even though he was still listening to every word. It was a strategic move I had learned when I needed someone to share personal information.

"My reasons are personal. No significant family or friends to speak of. Just me." I tried to emphasize my lack of desire to discuss my personal life.

"So, you're lonely," Kylan quipped and then calmly took another bite.

"No, I am not," I disagreed, polite but firm. "And don't think I didn't notice you casually asking about a boyfriend in there. In case you haven't picked up on this yet, I am not interested in a relationship at the time."

"Right, right. Because you're focusing on your *career*." He said, putting the word career in air quotes.

"Hey." I slapped his arm. "I am good at what I do."

"You are, Kate." He grinned. "You are too good at what you do. I don't think anyone could slow you down if they tried."

I ignored the compliment.

"Also, as far as the boyfriend thing goes, that wasn't me hitting on you." He finished as he looked away and took the last bite of his taco.

"And this lunch wasn't a disguised date?" I asked, attempting to out his plan.

He turned and his eyes fell on me. As he stared, I tried to reach into his mind. I had almost made the connection when his response startled me.

"No." Kylan beamed.

He stood and walked our packages to the garbage can nearest him. I stood from the bench, not believing his weak denial.

"If I wanted to ask you on a date, you'd know it," Kylan said.

My mouth fell open.

Did he always talk this way?

Kylan left me wondering and moved on from that topic with ease.

He continued the questions, and we walked back to our building. He was an annoyingly perfect gentleman. The rest of our conversation was platonic at best. Oddly, I felt more comfortable the longer we talked. Most of the answers I provided were lies mingled with gems of truth.

Anything about my past remained a lie. I was ashamed of what I used to be, and Alec's lingering threat made it dangerous for anyone to have this information. Human and Legend alike.

Kylan walked me all the way to my office and thanked me for having lunch with him. I attempted to stare long enough to finish the connection I had started in the park. All I needed was another second or two of unbroken eye contact and I would be in.

As if on cue, he turned around and headed back to his office before I could finish.

That just left me standing there, still staring at him before I turned and went in. I chided myself for not being able to get in faster. My eyes caught Lisa standing nearby as she misinterpreted the whole thing.

She came scurrying through my doorway a few moments after Kylan left.

"You went out to lunch with Kylan?!" she exclaimed.

I quickly reached past her and shut the door to muffle her squealing. My hands gripped the door as I saw Kylan standing just outside his office. He smiled proudly just before I closed my door.

"We ate lunch together," I answered and turned around to face her. I walked back to my desk and sat down. "I thought it was a meeting, and it wasn't but…"

"But it was really a date?" she finished my sentence for me and looked at me with her all-too-eager eyes. I returned her look with a firm reprimand.

"No, it wasn't," I corrected her and lifted my hand to hide a small smile creeping up my face.

"Oh, so it was just a meeting?" she asked, her tone showing she was obviously disappointed with the lack of details.

"No, it wasn't a meeting. It was just a lunch between two colleagues. We both have to eat, you know," I tried to clarify. She smiled anyway.

"Lisa," I chided.

"No, no, I understand. It was just lunch. I get it," she surrendered. "At least your crush notices you."

"Not a crush," I said. "And what do you mean by that?"

"Nothing, it's…it's nothing." Lisa shook her head.

I moved to one of the chairs near my office door and patted the one next to me.

She didn't meet my eyes. It even looked like she was beginning to blush. I could feel her energy spiking. She was nervous.

I touched her knee with my fingertips. I took some of her energy from her in attempt to clear her mind. She looked up at me as she calmed down.

My eyes stayed with hers as the energy drained. I didn't hear her words anymore as the flow of energy drowned everything else out. The longer my hand rested on her skin, the more I wanted to suck the warmth inside of me.

"Who is it?" I asked.

"Chase Kirchek," she blurted all at once.

My eyebrows shot up, and my hand fell off her knee.

I was grateful for the temporary distraction. It allowed me to stop pulling her energy. Something about the fact that I knew her helped as well. I didn't want to hurt her. Maybe that would have been enough to stop me.

"Chase? Really?" I questioned, bringing myself back. I could see the answer written all over her face.

She nodded.

When I almost jumped out of my chair from excitement, I realized that I had taken too much energy from her. Despite scolding myself for it, the buzz was intoxicating. The energy swirled inside my body, and the room itself seemed brighter, the colors intensified.

"When did this happen?" I prompted her, needing her to keep talking and keep my mind working on something else. Anything else.

"I've had a thing for him ever since he started here. Even when he was shy. He was just so cute, and he always greeted me when he walked by my desk. I know he is popular around the office now after landing the Grimaldi brothers' account, but somehow, I guess I just hope..."

She knotted her hands together. "I hope I have a chance with him."

Her wary gaze looked at me to make sure I didn't think she was crazy. When she saw my smile, she continued.

"I guess I also thought that since people look at me differently now, you know, that I'm not the lowest on the totem pole anymore, maybe he might consider going out with me," she finished her thought like it was painful. "Is that dumb of me?"

"Not at all," I said.

She let out the breath she had been holding. I waited for her to meet my gaze again. She smiled and ducked her head.

"Really?"

She had changed completely since the first time I met her. She was radiant now. Something inside of me wanted to make this happen. I actually cared about whether or not she was happy.

It was a nice feeling, even if it did seem out of place with a human.

"Just give it a little time." I shrugged. "You might be surprised."

Lisa brushed a stray curl behind her ear, as her other hand tapped on her thigh. She stood and turned toward the door. She lingered in the doorway to say one last thing.

"About you and Kylan. You know, it's just"—she looked at me just before she took the last step out—"you two do look cute together."

She hurried and nearly slammed the door closed behind her.

A smile grew on my face, one that only the empty room could see. I looked at the wooden door that Lisa had closed behind her. The door to my office I was starting to like at a company with people I was getting used to.

Maybe getting closer to these people wouldn't be as hard as I'd imagined.

Maybe.

CHAPTER
NINE

That afternoon, I dove into the books, trying to find any new leads, and came up with nothing.

I couldn't find anything linking back to the locket on display. It might have been too soon to track down an actual lead anyway. The longest I had been able to stay in a place while tracking leads was a year.

Instead, I focused on anything else.

During the day I went to work and found myself talking with others more and more. Slowly, the truths outnumbered the lies I had been supplying. It was good to have friends like Lisa, and even Kylan.

Despite his attractiveness, there wasn't any romantic connection brooding over every conversation. That didn't stop Lisa's not-so-subtle winks every time she saw the two of us together.

At the end of the day, my body was weary, and my mind was especially tired of hitting dead ends. I wanted to put the search on hold tonight and just sleep.

Well, maybe not sleep. I more wanted to lie on my bed

and think about nothing for a few hours. I shut down my computer, listening to the silence in the office. Everyone had long gone home.

I reached into my top drawer and grabbed a book that I had picked up from a library a long time ago. I held it in my hands and stared at the cover. The book was the first one I had noticed in my searches.

My fingers grazed the old leather binding. It was soft from being opened too many times.

At first, it was promising but turned out to be mostly useless. I brought it to work because it held a sentimental value of where this all started. It was one of the few things I carried from place to place.

Maybe it would spark an epiphany. I bit the inside of my cheek.

I had thought about it all day and nothing came to me. I threw the useless book on my desk and marched to my window.

A few remaining humans rushed in the street in work clothes. The rest had changed and were probably enjoying their evening. Their life was so simple. The longer I was around them, the more I was fascinated by their experience.

I was so wrapped up in my thoughts, I didn't hear him come in.

By the time I turned around, Kylan had walked in and picked up the book. I internally scolded myself for not hearing him enter.

"I thought everyone had gone," I said until I focused on the book in his hands.

The book. My eyes widened.

When my heart stopped, the silence was overwhelming. I watched him carefully, studying his every move in the next few seconds. His hand ran over the front cover. It was too late to hide the title.

"Legends?" he asked, staring into my eyes.

My heart rate sped. I scrambled quickly for an excuse in my mind.

"Yeah," I said, trying to stay calm through my pounding heart. "Just a hobby of mine. I'm fascinated by conspiracy theories. Pretty strange, right?"

I took a deep breath and remembered most humans did not even believe in Legends. I had nothing to worry about.

Kylan didn't seem to buy it.

He turned the book over in his hands and looked up at me. As his thoughts completed, he squinted.

"What interests you about them? Legends aren't even real." He shifted the book from one hand to another.

"Is any conspiracy or myth real?" I chuckled. "That's the point. It's just a fun read."

"I don't know," he mused, "People coming in the night and stealing your energy is more…creepy than fun."

He tentatively placed the book back on my desk. I stared into his eyes. He seemed to be shrugging it off, but I had to be sure. I knew I had enough energy. I just needed to use it wisely if I didn't want him to notice.

I focused on him and made the connection to his mind. I had tried getting in before and failed. Despite years of practicing, I was still fairly new to reading. Once I was in his mind, I quickly scanned through Kylan's thoughts.

He wasn't worried that I was a Legend. He was worried about my interest in them. He kept asking questions about why I would be looking into them. I realized he was not suspicious of me being a Legend, he was suspicious I would find something out. About him.

Then it finally clicked. He was a Legend.

My eyes widened, and I was so shocked, the connection between his mind and mine broke. That was why it had taken me so long to read him on the bench or in the office. He wasn't human.

"I felt that," he said and narrowed his eyes. "You couldn't have done that..."

He snatched the book from my table and threw it right toward my face. It was coming too fast for me to try and grab it. I sucked in a breath and reached my hands out. The air particles in front of me duplicated. The book halted before it reached me, hanging in midair.

At that moment, I was grateful I had enough energy in my body. Taking more than I needed from Chase and Lisa had proven quite useful. I looked directly back at him.

"Legend," he breathed, both surprised and amazed.

He smiled and relaxed his shoulders into the cool bravado he normally held. I used the dense air particles to force the book back at him. He caught it in midair as well. Once he did, he spun the book and set it gently on the table near the door.

All without touching it.

"Takes one to know one." I lifted my chin.

This time, I was smiling too. I had not met another Legend since I left the Shadows. It was a relief to know there was one person like me in this area. We looked at each other for a moment, taking it all in.

I took a second of focus away to destroy the extra cells I had created and turned the air pressure back to normal. It was a force of habit to clear my tracks.

"What do we do now?" I asked, breaking the silence.

"I think you should meet my family," he said as though it wasn't significant at all.

"Pardon?"

Out of all the answers to fit in this situation, that wasn't one of them.

"You'll see." He hardly comforted my wondering mind with his vague response.

I followed him out of my office, noticing the slight change when my body hit the denser parts of air around Kylan. He had left them the way he created them.

Both of us walked down to our cars. Once we were in the parking garage, Kylan looked around and then bolted to the car. He traveled the distance of the entire floor in less than two seconds.

I smiled and followed after him. I reached his car and reveled in the smile on his face. There was only one thought in my head.

Finally, someone to run with again.

"It's not fair that running this fast takes hardly any energy, but one use of your power and it's all downhill from there," I said, smiling.

"My thoughts exactly." Kylan laughed lightly.

I reached for the door handle. Kylan's hand beat me to it. My skin brushed his hand as I pulled back. Touching him now was starkly different from when I thought he was human. Nothing had really changed, but at the same time, everything just had.

When my skin grazed his, it seemed like sparks jolted through my arm. His eyes trapped themselves in my stare.

"How do you keep your secret?" I asked and couldn't break my eyes away.

Kylan just gently tilted his head to the side. Even the way he looked at me had changed from a few minutes ago. When his eyes scanned my face now, they didn't question anymore. They explored.

"You know, isn't HR kind of a hard position for someone trying to avoid…problems with humans?" I clarified and looked at the ground.

"I could ask you the same thing," Kylan opened the door and I stepped inside.

He was around the car in seconds and already sitting next to me.

"Isn't it hard to be around that many of them?" I asked again.

"Not unless you've never done it before." Kylan glanced at me.

I shook my head and turned my eyes away from him. I knew he understood. He continued on without skipping a beat.

"I find that hiding doesn't make you any safer. It doesn't really make sense, but being right in the middle of humans is where I feel the most…comfortable," he said, choosing his words carefully.

I looked up at him again. His soft green eyes made me feel like everything was going to be all right. For the first time since I stepped into the human world, I relaxed. His stare continued, his eyes roaming all over my face.

"What?" I stared back at him, raising my chin.

"I'm still just a little stunned. Meeting a new Legend is kinda exciting. Like the day you discover your powers, you know?" Kylan smiled and threw the car in gear.

"You found them all in one day?" I asked, a little too surprised.

"Yeah. I mean, they don't start developing until you're a few Legend years old anyway, but once they did…" Kylan said, his face falling slightly. "I had a father that didn't settle for mediocrity."

"You're not the only one," I said under my breath.

The drive from the office to his home was anything but silent. We both gushed about the annoyance of keeping secrets. The connection between us was instant.

We cruised past the tall buildings, through the streets of older homes that had been there for decades, even past the old museum. The scenery changed from densely populated to tree-lined streets and sparse houses.

The farther we went, the more I relaxed into my seat. My laughs slowly became real.

At that moment, I wasn't worried about anything. I was just me.

CHAPTER
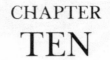
TEN

We pulled up to his house. It was smaller than I expected, considering his high-end HR job.

It had a large porch and was not very close to other houses. It had siding, wood shutters, the whole package. It even had a porch swing. All it needed was a dog napping under the tree, and it could have been in a Hallmark movie.

The cozy feeling of what it would be like to step through the doors tingled against my skin. We walked up to the double French doors on the side of the house.

Kylan stopped me before we went inside.

"My family can be a little...intense." He looked at the glass doors and then at the porch floor.

"Oh, I'm sure they are nothing like my family," I joked.

Too far. I shut my eyes and scolded myself.

Something about this comforting feeling on the porch made me forget who I was and who I was talking to. I shook my head and allowed my self-preservation instinct to kick back in.

"You have a family?" he asked, a little too interested. He must have assumed I was all alone.

"No, not anymore," I corrected him. He seemed interested in the story but I moved away. "That's a topic for another time. Let's go inside."

"Okay. I did warn you," he teased and opened the front door.

Before we even saw a person, I heard a loud, male voice yell, "Kylan's here!"

A tall man rushed from around the corner and almost toppled Kylan over in a hug. Kylan smiled over the man's shoulder and hugged him back.

The warm air floated over both of us just like I had pictured. We entered the living room, with the kitchen right next to it. The colors and design were a series of whites and grays, much like the design at the office.

I looked at the people standing there, both of them smiling at Kylan like they hadn't seen him in years.

"Of course, I'm here. This is my house, Derek." He smiled as he messed up Derek's curly brown hair.

"How have you been, bro?" Derek slapped a hand on Kylan's back, still smiling.

Derek's skin was darkened from an ethnic background I couldn't quite place. His muscles were thicker but not as defined as Kylan's. If it weren't for his silly smile, Derek might have been intimidating.

A small woman came out from behind Derek and gave Kylan a hug as well.

"Cassie, good to see you." Kylan brought her close, the top of her head only reaching to his chest.

Her auburn hair just barely brushed the tops of her shoulders, the ends flared in every direction.

She couldn't have been living here long because the sun

didn't shine enough for the dusting of freckles barely visible on her nose and shoulders.

Cassie's eyes trained on mine as she hugged Kylan. When she released him, Kylan turned around to me.

"This is Kate Martin," he gestured to me and put a hand on my back.

He did not force me to step forward, just left his hand there for support. I tried to relax my muscles where he touched me, but couldn't. I watched all the eyes switch to looking at me.

"She's like us," Kylan added slowly.

Their eyes lit up with understanding as they turned their gaze back to Kylan to confirm.

"You mean..." Derek edged.

He held Cassie in his arms and checked her reaction before looking back up at Kylan and waiting for the answer. It seemed like Cassie was the wiser of the two, and Derek knew it.

"Yes, Derek, she's a Legend. Kate, this is Cassie and Derek Challis," he said.

Derek looked like he could be Kylan's biological brother, even though Kylan explained that they weren't related by blood. They both had brown hair, though Kylan's was lighter and not curly. They also had the same wide smile.

"They just arrived a few weeks ago and have been getting settled in. They dragged their feet because they didn't want to leave our last area." Kylan shot a look at both of them.

"Hey, Florida was the best idea yet. Can you blame us for wanting to stay?" Derek joked and swiped a hand at Kylan, which he easily dodged.

Florida. That made much more sense with Cassie's tan.

As Derek hugged the woman closer, I saw their matching silver wedding rings glinting in the light.

"No, Florida is beautiful," I added, trying not to look like I was watching them too closely.

That had been the second place I ran when I got away from the Shadows. I wanted to maintain the sunshine, smiles, and openness. So naturally, I ran from one sunny place to the next.

"Yeah, but all it took was one of Cassie's art students finally looking up at her and asking, 'How old are you again?' and they were gone," Kylan joked back to Derek and Cassie.

"Gotta protect the family." Derek shrugged. "Can't be raising suspicion."

Kylan nodded and then paused before he looked around the room.

"Where is..." Kylan trailed off.

Apparently, someone was missing. I glanced around, nervous that someone was going to spring from the corner at any moment.

"Rachel?" Cassie asked. "She's late, as usual."

"Punctuality doesn't exactly run in the family," Derek added in a hushed tone.

"I may be older than her, but I can't control when she shows up or not." Cassie fought her own grin as she smacked him on the arm.

"Cassie and Rachel are sisters, biological sisters," Derek explained.

Legends rarely have blood siblings. Most of the time, a Legend was an only child because the parent only lived long enough to have one kid. Either the labs, humans, or other Legends caused the parent's untimely death.

"Well, that's my family for you." Kylan smiled at them.

"Do you live here together?" I couldn't stop myself from asking it.

They called themselves a family, but they were also grown adults. Somehow seeing them was different from all the Shadows living together in the mansion.

Kylan was the first to laugh.

"No, we don't," Derek answered through his own laugh. "This is Kylan's place. Cassie and I will be living a few miles from here. We just got into town. Rachel lives in West Haven. We just came over to meet you. He said it was 'important,' so we all came running."

I looked over at Kylan, who was sending a cautioned look to Derek.

"Well, it's not every day we meet another Legend. So, I wanted to introduce you to each other." He brushed it off.

Cassie, still behind Kylan, folded her arms across her chest and looked between him and me.

"Well, I'm grateful to meet all of you," I said to try and move the conversation again.

Honestly, I had no idea what to do. I had never met another Legend family other than my own. They were not a family in the human sense. Two of them were married to each other and the other two were blood siblings. I was still unsure of how Kylan fit into the picture.

Was he dating Rachel? So many questions and observations flooded through my mind. I tried to pick through each one and answer them myself.

Then I felt it.

The slight tapping on my mind. Someone was trying to enter and read my thoughts.

I immediately looked around to see who it was. My eyes quickly fixed on Cassie, who was already returning my stare. I narrowed my eyes at her, clenching my teeth together.

This was her.

Whether she was Kylan's family or not, it was rude to go poking around in someone's mind uninvited.

"Kate, I am sure you have plenty of questions, and we have some for you too, I bet. Come in and sit..." Kylan stopped talking when he noticed my fixed stare.

I felt her attempted connection and debated if I should switch it the other way to read into her mind or create a shock of pain so she would get out. Considering I used most of my energy at the office, I wasn't sure I had enough for either.

"Cassie, stop it," Kylan chided her.

She blinked, and the connection snapped. She turned and looked up at Kylan innocently as she folded her hands in front of her.

"What are you talking about?" She smiled harmlessly and then her grin turned wicked, pulling at the side of her mouth and giving her away.

"Aw, Cass!" Derek took over the chiding from here. "We don't want to scare her away. We just met her."

Cassie's mouth tightened into a thin line as she threw her hands up in mock surrender.

"Out of curiosity, who won?" Kylan asked quietly.

He knew what was going on between the two of us. He already knew I could read minds, and he must have known Cassie could too.

The only question left was who was stronger.

I don't know what kind of training she had, but I had no doubt of my honed skills. Reading may not have been the strongest talent of mine, but creating blocks against it was in much better shape.

If I had more energy fueling my body, she wouldn't have stood a chance.

"She did," Cassie huffed and tossed her hair back. "I couldn't get in."

Kylan looked down at me with his eyebrows up, a smile pulling at the side of his mouth.

"Wait, can you read minds too?" Derek asked me, but Kylan answered.

"Yeah, that's how I knew she was a Legend. She read my mind, and I remembered the feeling from when Cassie sometimes invades people's private lives." Kylan changed his tone and directed the last part to Cassie.

"I had to make sure she was the real deal. Plus, I didn't get anything anyway." Cassie rolled her eyes.

"You're strong enough to keep her out?" Derek mused.

Kylan looked impressed and proud, as if I was the new puppy he was showing off to his family and they all just saw me do a cool trick. I smiled at how impressed they sounded with me.

"What Level are you?" Derek finally asked. I looked calmly at him, ready to answer, but Cassie interrupted.

"Derek, you said we shouldn't be rude. Asking someone their Level when you just met them is rude." She nudged him with her elbow.

He didn't change his focus. He looked at me lazily, but in a way that I knew he was not going to look away until he got his answer.

"She's obviously strong enough to keep you out of her mind, which is impressive. It's an honest question," Derek responded, not looking away from me.

I didn't realize asking that was rude. Maybe it was like pointing or staring. Which apparently was not rude in this family, because all eyes were hooked on me.

I had always been honest, if not boastful, about my Level. Every Shadow was. Perhaps I should've kept it to myself.

"Kate, you don't have to answer if you don't want to,"

Kylan said and looked back at the others. "But I am kind of curious as well." He hurried and finished.

Cassie came from behind and smacked his arm just like she had with Derek. Kylan twisted away from her and lifted his smiling eyes back to me.

"It's okay, I don't mind," I answered, smiling and standing a little taller. "I'm a Four."

Gasps were just barely audible before the room fell silent. All of their eyes widened. The sound of the door opening cracked the tension filling the room.

"All right, all right, I'm here," a woman's voice called out from the back room as she stepped around the corner.

The woman looked like a more elegant version of Cassie, a little taller, with smoother and darker red hair. This must be Rachel. No freckles were visible on her face, but she had the same shade of brown eyes as her sister.

"A Four?" Cassie gasped, like knowing my Level was painful to her.

Derek's mouth fell open just a little.

"Who's a Four?" The woman stopped walking.

"Kate, this is Rachel McBride." Kylan rushed through the introduction. "Rachel, this is Kate Martin."

"Wait is she…" She slowly pointed toward me.

Kylan nodded, not even trying to hide his smile.

"That's as high as Kylan," Rachel sighed.

I looked back to Kylan now. *Was he the only Four here?*

I had never socialized much with anyone less than a Three. Compared to the environment where I grew up, I didn't think being a Four was that special. Kylan straightened, almost as if he was in the presence of royalty.

"Well, no wonder I couldn't get in." Cassie threw her arms in the air. "She's a Four! I had no chance."

Derek patted her shoulder and she leaned into him.

"Sorry." Rachel shook her head and reached a hand out to me. "It's nice to meet you."

I shook her hand and smiled. She stepped back to stand next to Cassie, leaning down and whispering a comment that I couldn't catch.

"What are all of you?" I interrupted.

Everyone went silent again. Apparently, that was not a good question to ask either. After a few painstaking seconds of pause, Kylan stepped in.

"Cassie and Derek are both Twos. Rachel is a One. And, I am a Four, obviously," he said quietly, almost as if he was happy that I was at a high Level, but didn't think the same way about himself.

Why would he want to hide his Level? I pulled my eyebrows together.

He had no reason to feel guilty for what he was born with. It wasn't a choice to regret.

Each Level meant you had one power and a certain caliber of strength. A Level One could have any of the five powers, but only one of them. A Two had any two of the five abilities.

Cassie had the ability to read, and something else. I couldn't tell anything from looking at Derek or Rachel yet. In theory, a Level Five had all five abilities and would be the strongest.

Being Level Fours meant Kylan and I had the most power. We each possessed four of the five enhanced abilities based on which diluted serum originally created our ancestors. The altered genes got passed down through generations, hence Cassie and Rachel both being Legends.

The values of the Shadows still pressed against my mind, making me shift my feet and fight a shudder. A Four associating with Ones and Twos felt wrong. Not quite as wrong as just mingling with humans, but still enough to make me quite uncomfortable.

I took a breath and straightened my shoulders. Either I could walk out the door, or I could learn what it was really like to live as they do.

The clear doors taunted me, reminding me that outside was only a few steps away.

Leaving would be comfortable, but I hadn't come all this way for comfort. So I stayed.

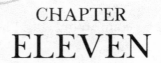

CHAPTER
ELEVEN

"Well, now that we've got that out of the way. Wanna sit?" Kylan motioned me toward one of the couches in the living room.

Cassie and Derek moved to sit on the white couch opposite us. When I sat, I looked at Rachel, who was still standing in the corner.

"Um, I'll just stand," Rachel muttered as she backed up.

"Why?" Cassie questioned, looking her sister up and down.

"Just…don't really feel like sitting down." She waved her hand and paced, trying to avoid eye contact with anyone.

I watched carefully. When I was really paying attention, I recognized it. The signs were all there. She wasn't excited or nervous.

She was high on human energy.

The vitality was practically pouring out of her body. Her eyes sparkled in the lights, and her body moved with a certain fluidity that comes from being completely satiated. I missed that feeling.

"Ugh, Rachel, again?" Cassie complained.

"I'm sorry! I would have toned it down, but Kylan texted and said we needed to be here now. I didn't know what to prepare for," she rambled and twirled her red hair around her fingers.

I smiled when I heard her confession. Her high was because she wanted it, not out of necessity. She was used to this level of energy, but apparently, the rest of her family was not.

It was almost refreshing to see normal Legends sometimes overdid it as well. The Shadows always took more energy than necessary.

The Shadow's mansion was completely hidden within sprawling plains. The nearest city was miles away. The previous owner was a multi-millionaire with no friends, and no one missed him once he was gone. The mansion was all ours now.

Besides the cities, the only other source of energy was the occasional hiker or two. That was exactly what Alec and I had found.

I stared ahead at the couple, their tent pitched behind them and the morning fire ready to cook breakfast.

It didn't take long for them to realize we weren't out here to enjoy the dusty scenery.

"Honey, get out of here." The man kept his eyes on us.

By the time she took her first step, Alec was in front of her and had grabbed her by both arms. She struggled for a moment until her body went limp as her energy coursed into Alec. He took a deep breath and let her fall to the dirt.

The man lunged for Alec. I flashed up behind him and grabbed the headphones in his pocket. I wrapped the cord around his neck and pulled.

He reached to push me off or remove the cord from his neck, failing at both. I used the cord to whip him around to face me. He clawed his neck where the cord left an indentation in his skin.

"What are you?" he managed to cough out as he half-stood, trying to look me in the eyes.

"Your worst nightmare," I answered him, and I stroked his hair back behind his ear.

His eyes were horrified, but he was too scared to move away. With his spiky hair and baggy clothes, he barely looked eighteen human years old. My hand touched the side of his soft face, and his eyes darted over to watch what I was doing.

"Please, don't do this," he begged, glancing at the girl's limp body on the hard ground at Alec's feet.

"I don't want to." I sympathized with him and watched as his eyes went wild.

"What?" he asked and looked at Alec again, who was slowly stepping closer.

"I don't want to kill you, any of you. I don't." I sighed and put my hand on his chest. "But I can feel your energy running just beneath your skin. I can imagine the rush when it floods into me. It's like nothing else. I'm sure you're a nice person, with people who will miss you. But right now, all I can think about is your pounding heart and the anticipation building inside of me."

I looked him in the eyes and watched as the light slowly drained out of them. He tried to stumble away, but my hands kept him pinned close to me. The rush of excitement flooded into every particle of my body.

"I guess it's not that I don't want to." I smiled and closed my eyes to revel in the feeling. "It's that I shouldn't want to. But it just feels so good."

As he took his last breath, his final energy burst into me. The sweet climax of vitality melded into my muscles, bones, and breath. I opened my eyes to a sharpened world around me.

Guilt should have been ringing in my ears, but it wasn't. I looked at Alec's smiling face, and everything else around me fell away.

"That was exactly what I needed," I sighed as I stretched my neck from side to side.

"Great, then let's go home." He offered his hand to me.

I looked at his open hand and then back to him. I rejected his offer by bolting toward our home, getting a head start.

"Nice try, Mara," Alec called from behind. He caught up and ran beside me long enough to look me in the eyes.

"I'm still faster." I focused ahead.

"Prove it," he whispered.

The race was on, and we both laughed. We were so high on the energy we had just stolen.

Nothing else mattered. And why would it? We were on top of the world.

Rachel and I were different. I killed to get the energy I wanted. Her eyes didn't show the remorse or anxiety from stolen lives. She was free, while the gravity of my mistakes crushed me.

What hurt worse was that I still caught myself wanting it. Life with the Shadows was a lot of bad, but it was also so easy.

Seeing Rachel reminded me of exactly how good it felt to have that kind of power pumping through my body. My fingertips tingled at the thought of filling myself up like that again.

I had not had enough energy in decades to bounce the way she did. For my own safety, and others', I needed to keep it that way. The threshold for taking a significant amount of energy and taking their life completely was still too blurred for me.

In that way, maybe Rachel was much better at being a

Legend than myself. She had enough self-control to stop. I had none.

"So, who did you meet first?" I leaned over to Kylan and asked.

I needed some form of distraction to keep my mouth from watering over how much energy I wanted, and how badly I wanted it.

"The first was Derek. We annoyed each other right away. He quickly became the brother I never had," Kylan said.

"Aw, you're gonna make me blush." Derek choked up for a moment and then dropped the act and smiled.

Kylan smiled, waving a hand at his brother.

"Then Cassie came along and swept Derek off his feet. Obviously, they've been inseparable ever since," Kylan added.

Derek lifted Cassie's hand, which he was already holding, and kissed it gently. She blushed and looked the other direction.

"Cassie found Rachel and brought her back to us," Kylan said and then leaned in and whispered, "The jury is still out on whether or not we actually appreciate her addition to the family."

"Hey!" Rachel piped up.

"So, it all started with this clown, right here." Kylan leaned forward and smacked Derek's knee.

"None of you have…" I started, not sure how to finish the sentence.

My hand reached up and tucked my dark hair behind my ear. Bringing up families was a sensitive subject for most.

It had been only two generations, almost three, since the original experiment. Because the average Legend lifespan was about ten times that of humans, their parents or even grandparents could have been in that lab.

Most of those families didn't have the chance to stay together. In the following decades, the labs hunted Legends down mercilessly to correct their mistake of us escaping in the first place.

Humans found out and continued the chase of the original Legends as a witch-hunt. The rest scattered into hiding or ran to the Shadows.

"Families?" Derek finished for me.

"Yeah," I said and put my hand down and sat a little farther back.

"Our parents are dead." Rachel answered for her and her sister while Cassie shifted uncomfortably in her seat. "Derek's parents joined a lab and disowned him when he refused to come along."

"What?" I asked in shock.

"Can't choose your blood." Derek shrugged and looked at the floor.

"Which lab?" I prodded, maybe a bit more than I should have.

There were two main labs that I knew of, both of them racing against each other. The one with the most promising progress to a new serum was in Louisiana. No one dared take them on. They had both Legends and humans on their side, all of them fighting for what they believed was right.

"The last time I saw them was on the steps of the lab in London. I have no idea if they're still there," Derek answered and then looked me up and down. "You're pretty brave to ask."

He smiled and actually looked calm, as if years and years had allowed him to deal with the heartbreak. A picture of hope for my future.

I shrugged my shoulders. Derek smiled and looked at Kylan, fluttering his eyebrows.

"Nice work, bro. She's a catch."

"No," I blurted. "We're not—"

"I will warn you though," Derek interrupted. "Don't ask any more questions about Cassie and Rachel's family."

I pulled my eyebrows together and looked at Cassie. She had her arms folded and locked her eyes with the ground. I glanced at Rachel, and she was looking down as well.

"It's not a story you want to hear," Rachel muttered and finally looked at me before she checked to see what Cassie was doing.

"Besides, we are each other's family now," Kylan finished and looked around the room at all of them. The girls looked up to him, and both of them showed the faintest smile.

Kylan's eyes were kind before his mischievous smile took over.

"Even though I found Derek when I didn't have the highest standards, at this point, I'm stuck with him."

"You want to say that a little louder?" Derek challenged, leaning forward from his seat.

Cassie was already looking annoyed at the two of them. Kylan sat up in response.

"Hey, hey, break it up you two," Rachel stepped between them and put her hands up.

A rush of air pushed them back into their seats. I could feel the new pressure against my shoulder closest to Kylan.

"Ah..." Derek smiled. "Looks like someone has some extra energy they want to play with."

Her hands dropped, and the pressure dispersed into the air. So, creating was her Level One ability. Rachel backed up while Kylan and Derek stood.

The brothers moved at the same time. Derek grabbed Rachel and pinned her arms behind her. Kylan put her in a headlock and rubbed his fist through Rachel's smooth hair.

The brothers laughed as Rachel scrambled to get away from them.

She may have been high, but it looked like both of them were still stronger than her. That's how it usually worked when a One went up against a higher Level.

In the tussle, they all tripped over each other and hit the ground. The three of them sprawled out and laughed before sitting up. The two men fist-bumped over her.

"They've fought like brothers since the day I met Kylan," Cassie sighed as she sat down next to me.

She looked at them with a knowing smile that said those two never seemed to grow up around each other. They may not have been blood-related, but they were brothers now and, to them, that was all that mattered.

"It's fun to have you here with us," Cassie added and leaned in close to me so she could speak loud enough for only me to hear.

"Thank you," I responded, caught off guard by her genuine eyes. "It's nice to be here."

"You must be something special," she continued. "Kylan hasn't smiled this much in a long time." After she finished, she stood from the couch.

Derek walked over to Cassie with Rachel following behind, which left Kylan by himself, sitting on the floor. He casually had one arm tossed over his knee as he looked at me and then away again. Out of everyone here, I was his person to go to.

It made me a little nervous. I was not a good "go-to" person.

Kylan moved to sit next to me again and after a while, we all talked and laughed the way Kylan and I did with each other.

For a moment, it felt like I was not just an outsider but

like I was one of them. That was a feeling I hadn't experienced in a long time.

We finally all decided to go home and get some sleep for the next day. Without energy teeming in my system, I needed sleep to extend the amount of energy I had.

Kylan stood and walked me to the door of his house. He closed the pristinely clean door behind him, but it didn't shut completely.

The warm air rushed through the opening to meet the cool outdoors. I stopped him before we walked off the porch, not wanting to leave. I hadn't felt this much at home since I left the mansion.

"Thank you for tonight." I touched his arm and changed the mood to serious. "It was nice to see others like me."

Kylan smiled at me. "It was nice to see *you* tonight."

"What?" I asked.

"You always have this guard up and only show the personality that you choose to," he said.

I tried to correct him, but he put his finger to my mouth.

"It was nice to meet the real Kate tonight. She is a lovely woman, and you should let her out more," he finished and pulled his finger from my lips.

I just nodded and looked into his inviting green eyes. The faint smile lines surrounding them and the slight upturn of a happy emotion made me not want to look away.

I wondered if I was safe with them. I saw no red flags, but I couldn't be too careful. Not after what happened with Alec and the Shadows. I never had my guard up with them because I felt I never needed it. I trusted them, and that had been a terrible mistake.

I wanted to be sure it would not be the same letting this family into my life. I remembered my former thoughts of how it was always safer to be alone. The feeling of being wanted and welcomed fit so well that it was hard to reconcile with my fear of Alec finding me if I kept looking for the necklace.

The two warring feelings couldn't exist together. One would win out.

Right now, the feeling of utter peace took the lead. The image of the necklace faded in my mind the longer I let the feeling warm my body. It wasn't abrupt like when Thayer forced an emotion on me. It was slow and melded into every piece of me naturally.

Kylan looked down to the ground and put his hands in his pockets. When his eyes looked back up to me, he opened his mouth to speak, but no words came out.

"Just kiss her already!" Derek shouted from inside the house.

I heard a punch hit against his body.

"Ow!" Derek blurted.

When I glanced over, I saw Cassie had punched him in the arm. He leaned back into the couch, looking at Kylan through the window and winking at him. Rachel giggled in the corner of the room.

Kylan closed his eyes and turned his head away from his family, trying to hide from the embarrassing moment they had just created. His hand pushed the door closed the rest of the way. The satisfying click let us know we were actually alone now.

"I'm so sorry." He tried to cover them up by stepping in between me and them. "They're normally not like this."

"It's okay. They're sweet." I shrugged off his family's insinuation. Kylan looked back up from the porch. Our eyes locked for a moment. The butterflies threatened to release from my stomach.

I echoed his own words back to him. "Besides, if I wanted you to kiss me, you'd know it."

CHAPTER
TWELVE

My front door clicked shut behind me. My mind raced through everything that just happened.

Kylan was a Legend.

His family was nice but far too nosy for my comfort.

I couldn't shake the excitement or the freedom of running in the parking lot or the warmth of a family around me.

Yet they were dangerous. All of them. But the feeling rushing through my veins was impossible to ignore. I wanted what they had. I craved it.

I eventually made it to my bed and stared at the ceiling all night long. I thought about the day I had just had. The memories replayed in my mind, just as bright as they were when I experienced them. Maybe that was what spilled over into the doorstep scene with Kylan. That night, my mind wandered to the place I used to call home.

I walked around the corner of the inner cobblestone courtyard that opened up to the sky. A grand balcony hung over all four sides, creating arched hallways underneath.

Commotion rumbled ahead before I even walked around the corner. Twenty or so Shadows were, from the sound of it, playing a game.

"Who's up next?" called Grae, the game leader. "Fiona and Marshall. Who else?"

Those two walked up to join him at the stone steps, which he stood on to be above the others.

Grae Finch joined the Shadows around 1950, which was a couple of decades ago. He had black skin and even darker eyes.

Alec allowed him to try out, and all of us were almost immediately impressed by his double talent in creating and changing. He got his mark within a month of becoming a Shadow.

The game today was simple. The contestants would shapeshift and try to hide among the crowd. It was the crowd's job to spot the person who was hiding as someone else and out him or her to the rest of the onlookers. The last person to be discovered would win.

Grae caught my eye as I walked by.

"Mara." He motioned with his hand for me to join them. "Care to show these people how it's done?"

Fiona and Marshall both looked at each other and their faces dropped. They knew they were up against the reigning champion, but Shadows were too prideful to turn down a challenge. They each turned to me and stared me down with matching blue eyes and black curls.

"I guess I could find time for one game," I admitted.

I grabbed the nearby column holding up the balcony and swung myself over to the stone steps they all stood on. The excited crowd beneath us watched with eager eyes. They cheered as I accepted the challenge to play the game.

Fiona and Marshall both crouched down in unison to prepare for their running start.

"Ready...go!" Grae called, starting the game.

The *twins flung themselves into the crowd, running so fast that I had trouble keeping track of where they went. I, however, stepped back into the shade, leaving Grae alone on the steps and the crowd looking the opposite way.*

The *crowd turned around in circles, trying to find the two contestants. They first picked out two of the exact same girl standing next to each other, except for the eyes. The real one turned to Fiona and outed her. Fiona changed back into her original form and accepted the jeers of those around her.*

She *was the first one out.*

Marshall *was a bit smarter and turned into someone who wasn't there and had similar eyes. However, that person walked around the corner and those standing around Marshall noticed the look-alike.*

He *was the second one out and, now, it was just me.*

People *tried to guess the people around them, but no one was admitting to anything. Granted, none of them saw me leave, so none of them had a clue who I could be. Grae noticed Alec standing on the balcony and called out to him.*

"Hey *boss, which one do you think she is?"*

The *person who looked like Alec stood there with his arms crossed over his chest, looking at the ground. All eyes were focused on who they thought was their leader.*

I *won.*

The *Alec standing at the balcony transformed back into me. The crowd went wild. I jumped from the balcony down to the rest of them, welcomed with pats on the back and clapping all around. Grae looked at me from the steps and gave a congratulatory bow. I nodded back.*

I *was practically royalty here. When I walked into a room, people noticed.*

It *was the only home I had ever known. They were the only family I had ever known.*

The rain pattered on my window, the soft morning light nearly completely blocked out. I turned my head to make sure that was what I was seeing.

I had lain here all night just thinking. I compared my life from then to now. So much about the world around me had changed. I worked a job and lived on as little energy as possible. I even caught myself finding ways to help people, even if they were human. These last few months had done more than all those years combined had.

I stood from my bed and walked to the grand mirror I had in the corner of my room. I looked at the woman inside. She smiled with satisfaction and contentment. I took a deep breath.

That was me now. Maybe I wasn't truly the Kate I had been introducing myself as, but I was far from the Mara that once stood in my shoes. I couldn't picture going back there, not after all I had learned to like about the humans and the other Legends.

When Alec and I were little, we played together and practiced our abilities on each other. We were friends. When we grew up, the feelings changed. In any phase of our relationship, I had never doubted him. He was a part of my family. I loved him. I had also been blind.

Alec and I were a perfect fit then.

But after decades away from the Shadows, I had changed and knew we could never fit like that again. Now, I thought about Kylan.

I looked back at the woman in the mirror, and she had a small smile on her face. Her eyes were brighter, as if they carried a happy secret.

My smile immediately vanished. I was just as blind now as I was a long time ago. I had made a commitment to keep my eyes open.

Maybe I did deserve to have relationships and be around other people who are like me, except that they were actually good. But that didn't mean closing myself off from suspicion or worries. I looked in the mirror and saw the determination reflecting in my eyes. I turned from the mirror and left the room. Today was another day, and I had things to do.

I threw myself into my list of to-dos. I waved politely to Kylan in the hallways, but other than that, we had little interaction. I spent my days following the motions of my human job. I conducted performance reviews based on the suggestions given previously and the progress since then. I finally got around to my follow-up interview with Lisa.

"How are things going?" I said to start the session.

She smiled and babbled about the respect she was getting now that everyone was beginning to understand how vital she was to the company.

"Mr. Lyle still remembered my name and bought me a new nameplate for my desk as an apology," she detailed for me. I nodded. "I feel more comfortable associating with the other employees, and so many of them ask for my opinion or help on their own projects. I finally get to share the knowledge that no one had even noticed until now."

She was glowing.

"I am so happy for you, Lisa," I commended her.

It felt like what I should say in this situation. It was different talking to her, harder than it was talking to another Legend. She smiled and dipped her head in modesty. Her tight, ringlet curls had finally been loosed from the constraint of the bun she used to wear.

The sparkle in her confident eyes was noticeable from across the room, as was her now-upright posture.

"You've done so much for me here," she gushed. "I'm really glad you came around."

"You had the potential to do this all along. You didn't really need me, you just needed a little push." I shook my head.

"Still," Lisa said. "It's nice to know I have someone looking out for me."

I didn't expect to be this close to a human. It still didn't even make sense in my mind. But I was proud of her and I loved seeing the positive changes in her life. I was rooting for her. I had never felt that toward a human before.

At the very least, any human was insignificant. At most, they were my source of energy and entertainment.

Every time I thought about where I came from, I was so disgusted with what I saw. I was a murderer that loved doing terrible things to humans as innocent as the one sitting in front of me.

I was an exact model of what people feared the Shadows to be.

Being around humans now just reminded me of all those pent-up fears about them. As much as I tried, I don't know if they would ever really go away, no matter how close I got to any human.

I finished up early every night for the next couple of days and left before Kylan had the chance to catch me. I didn't want to encourage any more attachment than had already occurred.

Kylan deserved someone who could give him and his family everything. What I had to give was a twisted view of love and the Shadows tailing close behind in continued vengeance. When I thought about giving up my search for the locket, I couldn't see a way that I would not harbor resentment for that choice.

That was hardly acceptable to bring to the table in any new relationship.

They were a threat to me, and I was certainly a threat to them. Especially to him. It was better this way.

CHAPTER
THIRTEEN

I arrived at work early and moved my keys to unlock the office. The door was already open.

Lisa stood inside. I leaned around the door and saw Chase across the front receptionist counter from her. I immediately stopped and hid behind the door before they saw me. I concentrated and listened closely.

"Should I pick you up around seven then?" Chase's voice was low and flirtatious, but still nervous.

I smiled, knowing that my subtle hints and subliminal messages about Lisa had worked. A purposely misspelled client's name here, a directed conversation there, and all he could think about was Lisa. Lisa. Lisa.

"Yeah, that would be great." Lisa calmly tried to contain her excitement. I could hear her words coming out too fast, but she was playing it off pretty well.

"Okay, I'll see you then." Chase finished.

Being privy to their conversation, I wanted to laugh at how they tiptoed around each other. They were both trying so hard to not give away their feelings. It was cute.

Someone else walked up behind me, and I turned around to stop the person from walking through. It was Kylan. I held up my finger to my lips, and he instantly shut his mouth.

"What's going on?" he mouthed to me.

Chase just asked Lisa out. I created the sound in his mind.

My mouth never moved. My body was still radiating from all the energy I gathered this morning. Kylan smiled at the happy news and also at me so easily using my talent.

Should we wait for a few minutes? I heard the words in my mind.

My mouth fell open when I looked back up at his smirk. I was shocked at how easily he entered and how clearly he created the thought. I scanned his eyes, and he didn't even look winded from the act. I caught myself envying his talent.

You're not the only Four, his voice echoed in my thoughts again.

I smiled.

We stood a few minutes, just standing there and looking at each other. I couldn't break my eye contact, and it was nice to see that he couldn't either. Even with my attempts at avoiding him, he was still interested. It was nice. Eventually, I turned around and walked into the office. Kylan followed a respectable distance behind me.

I snuck past Lisa's closed door. I listened carefully and could hear a faint scream of excitement coming from her. I smiled and hurried on to my office.

The rest of the day dragged on. I was thinking about the company's gala on Saturday night and picturing what dress I wanted to wear when I heard footsteps heading into the conference room.

Kylan walked by my door, and I paid attention as his footsteps followed the others into the room adjacent to mine.

I tried to focus on my typing, but the only thing my ears could hear was Kylan's muted voice—thanks to those human soundproofed walls—directing the meeting. The walls blocked humans from being able to hear, but for a Legend, it just took more focus.

My eyes drifted from my computer screen to the button that would part the wall and turn it into a one-way mirror. My fingers ached from tensing the muscles in them so tightly. The rationalizations flooded in.

It was a one-way mirror.

No one would be able to see me from that side.

It was technically my job to monitor the employees.

I couldn't fight my own logic anymore. I walked to my door and flipped the light off in my office to lower the risk of someone being able to see through the mirror. I briskly walked back to the button and weighed the pros and cons.

Deciding it was probably harmless, the button clicked under the weight of my finger.

The slats on the wall parted to reveal the happenings of the conference room. I looked in and found that Kylan had just turned the meeting over to John, who stood holding forms for everyone.

John passed them out and my eyes focused back on Kylan, who had just taken his seat near the head of the table.

As soon as he sat down, he stiffened instead of relaxing in his chair. His eyebrows furrowed slightly.

In an instant that felt like an eternity, a sly smile came across his mouth.

Then, without any other glancing around, he lifted his head and looked directly at me through the glass. While everyone else was watching John and oblivious to the mirror, Kylan stared straight into my gaze and winked.

I spun and faced the other wall.

Very smooth, I thought. I turned back around long enough to take one last glance and then shut the slats again.

The end of the day finally rolled around, and my fingers tapped quickly on the keyboard, typing up the most recent notes. I watched out of the corner of my eye at the words on the screen.

I reached for the next paper and it flew off the desk and landed on the floor in front of the door.

I looked up and saw Kylan standing in my doorway, smiling. He had his arms crossed over his chest and leaned casually against the metal frame.

His perfectly tailored suit matched his neatly placed hair. My eyes took him in, looking him up and down briefly before standing to retrieve the paper.

"Can I help you with something?" I asked as I walked around to the front of my desk where the paper lay on the floor.

Just as my fingers were about to touch the page, it flew from the floor and straight into Kylan's hand. He clutched it gently without wrinkling it, and his smirk grew.

"Well, I thought so. But now I'm second-guessing myself because you can't even seem to hold onto this," he mocked and waved the page he held in the air.

I snatched it quickly from his hand and waited for him to make another move.

He didn't.

"I'm sure I can handle it," I said walking back to replace the papers.

I leaned forward and put both of my hands on my desk. My eyes looked at Kylan, who was already approaching slowly.

"Glad to hear it." He grinned and watched as I shifted to the opposite side of the desk.

"What do you need?" I prodded.

"I need a date for the gala on Saturday night." He placed both of his hands on my desk and leaned forward as well. His face was only a few inches from mine.

"You said something about being able to handle that?" Kylan whispered.

His attractive smile remained in place, waiting. He even smelled amazing.

The gala was a huge, end-of-the-year event for the firm, and all the employees received an invitation, along with some other people that humans deemed important.

What piqued my interest was all the humans in one room together, everyone's energy running high. It would finally be a fun night for me to let loose.

No one would be suspicious of a sudden change in energy levels in a group that size. It was the perfect cover for a Legend to go hunting in the middle of a crowd. All I needed was a distraction for the humans to pay attention to besides me.

My heart pumped so loudly I could barely hear myself think. I was not worried about the necklace or about the Shadows. All I could see was all the fun and energy that lay ahead of me.

"Funny, that sounded more like a command instead of a request." I smirked.

I tried not to focus on him asking me out and leaned away from my desk.

I walked back to the bookcase and pretended to look at a book there to disguise my nervousness. I was fine avoiding him until he was actually in front of me. When he stood within my reach, I could not shake the desire to let go of everything else.

"Fair enough." He ceded my point and lifted himself off my desk.

He walked around it and stood directly in front of me, putting his hands in his pockets and trying a humbler approach.

"Would you do me the honor of accompanying me to the gala?" Kylan asked in a serious tone.

"Now that, I think I can handle." I nodded, accepting his invitation. He smiled and ducked his head in recognition of my willingness.

"Should I pick you up at seven?" he offered, walking out of my office.

"See you then," I confirmed, not taking my eyes off of him.

He turned and leaned against the doorframe again, pausing long enough to see my smile and then spun out of my office. I put the book back on the shelf and took a breath to steady myself.

My heart fluttered that he wanted me to come with him to the big event. My wary thoughts reminded me that I needed to remain vigilant.

I wanted to be around Kylan, but getting too close wasn't safe. For him or his family.

That night, I continued thinking about what I was going to wear for the gala with a new incentive. I decided to use one of my dresses I already had and improvise.

I stopped along the way and stocked up on as much energy as I feasibly could without being noticed. Altering the dress in the way I pictured in my mind was going to take a lot of effort.

With the winter season colors and the chilly air outside, I wanted long sleeves so the beautiful dress wouldn't be encumbered with a thick jacket.

I buzzed with energy when I arrived home and shot to my closet.

The original dress had black, cotton fabric and was too basic to catch anyone's eye and tonight was black tie. I closed my eyes and concentrated. I held the dress in my hand and envisioned what I needed it to be.

The plain fabric softened to a shimmering satin. The color lightened from black to a deep maroon color. The sleeves lengthened to reach my wrists.

I opened my eyes and held the gown gently.

The skirt trimmed down to hug my hips, but flared out to a full, floor-length skirt. The neckline was wide and high but the back dipped down to show the tops of my shoulder blades.

It was perfect. The satin shimmered in the sunset light coming through my bedroom window. The dress was elegant and intriguing with enough fabric to cover my skin from the cold air and conceal the dagger on my arm.

My heart skipped a beat, and I rushed to the bathroom mirror. When I was done with all the changes to my dress, hair, and everything else, even I was a bit stunned.

Kylan was going to drop dead. I smiled.

I heard the car pull around the corner, and I impatiently waited for him to walk to the door. I fixed a few stray hairs on my bun and looked myself over in the mirror one last time.

I was looking too beautiful not to have a good time tonight. I decided that for tonight only, I would enjoy myself. I would enjoy being with Kylan, and I would most certainly enjoy the looks on people's faces when they saw me in this gown.

I smiled at the thought of letting go for a night. My hands twitched at the thought of more energy.

The knock came and I opened it right away. The door swung open and revealed a gorgeous man donning a slick, black tuxedo. I scanned him from the bottom up.

A deep feeling fluttered in my body just from having him in front of me. When my eyes reached his face, I saw his expression, and that feeling exploded.

He was everything I thought he would be.

Kylan's jaw was hanging so low it might have brushed the ground. He held in his hand a single red rose. He just stood there, gawking, and looked like he wasn't even breathing. My smile pulled at my lips.

"You look...I...I can't even think of a word that would be enough to describe," he stammered until I cut him off.

"Thank you." I nodded and watched my icy breath float in front of my face. "You don't look half bad yourself."

His excited eyes tore into mine as he lifted the hand that held the rose.

"This is for you," he offered the rose to me, still trying to gather his thoughts.

I took the stem just above where his hand was. He moved his finger up to touch my hand before he let go. I pulled the flower up to my nose, and the scent relaxed me.

Roses weren't my favorite, but I still appreciated the gesture.

"Thank you again." I nodded and stepped out from the doorway.

Kylan offered his arm for me to take as we walked down the metal stairs, the dim streetlights lighting our way. I wrapped my free hand around his arm and held on a little tighter than I needed to.

He opened the door to the car when we arrived, and I tucked my gown inside. The whole time, he never took his eyes off me.

As he walked around to the driver door, I let my smile widen on my face. Tonight was going to be one I never wanted to forget.

We walked into the entrance of the gala. The warm air smoothed over the chill from the air outside. The room glittered with crystal centerpieces and bright chandeliers. It looked like a fairy-tale palace filled with beautiful people and smiles to go around.

The music was intoxicating, as was the smell of the decadent treats. Although neither was as enticing as the high energy coursing through the room.

I wanted that energy so bad I almost forgot that I knew anyone in the room.

Kylan's voice greeting Mr. Lyle pulled me out of the trance. I watched them shake hands, and I stepped over to hand my clutch to the well-dressed person taking them on the opposite side of the travertine entryway.

I pulled some of her energy and lost my sense of the surroundings again. My hand wanted to reach for more when I glanced at Lisa standing next to Chase.

That girl was so happy and nervous as always. I smiled and turned toward them.

She was wearing quite a daring dress for her personality. The floor-length silver fabric sparkled as it swished lightly around her feet. The sheer fabric for the sleeves went down to her wrists.

"My mother was from Argentina, and she married my father here in the U.S.," Lisa explained in a jittery voice.

Chase looked up from her long enough to notice me glancing back at Kylan. He was stuck talking to Mr. Lyle with his hand in a firm grip that he prided himself on.

I smiled again at the people all around me. I forgot about the energy in the room.

"Hey, look," Chase pointed to me and Lisa turned, her dress flowing around her movement.

"Kate, you made it!" Lisa said loud enough to catch my attention.

I walked over to greet her while Kylan finished up with Mr. Lyle.

"Yes, of course, I made it. I wouldn't miss a chance to dress up." I winked at her.

Lisa took a sheepish glance up at the man standing next to her. She linked her arm in his, and Chase smiled down at her.

"I see the two of you found each other all right." I nodded at their linked arms.

"Lisa was kind enough to come with me tonight, actually," Chase said, still gazing at Lisa. That kid was smitten. Lisa blushed.

"Well, Chase was kind enough to ask," she responded gently. Then she turned her focus back to me. "Did I see you walk in with Kylan?"

"Yes." I paused, smiling. "Yes, you did."

"Oh my goodness! So are you two a—" Lisa excitedly talked and reached for my hands but stopped the instant she saw Kylan walking up.

She hushed herself and tried to look like she was busy with something else, so as not to be suspicious. It was completely obvious but still adorable that she tried.

"Hey guys, you're both looking sharp tonight." Kylan came in and tried to refresh the conversation.

"Thanks, man. Looks like you scored yourself quite the date there." Chase was standing next to Kylan.

"Same to you," Kylan added as they shook hands. "Lisa, you look lovely this evening."

"Thanks," Lisa said, still dying to know.

I gently shook my head at her not to ask.

"We'll catch up with you later." She reluctantly accepted my advice.

Lisa and Chase both walked off to the dessert table.

Kylan turned to me, and I felt his green eyes staring at me as I turned to face him.

"Would you like to dance?" Kylan bowed and lifted his hand out to me. I laid my hand gently on top of his.

"I would love to." I put my hand to my chest, mocking as if I had been waiting all night for that.

In truth, I really was looking forward to it. He took the hand he was holding and guided me to the dance floor. He lifted his arm to spin me around and back into his arms. We stepped together with the slow music. One of his hands firmly held my lower back, and his other hand held mine in the air.

"So, does this mean we're dating?" Kylan asked frankly.

"Excuse me?" I blurted, shocked by his assumption and now wondering how best to answer.

"Lisa couldn't think of anything else besides that question. I'm guessing the only reason she didn't ask it was because I walked in on the conversation," Kylan explained and nodded over to Lisa, who was still taking glances at us.

I looked over to her, and she tried to casually look away. Lisa turned her attention back to Chase, who now had a whole plate of desserts and one in his mouth already, and she just laughed.

"You read her mind?" I tried to sound shocked and like I was scolding him. He just raised his eyebrows and looked at me.

"You knew I would," he mocked me back.

"Why did you want to know what she was thinking?" I asked, trying to make him feel pinned to the wall.

He pursed his lips and thought about it for a minute. He looked back into my eyes with glowing intensity.

"You got me there," he surrendered. "I wanted to hear what she was thinking because I knew it would be about you."

"Then why didn't you just read my mind?" I asked back.

"Would you have let me in if I tried?" he countered. He looked at me, already knowing the answer.

"No. But it would have been the attempt that counted." I smiled and laughed at his predicament.

He shook his head like he was mocking me. He took a moment to look into my eyes, but he didn't try to read my mind. He was just looking at me. He leaned his head forward and touched his forehead to mine. We were still swaying to the music.

If people weren't looking before, they certainly were now. His breath brushed across my face. Even his breath smelled enticing. My mind shut off higher thinking, and my heart took over.

This was exactly the kind of blindness that I had wanted to avoid.

"What if I tried to read your mind now," he whispered so only I could hear.

It was an offer, not a request from him, although I knew he was the one that wanted a look around inside. Part of me wanted him to. Then he could feel what I was feeling and see what I was seeing. Then he could know.

"Then I might not be able to stop you," I answered honestly for once.

Kylan pulled his head away and looked at me. I waited for him to try to get in. I braced myself for trying to keep him out.

"Then I won't even try."

It was too easy of a surrender. He took the moment to spin me out from him and then pull me back in.

"I don't want to do anything that would make you uncomfortable," he said.

I didn't remember the energy around me or that other people were even in the room.

My heart sank. He was too good, especially for someone like me.

The longer he was with me, the more ways I could see myself corrupting him, hurting him, or manipulating him. I wasn't good. He was. After I spun back into his arms, the feeling of discomfort crawled all over me.

He was an angel who had no idea the devil he held in his arms.

CHAPTER
FOURTEEN

The warmth from his body emanated near mine. For a brief moment, I forgot about all the ways I could ruin his life just by being with him. For a moment, it was just the two of us, spinning in circles.

But then the song ended, and Mr. Lyle interrupted the next piece with an announcement. He thanked everyone for coming and for being a big part of our success here. Kylan and I applauded at the end of his speech.

Once the applause was over, I felt Kylan's hand brush mine when he dropped his arms to his side. My whole body shuddered. This was too much.

Luckily, John from accounting interrupted that moment. He walked up behind us and slapped Kylan on the back. Kylan's hand disappeared from mine from the jolt of the back slap.

My heart resumed its normal pace.

"Hey, there you are." John walked around to stand in front of Kylan and outstretched a hand to shake. "I had been meaning to find you. I had a question about the report you left on my desk."

"Oh, come on, John. No shoptalk tonight. It's the weekend." Kylan put his free hand on John's shoulder. "I'll stop by your office first thing Monday, all right?"

"Okay, just don't forget, or Lyle's gonna give me an earful," John warned and released Kylan.

"Sure thing. See you Monday." Kylan returned the back slap.

They parted, and Kylan turned around to face me again. He looked like he wanted to talk, but something else caught my attention.

My eyes flashed to a man that I did not recognize from the company. I looked closer and thought he almost looked familiar. My heart turned to ice the second I recognized who I thought it might be.

Brown hair, five o'clock shadow, and a beautiful woman standing next to him. He looked exactly like Thayer.

"No," I wished under my breath.

I tentatively put my arm in front of Kylan and froze my breathing.

The man turned around. His eyes were too dark to be Thayer's, and he was wearing an ostentatious tie that Thayer wouldn't be caught dead in. Seeing his face quickly put my fear to rest.

It wasn't him.

My heart continued to race as the adrenaline calmed. I took a breath and allowed the oxygen to restore my body. When I finally allowed my eyes to drop to the ground, I felt a hand on my shoulder.

"Are you okay?" The voice broke my concentration.

I realized now that Kylan was staring and must be wondering what was going on. I looked up at him and cleared my throat, trying to focus my mind enough to form a sentence.

"I'm going to step outside and get some air. It's, uh, getting a bit warm in here." I pointed at the balcony and stepped away from him.

Kylan looked from me to the balcony door. I could see him wondering if he should follow me or not. I didn't wait for him to decide. I just turned and headed for the glass doors. My dress flowed gracefully behind me despite my hurried steps.

I pushed the doors open and felt the cool, night air waft over me. Another deep breath cleared my head. My hands released the warm, brass doorknobs behind me and the doors slowly closed. I stepped toward the stone railing. I took long, lingering steps as I thought about what was going on.

The event. This dress. The rose. That dance.

My emotions swirled inside of me, and I used my steady breathing as something to hold onto. This was too much for even me to deny later. Tonight was supposed to be fun, free, and no strings attached.

Seeing that look in Kylan's face and judging his body language, this had strings for him. I knew letting loose might come with risks, but I was not willing to put him or his family in danger by getting this close to them, even for one night.

If Alec ever found me, he'd find them too.

I not only wanted to keep them safe but keep myself protected and vigilant. The last few decades, I had been free and completely in control of my decisions. If I let this progress much further, I might not be.

But there was the ringing disappointment on top of all of these reasons. I didn't deserve someone like Kylan. My past ate at me whenever I watched him be chivalrous and perfect. He deserved someone like him. I wanted that for him because, despite my best effort, I cared about him.

My thoughts were interrupted when I heard the doors open and the sound of the party came pouring out to join me. I didn't turn around.

I just needed a minute longer.

A hand came bearing a drink and set it in front of me on the stone banister. The glass clinked as it slid on the stone over to me. I looked up at who I already knew was standing there. Kylan.

"You look like you could use this." Kylan said calmly. My hand wrapped around the short glass, and I moved it up to my lips. The cool water soaked my mouth and helped calm my stomach.

"Thank you."

He held his own glass and drank from it. He turned his gaze out into the night sky ahead. The building we were in looked over the outskirts of town, and the city lights were visible, along with a few stars. This whole night had been picturesque.

"Why do you want me around?" I asked pointedly.

My instincts were screaming to look inside his mind and get the real answer. I had enough energy left over to do it. My newfound morals were fighting strongly against that to allow him the privacy he deserved, especially in a moment like this.

He looked back up at me, confused.

"I like being around you," Kylan said, smiling. "And you like being around me too."

"What makes you say that?" I asked, smiling against the smooth glass pressed to my mouth.

"For starters, you keep coming around. So that's a good sign. Second, I can see the way you light up when you're around my family and me. Third, it's adorably obvious that you have a crush on me."

My jaw dropped open.

I gathered my thoughts before my rising emotions clouded in again. He took a step closer to me. I could almost feel his warmth through the frosty night air. The breeze cooled my skin, but the temperature was still rising inside my body.

"Am I wrong?" Kylan asked as he turned his eyes to mine.

"Absolutely," I said. Kylan smiled anyway.

"Are you sure about that?" he asked as he took another step forward.

My face was so close to his, I could feel it tingling. Our breaths visibly mingled in the cold air.

He brought his hand up and brushed the top of my shoulder and then let his hand trace down my left arm. I felt my body heat bloom underneath his hand. The tingling in my face now raced all the way down my body.

"Well, it's either that or I'd have to admit you are actually right." I didn't want to say it. The words just came out.

Kylan smiled at my surprise when I finally processed what I said. I lifted my glass again and drank down the rest of the water.

When I looked up, he was still looking at me and standing close enough to make my stomach twist even tighter. His other hand reached up gently and brushed my cheek.

His eyes locked on mine in a way that made the rest of the world disappear.

"Can I kiss you, Kate?" he asked so politely.

No beating around the bush, no clever line.

His face was close, but still far enough away to see his hopeful green eyes. He looked at mine, waiting for my answer. I hoped somewhere that his dad was smiling at his boy that he raised up well.

Out on the grand balcony with the oblivious party right inside was the perfect end to a beautiful night.

That's what made my decision harder. The inner struggle snapped the world back into my attention.

"No," I answered him quietly.

He pulled back, keeping his one hand on my arm and the other on my cheek. I closed my eyes to avoid looking at his face.

"What?" he asked, not in a rude way, but confused. "What's wrong? I thought we were having a great time…"

I could see why he was confused. I was confused myself. Even without looking into his mind, I understood completely that he didn't see what had happened. My stomach twisted as I thought through a response.

"Tonight was a dream. You have been so amazingly kind to me," I said calmly, taking breaths in between. "But we shouldn't…you shouldn't be with me."

"Why not?" he asked, almost vaguely intrigued.

"For so many reasons that I can't explain, it's a bad idea," I attempted and nervously took a step back. "For both of us."

"Shouldn't you let me decide that?" he asked and took a step forward.

"I can't," I answered.

In reality, I could tell him. I just didn't want to. Alec gave the exact same answer to me before I left the mansion. I can't. A sick feeling crept in as I thought about sympathizing with him.

"Kate, I don't mean to pressure you." He reached his hands back out and placed them on the outside of my arms. "If you don't want to move forward with anything yet, that's fin—"

"Ever." I interrupted. "Not ever, Kylan."

I wanted to be as gentle as possible with what I was about to explain.

"Thank you for everything you've done for me. But I

think it was a mistake to spend so much time with all of you. It's shown me a life I had only dreamed of, but one that I definitely don't deserve. I know this doesn't make sense, and why would it? Your life is perfect!"

I tried to laugh away the tension but I felt the mark on my arm as though it was warming my skin where the ominous dagger lived. It was always there to remind me of who I used to be. Despite my desire to change, I couldn't erase the guilt burned into my body.

This moment was proof. I would never be pure enough to deserve something like this. There was just too much to atone for. I mentally came back to the moment at hand by looking into Kylan's confused and innocent eyes.

"My life is not perfect," he affirmed. "You're only seeing what you want to see."

"Thank you for tonight, Kylan. Really." I watched his ambition dim in his eyes. "I just think it is time I left you all to yourselves. You and your family. You don't need someone like me in your world."

I looked down at the intricate patio floor beneath my feet. A tear welled up in my eye. It had been a long time since I said goodbye to someone I cared about. I had almost forgotten what it felt like. I turned around to leave, and I could feel Kylan's hand trying to stop me.

"Stay, Kate. We want you here," he attempted. "I want you here."

His request brought stinging tears to my eyes.

"I'm sorry," I breathed. I was partially talking to myself for all the pain I had created. The ache blistered inside me as his hand gently pulled on my dagger-marked arm.

There wasn't anything left for him to say. Nothing would change my mind. But then he whispered, "Please."

The word cut into my body and raked pain in strings

across my chest. I blinked the tears back and swallowed the lump in my throat.

"Let me go," I asked quietly without turning to face him.

His hand reluctantly fell from my arm. I walked toward the doors. I could see him still standing on the patio out of the corner of my eye as I pulled the door open. He was crushed, but at least he was safe.

I hailed a taxi to drive me home. I immediately changed out of my dress and hopped in my car. The engine roared to life, and I drove into the night with my lit apartment building growing smaller and smaller in the background.

I felt my heart begin to crush under the pain that I had been holding back until I was alone.

It all washed in. Kylan and his family would be better off without me. I just had to keep telling myself that. I would be undaunted now in my continued journey. It was better for the both of us if we stopped things before more feelings got involved.

This was the right thing to do.

This had to be the right thing to do.

I had allowed myself to hope when I shouldn't have. It was unfair to all of them that I used them to indulge my whim of wanting to experience being in a good family. In a month or so, his family would forget about me. Eventually, he would too.

Memories don't last forever. I knew that best of all.

CHAPTER
FIFTEEN

I couldn't stay here.

I packed what I wanted to keep and left the rest behind. I drove out of the city the next day and made an effort to forget about work and my life in Portland. I didn't even notice the city line once I crossed it.

My phone buzzed in the cup holder. Kylan Beck.

I clicked the button that could silence it and returned my gaze to the road. After a few more miles my phone buzzed again. Lisa Moreno.

The rings lingered. I decided to answer. My heart burned for her. If I was leaving, she at least deserved a goodbye. When I left the Shadows, I didn't say goodbye to anyone. Not Thayer, especially not Alec, not even Nikki. We had been friends, and I left her without a word. I left all of them with so many more things to say and that ate at me.

It was best to cut the tie now instead of dragging the guilt with me for however many years to come.

"Yes?"

"Sorry, is this a bad time?" she asked, her voice sounding unable to contain her happiness.

"No, no, you're fine. What's going on?" I beckoned.

"Chase kissed me," she tried to whisper, but it came out loud and clear.

"Lisa!" I exclaimed, mustering up all the excitement I could find. "That is amazing! So, give me the details. When did this happen?"

That was all she needed. She spent the next thirteen minutes describing what happened in detail.

At the sound of her joy, painful reminders of last night surfaced. From now on, it would be different. Last night was it. That was my chance.

An opportunity like that would never arise again. I wouldn't let it.

Maybe it was a good thing, though. I would have never been able to withstand the enticement of him offering himself up again. I juggled between the thoughts of believing I made the right choice and knowing I just made the biggest mistake.

Lisa noticed my silence.

"What's going on? I saw you two at the gala together last night and then you were just gone," Lisa asked intently.
She heard the pain in my breath before I had a chance to cover it up and shrug off her comment.

"Oh no, what happened?" Her tone matched the feeling I had inside.

"Nothing," I assured her with a smile, hoping it would convey through the phone. "Tell me more about Chase."

"That's not true." Lisa's statement stood in between me and my lie. "Something happened. It's all over your voice. You can tell me, Kate."

I could picture her crossing her arms in front of her chest

and tapping her foot like she did when she was waiting for something. Her firm words were almost intimidating. She had changed from the woman I had first met.

"Lisa, there is nothing going on between me and...and Kylan." I tried, and she didn't buy it.

I ran through the pros and cons of telling her. I could get it off my chest and, worst case scenario, I could pick up and leave later, and then nothing would tie me back here.

Maybe Kylan was too much for me to accept all at once. I couldn't handle it yet. But this, this was different. All she was asking was to indulge in a bit of girl talk.

Even as a Shadow, the closest female friend I had was Nikki, and that had been mostly superficial. The main reason I kept her close was that I was threatened by her beauty and skill.

Naturally, Alec had always been extremely proud of her. That's where our friendship came in. I wanted to keep her loyalty to me and her hands off Alec. I knew Alec would never betray me, but one can never be too careful when it comes to love.

Alec and Thayer found her in the heart of Mexico City, wreaking havoc with her abilities. People called her the Whisperer of Death. She was one of their first recruits with Alec's father gone.

After seeing her talent, Alec came up with the mark. The current Shadows all received one. He was first, I was second. I was only fifteen in Legend years, way back over a century ago, when my future was set in stone.

I hadn't heard Alec scream since his father was killed, and the sound of it still ricocheted through my mind as I looked at the new mark on his arm.

Nikki was destroying and creating a bond between the destroyed cells all at the same time. When she was done, it took a full minute before his screams stopped.

But Alec still smiled when he saw the small dagger.

The curves of the handle and the sharp point of the blade looked like it had been carved by an artist.

"Try to change it," Alec asked and held his arm out for me.

"Yes, please do," Nikki challenged.

She was incredibly smug for never having done this before. My power of being able to change cells was the best amongst the Shadows. If anyone could alter the mark Nikki had created, it would be me.

I concentrated on the skin of Alec's arm, but no matter what, the mark remained the same.

I reached out and touched the blackened dagger with my fingers. I closed my eyes and gritted my teeth. After a few moments, I opened my eyes.

The dagger remained.

"Brilliant." Alec smiled and pulled his own arm back. He ran his hand over the dagger and then looked up at me.

"This is forever," I warned him, and all he did was smile back.

"Once a Shadow, always a Shadow." He took my arm in his and looked deep into my eyes. This was exactly where I wanted to be.

"Your turn." Nikki had that same sick smile on her mouth as she grabbed my right arm. She lifted my sleeve to expose the skin.

I took one final look at her brown eyes before the pain scorched my arm.

I would always remember that day.

The decades that followed would be filled with torture, death, and domination for anyone we came in contact with. I was a permanent member of the Shadows and forever tied to Alec. Back then, that was all I wanted, but what did I really know at the tender age of only 155 years old?

I laughed at how truly little knowledge I had back then and how little experience I had with meaningful relationships. I knew all about regretting choices, but I so badly needed to tell someone about the swirling feelings inside me.

The more I thought about it, the more I was sure that I wouldn't regret talking to Lisa.

I took a breath and spilled it all.

I told her about the office banter. The strange lunch out, meeting his family, and the gala's events.

By the end, I felt a weight lifted off my shoulders as I breathed the last few words out. I thought the silent drive for a few hours was freeing. That was nothing compared to this moment. As the last word came out, I could finally breathe without the force pushing down on me.

This was freeing.

"So what about now?" Lisa asked. I thought about her question.

"What do you mean? What is there to do now? It's over. I don't even know if I wanted it to be, but it needs to be over. Does any of this make sense?" I asked for her confirmation that I was not strange.

Her reassuring laugh took that worry away. Maybe it was not just me with attachment issues. Maybe some part of this was just me being a normal girl.

"Kate, I saw his face at work today. He was hurt, but not ready to shut you out," she spoke softly. "I can also hear the hope in your voice. You are not ready to be done with this either."

The only problem was, I thought she was right.

"I can't, though. We would both be better off if we stayed apart," I tried to explain without revealing any details.

"Are you sure? Look, this is not saying you are going to marry him. All this is doing is giving him a chance. Just like you gave me a chance right now," she said in a bright tone.

I raised my eyebrows in surprise. I hated admitting when other people were right. When she didn't hear me answer, she filled the silence again.

"You let me in, and it wasn't so terrible, was it?" she edged.

"It's just that..." I started, being careful with my words.

"You have no idea what I would have to give up to stay or even to try. How do I know it's worth it?"

I had not said the words out loud. Somehow, it made the choice more clear. If I wanted to pursue a real relationship with Kylan or his family, I couldn't continue my search for the locket. Alec would catch whispers of it here and there.

I would have to truly disappear and cut my last tie to the Shadows. It was also the only tie I had to my past. It was the one thing I had never been willing to even consider giving up. For anything.

Until now.

"I don't know the reasons why, but you are holding yourself back. What I really don't understand is what could have made you want to do this. I don't need to know if you don't want to tell me. Just let me tell you this." She paused, letting the words sink in.

"You deserve to be happy. You do. No matter what. Happiness...happiness is worth anything," she finished.

I could hear the brightness resonate in her voice. It mimicked the feeling of Kylan holding me in his arms.

Her words penetrated the back corner of my heart. The part that held the sliver of hope that had almost been brought to the surface with Kylan on the balcony.

Here was this unknowing person telling me that I was

allowed to be happy. She had no idea of my past, or of the mountain of information that I was withholding, yet she didn't care.

She was my friend, human and all, and she wanted the best for me. She was also smart enough to see that me being alone was not it.

I already knew everything that could go wrong. It just didn't stack up to everything that could go well.

"I think you're right," I finally decided.

If I was going to do something, it needed to be now, before I lost my courage. I waited on the phone with the one question I needed the answer to before I made my next move, and Lisa already knew the answer.

"He went home early today," she responded to my unspoken question.

I turned the car around without slowing down first, feeling the exact amount of force needed to complete the turn without rolling the vehicle. I couldn't control my smile.

I sped down the road to hopefully catch him at home still.

My car flew down the curves in the asphalt past the city, past the old part of town, out to the houses dotting the green fields of trees.

When I made the last turn to the long road leading up to his house, my foot pinned the pedal to the floor. I slammed on my brakes and my tires screeched on his pavement.

I disregarded new smell of burnt rubber and focused ahead. Kylan was standing on the other side of the doorway as he shoved it open.

"Kate? What are you doing here? Are those marks from you?" he called out to me. I took the keys from the car and clenched them in my hand as I shot up to his porch.

"I like driving fast," I said.

He still looked at the marks. I marched up the steps and right up to him and that got his attention.

"Kate, what's going on?"

"Lisa is right." I started.

"Excuse me?" Kylan looked as confused as my mind apparently was.

"Maybe it wouldn't be terrible if we were together," I tried again.

That didn't come out right either. I sounded like a bumbling human. I looked into his green eyes and none of that helped me to clear my head.

"Okay…" Kylan tried to get me to continue. "So what does that have to do with—"

"I mean, we don't have to be together. I just, I was talking to Lisa and…We both deserve to be happy, right?" I stumbled on my words.

"Where are you going with this?" His eyebrows pulled together.

"I have spent so many years hiding from humans and avoiding actually having a life. I can't do it anymore. Especially not when I know what it feels like to live. There are a million reasons why I shouldn't be standing here, but all I can see is one reason that, for the first time in decades, makes me want to stay," I admitted, a smile pulling at my lips.

I took a step toward him without breaking eye contact, confident in my next statement.

"You make me happy," I whispered.

Kylan looked at me for a moment. The sun was reflecting in his eyes. They were soft and inviting, but he was looking to see if I was serious. I could see in his eyes that he was risking something too by letting me back in. He wasn't as careful the night of the gala, but he was now.

"I shouldn't have turned you down that night. I was

scared and caught off guard. I didn't want to drag you down to my level, and I was worried that if you and I were together, I might blur the lines between keeping myself safe and actually enjoying life. If your offer still stands, my answer is yes." I said with the last ounce of courage I had left.

"Yes, I want you to kiss me." I smiled.

Kylan took a step forward and put his hand where it had rested last night on my cheek. He brushed a lock of hair from my face and let a smile break across his face. He looked at me, his eyes gleaming with a thousand sunsets behind them.

"You couldn't have just made things easy for me, could you?" he teased as he leaned forward slowly and took my face in his hands.

"Where's the fun in that?" I smiled back.

He shook his head and closed the space between the two of us. As soon as our lips touched, I felt my heart double its pace. My hands felt his strong arms. My toes curled as the tingling sensation reached them too.

Warmth spread through my body. The overcast sun on my back, and Kylan in front of me. He was safe and warm, just like the sunshine.

Being in his arms, totally trusting and knowing it was a feeling I had not felt before. There was no edginess, no power struggle, nothing like what Alec and I were. The raw self-preservation instinct backed off. It wasn't needed here. We were the only two people in the world.

Him and me.

The rest of the day floated by like a cloud. Every thought of Kylan was followed by a smile on my face.

The next time I saw Lisa, she took one look at me and mirrored my smile. I ran to her and hugged her in front of the whole office.

"Welcome back," she whispered in my ear.

"Thank you," I whispered back, holding on to her.

She may be a human, but she was also shaping up to be a really good friend. That was something I had no idea I needed.

I waited for my smile to melt away. It didn't.

Back at my apartment, I just beamed at the tile floor like an idiot. I looked back over my life, and I compared my past to my present. I was happy now.

I caught myself wishing I could remember further back than meeting the Shadows. It was a couple of centuries ago, but I should remember something.

What if the Shadows had never found me?

I thought about the years of running. The crushing loneliness of not having a family or even a real friend. I had been on a chase for a locket that I wasn't even sure could give me all the answers I wanted.

I dreamed of the idea of having a mother and father that loved me. I recalled the warmth I felt from Kylan now. I wondered what it must have felt like to have someone care for you so unconditionally.

I wanted that. I wanted all of that. I felt a tear slip out of the corner of my eye and heard the soft crush as it landed on my pillow.

Maybe that should have been my life, I thought to myself.

I would never know for sure. I was left with endless possibilities and an eternity of imagining all of them.

Alec gave that to me.

The hate came piercing in my heart and the dream vanished. It was replaced by the crashing reality of my past life. I became sharply aware of how dark and empty this room felt. It was just me and my assorted daydreams.

The next time I opened my eyes, it was to the twinkling morning light coming through my drapes. I took a deep breath and reminded myself that I was one day further away from who I used to be.

I looked down at a sketch I had drawn of the locket on my small metal nightstand. My hand touched the edge of the paper, always close by. It used to be my only source of hope.

"Change is good," I muttered to myself, filling the empty air with the soft words.

I had something else to look forward to now. I lifted my hand from the paper. If I wanted to pursue this new life, then the hunt for the locket couldn't be a part of it.

I looked out toward the soft sunlight on the rainy streets. I felt my smile open as I thought of the opportunities this new day brought.

CHAPTER
SIXTEEN

One week had passed since our first kiss that afternoon on the porch. We had spent every second of time together that we could.

We walked through the streets of downtown. Both of us were feeling worn out from the few whirlwind days. Today was the first time I would be hunting with someone outside of the Shadows.

I was used to these trips being fast-paced and intense, but this one started out as a slow stroll through the city. We walked through the glow of the streetlights, and innocent strangers passed us by.

We had already been talking for over an hour, but I didn't mind the time. I was with him.

For the first time since I left the Shadows, I didn't worry about the necklace or about Alec. All I cared about was this moment. I wanted to breathe in every scent of musty concrete, fast-food restaurants, and the pines in the distance. I wanted to remember every second.

"Tell me about your family," Kylan said, continuing our conversation.

He pretended to bump into someone standing close to him. I watched carefully as he placed his hand on the stranger's arm and apologized. The faintest glow of energy swirled into Kylan's hand. He finished and turned back to me as if nothing had happened.

I stopped to think of how I would answer his innocent question.

As I paused, my eyes narrowed in on a little boy bouncing down the sidewalk with a tired parent trying to keep up behind him. I focused on the teddy bear that stuck out of his backpack. I moved the air around it enough to bump the bear out and onto the ground. I reached down and picked it up.

"I think you forgot something," I called to the boy.

He jerked around and sprinted back to me. I handed the animal to him and touched his bare fingers. His crazed energy flooded from his body into mine. After a few seconds, the boy thanked me and left, much slower this time. I took a glance at the parent's eyes and saw the relief.

Feeling the little boy's energy now pumping through me helped sharpen my thoughts. I took Lisa's advice and just started with being as honest as I could.

"I don't talk about them much. It was not a situation as ideal as yours here." I shrugged and looked away from him. If I was going to talk, I didn't want to see his reaction. "We were all friends. I was quite close with a few of them. In the end, it turned out to be more of an abusive relationship than a healthy one. I left and haven't kept in touch. In my eyes, we never were a true family. In a family, I always imagined there was honesty and trust. That wasn't the case for mine."

I finally looked at him. "You are lucky to have the family that you do. They may be strange in some ways, but even a human could see that you care about each other."

Kylan smiled at the joke. The relief I felt talking to Lisa

came again now talking to Kylan about my family. I would still never tell about my true past, but this was a start.

"How long ago did you leave?" he asked gently as he brushed the stranger behind him.

Another small amount of energy passed into Kylan. The man turned around and had a confused look on his face but kept walking.

"Just over twenty years ago," I answered and stared into the empty air in front of me.

This new place marked the sixteenth time I had changed my identity and appearance, all to avoid Alec figuring out it was the wrong decision to let me leave the Shadows.

"Do you miss them at all?" Kylan asked.

"No," I firmly answered. "I only miss the naïve feeling I had then. Everything was perfect before I looked deeper. Now, I carry that weight of them with me. I wish that could be gone like it was before."

"What happened? What made you decide to leave?" He wasn't being rude, just curious.

I still don't know that I had an answer for that question though, not one that I could safely share.

A woman stood in the middle of the sidewalk, arguing loudly on the phone. I touched her shoulder in what seemed like an effort to move her out of our way. She stepped aside as her energy jolted into my body.

"There were a lot of reasons. Things just kept stacking up until eventually, I knew I didn't belong there anymore," I said.

Kylan nodded along to my response.

"Your family is important to you, aren't they?" I could already see in his eyes how much he needed them.

"They mean everything to me. They are a bit crazy at times, but without them, I don't like to think of where I would be," he answered my question as he reached over and intertwined his fingers with mine.

"Would you ever want to have a family of your own?" I asked him, honestly wondering what he would say and admiring my own boldness. "Having kids, I mean."

Legend culture was different than popular human culture when it came to dating or marriage. Our reproductive systems were enhanced too and the altered genes were passed on, creating Legend children. Thus, here we are today with more Legends than the humans would care to acknowledge.

It took a while to notice that the normal course of aging had been slowed. Legend children needed years before they were old enough to thrive on their own. Then, maturing to an adult was just as slow. A child was a huge commitment already, but even more for Legends.

"If I found the right person to be with, I couldn't think of anything better than being a dad someday," he spoke calmly and firmly. "What about you?"

"I used to hate the idea of being tied down to a family. Then, I thought it would be okay but I was worried I would mess them up." As I spoke, I pieced together a conclusion that I had not yet taken the time to form.

"Now, I'm not sure. There is a part of me that believes I could be a great mother, and there is another part that doubts. I think you are right, though. It takes the right partner."

I looked down the sidewalk for my next target. I had to shake my head and remember that human weren't targets anymore. They were people that were kind enough to donate a little energy to us, even if it was unwittingly.

Even being away from the Shadows as many years as I have, I still had to consciously remind myself to think otherwise. I wondered if those ingrained ideas would ever go away, or if I would always be partly a monster. The latter scared me.

ANGIE DAY

Alec would be smiling if he could see my inner conflict now.

"For what it's worth, I think you would be a great mom," Kylan spoke up, drawing my attention back to him instead of in my own head. "I see you interacting with people, how much you've been helping Lisa, and how protective you are of your heart. You have an immense kindness in you, but you also have such fire and determination. You'd be perfect."

My breath caught as he described what he saw in me. My doubts melted. Tears stung the corner of my eyes, threatening to reveal themselves.

"No one has ever said anything like that about me before." My words choked partway through the sentence. I took a breath. "Thank you."

I looked up at his eyes now that I had blinked the impending tears away. My eyes and mind were clear as I looked at him. His caring smile was waiting for me once I looked up. He leaned forward and slowly closed the space between us.

His soft lips touched mine, and I felt the tears stinging again. My heart nearly pounded right out of my chest. He gently wrapped his arms around me, enveloping me in his warm embrace. My heart almost ached because I felt so close to him and so appreciated.

I looked out into the city again. I thought about the difference in feelings of now and then. It was a whole world away. I wanted it to stay that way.

That meant not giving any clues about my past. As much as I wanted to throw myself into this relationship, I was ever wary of Alec's threat still looming. I still watched every day to make sure I didn't recognize anyone from the Shadows.

The second I did, I knew it would be time to leave even if it was hard to say goodbye. I was on borrowed time.

Unfortunately, that was a problem of uncertainty that couldn't be solved by me thinking about it. I pulled myself back to the present.

"So, how old are you?" I nudged him with my elbow, trying to lighten the mood. It was a normal question even for humans to ask each other. The big difference was that our answers had far more years on them.

"In September, I will be two hundred and thirteen years old," he answered with a smile on his face as he whispered it to me. "Roughly, twenty-one Legend years old."

"Wow," I mouthed and tried to avert my gaze away from him.

"What?" Kylan prodded.

"I just thought you were a little older than that. You... um, you don't look that young at all." I shrugged my shoulders and tried to hide my smile.

Legends did not regard age the same way humans did. Two Legends could be centuries off of each other, and it was hardly even a concern.

"Why? How old are you?"

"Not two hundred and thirteen, that's for sure." I faked a grimace and looked at him.

"Kate..." he edged, wanting me to answer.

I couldn't take the tension anymore. "I'm two hundred and forty-three."

His shoulders relaxed the instant he heard the number. Then he saw my teasing smile and finally caught on. I just shrugged my shoulders when he narrowed his eyes at me.

"You knew that wasn't...You're totally messing with me," he accused, and I nodded my head without a shred of guilt.

"Yeah, I am." I smiled back at him. I saw the smirk on his own face.

"What if I don't want to be dating an older woman?" He backed up slightly and looked at me with slight aversion.

"Oh, be honest. I don't look a day over two hundred," I fluttered my eyes at him, and he broke into a smile.

We spoke a little too loudly for all the people around us. However, no one was actually listening, nor would they think we were serious.

"I suppose you do look good...for your age," he said and looked down at the ground.

I shoved him hard enough that he stumbled into another person. He caught himself and took the human's energy as he apologized.

"Well, I think you're stuck with me anyway." I smiled and looked over at him.

He smiled back, and everything else went away. I no longer saw the city, the people, or the grand sky that was finally clear enough to see a few stars. All I saw then were his bright eyes.

"Good," he answered and put a hand on my cheek, and we both stopped walking.

He brushed his finger from my cheek to my ear. His eyes told me something serious was coming. My heart told me that I wanted to hear what he had to say.

"I am sorry about what you went through. I hope your future can make up for the past," he wisely added.

"I think it already is," I said and stared into his eyes.

I moved forward and wrapped my arms around him. He pulled me in for a comforting hug. I could smell his scent on his shirt. I buried my face in further. Having him all around me felt like what I had pictured a home to feel like. Safe, warm, and happy.

I thought about my future with Kylan.

If the Shadows never came back around, I wouldn't

have a reason to run anymore. Maybe after all these years, Alec had finally given up. Maybe I was safe, and I just didn't know it.

"Wait here," Kylan said through the chatter. He was looking at an ice cream shop. He paused before he lifted his hands from my shoulders and walked toward the building.

"Don't you need to know what kind I like?" I called out to him. He turned just before he walked in the door and flashed a knowing smile at me.

"No, it's a surprise." He shrugged.

"Okay, just anything besides mint or—" I raised my hands.

"Sur-prise," Kylan repeated and winked.

I just smiled back at him and shrugged my shoulders. He went inside without another word.

I stood on the street and watched all the people passing me by. I noticed a man walking toward me. He seemed to have his eyes trained on me as he moved closer. I tried to avoid his stare, hoping he would just go away.

The closer he got, the more I realized that wasn't going to happen. The man looked like he had just stepped out of a library. He had glasses, a wrinkled shirt, and had gone at least a few days without shaving. He walked right up to me and just looked at me for a minute before cracking a grin.

"You're one of them. Aren't you?" he asked jabbing a finger in my face.

I took a step back and was shocked at how close he was standing to me. I thought of the possibility that he was just some crazy conspiracy theorist, but I also considered the chance that he might actually know something.

"Excuse me?" I asked him politely as I tried to deflect his question.

"You know, one of those mutated people," he said.

"I don't think…" I stiffened as I watched him more carefully.

"A Legend," he talked over me.

My stomach dropped. The blood pumped in my veins, preparing my body for attack. My eyes narrowed and focused on the one threat standing in front of me.

No one around us had stopped walking or looked over. It was almost like he didn't want anyone to hear us. He just wanted to know. Judging by his intellectual appearance, he wasn't just insane. He might have been a bit deprived of vitamin D, but he was coherent.

"I don't know what you're talking about," I tried to say without clenching my teeth. I took a step toward the door of the shop that Kylan had entered. The man stepped in front of me.

"I've been watching you walking down the street." He smiled even wider now. "I know."

My hands yearned to throw him into the window to get him to stop talking. After, I wanted to wrap my fingers around his fragile neck and force his energy into my body.

My breath throbbed as I thought of the familiar feeling of someone's final energy coursing into my veins. I could recognize it anywhere.

"Imagine what the others will say when I tell them that I turned one of you in. They won't even believe me! I wouldn't even believe me. But you are real. You're right here," the man prattled, a growing excitement that I couldn't wait to rip away from him.

I turned to look at him again, his back to the street. He eyed me like he had found the gold at the end of the rainbow.

He didn't even bring backup to take down a Legend. He was alone and quite useless. Not only that, but he didn't just walk up to a regular Legend who might be scared enough to comply with him.

He had walked up to me and he was about to find out just how deep he had dug his own grave.

I hadn't tracked the locket in a while, so any of my trail left behind would be cold. For now, the danger was suspended. Alec didn't have a reason to pry here anymore.

Maybe that idea made me bolder than I should have been. I was tired of watching myself and always being cautious. The impulse to do something I shouldn't raced in my veins and, for once, I didn't stop it.

I smiled at the desire to have some fun at this poor human's expense. I decided to test his knowledge a little further. If he knew this much about Legends, maybe he would know other things. I glanced at the building where Kylan was still waiting for the ice cream. I consciously turned my back to him and faced the man completely.

My sharp gaze locked on his.

I reached down to my right arm and pulled my sleeve up above my elbow. The second the man saw the mark, his face turned white and his mouth finally stopped moving.

I smiled.

"Now, even if that were true, wouldn't it be incredibly stupid to confront someone like me?" I asked.

I put my free hand on my hip and he locked eyes with the dagger mark on my arm. He tried to take a step back. I followed him and took a step forward.

He froze, unsure of what to do. I didn't bother hiding my smile. I'd been running scared of the Shadows for years but now this mark on my arm finally had a use again.

"You're a...a...You're real," he finally breathed and looked up at my eyes again. I pulled my sleeve back down to my wrist.

"Real or not, we're definitely dangerous." I smiled.

I felt exactly like I did as Mara, powerful and in control. The energy from the day coursed through my body as I straightened my shoulders. The man gulped in front of me.

Nothing could replace the feeling of being a strong Legend encountering a cowering human. The utter power was intoxicating.

The sight of Kylan stepping around the corner, ice cream in hand, broke through my thoughts. His footsteps approached, but I kept my eyes on the human.

"Kate, who is this?" Kylan asked, immediately sensing the tense situation.

While I was busy planning the man's death, his voice reminded me of all the work I had put into becoming a different person.

"He's one of them too. Isn't he?" The man said despite clearly having the good sense to be quiet a moment earlier.

"Does he mean..." Kylan asked me now.

"Yes," I answered firmly and didn't take my eyes off the man.

The longer I stared, the more he seemed to conclude it was probably a bad idea to approach me. The fear trickled into his eyes.

"Sir, I think you are mistaken..." Kylan started. I raised my hand to stop him from talking.

"He already knows," I said back to Kylan, "but that will change."

I focused my eyes on the man and watched the fear bubble up. At least he was smart enough to be scared. In such a public place and with Kylan watching, I wouldn't hurt him.

Maybe I wouldn't even if we were alone. At this point, it was hard to think of anything past self-preservation.

I had ample energy flowing in my veins, and with us just out of sight from the people on the street, I didn't mind expending it. I snapped the connection into place between his mind and mine.

Just before I manipulated the first connections, I was interrupted.

"Stop." Kylan's voice was strong and authoritative. "You can't just change his memories. You don't know how that will affect him."

"It's better than destroying the memories completely. That would definitely affect him. What do you want me to do?" I threw at him a little more harshly than I wanted.

I turned to look at Kylan now instead of the man. The second my eyes were off of him, he tried to step away from us. I snapped my hand out and grabbed his arm. I pulled him even closer to me.

"You're not going anywhere." I glared into the man's eyes and then looked back at Kylan.

I wanted him to see that this was our only option. Kylan set the ice cream on a stone ledge that used to be a window. He walked up to the man with his arms raised in surrender.

Seriously? I thought.

That was the one thing he could think of to do?

"Look, we aren't going to hurt you." He tried to reason with the human that was shaking scared in my hands.

"Liar," the man gasped.

I clenched my jaw and sucked in a breath through my teeth. My grip tightened on the man's shirt until my knuckles turned white.

"That isn't going to work. Can't you see? He's already scared." I shook the man I held.

He was breathing even faster now. I just wanted to rip his energy from his body and be done with it all.

"Maybe if you hadn't threatened him, he wouldn't be." Kylan looked sharply at me now.

I stared back into his eyes.

"Maybe if you hadn't stopped me earlier, he would already be walking away." I raised my eyebrow at him.

"No matter how fun it is, you can't just manipulate people..." he started.

"How fun it is?" I clarified, taken aback. "What would you know about that?"

I hadn't seen Kylan so much as a raise a finger against a human. He didn't even seem to enjoy taking their energy. In that moment, I looked at him and didn't see a perfect model. I saw a man with his own set of struggles.

Whatever glimpse of the past flashed in his eyes quickly left when he shook his head and refocused his stare.

"You can't manipulate them just because they are humans, despite everything that you believe about them," he continued, but it sounded like he was reassuring himself instead.

"Changing his memories is me being generous." I raised my eyebrow at him.

I hoped he would understand how hard I was trying to do the right thing and how much I just wanted a little slack.

Killing his memories would destroy the parts of his mind that held them. It would cripple his brain function from here on out.

"This isn't right," Kylan said, not budging at all.

"There isn't a right choice here," I said, hoping he could see how backed into a corner we were and all from some pathetic human.

I threw my hand in the air, inviting him to come up with a more viable solution.

"I won't be a part of this," he answered coldly.

I looked at him and knew that he meant every word. However, I had so much more to lose than he did.

"Then don't watch," I repeated, just as I did many years ago. I was never good at meeting people's expectations.

The shock in his eyes hurt me inside, but not more than the threat of being exposed. At best, he and his family would have to move.

For me, rumors could travel back to Alec that a Shadow had been sighted. I would be on the run with him close behind me.

I could understand his frustration, but I couldn't explain how I had so much more to lose than he did.

Kylan took my suggestion and walked away. He walked out into the main sidewalk and left me behind with the frantic human. I took a moment as I watched him leave. I thought of ways I could fix this later. The fast-paced breath of the man I was holding brought my attention back.

I moved my eyes and they burned into the human's. This insignificant person caused a rift between me and Kylan.

I pulled his energy from his body with my other hand that gripped his arm. The warm thrill floated through my body and I never wanted it to end.

My knees got weaker the harder I clenched my hand on his skin. I might have drawn blood if I kept going. And I wanted to keep going.

As much as I wanted to make him suffer, or as much as I wanted to hear him beg for me to be merciful, I knew I shouldn't.

Years of retraining my mind had taught me how to hold back, even if I didn't want to listen. My weakness was that part of me still enjoyed it.

A big part.

And in this perfect situation, I had every reason to cave and fill my craving.

Then I remembered Kylan. I forced myself to stay calm. If I didn't want to be a Shadow anymore, then I needed to act like it, especially in times like this.

I took a few breaths, letting the humid aid bring me back to the moment, back to the human who was losing energy fast. I focused on what I wanted to do in the first place.

I released my touch on his skin, feeling the ample energy fuel my body. I concentrated, entered his mind, and changed the events of what had just happened.

"You met a stranger on the street and offered her directions," I said, gripping him as tightly as I could without breaking any of his bones.

As soon as the memory solidified in his mind, the fear vanished from his eyes. I dropped my mental hold on him and released him from my hand. He blinked for a moment and then looked up at me.

"It's really not that far from here. Does that help?" he asked, confirming that I knew my way around now.

"Yes, thank you very much." I smiled and nodded.

"Well, good luck." He waved as he walked a little slower toward the main sidewalk.

I sighed as I waited for my body to reconcile the loss. I waited for a second more, and then walked out too.

My eyes searched around for Kylan, but he was already gone. I looked down at the two ice creams, melting on the ledge. One of them looked like strawberry.

He got it right. I smiled.

I took a moment to breathe. This was something I could still fix. I had to. I realized how much Kylan was worth to me. If he hadn't been there, I may have taken that man's life instead of only adjusting his memories. No one else would have stopped me from doing worse. No one would have known how.

But he was kind and sweet and good and someone that I wanted to emulate.

Just being around him made me want to be better. Even if my better still wasn't quite good enough.

Perhaps one day it would be.

CHAPTER
SEVENTEEN

I had rehearsed my apology all night, and it still didn't seem ready.

I set down my stuff in my office and took the walk of shame over to his door. Before I arrived, my eyes caught Lisa answering her cell phone.

"Yes, this is her," Lisa said, her face pulling in confusion.

I paused, sensing the tension in her voice. She stared ahead, glancing up at me before the color in her face drained within seconds.

"What?" she breathed, almost too quiet to hear.

She darted into her office and closed the door, not hard enough for it to click shut. I walked closer, listening to see if I could hear the other voice on the phone.

"...know this is difficult news...we apologize for your loss..." the voice said, a little too muffled to catch the rest.

"Thank you for the call," Lisa said dryly.

I heard her tap the screen to end the call, and I didn't wait another second before pushing open the door.

She stared at the back wall with wide eyes and a blank expression. She rested the phone in her lap, not breathing.

"It's my mom," Lisa said, her voice totally void of any emotion. "She was in an accident."

"Is she okay?" I asked, walking in and closing the door behind me.

"They took her to the hospital, but she was already gone. They said she wasn't injured. She just stopped..." Lisa explained, most likely repeating the words she had just heard on the phone.

My ears perked up at the explanation. Normally when someone was uninjured, young, and involved in something that could have led to their death, I always jumped to the same reason.

"What do you mean?" I asked, hoping I was wrong.

"She stopped breathing, they said." She shook her head. "It doesn't make sense."

It wouldn't make sense, at least not to a human. I pulled a chair next to hers and sat close enough to touch her, acutely aware of the fact that I was a Legend and she wasn't.

"I'm so sorry, Lisa. Were you close to her?" I tried to focus on her instead of the situation that most likely happened.

"Not really. We haven't talked in years," Lisa started, and I let her talk. "You know how Mr. Lyle's been paying for college classes for me? Well, I was going to graduate in the fall, and I planned on calling her. Maybe if she saw me accomplish this, she might forget all the ways I disappointed her by being an assistant for so long. I just thought...I just thought I had more time."

"I bet she would have been proud of you." I smiled, reaching my arm around her shoulders.

Human lives were so short on their own, but I hadn't

really thought about what it would feel like for them. Seeing the pain, masked by apathy on her face, made my stomach twist uncomfortably.

How many people had I done this to? How many families had I left wondering?

"How do you know? How can I know anything she would've done? It's just... it's all over." Lisa's voice finally cracked.

A tear glimmered in the corner of her eye. She let her head fall forward, her unruly curls tumbling in front of her face.

"I remember the day I lost my father. He wasn't the warmest person, but he was my dad, you know? It still hurt the day he died. It hurt like nothing I had ever felt before." I pulled her into me as her sobs shook through her body.

My voice held steady, but only just barely. I avoided looking at Lisa. Instead, I stared at the beige wall in front of me and thought about that dreadful day.

I tasted the adrenaline pumping through me.

The lab had been kidnapping Legends and torturously taking them apart to see how the serum affected each part of their bodies. Every cell had to be analyzed. The pain of that feat would be agony to the Legend on the table.

I stared ahead over the sharp mountains at our target.

The fight should have been easy, and when we went up against the humans, it was. Then the Legends came out. We hadn't expected them to have an Extractor.

Charles wasn't biologically my father, but he had taken me in and made me a Shadow. When that Extractor wrapped a hand around Charles, I couldn't stop myself.

I screamed as loud as I could, "No!"

Charles turned and looked at me just as the other Legend

grabbed his arm. I saw his shoulders begin to droop and his eyes roll back in his head.

His energy was fading too fast.

An Extractor, one that could take energy not just from humans, was extremely rare, and I had no idea how the lab managed to snag one.

I turned my attention back to Charles's slowly sinking frame. I bounded forward, trying to reach him. Charles had enough energy to put his hand out to stop me.

"Run," Charles croaked before his eyes shut.

I looked at the Legend that now had Charles's energy coursing through him. My eyes narrowed and my temper flared. I hated the look of triumph in his eyes. He stepped over the only parent I had ever known and made his way to me.

My eyes darted around. There were only a few of us left.

Alec's worried eyes locked on mine. Just as Alec grabbed me, another Shadow lunged for the Extractor. We made it to a hill about a hundred yards away. I finally threw off Alec's grip and stopped running.

"Come on, Mara, we have to run. He'll find us later," Alec urged and tried to reach for me again.

"Your father won't be coming home," I said, my voice breaking.

Pain seared into Alec's eyes. He darted to the top of the hill to get a view of the body that once held all that his dad was. Tears stung as I watched Alec's shoulders fall.

He was gone. The man who raised me was gone. My heart shattered.

Without even thinking, I narrowed my eyes on the last standing Legend that took his life. The human scientists had begun to pour out of the building now that it was safe.

If they wanted a monster, that's exactly what they would get.

I let out a loud scream as I focused all the energy I had on that building. I commanded all the inanimate cells to change. The building erupted with fire as the humans inside screamed.

I didn't even flinch when the heat from the flames touched my face.

I locked eyes with that lonely Extractor, and I wanted him to feel the pain that now burned inside. He tossed on the ground helplessly as the flames from the building slowly enveloped him.

Once I heard his heart stop, I released my concentration. The flames tempered slowly and burned sustainably on their own.

The surrounding rock couldn't support the fire and it slowly puttered out.

Pain washed back over me. I would never see Charles again. I turned to see Alec next to me, his mouth wide open. Despite my constant trying, I had never achieved that level of power again. I had no idea where it came from or where it went.

All that remained was hate.

That hate and anger felt different now, holding Lisa in my arms and seeing just how much humans feel.

I reached and grabbed a tissue for her. She yanked it from my hand and slowly lifted her head.

"The funeral is in a week, in Texas. My aunt is probably already making the arrangements," Lisa said, her voice still shaking.

"What about your dad?" I asked.

Lisa rolled her eyes and shook her head. Her hands shifted in her lap.

"He left us when I was little. We haven't talked to him since, so I doubt he'll be there." Lisa lifted the tissue to her face again.

"Let Mr. Lyle know, and then you should go. Even if everything is taken care of, you'll feel better just being there. I would have given anything for a few more moments with my father." I smiled, fighting back my own tears.

"I can't just leave." Lisa shook her head faster. "I have

two assignments for college. I have a project that Mr. Lyle wanted on his desk yesterday. I'm not just—"

I grabbed her other shoulder and turned her to face me. She looked up reluctantly.

"Lisa, go." I stared into her eyes. "Life is short, and you can't miss moments like this."

She nodded and immediately started sorting papers on her desk. I didn't know what else to do, and I had another person that needed me down the hall. I started moving toward the door.

"Hey, Kate?" Lisa called.

I turned and looked at her drying tears and fidgeting hands. She stopped for a moment and just smiled at me. "Thank you."

"Let me know when you're leaving?" I nodded to her.

"I will." She wiped under her eyes and looked back down at her desk.

I closed the door behind me and took in a breath before I went to Kylan's office. My shoulders lifted slightly.

I walked in on him typing on his keyboard and intently watching the screen. He looked up at me as soon as I walked in.

"I'm sorry, about yesterday," I started as I walked through the doorway.

"Shut the door," he ordered as he stood.

I paused for a second, worried that this was going to turn into the second version of the same argument. That's how it always happened with Alec. But I did as he asked.

As soon as the door clicked shut under my hand, Kylan stepped around the desk.

"I should've handled that situation differently." I sighed. He reached his hands up and placed them on my shoulders.

"No, I'm the one who should be sorry," he said with

sincerity. I looked up into his eyes, confused. "You were just protecting us. I can see that now."

"But you were right. We shouldn't tamper with their lives just because we can." I put my hands on him as well. This apology was going much better than I expected.

"You were right too. Sometimes, you have to do things that you don't want to," he said, moving his hand up to my face.

His apologetic eyes showed me that he understood my reasoning. Seeing him reacting so rationally to what could have been a big argument reminded me of the caliber of character he had.

As I looked at him, I wondered how we ever crossed paths and was grateful for whoever made it happen.

"I'm so glad you feel that way, because I really didn't want to fight with you," I sighed and finally smiled for the first time today.

"Why? Are you worried you would lose?" he taunted and smiled at me.

"No, I'd be more worried about not rubbing it in. I'm a prideful winner," I joked back with him. He smiled even wider and leaned closer to my face.

"Let's not risk it then," he whispered almost against my lips.

"Deal," I agreed with him and waited for him to close the space between us.

After one, far-too-short kiss, he leaned away from me again.

"Hey, how about we go to your place tonight?" he offered. I stood with my mouth open for a moment, trying to find words. I had spent most nights at Kylan's house for dinner, with his family, and spending time with him. He had not come to mine yet.

I thought about how fast I could clean the place so nothing personal or relating to the Shadows was out.

The other main reason I had never invited him over was that my home has been my personal space. I go in and out, and no one else. It was a world that I could entirely control.

Having someone else in there would mess with the balance of things. I would be sharing my safe space with him.

Even back at the mansion, I had my own room. Alec had only gone in a few times. It was my space, and I needed it.

I wanted things to be different with Kylan. That would mean sharing more with him and opening up more to him with things I had never done before.

"I think I can do that," I answered confidently, even though my mind was still reeling.

"Good. Then you better get out of here and stop distracting me." He smiled and kissed me one more time before nudging me toward the door.

I tried to hide the smile as I left his office, but it didn't work very well.

After a long day of working, I listed every personal thing in my head that I owned and all the good hiding places.

As any normal girl would before a date, I assumed.

If I wanted this relationship to work, I had to invest something. Tonight was the first step. I left my office and met Kylan in the hallway.

"Hello beautiful." He smiled and locked his door. I walked up to him and planted a small kiss on his cheek.

"Are you all ready for tonight?" he asked.

"Yeah, I just need to grab something on the way home. I will be just a few minutes." I stalled to give myself time.

"Need time to hide all of your stuff?" he asked.

"What? No... I just..." I started, shocked and trying to think of a lie.

"I'm joking. I'm gonna head home and change, and then I'll meet you there. Is that enough time?" he raised his eyebrows, waiting for my answer.

"Well, only if you drive slow," I joked back.

"See you in a few minutes." He smiled.

CHAPTER
EIGHTEEN

I rushed in the door to my apartment, scrambling to hide anything I did not want him to see.

I changed my clothes from my business attire to jeans and a shirt. The shirt I had chosen didn't have long sleeves to reach past my elbows.

My mark taunted my choice as it stood completely exposed. I quickly grabbed a button-up sweater to match and pulled that over my arms, leaving the front open. I was walking through the small hallway when I heard a knock at the door. I paused.

It all had to be in place now because there was no time left. He was here.

I walked to the front door and took a deep breath to calm my heart and also to allow myself a moment to gather my thoughts. I was inviting him in, and this was a big step. I put my hand on the doorknob and turned it.

My heart rate slowed.

"Was that enough time?" he asked with a smile.

He wore a t-shirt and a zip-up jacket yet looked every bit as good as he did in a suit.

"Yes, perfect timing," I said and was about to take a step aside so he could come in when he pulled a bouquet of flowers from behind his back.

"Actually, I'm a bit later than I was hoping. I had to stop and get these," he excused and handed them to me.

The bright red daylilies were bunched tightly in new paper. I smiled. They were a flower that could withstand a lot more than others. They were hard to kill which made them my favorite.

"How did you know?" I asked.

Kylan smiled and tapped a finger on his temple. My smile fell from my face. If he had read my mind, I hadn't felt anything.

"I'm joking. Actually, Lisa gave me the tip. Said she saw you doodle them in the corners of your notes," Kylan said.

My shoulders relaxed.

"Thank you." I nodded and stepped aside. "Please, come in."

He stepped through the door and took a quick look around. I locked the door behind him. He turned to get a full view and then looked back at me.

"This place is nice," he said easily.

"Let me get some water for these, and then I can give you the grand tour," I explained as I headed to the kitchen for a tall cup. I didn't have a vase—because I honestly never thought I would need one. He chuckled when I pulled the cup from the top shelf of my cabinet.

"Next time, I'll bring a vase." He laughed.

"Oh please, don't mock. Do you have a vase sitting at your house?" I asked.

"No, I don't. Although I am not expecting strapping young men to be bringing me flowers," he explained.

"Well, neither was I." I shrugged as I filled my cup.

I proudly set the flowers in. They drooped to the sides of the wide cup and did not look as pretty as they did all bundled up. I pushed a few around to group them together to no avail.

"Kate, it's fine. They don't have to look perfect." He took my hand off the flowers. "You already do."

I looked at him for a moment and took in the cheesy compliment.

"Wow, how smooth was that line?" I grinned.

"I know, right?" He played along with a mischievous grin. "In all honesty though, you do look great tonight."

His eyes stayed locked on mine until they finally closed because our faces were too close to get a clear view.

His lips kissed mine gently, and then again, and again. He pulled me close and hugged me to him. I tucked my chin over his shoulder and leaned into his arms. We pulled away from the hug and looked at each other again.

"How about that tour I've been waiting for?" Kylan asked.

I smiled and walked him through each room. It didn't take long before we made it back to the living room and sat on the couch.

"You have a lovely home," he commented, but something seemed off.

"Is there anything else you want to say?" I prompted.

I could see the thought process going back and forth in his head to decide if he actually should say what was on the tip of his tongue.

"It's immaculate. Do you actually live here?" He finally glanced at me, cringing.

"Do I what?"

"There are no personal belongings out, no photos, no trinkets. Everything is just too perfect," he said.

I looked around the apartment and understood what he was seeing. This was not a home I lived in, this was the model home I had carefully prepared to show off.

"I was worried about you coming over and seeing all of my personal things. I like you so much already, and I just want you to like everything about me. So I didn't show you anything, and now I can see that may not have been the best choice." I wrung my hands as I explained.

"Kate, I like you the way you are. You don't have to hide your things from me, I want to see them all. What I have seen so far, I like a lot." He smiled at me and placed his hand over my nervous, moving hands.

"Okay, so ask. I will tell you anything you want to know." I challenged both him and myself.

"All right, do you honestly keep your bedroom that clean?" He raised an eyebrow.

"No, all my clothes are shoved in the floor of my closet, collecting wrinkles," I explained, maybe a little too in detail.

"Wow, okay. Um, what about pictures?"

"I am not a big fan of photos on the wall. It's only me, and I don't want a whole bunch of pictures of myself to stare at." I satisfied his question.

Then I thought of the one photo I had removed from the bookshelf. I brought the small, wooden frame back with me to the couch.

"This is the only photo I have." A beautiful golden retriever stood in the picture among a few pine trees. "This was my dog, Alvie. I had him a few years ago, but he died before he got much older than a puppy. I took this picture on a camping trip. For a while, he was my only friend, so I kept the picture."

Kylan looked at the photo he held in his hands and smiled.

"He looks like a gorgeous dog. How did he die?" Kylan asked.

"The vet said it was a heart attack. Just out of the blue, and he was gone one day. You can imagine what thoughts spiraled into my head from there about mortality and how we need to appreciate the time we have...Anyway, he was a good dog. I even miss him sometimes still," I sighed.

I took the photo and allowed the air around the frame to lift it. It floated away from my hands and gently settled on the end table by the couch.

"How often do you use your abilities? Do you practice at all?" he asked, already having his own answer in mind due to the use of my abilities to move the picture.

"Fairly often, I guess, when I have the energy. I just use them for little things here and there. I used to practice and try to improve my skills a lot. I have mostly stopped now. I can tell when I try new things that I am getting a little rusty," I explained.

He nodded as he listened to me and it felt oddly good to talk.

"Do you practice?" I asked.

"I help the others with their skills. Rachel insists that she is a Two and just hasn't broken through the other Level yet. Sometimes I use mine for demonstration, but I don't develop mine just for the sake of improvement anymore," he told me plainly.

"You're a Four, though. You must be curious about what you can do?" I prodded a little.

He looked away from my eyes and stared at the floor. He silently shifted his position and looked around the room.

A speck of light shimmered in the corner of my vision. I turned and found that it wasn't just one. The air in the entire room held fluttering, glittering specks around us.

My heart raced at the floating magic.

The dim lights in my apartment threw tiny rays of light into each speck. My breath stopped as I looked at Kylan.

Without closing his eyes, or using much concentration at all, he created a starry night exactly where we sat. My eyes widened and my lips parted as I tried to force my mind to believe what my eyes had just seen. Creating was definitely his talent.

"I have a pretty good idea of what I can do." A small smile crept up on his face as he saw my reaction.

He blinked and let out a small breath. As he did, the glittering specks fell to the ground, covering the carpet.

"Perhaps the better question is what can't you do?" I asked, still amazed at the brightly shining star and his ease in adding to it. I looked at him happily only to notice that the smile had melted from his face. I could see the guilt forming on his face.

"Based on my family history, I don't doubt that I could be capable of so much more. I'm just content where I'm at." His mouth tightened at a memory. His eyes drooped in disappointment.

"What Levels are your parents?" I asked in a quieter tone. I touched his arm to let him know that I wasn't judging and that I was here to help. He had no idea the kind of past I came from. I could never judge him for his.

"They were both Fours. Some of the strongest, actually. My mom was gentle about her abilities, but when you got her angry, you knew you were in trouble," he snickered as he was probably recalling a memory of his mom.

Then his smile faded.

"My dad insisted that we were never good enough and we could always try harder. 'Sleep is optional,' he used to say to us. My mom and I left when I was still little."

He stared at the tan carpet in front of him, looking at his hands like they should be holding something.

"Where are they now?" I encouraged him to keep going.

The more he opened up, the closer I felt to him. I wasn't the one who was sharing, but I still reaped the rewards. I was glowing inside at the thought that he trusted me enough to share this with me.

"They are both dead. My mom died when I was about fourteen Legend years old. I'm not sure what became of my dad. I assume he is probably gone. Something tells me that he wasn't the type to live out a long life. He was more the type to go out with a bang."

He let out a small, forced laugh.

"Is that why you don't practice your skills? Because of your father?" I softly tried to clarify.

"Kind of. I just think I have enough power for what I need. I don't need to be dominatingly strong. I can just be me, and I am fine with that." He looked back at me, waiting for my silent approval. I nodded.

"How noble of you," I tried to hide my sarcasm.

The more I got to know him, the more I knew that my past would be a deal breaker for him. As sweet and forgiving as he was, no one could simply overlook years of murdering people and enjoying it.

Whether I liked it or not, I was capable of that kind of life. That was something I couldn't change. The only thing I could change was my future.

By not sharing my history with Kylan, I was looking to the future instead of drudging through the past. I looked at his green eyes and all I could see was the possibilities ahead of me.

"Okay, next question?" I asked him as we both sat back in more comfortable positions on the couch.

"Let's do…most embarrassing moment." Kylan narrowed his eyes as he found the question he wanted to ask. He waited expectantly and excitedly for his answer. I thought for a moment and then my eyes popped wide open when I realized what answer I would give.

"Oh, I've got it." I drumrolled my own hands on my legs. "So, this is back when I was a doctor in South America and—"

"What? You were a doctor?" he asked.

In each hometown, I changed what I did for a living. During my time away, I went on to be a student abroad for a few years—a doctor, a historian, and anything that would teach me more about humans or about the necklace.

"Yeah, it was just after I had left my family, and I wanted to do something totally different. I was in such a small village that I didn't deal with too many patients at a time, and I pretended that I couldn't learn the language to keep any of them from getting too comfortable with me."

I smiled at the happy memory and looked to see Kylan was no longer paying attention.

"You're incredible." Kylan looked at me with starry eyes.

"Far from it actually…" I started, but he didn't let me finish.

He leaned forward and kissed me. His hand immediately followed to pull my face closer. We each kissed slowly, but that rapidly changed. My logic completely shut down when I heard him breathe faster and felt him pull me even closer to him.

My hands moved up to his shoulders automatically, as my fingers clutched the collar of his jacket. Without any hesitation, he granted my unspoken wish. Before my next breath, his jacket was off and his hands were back to tangling themselves in my dark hair. My heart slammed against my chest as his hand moved from my hair to my cheek to my shoulder. A tug on the fabric of my sweater pulled it over my shoulder. The open front allowed the sleeve to travel down my arm.

My right arm.

My attention snapped back immediately just as the sweater was passing my elbow and the skin near my mark began to burn.

"Stop," I gasped as I yanked my face away from his.

I grabbed my sweater sleeve and held it firmly in place, not letting it slip down any farther. A few centimeters more, and the hilt of the dagger would have shown. I tried to calm my own breathing.

He didn't see anything. I tried to convince myself.

That wasn't the problem, though. The problem was that I almost let him. I finally looked back up at his confused eyes.

"Are you okay?" he asked tentatively.

He glanced for a second at my arm that I had just covered again. I sat up and moved back to my spot on the couch next to him.

"Yeah...I'm fine," I stammered.

The only way Kylan wouldn't be suspicious is if I really sold this next moment. Unfortunately for me, that meant playing the scared girl card. I gulped, and my pride went down with it.

"I just...I just don't want to move too fast. I'm not sure I'm ready for anything like that," I said and tried to make my eyes as sincere as possible.

Even I hardly believed my own lie. The truth was that I wanted Kylan as bad as he clearly wanted me. Letting him in that way would mean telling him all about my past. I didn't think tonight was appropriate to bring up the startling I-am-a-reformed-serial-killer type of conversation.

I watched Kylan's eyes change from confused to disappointed. I knew it would be coming, but my heart still ached inside my chest.

"I totally misread that..." His voice trailed off.

He looked away for a moment and gathered his composure. He sat up straighter and looked back at me with fresh eyes, but I could still see the confusion lurking behind his bright attitude.

"Please don't take this personally. It has nothing to do with you." I tried to smooth things over. As soon as I said the words, I realized how cliché they sounded. I wish I could accurately describe how true they were.

"Look, I don't want to push you into anything before you are ready," he said, and I dropped my gaze to the floor. He put his finger under my chin and brought my eyes back up to his.

"I care about you too much to do that," he finished his statement. I smiled and let out a breath.

"Thank you," I whispered back to him.

He believed me. It almost hurt more that he did. I was a little too used to lying, even to the people I cared about.

"All right...um...your turn. What's the thing you are most afraid of?" I asked him a piercing question in return.

He let a laugh before thinking of his answer. He looked me right in the eye and forced his shoulders to relax.

"Being alone," he answered thoughtfully. "When I was growing up, I had my mom. After she was killed, I had no one in my life at all. Now, I have my family. Seeing both sides, I am my best self when I have others around me."

"Well, I can tell you firsthand that it pretty much sucks. It's great to have the freedom, but with no one to share life with, it's just empty opportunity," I explained.

He nodded with eyes full of sympathy.

"What's the worst thing that ever happened to you?" Kylan asked softly.

His tone of voice told me he would treat the answer with the respect it deserved. I scanned my memories for a moment, but I already knew the answer. I recalled vividly the day that everything changed for me.

"The day I lost my father," I started. "I guess he wasn't biologically my father. He was the man who loved me, raised me, and taught me everything I know. So, to me, he was a father."

"I'm sorry," Kylan nodded.

"He was killed. We had a bad run-in with an Extractor. He took my father's life right in front of my eyes. I can still remember the life draining from his face." Nothing could stop my voice from breaking now. Kylan reached over and held me in his arms.

"How did you make it out?" he edged slowly, not wanting to press too far.

"We ran. The only ones left alive were me and..." I stopped that sentence, not wanting to dive into the Alec situation just yet.

"After I was a safe distance away, I looked back and... I killed him," I spoke gently.

I didn't want to reveal the kind of skill I had honed. I took all precautions, even with Kylan. Maybe especially with Kylan. I didn't want him drawing any conclusions. I hung my head.

Up until now, I hadn't admitted that I had killed anyone before. As a Shadow, it was a badge of honor. As a regular Legend, I didn't imagine that was a point in my favor.

Kylan reached over and lifted my chin, so my eyes had to meet his gaze. What I saw was not what I was expecting. His eyes were soft, and a sad smile formed.

"You are not the only one who has taken a life," he muttered, almost too low for me to hear. His eyes filled with understanding. "Sometimes, you would do anything for the person that you love."

"All I wanted was to make him proud. He may not have had the kindest way of going about things, but it was all I had known a parent to be, you know?" I shrugged.

I needed to defend him and the way of the Shadows, even if I knew it was wrong. I didn't want anything to stain the memory of him.

"Kids rely on their parents. That's normal. It's not wrong to think that he was a great man, even if he made bad decisions." Kylan comforted the exact fear I had. "I've caught myself thinking the same thing about my dad. Not that my mom was perfect either, but compared to my dad, she was an angel."

"I loved him like a father, and he was ripped from me. It's not easy to forget." I spoke softly, not wanting to cause any further tears to come erupting through. "After years and years of moving through all the stages of grief, I think I've finally accepted it. Hence, me trying to live near humans. I've been reworking my thinking to accept that not all humans are bad. The ones I encountered on that day probably had their reasons, and though it does not justify what they did, it does help dull the pain."

"You are incredible, you know that? Most people would just use that as an excuse to hold a grudge indefinitely," he said.

I saw the admiration in his eyes. If I couldn't tell him everything, I at least wanted him to know that I wasn't perfect. He deserved at least that much honesty.

"I wish that were the case. The Extractor... I constantly tried to give him the benefit of the doubt. The most I can muster is that just not thinking about him at all is easier than fighting the pain. I don't know if I could ever forgive him. If I ever saw him again, I don't think I would change what I did," I admitted.

I couldn't help the hate from seeping into my heart. He was helping those vile humans. Reliving the memory brought back the rage that had once ruled me, the rage I had worked so hard to overcome. I saw Kylan lowering his head out of the corner of my eye. He looked like a new burden had been placed on him.

"I think a lot of people would agree with you. An Extractor is always a threat. That's just how it is." He spoke slowly, like he was reciting something he had always been told. "I don't blame you for doing what you did."

He looked at me with a tight smile on his face, his eyes still holding back a sadness that I couldn't understand.

"Are you all right?" I watched his eyes for a real answer.

"Are you?"

"I'm getting there," I answered honestly.

"Me too."

"You know what I think?" I asked and almost started with my next statement.

Kylan cut me off by looking into my eyes too strongly and said, "Give me just a second, and I will…" he smiled and focused on me like he was concentrating.

I smacked his arm and broke his concentration. He smiled. I leaned forward and kissed him. It sent chills down my spine until my toes tingled.

"I think we're gonna be fine. It just takes time," I spoke softly with his face so close to mine that I couldn't focus on his eyes.

"I think you're right." Kylan nodded and kissed me again.

This time, neither one of us had the power to stop. We just sat there, sinking further into each other.

That night, I took the picture of the locket that had ruled my life for so long and tucked it into the first book that launched this journey. Both of them sat on the table in my kitchen, ready to be packed up. I didn't want any reminders of my past.

These two had been with me over the decades, and after tonight, I was finally ready to give them up. I knew what I wanted now, and it was something that this old necklace couldn't give me.

CHAPTER
NINETEEN

"Come on, they're already here," he reminded me as he hurriedly led the way into the trees.

I walked away from the car, holding towels and bottles of water. Just around the corner, I could hear shouting and splashing. Kylan had taken me to his new favorite spot in Oregon, and all the family was here. It had been a while since all of his family had gotten together like this.

We stepped out into the clearing, and I could see what he was so excited about. It was beautiful.

The large pond was about twenty meters long and had rocks surrounding it. A cliff overlooked the water and had a small waterfall cascading into the pool below.

It was the beginning of spring, and the water was still cold enough to keep the humans away. Cassie and Rachel were at the top of the rock, getting ready to jump. Derek was out of the water with his phone up to take a picture of the two of them jumping off. Cassie was the first to see us.

She looked up and gave us a fast wave. "Hey Kylan! Watch this."

In perfect synchronization, they both flipped in the air. As they neared the water, they straightened out and dove headfirst into the water below, leaving two small ripples where they entered seamlessly.

Kylan ran down the hill and came skidding to a stop just in time to drop the bags, remove his shirt and shoes, and take the next leap up onto the outer rock.

He stood for a moment on top of the rock for all the world to see. The midday sunshine hit his body, and his skin glistened. It took me too long to realize that I wasn't breathing. Kylan turned around to look at me one last time.

"Come on, Kate, you're missing the fun!" he shouted as he dove headfirst into the water.

I set my stuff on a rock surrounded by dirt at the top of the hill with the rest of Kylan's things. I pulled my shirt off to reveal my long-sleeved rash guard that covered my swimsuit and the infuriating black dagger mark on my arm. I pulled the zipper down on my shorts and stepped out of them.

I heard a loud whistle from down at the pool. I turned and saw Kylan checking me out. It was my turn to smile.

"Are you coming in? Or did you just come to sunbathe?" Derek taunted from inside the water.

Kylan threw a splash of water at his face. Derek turned his head just in time to miss most of the water.

"Kate, show us something cool!" Rachel cupped her hands around her mouth.

She and Cassie had made it out of the water and were heading up the rock again. I took a deep breath and took my stance.

I ran full-speed toward the rock barrier of the pool. My steps crushed the soft dirt beneath. My first foot hit the hard rock. On the second step, I shoved off the rock.

I launched into the air with my body laying out flat,

parallel to the water. I flew far enough to miss hitting Kylan in the water. Not an inch too far away though, just enough to make him flinch.

At the last second, I tucked into a front flip and, when I finished spinning my feet entered the water.

Under the water, everything was silent. I could only hear my heartbeat and my strokes in the water.

I broke the surface and the silence shattered. My ears filled with the cheers of those around me.

Derek swam over just to give me a high five hard enough to knock my arm back into the water.

Kylan reached me just after and wrapped his arms around me. We both began swimming to the edge of the pool. We had just reached the area where we could touch the bottom. Kylan kept stepping forward, revealing more of his body from out of the water. He stopped walking long enough to turn to me.

"You never cease to amaze me, Kate," he whispered for just the two of us.

"Hey, let's not forget your incredible dive." I smiled. "I would give that at least a three out of ten."

Kylan held back a smile and glared at me instead. He pulled my face to his and planted a kiss in front of his entire family.

He broke the kiss and waded through the water to the edge of the pool.

"Nicely done, man. I thought she was going to be too good for you," Derek joked.

Cassie threw him a hard look. Kylan took a small bow facing the rest of them. Derek and Rachel laughed and gave him a brief applause. I smiled. It was good to see them so happy as a family.

Cassie stood and came over to me. Kylan switched places

and sat next to Derek. We both stood on the edge of the water, dripping wet.

"I'm so happy you guys got together," she spoke softer than her usual shrill tone. "I have been with Kylan a while, and I'm glad to finally see him so happy again. It's been a long time."

"What do you mean?" I echoed her hushed tone.

"He hasn't brought a girl home since his last major relationship about, oh, twenty years ago. Since then, it has just been him," she shrugged.

"What was she like?" I asked another question. If she was willing to tell, I was willing to pry.

"Her name was Halle. She was nothing like you. She was very powerful, and she knew it too. Kylan was crazy about her, but she didn't want to live a life like we all do. She wanted to be…superior." Cassie shared more and more the longer I let her talk.

"They were good for a while, but eventually, they both could see it wasn't a good fit. Kylan was devastated. He could see all of us being happy, and he wanted the same thing. We didn't see him for about a year. Then he showed up and said he wasn't going through that ever again. Then he brought you home. None of us were surprised when we found out you were a Four, I guess. Kylan is drawn to the strong ones. He tries to hide it, but we all see the, uh, the burning desire to be strong. It's ingrained in him," she finished.

"And you are worried I'm going to do the same thing to him?" I asked.

"Let's just say if Kylan is finally open to the idea, then we'll be too. To be honest, I like you. Rachel is sad we don't know much about you. We just want to look out for Kylan. He's what makes us a family." She smiled.

I loved how much she cared about him, how much they

all cared. Cassie's smile fell to a serious look when she turned her face up to me. "All I am saying is, be careful with our boy."

"I honestly care about him, Cassie," I assured her. "I have no intention of hurting him."

She looked me over and did not appear to be buying my answer. Her eyes glared back into the clear water in front of us. "Neither did Halle."

Kylan looked over and saw the look on my face before I could hide it. His smile disappeared, and he immediately came over.

"What's going on here, ladies?" he asked, looking mostly at Cassie. She shrugged and smiled back up at Kylan.

"Nothing, we were just talking," she finished and stepped out of the water.

She looked pointedly at Kylan and then took one last glance at me. I nodded to let her know I understood what she meant. She took that and sauntered away.

Derek stood to greet her and quickly threw his arms around her. He picked her up and spun her in a circle. Her dark red hair ponytail, glinted in the sunlight.

Kylan took her place beside me. "Are you all right? You look like you just saw a ghost." He looked into my eyes and placed his hand on my knee.

"I'm okay." I swallowed. "I was just wondering. If I gave you a rematch, could you come up with a better dive than that classic headfirst one you pulled earlier?"

I bit my lip and raised my eyebrows to offer my challenge, hoping he would take the distraction.

Kylan's eyes flashed in utter excitement. He squeezed my hand and nodded at the rock behind him. "Meet you at the top of the cliff."

We took off. I actually ran to the top and Kylan jumped,

caught the front of the rock, and swung himself up to the top. We both met at about the same time.

"Ah, look who's impressive now." I allowed the sarcasm to drip through my words.

Kylan smiled a crooked grin and took me by each hand.

"For my next trick," he said as he turned me around so my back faced the open water. He faced me. "I am going to need your help."

I stood still as he moved his hands up over my clothed arms and reached the bare skin on my neck. He took my face in his hands and pulled me close. His lips met mine in a deep kiss that made my head spin. His tongue just barely grazed my mouth.

My mind went wild, and my body froze.

Kylan had never kissed me with such intensity before in front of other people. The thrill was intoxicating. My heart answered the call and pumped blood to every extremity.

Just as I was running out of air, Kylan gently moved his hands to my shoulders. The kiss broke, and his entire body weight pressed down from his hands to my shoulders.

I opened my eyes in time to see Kylan do a handstand on top of my shoulders and use that momentum to twist in the air and glide seamlessly into the water below.

He swam back up to the top and looked back up at me, grinning from ear to ear.

"Thanks for the lift," he called from the bottom.

I smiled down at him. My heart leaped in my chest as I looked down at him and around at the others. This was a life I couldn't even think to imagine.

For the next hour or so, we splashed around. I took a break to sit on the edge of the pool. Rachel found me.

"Are you cold?" She pointed at my rash guard.

It was meant to cover the mark on my arm. The black

sleeves acted as a perfect barrier, even when they were soaked.

"I guess I'm just a little more conservative. I just feel strange not being covered up," I lied.

I noted Rachel's olive green, one-piece swimsuit that didn't leave much to the imagination. Although, compared to Cassie's outfit, Rachel's looked conservative.

"Oh, please, you don't have anything to worry about," she looked me up and down and scoffed.

"Thanks." I turned my gaze to the ground, trying to hide my smile.

"Plus, it's not like that shirt is hiding much anyway." She leaned in close, not wanting anyone to overhear.

Her point was accurate. The rash guard clung to my body from being wet. Everything underneath had a visible outline through the shirt. However, I didn't actually care about how others saw my body. I knew I looked good and to me, that was all that mattered.

"I know," I whispered back, turning my face up so she could see my smile now.

Rachel laughed and we both relaxed. I definitely felt more comfortable around her than I did around Cassie or Derek.

After a pause, she looked down at the dirt, dragging her finger through it to form a circle. I waited, not sure where she was planning on taking this conversation. She didn't say anything.

"Rachel, how about you just say what's on your mind?" I asked.

She shot her eyes back up to me. Then she smiled at the fact that I knew she had another angle. She was quick, but so was I.

"It's just that you seem too good to be true," she edged, watching me. "I mean, you seem nice and polite and modest and funny, and Kylan is obviously head over heels for you. I just wonder if that's all you are."

I thought about her question. I looked at what I'd been showing of myself to Kylan's family. Rachel was right. Based on what they had seen, I was too perfect. I laughed at how wrong that assumption was. My mark on my arm began to burn and reminded me of its forever presence.

"I'm far from perfect, trust me," I tried to console her suspicion.

She just waited and even tapped her finger on her knee to let me know that she was waiting for a better answer. I took a breath and dove in.

"For example, the first time Kylan tried to kiss me, I actually turned him down," I continued.

"What?" Rachel smiled at the idea that I had actually made a mistake.

"True story. He asked if he could kiss me and I flat-out said no. I thought I was making the right choice and then later decided that, yes, it was stupid of me. So, then I marched over to his house and...well, you know the rest."

"Hmm." Rachel thought about this information for a moment.

"Or one time, I forgot that cars need gas, and ran out in the middle of nowhere. Oh, when I was really little, I loved telling humans that I could change things with my mind, and then my father swore never to leave me alone in public again. There have been quite a few thoughtless moments in my life."

I laughed, remembering how many little mistakes I had made and how much those little mistakes meant nothing to me. But it meant something to her to hear them.

"Maybe you're just as messed up as the rest of us," she said and laughed along with me.

"What about you then?" I turned the conversation back on her. "What's something you don't like telling people?"

I figured if I was sharing, then she should too.

Rachel took a breath in and a quick glance around to make sure no one was paying attention. She looked at me for a moment before she spoke.

Her face was judging whether or not I could keep a secret. I waited patiently until she must have found what she was looking for.

"Before Cassie found me, and before I came to this family, my life was...different," she whispered.

Either the others didn't know or she didn't like talking about whatever it was.

"I was living in New York and was ridiculously wealthy. I used my abilities to play the stock market, embezzle funds from the companies I ran, and I cheated a lot of people out of their hard-earned interest and investments. I was incredibly good at what I did, and nobody questioned me." Rachel's eyes lowered to the ground as her story came pouring out.

Her fingers distractedly moved the dark brown dirt around in different shapes.

"Cassie came to my front door one day, and I almost recognized her by the resemblance alone. She explained that we were sisters and that she had a wonderful family. At first, I couldn't believe it was really her. We were so young when we got separated. But she asked me if I wanted a better life, a family again. Cassie knew everything that I had done. It was part of the reason she was able to find me, actually. Yet she still accepted me."

My heart glowed in my chest. Rachel had a dark story, and yet here she was with the rest of them.

A bright hope bubbled up as I listened to her.

"I met Kylan and Derek next. They were so excited to

see me and happy that Cassie had found her long-lost sister. It all kind of sounds like a fairy tale now that I look back on it. Before she came to find me, I was aware of how empty my life was. Money was the only thing I thought could fill the void but, man, was I wrong. After being with them for as many years as I have, I can clearly see that this was the life I had wanted all along." Rachel finished her story and still did not look up from the ground.

She kept her head low and waited until she felt safe enough to look up and see my reaction.

I reached over and touched her bare knee, her skin warm to the touch despite the cool breeze.

She finally met my gaze.

"I think I might be a lot like you. I'm not exactly proud of my past. Since, um, changing my life around, I still wonder if I even deserve a better life," I said a little too easily.

Rachel's confession gave me more hope than Kylan's unconditional love alone. The whole family treated her like she was no different than them.

"If I can come back, then you certainly can too," she said.

Rachel reached her chilly hand and placed it on top of mine for comfort. Her soft, accepting eyes waited.

"I mean, it's not like you were like a murderer, or worse, a Shadow. You're probably just fine," she added at the end with a laugh to break the tension.

My heart plummeted in my chest.

"Yeah, that would...Both of those would be bad," I muttered to myself and agreed with her comment.

"Come on, I brought lunch for all of us." She lifted her hand and patted my leg as she stood.

I nodded and tried to smile. I breathed and remembered that they didn't know anything yet. For now, I was still just as safe as I was before.

"Thanks for the talk, Rachel," I finished before she walked away.

"Thanks for listening," she added and turned around to prance toward the bright-red cooler of food.

I took a moment to myself and just sat there. I watched the sun on the water. Despite my hope for redemption, I reminded myself that my past was unforgivable. I tried to keep the looming, pessimistic doom out of my thoughts but with that blow, it was going to be hard.

Rachel walked over to the cooler and opened the creaky lid. She handed out the chicken sandwiches and all the snacks to go along with it. My mouth watered instantly. I hadn't realized how hungry I was. As a Shadow, we hardly ever wasted time with actual food, we just kept ourselves filled with human energy.

She handed Kylan and Cassie two apples and took one out for herself. She immediately sat down on the nearest rock and took a bite. Derek was giving Cassie the sandwiches when he noticed the apples come out.

"Hey Rach, do you have another one?" he asked.

"No, I only brought three," she said, stroking back her hair. "Make one yourself."

"No way. You're the one who always has enough energy to spare. Plus, you were in charge of food." He shook his head.

She glared at him lying on the ground next to Cassie basking in the sun.

"Fine," she conceded.

In a matter of seconds, a plump, red apple sat just inches from her face. She opened her eyes and released her breath.

She smiled and, without warning, she whipped around and shot the fruit at Derek. As it neared his head, Cassie snatched it and rolled over to look at Rachel.

"Play nice," Cassie warned her and held out her hand as the apple dropped to meet it.

She politely handed the apple to Derek without looking away from Rachel. Derek immediately took a bite.

"Excellent work, sis," Derek called out to Rachel as he waved the bitten fruit in the air.

Cassie kept staring at the apple, even as Derek lifted it to his mouth to take another bite. The edges of the fruit turned black, slowly covering the whole thing in a nasty, dark color.

Derek saw it and dropped it immediately. The lump of black crushed into the ground.

"Oh, whoops." Cassie grinned and took a glance at her sister.

Destroying. That must be Cassie's second Level.

"Here we go," Kylan muttered.

I glanced over at him but he just kept watching Derek. I turned my eyes back to the happy couple.

Derek looked up at his wife and didn't say a thing. His mouth thinned and his eyes narrowed as he focused on the sandwich Cassie was holding.

The same thick shade of black that now covered the apple overtook the sandwich, piece by piece. Cassie tossed it away from her before it had even fully disintegrated.

Her eyes shot down to look at Derek, lying on his stomach and grinning up at her.

So, he could destroy too.

"Touché." She glared at him.

Derek smiled and grabbed her with both of his huge hands. He pulled her down to the ground on the other side of him, her body flying over his. They stopped laughing when Derek kissed her. Cassie stopped shoving him away and pulled him closer instead.

"Oh, break it up, you two," Rachel called and tossed a handful of dirt at them.

Derek broke the kiss and looked up at her. He looked down at Cassie, and without talking, they both knew what to do. They shot forward and grabbed Rachel by either arm. Together, they launched her from her seat on the rock straight in the pool in front of us.

Her body crashed through the surface of the water, cutting off her scream. She popped her head up to the surface with her auburn hair slicked back from the water and a smile across her mouth.

This is what a family was like? I wondered, a smile forming on my own face.

I looked over to Kylan. His wide grin matched Derek's as they high-fived each other. Both of them barreled into the water together with Cassie bouncing behind them.

That was what I wanted to have one day, what I wanted to deserve one day. I thought of the mark on my arm. Maybe today just wasn't it.

CHAPTER
TWENTY

"All right, what's on your mind?" Kylan asked as soon as we stepped in the door of my apartment.

He shut the door behind him and waited until I put my bag on the ground and kicked off my shoes. My bare feet pressed against the cold tile floor. Kylan stood still by the front entry, waiting for me to talk.

"I thought you said that your family didn't use their abilities that much?" I commented, redirecting the conversation.

"No, I said I didn't use mine that often. They sometimes do. Today was kind of an exception, though," Kylan explained, keeping his eyes focused on me.

"Okay." I shrugged my shoulders and walked into the kitchen, hoping he would keep talking.

"But that's not really what you're thinking about, is it?" Kylan pushed further, following me into the kitchen. He touched my shoulder and softly pulled me around to face him. Asking with his eyes for me explain. I had to give him something.

"Cassie told me about Halle," I muttered as I looked at him steadily.

This wasn't the main confession weighing on my mind, but it was a start. I watched his eyes as the care for me faded, and the anger at Cassie began to win over.

"Ugh, that girl," he scowled. "She has the biggest mouth of all of them. Even Rachel is better at keeping secrets than Cassie, I swear." He rambled and tried to play down the information. I waited.

"Why did she think it was important to say something?" I asked him directly. Kylan paused for a moment and ran his hand through his hair.

"You have to understand that Cassie has a big heart, and she cares a lot about the happiness of others…including me. She saw me fall for Halle, and it hurt Cassie just as much when we split. She probably told you because she is being protective of me." Kylan gently explained.

"Does she think I'm going to hurt you?" I tried not to think of all the ways that I could hurt him. Ways that I wouldn't even have to try that hard.

"No." Kylan answered firmly this time. "But that's the problem. Every one of them is hoping that I will find someone to be happy with. When I brought Halle home, they thought she was the one." He paused just long enough to show the sadness in his glimmering eyes.

"We all did."

He looked anywhere else in the room instead of at me. After a breath, he stepped forward, still keeping his eyes on the ground.

"That's always the problem with falling in love. That's also what makes it such a rush when you meet someone new. The possibilities are exhilarating," he finished and looked back at me.

"Do you think that I would hurt you?" I asked him with the quietest voice.

He leaned forward and placed a gentle kiss on my lips. He pulled back and rested his forehead against mine.

"I hope not," he whispered. I could see the muscles in his arms flexing from straining to find the right words. "I would never see it coming…I'm crazy about you."

"Me too," I whispered back to him. I watched his smile widen.

He kissed me again, this time with more excitement than the last. I couldn't wish him harm.

His hand wrapped around my back, and he pulled me into him. Our lips blended together as our hands explored. He was nervous, and yet there he was, trusting me with his heart. Maybe I could learn to loosen up around him.

He reached up and touched the back of my neck. His hand carved a path through my damp hair. I could stand to share more of my life with him. Not the past, but the future was shaping up to be more of a possibility.

My breath caught as his hands laced fire across my body. He lifted me up and walked me over to the kitchen table.

As soon as he lowered me down, something pressed into my leg. I turned my head to see the book about Legends on the table.

I shoved it to the side and looked back up at Kylan, but he wasn't looking at me anymore. His eyes had fallen to the book.

Then he stopped. His hands were gone but the heat still lingered.

His fingers brushed the paper tucked under the corner of the book I had just moved. He pulled out the piece of paper that showed the sketch of the locket face. He looked at me curiously.

"Oh, sorry. I didn't mean to leave that out." I tried to reach for the paper.

Kylan pulled it away from me. I leaned back on the table, trying to slow my breathing. My heart still raced from the kiss.

"What is this?" he asked and looked at the paper he was holding.

I knew exactly what it was—the locket I remembered seeing in the safe. The intricate design on the front was not quite done justice by my drawing. I hadn't even drawn the chain, so it actually just looked like a fancy oval.

"It's nothing, I just forgot to put it away," I said, reaching for the page one more time.

Kylan stepped back, holding onto the image. The look in his eyes caused a knot to form in my stomach. My hand fell, and my heart thumped.

"Did you draw this?" he asked, turning his attention back to the paper.

"Yes," I answered warily.

He looked from the paper to me. When he looked back at the paper, he had a different expression on his face. He tilted his head the way he did when he was trying to figure something out.

"I've seen this before," he mused as he looked the drawing over.

"Wait, really?" I asked, my vision focusing on him alone.

The rest of the room faded away. I couldn't see the oak kitchen cabinets, or the dark countertops, or even the painted wood table I sat on.

All I could see was him, and his eyes as they recognized the image. The image that I only knew of three people who had seen it before.

He shouldn't know it. It had to be a mistake.

"Is this a necklace?" Kylan asked and turned his head toward me for the answer.

My breath caught in my throat. Even if he had seen the design, he shouldn't have been able to guess it was a necklace. Unless he already knew what it looked like.

My mind detonated into a thousand thoughts.

"Yes, it's a locket." I nodded and waited in silence for his explanation.

Inside, my mind was anything but silent. I studied his eyes, his hands, and his entire body language. I searched for any clue as to how he could know about this.

"I can't quite place where I have seen it." He spoke slowly and kept thinking. "Where did you get this image to draw the picture?"

"I just saw it in my mind, like a dream, and couldn't get it out until I drew it on paper." I rushed my answer.

It was mostly true, but I wasn't concerned about giving him more information about it. I was concerned with how much he might have already known.

Without warning, his grip tightened on the paper, almost crumpling it in his hands. My ears heard the crunch as his eyes narrowed.

"No," he breathed.

His eyes skimmed across the image over and over again in a matter of seconds until they finally shot up to look at me.

He was confused. He had a question in his eyes. I only wondered if it was the same one that I had in mine.

"I know this necklace," he said as he stood to his full height immediately and took a step back from me.

I wasn't sure if I wanted him to know more or if I wanted him as far away from this as possible.

"What do you know?" I asked.

I reached my hand out to him and he pulled his arm farther away from me. We knew so much about each other, and we cared so much about each other. Yet in that moment, I was staring at a stranger. His eyes showed the same lack of familiarity.

"How do you know about it?" he accused and rushed forward.

I jumped off the table and held out my hand to warn him not to come any closer. To his credit, he stopped, but his expression didn't change. His blazing eyes bounced from the paper to me.

"I don't know anything about it," I tried to explain, taking a step back from his rage.

My eyes snapped back and forth between the piece of paper and his burning eyes. My fists clenched at my sides as I took slow, steady breaths.

"Then why do you have it?" he interrogated faster, never taking his eyes off me.

"I think it has something to do with my past," I forced an honest answer again.

Kylan was not getting the whole picture, but I was trying to tell as much truth as I could. The tattooed mark on my arm awoke. This was a moment that I was dreading. He knew something about me by seeing the necklace. If he knew enough, he could easily piece together exactly where I saw the image.

"Who sent you?" Kylan's eyes narrowed as he scanned my face.

He seemed to look for any kind of recognition, I just didn't know why. Based on the necklace, he thought he should know my identity.

How much could this necklace possibly mean to him?

My mind raced through the scenarios. I thought of the quickest exit through the window, which he was blocking. My next-best option would be the door, which was locked.

"No one sent me. I came here on my own. I came looking for the necklace…and for…" I started, but realized that nothing was really getting through to him.

"Me?" he accused again.

"No," I answered firmly.

If I had known Kylan would be in Portland, I would have come much sooner. Even if the Shadows were still prowling around, I would have risked them seeing me. He was worth almost more than my own freedom.

This necklace was going to ruin all of that.

"Kylan, you have to tell me what is going on," I begged, hoping he could see the pain in my eyes, the worry.

"You don't know who this necklace belongs to?" he asked, quieter this time.

"No. The closest I got was a museum that had a picture of someone holding it." I shrugged, hoping the tension would ease.

"The night I ran into you." He raised an eyebrow.

His face finally softened. Something about my answer put him at more ease than before. So many questions still swirled in my mind. The fragile peace that had formed between us told me that now was not the time to press for answers.

"Yeah, actually." I remembered seeing him in the streets as I was looking over the registry from the opening day of the museum.

"I'm sorry. I didn't mean to…" He shook his head.

He took a breath to rid the last bit of anger from his expression. When he looked back up, the kind green eyes returned.

I relaxed, knowing that the threat was temporarily gone. I wanted to force myself to be quiet, to not push anything further. I knew it would be wise, but my curiosity burned out of control.

"Kylan, do you know where this necklace is?" I asked, now advancing on him instead.

"I haven't seen it in centuries. I don't even know if I'm thinking of the right one. I shouldn't have just assumed like that." He shrugged his shoulders.

His eyes looked more at the ground than they did at me. He wasn't lying, but he was hiding. I could see the stress racing across his eyes. I could hear that his heart hadn't slowed at all. He was brushing this off on purpose. I didn't need to read his mind to know that.

"The necklace that you are thinking of, could you find it?" I asked, trying not to press too hard but not being able to ignore the rush of being so close.

In decades, no one had recognized the necklace or even its origin. It was a complete mystery. To be fair, I was working off a picture of the locket alone, but this was the first time anyone had looked at that image the way he just had. Somehow, he was my answer to my longest-standing questions.

"If I see anything like it, I will let you know," he said.

My hopes crashed as I realized that was all the response I'd be getting tonight. I'd never been this close. Until he trusted me, I doubted I would ever get any closer.

"Under one condition," he added, finally looking me in the eyes.

"What is that?" I asked, expecting some sort of one-sided trade that Alec would try to negotiate.

"I want to trust you, Kate. You have no idea how badly," he started and let his heavy hands fall on my shoulders, like he was scared to let go.

"I know." I nodded, staring at his face twisted in wary confusion.

"Please don't give me a reason not to," he warned with his green eyes filled with worry.

I could see it. In that moment, I was a wild card to him. I had offered more mysteries than answers. He had no reason to trust my shady past that I had shared or the negatively affected person that I was at that time.

If I were him, I would not fall for me. I would run.

But he stayed.

CHAPTER
TWENTY-ONE

Kylan

"Okay, walk me through this again." Derek sat on the bed, refusing to help me rifle through the boxes.

I shifted the box in my lap to the floor as I grabbed for the next one, tearing open the flaps that held it closed.

"The locket," I started. "I know I left it in one of these boxes."

"Well maybe if you didn't cart so much stuff around from place to place, you wouldn't have this problem," Derek chided.

"Some of us are sentimental." I rolled my eyes. "Get your butt down here and help me."

"Fine," Derek grumbled and knelt on the ground next to me. "So, this is your mother's locket? Wasn't that the one you gave to that weird museum here forever ago?"

"I didn't give it to them. It was a loaner for their event." I pulled out the photos that rested on the top of everything else. "But I got it back, so it has to be here."

"Okay, and she knows about it somehow?" Derek asked as he pulled a box from the bottom of the closet. "Are you sure it wasn't just some other old locket?"

I stopped and glared at him. As helpful as having a brother was, it was definitely annoying sometimes.

"It was the last thing my mom gave me before she was killed. I'm not just going to forget what it looks like." I shook my head at him before going back to the box.

"But how is that even possible?" Derek asked.

"I don't know," I answered.

I thought about my conversation with Kate. She couldn't have known about it, but she did. Fear shook through me as I tried to think of a way out of any of this.

"You don't talk about your family that much," Derek mused as he slowly opened a box. "Not that I'm one to judge, but still. Maybe it has something to do with her knowing about the locket?"

I had reached the bottom of the box I had. Still nothing. My face warmed from Derek's question. I shook my head.

That's not possible. Kate couldn't be connected to my past. It just didn't make any sense.

I moved to grab another box from the closet, but noticed something in the one Derek held. A red velvet case, tucked in the bottom corner.

"That's it," I breathed.

Derek clutched it and handed the case to me. My hands touched the familiar velvet as it crushed under my fingertips. I pulled the lip open and looked down at the ornate design on the front of the golden face.

The oval was almost two inches long, with a chain thick enough to support the weight of it. I ran my thumb over the raised parts before I tucked a finger under the chain, lifting it out of the box.

Waves of nostalgia washed over me. This reminded me of my mother more than anything else I owned. She always wore it.

I stopped. "I don't know what to do."

Before Derek could answer, the high-pitched, arguing voices of Cassie and Rachel interrupted.

"We both know that would never happen." Cassie stormed into the room with her sister following close behind her.

"You can't possibly know that!" Rachel shouted back at her.

It didn't matter what they were arguing about. They could fight and then be thick as thieves one minute later.

Both of them stopped when they saw me holding the locket.

"Your mother's necklace?" Cassie asked. "Why are you bringing that out?"

"Because, apparently, Kate has been looking for it? And Kylan is deciding if he wants to give it to her or not," Derek answered for me.

"What? How does she know about it?" Rachel asked.

"Don't know." I shrugged. "She kinda didn't tell me."

Cassie and Rachel both moved in unison as they sat on either side of me. Each of them put a hand on my shoulder or my arm. A small amount of relief tickled my spine. As infuriating as they could be, I felt better with them around.

"You love her, don't you?" Rachel stared with her thoughtful gaze.

"I don't know. It's been less than a year that we've even known each other." I dropped my shoulders and looked at the locket. "With all of this, I'm not sure if being with her is the best idea."

"Then, let's leave," Cassie suggested. "Let's pack up tonight and be out of here in the morning."

"I can't just bail. Kate's expecting me later tonight." I shook my head.

"Sure you can. Shoot her a text, or just don't say anything and move on," Derek added, joining her.

"No. I wouldn't do that to anyone, let alone her." I narrowed my eyes at him.

"Come on. We could go to Australia like we've been talking about. Or I hear Rome is especially nice this time of year," Cassie continued.

"No, no. You always get to pick." Derek glared at her. "I have been wanting to go to Singapore for a long time—"

"Stop!" I raised a hand. "You two are relentless, and I see what you're trying to do."

"What?" Cassie asked with big, innocent eyes.

Too bad her mischievous smile always gave her away. I smiled as I lowered my head.

"The more you talk about leaving, the more it makes me want to stay," I answered.

"Does she feel the same way?" Rachel asked.

"I don't know." I shrugged. "I just keep having this thought that if I show her the necklace, she'll disappear."

Cassie wrapped her arm around my shoulder and hugged me. She had to pull me down because even sitting down, I was still taller than her.

"You've got two choices. You can walk away, and we won't ever talk about it again," Rachel offered.

"Or you can go meet her and find out for sure," Cassie finished.

I touched Cassie's arm around me, holding on to her to remind me that everything was real and happening whether I liked it or not. I took a deep breath.

"What if…" I edged. "What if tonight is the end of everything?"

"Then good riddance," Derek scoffed. He put the box he was holding aside and looked back at me.

My eyes locked on him, still sitting casually in front of me. I narrowed my eyes and tilted my head.

"What did you say?"

"You sound like me before I asked Cassie to marry me." Derek shook his head. "If she's not there with you, then dump her and move on."

"You don't know what you're talking about." I moved my hands to my lap.

"Yeah, I do. You just don't want to admit it." Derek shrugged. "Just leave her."

"Stop." I rolled my eyes and stood to put the first box back in its place.

"Why? She's being shady and won't tell you stuff. You're being a scaredy cat and won't ask her." Derek stood and followed me.

The anger burned in my fingertips. I set the box down and handed the locket to Rachel, who was slowly backing into the corner with Cassie.

"Dump her. She's not worth it." Derek moved forward.

Each step closer ignited rage up my arms and into my chest.

"Stop talking." I clenched my fists at my sides.

"No. You're making a mistake, and I'm not going to watch you throw your life away for a silly girl." Derek stared at me.

I didn't even feel my hand move before it knocked against Derek's jaw.

"Shut up!" I shouted as Derek's head snapped to the side.

"No." Derek shifted his jaw as his eyes winced.

He jumped forward and wrapped both of his arms around my hips. Both of us flew back, and Derek landed on top of me. Pain shot up my spine.

"You're just mad because I'm right," Derek growled.

I grabbed him and tossed him off of me, quickly getting up on my knees to be level with him. Derek didn't punch, didn't advance at all.

"You're not," I snarled back at him.

I moved on my knees and grabbed for Derek. He dodged my hands in time and shoved me into the scattered boxes.

"You're in love! You're too blind to see that she might be bad news for you," Derek said.

I yanked myself up and clamped my hands in Derek's shirt, shoving him on his back.

"She might be!" I shouted in his face, my fists still clutching his shirt. "She might be the worst thing that ever happened to me, but I don't care. Wanna know why? I love her. I care about her more than knowing whatever she's hiding. No matter what happens tonight, I want her in my life. I want to try."

My breaths came in short spurts as I looked down at him. He just smiled back up at me. He released his hands from me and held them up in surrender.

"If you're willing to fight for her, then she's worth it," Derek said, nodding.

I laughed and collapsed on my back next to him. He was the only person who could get me this angry. I shook my head.

"You're the worst." I smiled.

"Coward." Derek shoved a hand against my shoulder.

"Idiot." I jabbed an elbow at him.

Cassie came to give Derek a hand up. As he stood, Rachel came to stand over me, holding her hand out and wiggling her fingers.

"You know, you could have just talked to him." Rachel rolled her eyes at Derek.

I took Rachel's hand and pulled on her to help me stand

up. I noticed the pain smarting on my sides from getting knocked around.

"Eh." Derek shrugged. "I'm much more of a physical learner."

"Thanks." I reached a hand to him.

"What are brothers for?" Derek shook it and smiled.

He put his arm around Cassie as she inspected his jaw, the bruise already starting to form. Derek didn't have enough energy to heal it quickly. Neither of us ever did.

"Kylan, look at me," Rachel said. "We love you and we'll support whatever you decide."

She lifted my hand and let the locket fall into my open palm. The metal was cold from being in her ever-chilly hand.

"Plus, I kinda like her," Rachel smiled.

I wrapped my fingers around the locket. Thoughts raced through my mind, but none of it made sense. I wanted the world around me to stop spinning long enough for me to have a coherent thought.

"Thank you." I nodded to her.

I spun the locket face in my fingers, watching the light glint off the still-bright gold. I took a deep breath, hoping it would clear my head. It didn't.

Kate was endearing, exciting, and dangerous. I wanted the person who danced with me at the gala, and even the one that turned me down, but not the one that potentially threatened my family. I looked at them. Rachel's sweet eyes, Cassie's mischievous grin, and Derek's easy smile.

I had to protect them. I looked back at the locket. I also needed to know for sure. I raised my eyebrows.

"You guys think I'm crazy, don't you?"

What I didn't say was that even I thought I was crazy for wanting to see her tonight.

The locket. The secrets. None of it connected in my mind.

I looked at my family, hoping they would trust me enough for this. Cassie glanced at the ground. Rachel looked at Cassie. Derek looked straight ahead to me.

"Go get her, bro." He smiled.

My fingers wrapped around the locket, feeling the metal warm with my body heat. Every nerve in me awakened to full alert. I gulped.

Tonight might change everything, or might even ruin everything. But she was worth it.

At least, that's what I hoped.

CHAPTER
TWENTY-TWO

That was the longest four hours of my life.

Kylan had insisted we meet far away from anyone, so we walked arm-in-arm through the trees outside of the city. The sun was just starting its descent to the horizon. The air was crisp, and there were clouds in the sky that already reflected the pink glow from the sun.

It was a perfect evening.

I looked over at Kylan's face to make sure he was still standing there beside me. His eyes faced forward. What had happened after swimming with his family had been a jolt to both of us, and we were trying to move past it. He held my arm firmly in his. I could still see the care in his eyes.

"If you could go anywhere in the world, where would you go?" I asked and gestured out with my arms like the whole world was in front of us.

I had to do something to break the tension. I knew Kylan may or may not have the one thing I had been looking for. But that wasn't all he was worth to me. I needed him to see that.

"Anywhere?" Kylan confirmed.

"Yes. Forget about time restrictions or money. Where would you want to go?" I eagerly prodded further. Kylan looked around and thought long about the answer.

"Okay, got it." He nodded curtly and casually looked over at me. His mouth didn't move at all to start talking.

"So…" I nudged him on, and he finally cracked a smile.

"Oh, you wanted me to tell you right now?" he joked, and I lightly punched his arm.

"Come on, I'm serious." I smiled.

"Mine is probably not a typical answer," he started, and I waited for him to continue. He looked at me and said, "If I could choose to go anywhere in the world, I would go home. I would be with all of my family."

I looked at him in slight awe and first thought about how illogical that response was. The world held so many amazing places like Asia, New Zealand, or even New York City. Out of all of those, he would choose a familiar place. But that made sense for him, with how important his family was.

"It's the people that make the place," I said.

"Exactly." He seemed a little surprised I understood.

On some level, I did. When I was a Shadow, we loved being in exotic places with fancy things, but what really mattered was who surrounded you. Maybe even my twisted family had at least one thing right.

As I thought about how happy I could be here, a thought crossed my mind.

I was back in the mansion. The Shadows surrounded me and praised me. I had Alec by my side. Triumph flooded through my chest.

I shook it out of my head. Nothing about this moment should have made me think about being back at the mansion, especially not happy to be there.

A strange feeling came over me. I became wary of my surroundings. I listened and held my breath to concentrate.

"Do you ever think about the future?" Kylan's voice broke my concentration.

"What?" I asked, trying to come back to the situation I had just momentarily left.

"I mean, where do you see yourself in, say, five years? Where do you see us... in five years?" He clarified his chary question.

I thought about my logical response. As I did, I looked at him and soon realized it was not a logical response he was looking for. I saw a flicker of hope in his eyes. He meant our future together.

"I see myself being as happy as I am now." I tried to give an obvious answer so now it was his turn to talk. He was stuck with the risky answer now.

"Do you see us still together?" he asked, dodging my setup.

Clever move. I took a breath and wondered why he would be asking these questions. The smile hiding in the corners of his mouth gave a clue that this was not a breakup talk.

"Yes," I answered firmly.

One of us was going to have to stop beating around the bush. I kept my eyes forward as we continued walking toward nothing.

If I was going to be vulnerable, I did not have to stare at his face to see his initial reaction and open myself up to the possibility of him not feeling the same way.

"What about ten years from now?"

I looked back at him. He still had that hidden smile.

"Why?" It was my turn to ask now. "Where do you see yourself in ten years?"

"Right where I am now," he answered without breaking

eye contact. I took a sharp breath in. In ten years, he still wanted to be with me. How could he see that far into the future? How could he know? We had only been together for a short time.

"I mean, not right here, obviously. I'm okay if we live in a different place. But I see myself with you. Even in ten years from now." He looked at the ground and kicked a small stick that was between us.

He looked back up at me to read my face. I now had enough time to process what he had just suggested. He wanted to be with me. He still wanted to stay.

"What about you?" he asked me.

"What about me?" I teased and gave myself more time to gather my composure.

"I love you, Kate," he breathed.

I took a quick breath in as utter glee filled my entire body. I could almost feel the happiness shooting out of my fingertips. I moved my hands up to his shoulders and paused for a moment as I realized what I was holding.

He was my chance.

With him, I could learn to live a different life. I could learn to enjoy a different life. I may even get the necklace and the answers I had spent the last few decades searching for. Maybe Rachel could even show me the ropes on how to take more energy without hurting people.

I could have everything I wanted.

My mind raced through what our future could look like, what I could look like. Once I got a clear picture, my entire body craved it. I don't know if I was ready to give everything else up, but I knew I was willing to try. When I saw his green eyes say the same thing, I wanted to shout to the world what I felt.

Despite my total joy and a smile breaking across my face, I heard something.

A distinct whisper in my mind.

Mara.

The voice sounded far away. It was such a faint sound, I almost missed it completely. I listened more closely, hoping it was just my overactive mind playing tricks on itself. I waited in silence. After a few seconds, I was sure it was just my imagination.

Mara.

Now the voice sounded as if it was right next to me. It was impossible to deny it now. Tragically, I recognized its owner. My fists clenched at my sides.

Alec was here.

His mental voice was impossible to mistake. I had heard him call my name many times, and it was a sound that still haunted my occasional nightmare. But I was awake. Which meant this wasn't a dream, or even a nightmare. This was real.

The concern now flooded from my thoughts to my facial expression. Kylan could see the fear pouring into my eyes.

"Kate, if that worries you, we can move slower. I don't mind. I just want to be with you." Kylan tried to backpedal his forward advance from earlier.

The pain hit me that he would even assume that my worry would be because I didn't feel the same way. I wanted to shout from a skyscraper that I loved him too.

But if Alec was close enough to plant a thought, he knew exactly where I was. I couldn't run fast enough. But Kylan still could, and I didn't have time to explain why.

"Leave," I urged him, begging with my eyes to just do what I asked.

"What? What's going on?" He needed an explanation. One that we didn't have time for right now.

"Please, just trust me. You have to get out of here now." I lowered my voice to ward off any faraway listeners.

I gave him a hard shove in the direction we had just walked together.

"I don't have time to explain. If you love me, go now," I begged, but Kylan remained standing exactly where he was.

Mara.

The voice echoed loudly between my ears.

I cringed at the sound that only I could hear. My wild eyes looked for a way to get him as far away from me as I could.

"Kate, I'm not leaving you. Just tell me, what is going on?" Kylan asked me as he stepped closer to me again.

I looked at his eyes with the sadness that comes when you know you may never again see the person you love. My heart began to feel the ache of never holding him close.

"I didn't just want the next ten years with you. I wanted centuries," I murmured as I leaned up and kissed his mouth gently.

A deep, throbbing pain spread through my entire body. He looked at me with a wild pace, trying to understand the situation. I calmed myself with a breath, knowing he wouldn't look so confused for long. I had plenty of energy to start with and using it to make sure he was safe was the noblest cause I could imagine.

"Go, Kylan. Please."

I looked deeply into his eyes and planted the strongest thought I could muster. I planted a thought of me wanting and needing him to leave. If he wanted to please me, this was the way. I forced that thought onto the front stage of his brain. He blinked as he tried to expel the foreign idea.

Despite him fighting, the thought ran through clear. He had to leave. Now. Every synapse in his brain told him so.

He had not kept up his guard for my level of strength. Unfortunately, this was now to his disadvantage because I had control.

I never told him the true level of talent I possessed, that I had practiced over the last few decades. Now, this secret came to my advantage.

As the thought penetrated the logic center of his brain, his face changed. He actually wanted to leave like I had asked.

This was an invasive maneuver I swore would never do to someone like Kylan. But the alternative was unleashing Alec's powers on his mind. Powers that I knew I may not even survive.

"Okay, I'll go. Come find me at our bench under the tree." He surrendered and pulled my hand up to his mouth, kissing it lightly.

"I love you, Kate," he whispered.

Those words echoed in my mind as Kylan turned around and ran away from me. A tear slipped from my eye as I watched him disappear in the distance. He never stood a chance against my power once he had opened his mind to me.

That was the problem with trust. It can be the best thing or the thing that undoes you. My high spirits sank as my energy faded and Kylan's presence vanished.

The dark, hungry, familiar hatred crept into my body. The weight of my past fell back on my shoulders. My hairs stood on end as Alec's presence neared. I leaned against a tree for support. I was alone, facing my worst fear.

My nightmare was becoming a reality.

Years of running, and I was caught, unaided and unprepared. I had enough energy remaining to pull one major move, but that was it.

The tough facade of the person I used to be filled my body. I may be unprepared, but I was not weak.

This was the fight I knew would be coming, the one I had been waiting for and carefully avoiding. I straightened to stand tall as I heard footsteps come up behind me.

The very temperature in the air seemed to drop with the sun. The footsteps stopped. My body stiffened.

"Mara." The voice was audible now, not just in my mind.

CHAPTER
TWENTY-THREE

I turned to face him.

Alec stood there in all his glory, hair gleaming in the fading sunlight and indigo eyes piercing through the air. He stood tall and strong like he had been long awaiting this day. The boiling anger came flooding back, all the way down to my fingertips.

"I almost didn't recognize you. But one look at those eyes…It's really you. It's been a long time." Alec's soothing voice coursed through the air.

"Not long enough."

I stood still. I had to focus hard if I was going to keep the upper hand against an opponent like Alec. I had already let him in once, so he knew his way around. He was my most dangerous enemy.

"Why are you here?"

"For you," he admitted easily.

He stepped closer and closer to me. Running was pointless and stepping away would only show my intimidation. He finally was within reaching distance of me. My heart sped up as my adrenaline spiked.

Looking at him brought back all the memories, all the years growing up, and all the pent-up feelings. My skin could barely contain the raging emotional storm inside me.

"How did you find me?" I asked, gritting my teeth.

"You know how." Alec smiled, flicking his beautiful blue eyes between my mouth and my eyes. "Short answer is I've known where the trail to the locket ended all along. I just had to wait for you to figure it out. The long answer is that you left a little trail of your own behind."

"What do you mean?" I asked, already feeling the blood rush in my ears.

"Well, a certain old museum curator seemed to have a difficult shift with a woman who never returned her books. And then a worn-out professor had a very stressful day that magically got better when he helped a woman find her way downtown. Want to know what both of those people had in common?" Alec smiled.

"Me," I finished, shutting my eyes.

I hoped that if I couldn't see Alec, I wouldn't have to face the fact that I led Alec straight to me by getting distracted with Kylan.

"Yeah. You. Well that, and now both of them are lying six feet underground somewhere. Nikki took care of the exact details," Alec finished.

My gaze shot up to look at him. His cruel smile pulled at his eyes. He tapped his fingers on his leg, waiting for the full amount of guilt to hit me. I swallowed and straightened my shoulders instead.

"Two witnesses and you still took so long to confront me. I've been here for almost a year," I said, crossing my arms in front of my chest.

He appreciated the sarcasm. I appreciated the stalling time. Alec smiled when he saw me take that stance. I waited.

"You were hiding in the middle of humans. Something I did not expect, I will give you that." Alec smiled.

"Now you see how far I will go to get away from you," I snarled at him.

"Baby, did you not miss me?" he asked, his dark blue eyes catching in the last bit of light.

They cringed at the edges from being unwanted. Then his wicked personality flared again, and I knew he wasn't hurt by what I said. He reached out and touched my face.

"I missed you," Alec sighed, so soft and sincere.

A familiar temptation tingled where his hand brushed my cheek. The small, suppressed part of my mind that used to yearn to obey him rustled awake. The guilt of rejecting him pooled in my stomach.

I pulled my face away from his touch.

Childhood friend or not, Alec and I no longer wanted the same things. We weren't the same people that stood face to face all those years ago.

"You came all alone?" I asked and glared into his eyes. "Do you think that little of me?"

I smiled at his assumption that I would come quietly. Alec smiled too easily. There was still something I didn't know, and he was reveling in it.

My smile fell as soon as I heard the second pair of footsteps from behind him.

"You know, it hurts that you didn't even notice I was here," Thayer said as he stepped from behind the tree.

His glittering smile was the first thing I recognized.

Butterflies released in my stomach before my mind could reason otherwise. Thayer had mastered how each emotion presented in the body so that he could replicate it by creating the correct hormones or triggering the right responses.

He could make you love or hate anything he chose.

He wasn't great with mind games, but he could crumble your emotional resolve without blinking. He had a hold on everyone he laid his shining eyes on. How appropriate that he excelled at manipulating emotions.

"Yes, you can't go anywhere without your *sidekick*." I laughed at myself for not remembering that those two were joined at the hip. "Thayer, I think I missed you least of all."

"We both know that's not true." Thayer grinned.

Alec stood behind me now, facing Thayer on the opposite side. They circled me slowly like I was the prey of their little wolf gang.

"I couldn't just leave him at home. You know how restless he gets when he is left out of the loop." Alec joked about old times as if they were fond memories for both of us.

I glanced at Thayer's eager stare. "Insatiable."

He smiled and winked at me. I shifted my feet.

"I missed you too, you know," Thayer said. "Things just aren't the same without you there."

He focused his bright brown eyes on mine.

Desire ignited my skin as it entered my body. I broke eye contact and shoved the feeling away. When I looked back up, I glared at Thayer in response. He let out a small laugh that raised goose bumps on my arm.

Thayer was no easy feat to overpower. I began running through ideas of how I could possibly get out of this. Thayer may be a manipulator himself, but he was also quite easily manipulated.

He wouldn't present near the challenge that Alec would. If I kept my mind in control instead of allowing my emotionally susceptible body to be in charge, I could survive.

"Come on, Mara." Alec came up from behind me and laid his arm across my shoulders.

I shuddered at his touch.

"We want you back." Alec turned me around to face him. "All of us."

"What do you mean all of...?" Before I could finish, the sound reached my ears.

I could hear them all now. My attention was too divided before. I always fell for that. I could focus my mind extremely well on only one thing at a time.

"Well, everyone was so excited to see you, and they all wanted to come. And you know me, I just can't say no when it comes to you." He smiled wickedly as he knew my only chance of escape melted before his eyes.

I looked around and watched as they all stepped out from behind the trees. I remembered no more than twenty Shadows when I left.

At least forty Legends, maybe more, surrounded me. They all donned the same black mark on their forearms. The familiar rush of excitement from being near so much power and talent crashed around me. I was among the entirety of the Shadows.

I thought of that future I had almost committed to with Kylan. That future was so clearly gone now. I could never find a way out of this, and the look on Alec's smug face told me he would never let me go again.

Decades later and the game was finally over, just when I was about to win.

"So, what do you say? Are you ready to come home?" Alec took me by both hands.

I was too overwhelmed to protest his touch. Alec knew that. My eyes still snapped between all the people around me. I recognized only about half of them. I stretched, but I couldn't see Nikki or Grae yet.

My attention moved back to the immediate threat. Thayer walked behind me, his beady eyes watching me.

"Come on, Mara, you know you want to," Thayer begged gently.

He was close enough that I could feel his breath. His voice made my heart want to sing. I took a breath to calm my racing mind and tense body.

"Oh, you know me. I don't go down without a fight." I knew my icy eyes were stone cold as they stared back into Alec's.

False confidence was all I had at this point. He smiled as he accepted my challenge. He always made me nervous when he gave that knowing smile. I instantly hoped this wasn't a trap.

"Very well, if it's a fight you want," he changed my words as he pulled me in.

He put his hand up to my face again and stood unnervingly close to me. He still acted as though he had a romantic pull on my heart. My body still responded as though he did. Despite years of making him a villain in my mind, I couldn't convince myself completely.

I searched his gaze for what he was hiding. Then, something in his eyes changed. A new spark of supremacy gleamed as he continued to speak and slowly stepped back.

"You are worth whatever it takes. Because I don't just want the next ten years with you," he recalled the words I had just spoken.

I took in a sharp breath.

"I want centuries."

Alec leaned back to fully take in my reaction, clearly proud of himself.

"No. Alec, leave him out of this," I commanded him as I stepped forward.

I actually drew him closer. If I was ever going to beg, it had to be now.

He smiled as I pulled him into me. Goose bumps raised on my arms at seeing him happy about his victory and my loss. I didn't even stand a chance against Alec and the Shadows. If Kylan was here...

"Take me. Just me," I offered quickly.

Watching Alec's smug smile was hard enough, but begging him for anything was the worst kind of torture.

I allowed him to run his hand along my cheek. He leaned in close to my ear. My fight response came boiling up. I wanted to punch him almost more than my muscles could restrain me from doing so.

I fought the urge and allowed him to lean closer as my stomach twisted. Just as his lips brushed my ear, my body shuddered.

"Not a chance," he whispered.

I threw him off me, and he stumbled backward as his bright chuckle came out. To him, we were just playing, teasing each other as we always did. He held no concern for a life he might take, even if it was a Legend. He only had eyes for me.

"You wanted a fight, you got one." Alec raised his arms out to either side.

The Shadows took the cue and began shouting and cheering. He was their king, and they had just won. For once, I was powerless among them.

"Shh. Listen closely, Mara. Here they come now." Thayer leaned in to whisper near my ear.

The close proximity normally would have bothered Alec, but he was too busy gloating to notice. Thayer stepped even closer and held my arm to make sure I didn't run.

I listened for Kylan's voice, but couldn't find it. Nikki was chattering and whoever else was with her was silent. But there was no screaming, no sound of pain.

I only heard two sets of footsteps approaching. I knew he wouldn't be walking with them willingly. Even Nikki couldn't threaten him enough to do that.

Maybe they hadn't found him. Alec looked over and saw the flicker of hope in my eyes.

"Listen closer," Alec warned, his eyes now trained on me.

I stared back at him and listened closer. Then I heard past the two footsteps. My ears twitched at the sound of something dragging. I could tell by the smile peeling across Alec's face that I had found the right sound.

That was Kylan.

I saw two Shadows come through the trees from the direction I had sent Kylan. Nikki walked on the right, her black hair pulled in a beautiful, long braid. Grae walked on the left, his nearly black eyes looking directly at Alec. In between them was Kylan, face down in their arms with his feet dragging behind them.

I rushed forward to help him or even just check if he was still breathing. Thayer moved before I had taken two steps and pulled both of my arms behind my back. Despite my mental strength, I wasn't a match for Thayer's physical strength.

His father had been given more muscle enhancement drug than most, making Thayer historically stronger than most Legends.

Alec knew this, and it was why Thayer was his second in command. He only obeyed Alec. For Alec, that meant that all of Thayer's power was at his disposal. Although, to Alec, everyone was at his disposal.

"Shall we see who our Mara has been fraternizing with?" He rubbed his hands together eagerly.

The Shadows cheered him on.

The excitement of the moment, and the excess energy

he no doubt consumed prior to this, caused him to almost bounce as he walked over to Kylan's hanging head.

I pulled against Thayer's arms harder. I had to stop Alec from hurting him. The harder I pulled, the tighter Thayer held me. I wasn't going anywhere until Alec gave the word.

Alec reached over to Kylan and grabbed a fistful of hair. He yanked upward to reveal his face. Alec looked at him and immediately his glib expression fell.

He released Kylan and sharply pulled his hand back as if he had touched something hot. Kylan's head flopped back down lifelessly.

Alec took a staggering step back. I looked at Alec, to see what was going on. He looked back at me finally and glared with true anger. The playful sarcasm was gone as his eyes seared into me.

"Well played," Alec spoke through his teeth.

My eyebrows pulled together in confusion. Alec turned back to Nikki and nodded for her to wake him up. She ran her free hand through Kylan's hair and kindly looked down at him. A smile peeled back across her perfect teeth.

Kylan's scream pierced the air as he tumbled onto his hands and knees.

"Stop it, Nikki!" I shouted.

Nikki's startled eyes looked up at me. She immediately obeyed and gave up her hold on Kylan. His body finished dropping to the ground in silence. Nikki's gaze bounced from me to Alec, her loyalty divided.

Alec still stared at Kylan on the ground as he stirred to consciousness.

After a few painfully long seconds, Kylan eventually hoisted himself back up onto his hands and knees. He lifted his head and squinted to see where he was.

The first thing he locked eyes with was Grae's black dagger showing proudly on his bare arm.

Kylan froze, his eyes widened.

"Hello, Kylan," Alec called from a few feet away.

"Alec," he muttered as he finished turning his head to finally meet the Shadow leader's eyes.

CHAPTER
TWENTY-FOUR

Kylan stood slowly from the ground and settled his gaze on Alec.

His body seemed weaker than when I left him. I tried not to think of what Nikki and Grae had done to get him here. He took a step forward and went to raise his hand toward Alec.

His movement halted when he spotted me trapped in Thayer's arms. Kylan's face flushed.

"Let her go, Alec. She has nothing to do with this." He nodded toward me.

They knew each other? I was truly confused now. My mind tried to connect how the two of them could have ever crossed paths.

"Excuse me?" Alec seemed genuinely confused.

He stared intently at Kylan, not wanting to take his eyes off him. It almost seemed like he was nervous about Kylan being so close to him.

"You two know each other?" I asked.

Alec looked at me as he finally understood what was going on. His eyebrows raised and his smile returned.

"We're brothers," Kylan answered me, still clearly unaware of my role in this.

The bystanders gasped as they took in the news. Nikki's mouth fell open behind them as she glanced at Thayer and Grae to see if they knew. They didn't

They looked just as shocked.

Between Alec and Kylan, the family resemblance was barely recognizable. Kylan's face was softer, tanner, and when he smiled my skin didn't crawl. Overall, Kylan didn't quite level up to Alec's sharply beautiful features, sculpted cheekbones, or defined eyebrows. True, Kylan was handsome beyond belief, but Alec was breathtaking.

"Nicely done," Thayer leaned into my ear and muttered his sick congratulations only to me.

Twisted relationships had always intrigued him. At least I knew that one thing about him hadn't changed.

I flinched at his voice, and he chuckled. That familiar flutter of anticipation rushed into my body. I elbowed him as hard as I could. My elbow connected with one of his ribs before he could stop my swing. I smiled.

"This is too good." Alec smiled wider as he put together the fact that we had both been keeping secrets.

I hardly blamed Kylan for not telling me that his brother was the leader of the Shadows.

After all, I didn't tell Kylan that I had dated that same person either. Alec wasn't exactly someone to be proud of claiming, unless you were a Shadow. Maybe Alec and I knew both sides of this story, but Kylan still didn't.

"Alec, I have never wanted anything to do with you. I still don't. It's petty, even for you, to drag this innocent woman into your mess," Kylan growled.

My eyebrows pulled together. He didn't seem to know the mental influence or destruction that Alec could have.

"Innocent?" Alec turned toward me. "This is the one you chose. Out of everyone in the world, you picked my similar—but ever so inferior—brother. I'm impressed by the irony alone, but also the fact that you never told him? Who would want to spend the rest of their life with a liar?"

Then he turned his gaze to Kylan. The look on Alec's face didn't change. He was taunting both of us.

"How long did you think you could keep it up?" Alec finished, still looking over his brother with the most intense disgust. Seeing that look lit the defensive fire inside of me.

"He is not inferior, Alec. Kylan is twice the man you could hope to be." I was infuriated that he would insult the man I cared so deeply for.

Thayer's hands relaxed against me, still distracted by the reveal. I took the opportunity and pulled away from Thayer. He let me slip right through his hands, too shocked to stop me.

I ran toward Kylan immediately.

"I'm so sorry, Kylan. I should have never brought you into this. I never wanted…" I tried an apology.

Kylan reached around and took both of my arms in his hands.

"Kate, what are you talking about? You know him?" Kylan asked as he tried to calm my fast-paced speech.

He glanced at my covered right arm. I stopped talking as soon as I saw his eyes move.

"Yes, Mara, how do we know each other? But more importantly, how much do you two know about each other?" Alec edged as he stepped closer to Kylan and me.

He was trying to figure something out. He already knew I didn't tell Kylan everything, so there shouldn't be anything else that he would need to find out before making his final move.

Kylan released my hands and stepped around me so he was between Alec and me. Alec continued but seemed like he was taking his steps carefully now that Kylan stood in his path.

"Take one more step, Alec, and I swear…" Kylan started his threat before he took a glance at me. Kylan paused, almost stumbling over his feet. He needed energy, and there was not a human in sight. Alec smiled.

"You'll what?" Alec stepped closer to him and then waited. I watched Kylan relax his muscles. He looked at me as he decided not to continue the threat on Alec.

"That's what I thought, brother." Alec grabbed Kylan by both arms and stared at him straight in the face. "Women, right? They have such a hold on us. Sometimes we can find ourselves doing anything for them."

Alec patted Kylan on the shoulder and then released his grip on him. I had never seen Alec so excited about boasting. The look on his face was pure joy.

"You have done a number on him, Mara. Excellent work." Alec winked at me.

"Her name is Kate." Kylan threw the words to Alec but turned back to look at me.

I backed away from Kylan slowly. The one secret I had kept from him was about to be released. Regret trickled in as I reminded myself that I should have told Kylan long before this day. Yet, here we were, in the worst circumstances. The helpless remorse instantly flooded my system.

"Is it?" Alec asked Kylan back. I saw the moment of confusion on Kylan's face and lowered my eyes from his gaze.

"What's going on?" Kylan asked warily.

He must be assuming the secret I had been carefully avoiding.

"Kylan, it gives me an immense amount of pleasure to be

the one to break the bad news." Alec walked past Kylan and continued toward me. He arrived in front of me and stared directly into my eyes. "She is one of us. A Shadow. The very thing you hated and swore you never wanted to be a part of. Not only that, she was one of the best. Quite the killer, and also quite the kisser, I might add, but you probably already know that."

I didn't return Alec's stare. I looked straight at the ground. I couldn't meet either of their eyes. Alec's grin would crush me and Kylan's betrayed face would as well.

"No," Kylan said.

Not a question, a statement. He was sure that the woman he loved couldn't have been affiliated with something so vile. It wasn't in my nature, according to him. I gulped, knowing how wrong he was.

"Oh, yes," Alec assured him, bursting with excitement. "You want proof?"

Alec stared down at me. I raised my face to meet his unrelenting stare. The flame of triumph burned in his blue eyes just as I imagined it would. Kylan remained silent.

Nothing I could say would fix or ease what came next. Alec stepped around me and grabbed my right arm. He took the bottom of the sleeve on my denim jacket and yanked it up past my elbow. Alec held my arm out proudly for Kylan to see.

The black dagger shimmered in the fading sun and stood in stark contrast to my light skin. I watched as Kylan took in the sight before him.

I didn't struggle against Alec. I was too engrossed in watching Kylan's face fall. The proof was undeniable.

Only Shadows carried a mark like this. Black, ominous, and permanent.

"Kylan, I'm so sorry. I should have told you." I whispered

for only him to hear. Kylan looked hurt, then angry. He moved his gaze to Alec.

"You did this to her," Kylan accused Alec. The hope of my innocence still shone in his eyes. He stood sure of himself. My eyes couldn't look at his hope anymore.

"She did this of her own accord. She used to be my right-hand girl. We grew up together, fell in love. I probably know more about her than anyone on this planet."

"You don't know me anymore…" I muttered and looked at the ground.

"Baby, I do. I know you've had your time with the humans and…" he glanced at Kylan, "anyone else along the way. Now you know what the other side has to offer. It's not everything you imagined, is it? I can see it in your eyes now, how much you want to come back. Face it, that life doesn't compare to the one you had."

I locked my gaze on his deep blue eyes, and my mouth immediately went dry. He looked back at me, his chin lowered, eyes tearing me apart. A smile pulled up the left corner of his pink lips. I trembled in front of him.

"Isn't that right, Mara?" Alec asked. The pit in my stomach sank deeper.

I couldn't deny the truth in what he said. I hung my head in shame of the past I had buried being strewn in front of me. The memories of the horrible things I had done came racing back through my mind.

I was not that person anymore, and I wasn't even sure I wanted that life anymore. Or Alec.

"No, you're wrong." I shoved him away from me.

He bounced right back and his hands latched on either one of my arms, pulling me close enough to feel his warm breath on my face. The threat in his eyes bled into the air.

"I'm never wrong," he whispered so close to my face.

"You want to know why I'm right? Because I know how perfect you seem to everyone else—Shadows, Legends, everyone. They all believe it. But I also know that you have always had two weaknesses."

My skin went cold the longer his eyes raked across me. I didn't fight against his strong grip. I couldn't force my body to obey. Even my eyes remained frozen in his gaze.

"First, you know exactly how it feels to live like we do and, deep down, you don't want to give it up. Even if it means you can't reconcile that with whatever conscience you've created for yourself. You want the energy as badly as I do," he said.

I halted in his grip. As much as I wanted to deny what he was saying, especially in front of Kylan, I couldn't. After all these years, I could never kick the urge or even dull the desire. I wanted him to be wrong. I wanted to prove that I had become better after all this time away. There was one major problem with that.

Alec was right.

"The second?" my voice croaked out finally.

"Your second weakness? That one's easy," Alec looked me up and down as he pulled me closer to him.

"Me." He smiled.

My face was just an inch away from his, and my body exploded with emotions. Every cell in me mobilized into action as my mind tried to do the exact opposite. My hands wanted to reach out for him, but my good sense wanted to throw him away.

The result was me standing in front of him, not able to move at all.

The annoying, knowing smile returned to Alec's mouth. His obvious pride snapped me out of the trance he created.

My eyes burned into Alec's gaze. I couldn't discount the

truth in what he had said, but he no longer understood the full picture. I pulled myself from his hold and took a step back.

As soon as I was a safe distance away, Thayer came up from behind and immediately restrained me.

"You should have left me alone," I said, glaring.

"I need you with me, Mara, I always have. Because there's one thing most people don't know about me," Alec whispered, daring to step closer again. "You're my weakness. And despite everything, I love you."

I looked into Alec's eyes as he spoke. He wasn't lying. He needed me.

"If you love me, you would want me to be happy." I threw his excuse back in his face.

"You will be, baby. Soon," he assured me in the sweetest of voices. It had just enough double meaning to make my skin crawl.

Of all the terrible things I had done and seen, Alec was by far the most twisted. He reached up and placed his hands on either side of my face. I couldn't avoid looking into his hungry eyes.

"We can do this the easy way or the hard way," Alec warned me.

I threw my head forward and hit his skull with mine. He jerked back and his hand flew to the new pain throbbing in his skull.

The same pain ricocheted through my forehead. He looked back up at me with eyes squinting from the blow.

"You really do want a fight, don't you?" he challenged me. "Then, I'm not sorry for what you are about to feel." His eyes darkened as he focused on me.

I held my ground and stared back at him. Avoiding eye contact wouldn't be enough to break his concentration.

I would have to stand against him. I focused all my energy

on keeping my mind blank and protected against his invading power. Alec nodded to Thayer without breaking eye contact with me.

"Just give in," Thayer hissed the words in my ear. "Let the Mara we all know and love come out to play."

Thayer dragged his finger up my arm, distracting my physical senses. His breath chilled my skin. His body pressed tighter against mine. He was trying to overwhelm me to prepare for what was about to happen next. My eyes finally focused on Alec just a second too late.

Alec honed in on the logic and memory areas of my mind, without much luck in gaining access. My resolve held strong. I wanted to conserve my energy for an offensive attack, not waste it on defending myself.

But I couldn't let him win. I held my breath and tried with every bit of determination I had inside of me to hold the block.

Then Thayer came, so quietly, and softened that resolve. I could feel the happiness of being with Alec and the Shadows. I felt peaceful seeing him in front of me. As much as I tried to tighten my muscles and my concentration, my body just relaxed. I was calm.

Once that happened, Alec pierced into my mind. The pain burned through my whole body. I let out a scream and tried to pull away from Thayer and Alec, the sources of my pain.

Despite Thayer's stronger attempts to keep me calm, all my muscles tightened in defense. He switched his tactic and went for a stronger emotion.

My heart twisted as it changed from hating Alec and wanting to gouge his eyes out of his head, to an all-consuming desire for him.

My body changed to match. My long hair lightened to the

shoulder-length, glittering blond hair it once was. My fierce cheekbones matched my threateningly arched eyebrows. My clothes remained the same, but my body felt unrecognizable, apart from my everlastingly blue eyes.

Once the pain reached its peak, it started to break. After the pain, a sweet release relaxed my muscles as my need for Alec intensified.

The darkest parts of my mind seemed to awaken out of a century-long sleep. My ears burned as he called my name. My heart soared with him near me. My mind obeyed as his command beckoned. It was a familiar routine that I had been long trained to perform.

Alec called, I answered.

The pain was replaced with a deep satisfaction that clicked into its former place. The piece of my mind that still cared for Alec came flooding back naturally now.

Thayer's hands relaxed against my arms. I thought it would hurt, but instead, it felt like coming home.

I opened my eyes and watched the world unfold around me. My new perspective changed how I processed what I could see, including the man with haunting blue eyes just inches from my face. I looked at his expectant, hopeful gaze and automatically smiled.

I took my first breath, and Mara awoke.

"Mara?" Alec breathed, still catching his breath from the effort he had just put forth.

I looked around but my eyes came back to his face, to my Alec.

My memory held only good thoughts about the man standing before me.

"Alec," I breathed back with a smile inching up my face.

CHAPTER
TWENTY-FIVE

Alec returned my smile with his own. Thayer dropped his arms, and I let mine fall to my sides freely. I drew in an easy breath.

Alec took a step toward me slowly. Once he got close enough, I pulled him into my arms. He hugged me back tight enough to force my breath out of my body.

"Oh, I missed you, baby," he purred into my neck.

I laughed as his breath tickled my skin. I pulled away and looked at his eyes. They were just as enticing and beautiful as always. I noticed the situation around me and looked at everyone standing and watching the two of us.

I noticed a man standing that did not seem as excited by my change, but every bit as attentive. I looked at his face and tried to place him with a name or a memory.

He looked familiar. I just couldn't seem to tell how.

"Kate," the man said as though he couldn't believe what he was seeing.

Kate. That name sounded familiar.

He looked at me like he was watching something

being taken away from him. He didn't move forward, he just stood and looked at me deeply. He tilted his head to the side as if he was coaxing me to remember something. I had seen that head tilt before. I pulled my eyebrows together.

How could I have seen something and not remember it now?

I looked at Alec for confirmation that this man was a stranger.

"Ready to go home, Mara?" Alec spoke a little faster than normal.

He was nervous. He still wore all his bravado on his sleeve, but his voice told me everything. There was something he did not want me to know.

I looked back at the man and raked through my memories to place him in one.

"Kate, I love you," the man said again, this time more fervent despite his obvious exhaustion. "I don't care what you did in the past. All I care about is who you are now. I want to be with you. I want you, Kate." He finished his brave confession with a quiet, "Please."

Kate.

That head tilt.

Please.

My mind started processing what I just beheld and finally placed them all together. A barrier burst in my mind and memories came flooding back in. I scanned through them like I was watching a movie of my own life.

Kylan. I remembered.

I knew him. I loved him.

My body felt wrong. My face, my hair, and everything was off. I was no longer Mara, I was Kate.

I looked back at Alec and began changing my appearance back to Kate's self. My hair darkened back to the chocolate color. My facial features became more curved and less intimidating. I looked like the Kate in my memory.

Alec's expression fell. He had lost. I took that moment of surprise when everyone just saw him fail and used it. I took that brief moment for the only attack plan I had left. I only had enough energy for one bold move, and this was the only chance I was going to get.

I thought of how much Kylan meant to me and how desperate I was to save him. I reached into the mind of everyone around me. I had access to everyone but Alec. But with his guard down in this brief moment of shock for him, I got into his mind too.

I focused every ounce of energy I had left and closed my eyes.

Then came the screams.

Everyone heard a penetrating ring ricochet inside their heads. Everyone but Kylan and me. They all clutched their heads, gasping or screaming in pain. I opened my eyes long enough to watch them all fall to the ground, unconscious.

The last person to drop to the ground was the most satisfying of all. Alec's limp body finally hit the ground, and a wave of relief flooded through me. I looked around briefly to confirm that there wasn't anyone left standing. Kylan looked around in disbelief.

"Are you sure you're only a Four?" Kylan muttered as he looked around at the hoard of limp, unconscious bodies.

He finally turned to meet my gaze. I smiled and accepted his praise of my unknown talent. Up until now, he had not fully seen what I was capable of doing. This psychic blast was one of the greatest feats I had been able to perform. Unfortunately, it took the toll of a lifetime on my body.

"Kylan, I love you too," I answered.

My legs shook beneath me until my knees buckled. I no longer had enough energy to hold myself up. I barely had enough to keep my eyes open.

"Get out of here," I said and struggled to focus on anything. All I knew was that I had to get Kylan out of here.

"What? Kate, there is no way I am leaving you with these monsters. You and I both know what they can do. Come with me." He stepped closer to me and put his hand on one of my cheeks.

"I c-can't," I sputtered.

My body was too weak to stand on my own.

"I'm not strong enough to carry you. Please, you have to stand." Kylan breathed as hard as I did.

I leaned into his palm. His warmth radiated from his hand to my cool face. The warmth fused into me. I looked up into his eyes, and I stood a little taller. I loved him, and that seemed to give me just enough to keep going.

My eyes concentrated on the person standing in front of me. Kylan seemed to sag from a lack of energy. He too could barely be able to hold his own weight up. I hadn't noticed how drained he was before. All I could think about was getting him away from here. I raised my head away from his hand, and he collapsed to the ground.

"Kylan?" I shook his shoulders, but he just continued his descent to his knees. He was awake but not strong enough to stand.

"Come on, get up. You have to get out of here." My hushed voice still caused a person to stir to consciousness behind me. I shook Kylan harder, unable to pick him up, but nothing happened.

Before I could think of a way to help him, Alec stood. He shook his head to clear his mind and brushed off the dirt. He met my gaze, impressed. He then looked at the ground where Kylan was trying to remain kneeling upright. Alec's face looked puzzled for a moment, then he looked back up at me.

"Bravo with that little stunt." Alec grinned until he noticed Kylan. He shook it off and focused on me. "I'm truly impressed. I haven't seen that kind of power coming from you since the day we attacked the lab in Canada. I will admit, I didn't think you had it in you anymore."

Alec brushed the leaves off his clothing, as if whatever had just happened was inconsequential.

"You've always underestimated me, Alec." I looked him in the eyes.

I knelt down to hold Kylan. I glanced down at him quickly. Kylan shook his head as he tried to focus his eyes.

"Maybe. Or maybe I know you just haven't lived up to your full potential yet," Alec retorted as he stepped closer to Thayer, who was still lying on the ground.

A small thud sounded as Alec's boot kicked into Thayer's shoulder. Thayer's eyes flew open, and he groaned from the lingering pain. He clutched his head as he shifted his legs underneath him. The leaves crunched as he slowly stood with Alec.

"You would know all about failed potential, wouldn't you? I'm sure this is exactly what your father had in mind for the Shadows. Organizing them in full force to come pick up a girl? He would be so proud," I mocked him.

I knew the pressure that Alec had from his father to make the Shadows greater than ever before. I spent long nights consoling him and confirming that he would one day be a great leader.

If anything was a tender spot, it was Alec's relationship with his father.

Alec smiled and pretended as if I had just stabbed him in the stomach.

"Ah, you got me." He overly faked pain in his abdomen and then abandoned the act.

"If you want to talk about disappointments, you are dating the biggest one of all." Alec looked down at the groggy Kylan, who was still kneeling on the ground against me. "I mean look at him. He never had the stamina or courage to be anything. He ran away from his own family only to suppress all that power he was born with and live a simple life. Quite pathetic. My only regret is that Father isn't here to see him now," he said.

Alec's eyes watched Kylan with the same disappointed disgust that Alec believed his father would have had at this moment. He then shifted his gaze to me.

"Well, enough about the past. Let's focus on the future." Alec continued waving away the accusations I laid on him. "Time to come home, Mara."

I stood and stepped in between Kylan and Alec. Alec smiled.

"Why? Why can you not just leave me alone?" I threw back at him.

If he wanted to talk like he was acting rational, I could attempt to reason with him. Alec stepped closer to me and lowered his head so he had to look up to me. His big blue eyes begged me to listen.

In the most innocent way possible, he reached forward and took my hand in his.

"You'll see, baby, I promise." He smiled kindly, and his dazzling face brightened.

In his twisted mind, he must actually believe he was doing the right thing. I scowled at him and moved my face away.

"Stop calling me that," I ordered through gritted teeth.

That only made his smile widen. His eyes locked on mine and I already knew the threat resting on his tongue.

LEGEND UNDONE

"You have two choices. Come quietly and never leave again, and Kylan can stay here, untouched. Or I will kill Kylan right now, and you can try to fight your way out as we drag you all...the way...back."

Before I spoke, Kylan did. "He's bluffing, Kate. He can't kill me," he said through clenched teeth as he tried to steady himself.

Unfortunately, with both of us so drained of energy, there wasn't a choice.

"You look like you are struggling a bit there?" Alec chimed in, focused on Kylan now.

He put his hand on the back of Kylan's neck, forcing Kylan to turn his face toward Alec. Kylan's eyes narrowed, staring at his brother.

"Too bad there isn't any energy around for you to siphon, brother." Alec taunted.

"Get your hand off me," Kylan spat as he slowly stood up.

He held onto me to lift himself to his feet. Kylan pushed Alec's hand away and turned his focus on me.

"If you leave now, I'll never see you again. I won't risk that." Kylan held my face in his hands.

"He will kill you. My life isn't worth yours," I tried to explain back to him.

"Seems we are at a bit of a standstill," Alec interrupted. "Unfortunately, I don't have time for rock, paper, scissors. We have an important appointment at home."

"Sage doesn't like to be kept waiting," Thayer added.

I raced through my memories and could not place that name. I looked at Thayer, who shook his head slowly.

"Who is Sage?" I asked.

"She's new," Thayer answered. "And you are going to hate her."

Alec threw him a sharp glance to shut him up. Thayer caught Alec's eye and then looked at the ground.

"Since we don't have time to waste, take them both. After all, I haven't seen Kylan in ages. We have some catching up to do." He didn't bother looking at Kylan. He only had eyes for me now.

"Nikki, Grae, grab my brother and let's go home," Alec commanded.

They both lunged forward and ripped Kylan out from under my hands. He did not have the strength in him to fight back and wouldn't until he could replenish his energy.

I watched his tired eyes as they yanked his body in the other direction. I jumped after him, and Alec grabbed my upper arm and yanked me back toward him.

My body pressed up tightly against his chest. I could feel his breath racing. Thayer moved to help hold me down.

"No worries. I'll handle Mara," Alec snarled.

His eyes chilled my soul and halted my movement. I could see the anticipation for this moment and the excitement for the future. I saw my upcoming fate in his deep, cold, blue eyes. I knew exactly the life he had in mind for me.

Goose bumps raised on my arms as an icy shiver shook my body.

CHAPTER
TWENTY-SIX

The mansion appeared as we crested the hills surrounding it. I looked down and saw the home of death sitting calmly in the middle of the valley. The crunch of so many footsteps across the baked dirt and dry grass was the only thing I could hear over my own breathing. The cool breeze brushed over my skin with an eerie welcome.

It had been twenty-three years since I had laid eyes on these rock walls and tall pillars.

The beautiful white stone and the metal-cased windows reflected the iron lights on the outside. It looked exactly as I remembered, as if I had never left.

The lower we stepped into the valley and closer we approached, the more it towered over me. It resembled a prison more than it did a home.

I stood tall as I walked through the front doors once more. My eyes reluctantly met the expanse of the stone floor, high ceilings, and dark wood furniture in front of me. The foyer instantly smelled of the familiar dry air and hunger for power.

I watched Kylan get dragged off to the dungeons.

I could only imagine the things that would happen to him from here on out.

I was led down the opposite hallway. We walked past the open courtyard filling with Shadows and back into the storage rooms. They were off the beaten path, but not nearly as hard to break out of as the dungeons were. That told me that this was just a stop along the way.

They opened a door to a nearly empty room. The only thing in there was a metal table sitting near some cabinets in the right corner. The light was a single bulb dangling from a gold chain in the center of the ceiling. The light didn't even reach the back corners of the room.

Thayer and Alec escorted me through the doorway. Alec turned to Thayer and nodded for him to leave. Thayer seemed to be looking around the room for something, and then he slowly left. When Alec heard the door shut, he looked down at me. I paused for a moment to make sure that we were alone in the room.

When I didn't hear anything, I snapped into action. I didn't have enough energy for a mental assault, and going up against Alec wouldn't be smart anyway. I did have just enough energy for this.

I yanked my arm from Alec's grip and reached for the only thing in the room, the table. I grabbed the bar that spanned between the two legs and ripped it off. The metal made a loud sound as it broke. I spun, knowing Alec would have followed me over here. Without marking his location, I shot the jagged bar forward and heard it plunge into Alec.

It landed just underneath his collarbone. I dropped my hand and tried to step away.

"Ah," Alec groaned, and pulled out the bar.

He held tightly onto my arm—despite the injury—and took a heaving breath. Blood soaked through his dark shirt.

Within a matter of seconds, the wound glowed with a faint yellow light. My jaw dropped as his blood stopped running far too quickly. Alec swiped a finger where the open wound should have been.

He took a lazy breath and looked back down at me with disappointment.

"That's the best you can do?" Alec taunted and tossed the bar in the corner.

His blood streaked across the tan stones as the metal piece clattered to a stop. Alec stood to his full height and smiled.

I didn't bother hiding my surprise. I had never seen anyone heal as quickly as Alec just had. His eyes narrowed, waiting for my next move.

"How high are you?" I breathed, still amazed.

Excess energy healed wounds faster than normal. But that kind of wound should have taken hours to heal. I had just watched it close in less than a minute.

I was completely outmatched. My body was running dangerously low on energy, and Alec was still flying high.

As long as things were so uneven, I didn't stand a chance. However, with Thayer gone, I planned on using every second I could to get out of this situation.

"I told you. You are worth whatever it takes." Alec's voice floated into my ears.

He pulled me unnervingly close to him. I could hear his heartbeat and feel his breath on my skin. His strong grip remained glued to my arm and his eyes never left mine.

Anticipation and vengeance built in his stare. The deeper I looked, the more I saw.

A thought crossed my mind of just how many people had to die to get Alec to this level of power, this amount of utter domination.

Then my imagination became real.

I saw their faces, their scared faces. Alec touched them and all of them crumbled within seconds. Person after person flashed across my vision. Men. Women. Young. Old. No one was safe from him. I felt all of their energy as if it were my own. I sensed their fear as if I was standing in front of them.

I couldn't count them all. It must have been hundreds.

That's when I realized these images weren't coming from my imagination. They were memories. Alec's memories. He was showing me everything he had done to bring me back.

"Stop," I begged.

I shut my eyes and turned my head to the floor to rid his hold on my mind. I was too weak to fight him off. If he wanted to get in again, he could.

The silence broke when my phone buzzed in my jacket pocket. I automatically reached for it when Alec caught my hand.

"Ah, ah, ah," he chided and reached into my pocket for my phone.

He pulled it out and immediately moved it out of reach. I grabbed for the phone, but he took it farther away. He held out the phone for both of us to see the screen.

"Who is this?" Alec asked me.

Lisa Moreno.

It would probably be the day she was leaving for her mother's funeral, or maybe she'd just arrived. Either way, she called me just like she said she would. My heart wrenched in my chest when I looked at Alec's cold, intrigued gaze.

He ended the call and looked back at me for the answer. Alec skipped the opportunity to torture me with her name. In fact, he was careful not to say her name.

Was there someone else here?

"No one," I answered back too fast.

I remembered all the humans he so thoughtlessly killed. The ones I had just seen flash across my eyes. To him, she would be just another body in the pile. He smiled when he saw the concern on my face.

"Is this 'no one' a human or Legend?" Alec asked and I hated the morbid curiosity in his eyes.

"Legend," I lied, hoping he would believe me.

It would be much better for him to think I had found another Legend friend than for him to think I was actually close to a human. Alec didn't tolerate any human-to-Legend relationships of any kind.

"You're not a very good liar anymore. Anyway, I don't see why you would be protecting a human," he teased and raised his eyebrow. Then he remembered something. "Right. Kylan. Don't tell me you've gone soft toward them."

"Not soft. Better," I spoke through my teeth.

"I think 'better' is a relative term." He shrugged and looked at the phone again. "Should I tell Grae to go look for someone in Portland by the name of—"

"No," I said, almost shouted.

"Not Grae? What about Nikki?" Alec shrugged watched me out of the corner of his eye.

"No!"

I despised Grae and how much he kissed up to Alec. Of course, Alec knew that. But subjecting Lisa to Nikki would be intensely worse. Alec smiled at my reaction. He always loved to play games with me, and I was giving him exactly what he wanted.

"All right, I'll make you a deal," he started and tucked the phone in his own pocket. "If you promise not to fight me, I'll forget I ever saw her name."

"Ever? I won't promise that." I glared back at him. The more I threatened him, the more he smiled.

"What about just for the next twenty-four hours? Would that be worth her life?"

"Why?" I asked.

"For reasons you don't need to know, I would prefer you to...cooperate," he said.

He stared into my eyes with the same cold stare that had haunted my nightmares for the last few decades.

"Let me remind you how generous this is," he threatened.

The words he said made my mind recall that I had told the same thing to Kylan when I needed to change the human's memories. As much as I didn't want to think about it, Alec and I were still a lot alike.

"Fine, I won't physically hurt you, but I won't let you in my mind willingly," I explained.

He should know that me being cooperative and me giving up were two different things entirely. From the sadistic smile that came across his face, he did know that.

"Baby, you know I wouldn't want you if you did. I love a good challenge," he said and put his hand under my chin.

I didn't pull away, as I had promised not to. I needed Alec to hold up his end of the bargain. He lifted my face, forcing me to meet his gaze.

"Hand me the phone," I demanded.

I took a step toward him, his hand still under my chin, so he didn't have to pull on my arm anymore to keep me close. I didn't want him having any ties to my home or any of the people that I knew. He looked at me for a moment, puzzled.

"You don't trust me to keep my promise?" he asked.

Instead of his eyes showing hurt, they lit up with pride. He wanted me to be cynical, just like I used to be.

"The phone," I ordered again.

He reached into his pocket and handed the phone to me slowly. I pulled my arm out of his and he let me go.

I took the phone from him and immediately dropped it on the floor. I stomped on it as hard as I could and listened as it shattered under my foot. The various pieces of glass, metal, and plastic scattered in shards.

Seeing that it was destroyed, I relaxed my shoulders.

"Just remember, I'm not the bad guy here," Alec whispered to me, so quietly.

When I looked into his eyes, for a moment I saw the child I grew up with. I saw the blood near his shoulder and how he still held that arm carefully. I heard him breathe faster the longer he was with me.

I snapped out of the trance and balled my fists, not wanting to fall for his tactic.

Thayer burst through the only door in the room with a human teenager in tow. The kid fought hard against Thayer's grip, but it didn't even faze him. He just continued to drag the kid along, almost annoyed by the flailing person he had to control. The boy looked at me and Alec for help with wild eyes.

I winced, knowing his upcoming fate.

Thayer forcefully tossed the kid into the dark corner of the room, where he disappeared. I followed the trail with my eyes. The light from his energy exiting his body brightened the area surrounding him. Soft, swirling energy illuminated up to a female's face.

Someone else was in the room, and she had just seen our entire conversation. The energy bent around her fingers and into her body. The light diminished as it absorbed through her skin.

"Mara, this is Sage Trevan," Alec introduced me.

The woman stepped out from the shadows and under the dangling light. Every part of her body was all varying shades of the lightest white.

Her pale skin was almost translucent. Her hair was so blond it was almost white. The long tresses shimmered in even the dim light.

The only thing that stood out was her eyes. The bright red color surrounded her dark pupils. She used those shocking eyes to look me up and down and then over to Alec.

"You couldn't go outside and get your own energy?" I motioned to the heap of bones lying in the corner that used to be a kid with a future ahead of him.

The woman glanced at the kid lying on the floor and then flicked her creepy eyes back over to me.

"Here we go," Thayer muttered gleefully. I looked at his smile as he waited for Sage to respond

"It's such a beautiful day and, honey, you could use the sun," I added, eager to push her limits.

Just my presence in the mansion made the Mara personality come screaming back to the surface. Sage said nothing. She just glared at me with her crimson eyes.

"Sage doesn't do sunshine," Alec remarked.

I gawked at Sage and noticed she hated it. If she lost her concentration, Alec couldn't use her against me. But her pale face smoothed into a faint grin.

"The Louisiana lab wanted to improve their original invention." She recalled the story.

I cringed on the inside. Scientists with new ideas were never a good thing.

"They wanted to nullify the threat Legends posed to humans by making the skin sensitive enough that it couldn't take in energy, or at least not quickly."

I turned when I heard Thayer's scowl.

"After all the chaos they caused to create us and then in trying to destroy us, you think they'd just cut their losses and leave us alone." Thayer shook his head and his hardened gaze was returned by her.

"They can't do that. They have to perfect their creation and bring joy to all the world," Alec mocked lightly, eyeing me longer than he should before turning to her.

"Please." Thayer scoffed and returned his look back to Sage. "What do you think? Is this joyful for you?"

"That's not exactly how I'd describe being kidnapped and experimented on. Obviously, the plan didn't work out like they hoped. I can't withstand sunlight, but energy can still pass freely." She calmly explained why she more closely resembled a ghost than a person.

"How did you escape?" I asked, honestly curious.

"I gave them what they wanted. I pretended to weaken each day from not being able to take in energy. They finally let their guard down long enough for me to escape. The second I walked outside…it was the last sunny day I ever willingly walked into." She finished her story and looked idly at her pristine nails. She acted like she didn't care at all.

"Remember now?" Alec's hand brushed my arm. "They are the enemy."

I can't see much difference between them and you, I thought, and allowed Alec to hear in my mind. I noticed the faint grimace when he understood what I thought of him.

I took a step away from him but realized that just made me take a step closer to Thayer. I watched his smile out of the corner of my eye. Despite how he made my toes curl, Thayer was the lesser of two evils here.

I looked back at Sage, who seemed shocked that I would turn away from Alec, as he was the leader. They obviously hadn't filled her in on the whole story yet.

"I hoped for the day I could repay the favor." Sage's eyes glimmered with revenge as she clicked her nails together. "My wish came true when I met Alec."

She looked at Alec like a partner in crime. If she wasn't eerie on her own, the red eyes were not helping. Alec bowed his head to her like he was a gracious leader.

I tried to ignore the flame of jealousy boiling in my stomach. I still hated Alec, but I hated seeing others with him even more.

"We found her hiding out in an obscure cave. She had been luring humans there and taking their energy, so she never had to leave. Years of that practice made her mind-creation skills almost a rival to mine." Alec smiled at me now.

"Almost." Thayer winked at Sage.

"Alec found me and offered me a place among the Shadows. No tryout." She glared at me.

I looked down and saw the fresh mark on her arm. I raised my eyebrows.

"No tryout? That's not possible..."

"Relax." Alec shrugged and brushed a dark hair out of my face, and I glared at him. "She still had the same stakes as everyone else. We marked her right away, but I told her that if I didn't like what I saw, then I'd kill her myself."

I looked back at Sage now, who was errantly pulling her sleeve higher to show off her new mark. The skin was still slightly red around the edges from the pain. Mine looked like that for a week after Nikki marked me.

She was so new, and Alec already trusted her enough to help handle me. Then I tried to remember that I shouldn't care about any of this.

"I couldn't turn down such an honor. Who could walk away from a life like this?" Sage gestured to the mansion surrounding us, like it was the safest place in the world.

"I can only think of one person who would," Thayer remarked quietly from behind me.

I whipped around and lunged for Thayer but didn't actually touch him. Alec said I couldn't fight them, but he didn't say anything about scaring them. Thayer jerked back automatically, even though he knew how little energy I had left. The ability to still intimidate him made me smile.

"Don't worry, she's not going to hurt you," Alec laughed.

"Are you sure?" Thayer asked, crouching a little lower.

He took a tentative step closer to me now, testing my limits. I didn't move. He relaxed.

"She has someone she's protecting. A girl," Alec said, running his hand across the back of my shoulders, pulling my brown hair out of the way.

I spun immediately and glared into his eyes, my hair flying out of his hand.

"Oh, I love girls," Thayer said in a low voice.

My stomach turned and I stared him down. He just smiled proudly and took another step toward me. I didn't move again.

"A human girl," Alec continued.

I realized now that he promised to forget her name, but not anything else. I wasn't the only one looking for loopholes in the deal. I wish I could say I was surprised.

"Even better." Thayer smiled down at me and rubbed his hands together.

He moved even closer to me, close enough for me to feel his breath in my face. I put my hand on his chest and shoved him away from me. He just laughed and stumbled a few steps back.

I rolled my eyes at the both of them. No matter how old they were, they still acted like little boys, especially around each other. It was a lot like Kylan had acted with Derek. My heart sank, and I shook off the thought to focus back on what was happening.

I moved my gaze back to Sage. She was standing with her arms crossed over her chest, clearly not impressed by the reunion taking place in front of her.

"Judging by the fact you are still alive, you must be quite the catch. What Level are you?" I asked, changing the subject. Her wicked smile preceded her answer.

"I'm a One."

I raised my eyebrows and couldn't help but look over at Alec in disappointment. He hid his smile and watched Sage closely.

"A One? You thought a One could bring me down?"

His lack of confidence in my ability to defend my mind made me even more excited to try and prove him wrong. His smile didn't waver as he looked at Sage.

"Honey," she mimicked my earlier condescending tone, "I only need One."

Her voice seared into my mind without much effort, creating a painful ring between my ears with each word. I hissed and stumbled back, trying to force her out of my head.

"Mmm. Alec, I like this one." Thayer looked Sage up and down.

Jealousy sparked in me again, this time too quickly for me to believe it actually came from me. I shot Thayer a glance. He smiled just long enough for me to see.

"This shouldn't be too difficult." Sage cracked her knuckles obnoxiously.

"You might be surprised by her." Alec talked as though I wasn't standing right next to him.

I kept my eyes focused on Sage. She didn't break eye contact until she was standing directly in front of me.

"I can tell you this is going to hurt," she said and finally seemed like she was acknowledging my presence in the room. "I just can't tell you that I will feel sorry about it."

She reached up and put one hand on the right side of my face. Alec put his hand on the left side of my face. They both stood in front of me.

My eyes bounced between the deep blue gaze from Alec and the scathing red gaze from Sage. Thayer moved behind me and placed his hands on both of my arms.

I knew what they were planning as soon as they both closed their eyes. Alec wasn't strong enough on his own to suppress the decades of memories that I had made away from the Shadows and, at the same time, create blocks to prevent them from coming back. But there was nothing I could do to stop him now.

Sage was being honest. The pain was excruciating.

The only thing keeping me from dropping to the floor was their grip on me. I reached up and grabbed Sage and Alec's hands, hoping it would lessen the pain. It didn't.

I watched the last few decades play through my mind. After each place and personality flashed across my memory, it was ripped away, leaving a stinging pain in its absence.

The next one would follow and then be torn away just as quickly, more pain plunging into my head. I could feel my mind slashing itself apart to reveal every memory and thought I had since I left.

Alec was reading and altering my memories. Sage was creating blocks to cover the past I wasn't supposed to know about. It hurt to have my memories manipulated against my will.

Despite my effort to protect my mind and put up a fight, my strength couldn't compare to the three of them so high on energy.

I couldn't breathe. I couldn't fight. I could barely even stand. My entire body shook with desperation to get away from the source of agony crashing through my mind. I had no idea the amount of time that passed. It felt like years.

Eventually, I blacked out from the pain. My consciousness slipped away. I stayed aware only long enough to feel Alec move me to the table in the room. The stiff metal pushed against my limp body. My ears strained to hear the last bits of conversation between them.

"What about this body?" Alec asked quietly.

Every word they spoke brought a resounding pain to my head. I strained to listen through the groggy, half-conscious state I lingered in.

"Her mind will no longer remember this form. She will change back without even trying. She'll look like her old self before she wakes," Sage explained.

Then everything went black and finally, finally the pain ceased.

CHAPTER
TWENTY-SEVEN

Hard metal pressed into my back, warm from my body heat.

The ache of sleeping on such a stiff surface sliced through my unconsciousness. I stirred my muscles awake. Finally, my eyes opened to see the empty ceiling above me. I took a breath in and let it penetrate the bleary corners of my mind. My vision sharpened as my head cleared.

I sat up on the table, shifting to the cold part that my body hadn't been touching. The aches flared at the slight movement.

I reached up and moved my blond hair from out of my eyes. My rigid muscles shifted. I turned my head around to stretch out my neck. When I looked down, I noticed a pastel skirt around my waist extending to just above my knees.

What was I wearing?

The clothes were unusual. Everything was too fancy, too feminine even, for my taste. Even my shoes were clearly not made for any kind of running.

I swung my feet down to reach the floor beneath me. I

reached to my shoulders and took off the tight jacket that restricted my movements. I threw it to the floor.

Something moved behind me. I paused for less than a second to locate where exactly they were. In one motion, I jumped forward off the table and spun around to see who was lurking.

Alec stood from the chair he was sitting in. He looked at me with a concerned expression as I stood low in a defensive stance. My mind took a moment to decide how to react, slugging through the remaining fog.

"Mara?" He let my name linger in the air between us.

Something in my mind shifted as his sweet voice reached my ears. His strained eyes held the weight of centuries in them. I knew those eyes.

"Yes," I breathed as my smile grew.

He returned the grin and ran toward me. He shoved the table out from in between us in one motion. The metal legs screeched across the stone. I reached out and threw my arms around him. He hugged me so tight that I could hardly breathe.

"It's nice to see you too," I laughed into his neck with my limited air supply.

He loosened his grip enough for him to pull away and look in my eyes. When I looked back at him, all I saw was beauty, cunning, and enough power to shake the world.

"I missed you," he sighed.

His voice sounded like he had not seen me in years. He held me like he was afraid I would run from him if he let go.

"Missed me? What are you talking about?" I asked him.

"You don't remember?"

I searched through my memory and shook my head. He seemed to be holding back a smile.

"We got into an argument. You stormed off and no one

saw you for days. We went looking for you, but someone else had gotten to you before we could," he said.

He paused and watched my face as I processed what he said.

"Who?" I asked him to continue the story.

"An Extractor," he continued. I took a sharp breath in. "You were not in good shape when we found you. We raced you back here, and after a few hours, well, here we are," he finished.

"Wow, that'll teach me not to go out on my own," I chuckled.

"But you're safe now, and you are home again." Alec held my face in his hands.

"Thanks to you," I said, smiling.

I leaned forward and kissed him. My stomach tightened, and my toes curled in excitement. My deep desire for him resonated through my body. Every muscle, every waking nerve belonged with Alec. The need for him spread all the way to my hands that pulled him closer to me. He was my best friend with whom I happened to fall in love. He was my fairy tale. I pulled away to look at him. He stood tall and proud like he always did.

Alec.

A knock came on the door and before either of us spoke, it pushed open. Thayer poked his head around the corner. He saw me and looked at Alec before saying anything. Alec smiled and pulled me closer into his arms. Thayer's shoulders slightly relaxed as he looked back over to me.

"Mara, you're okay," he said, smiling at me with those familiar gleaming teeth. "We were worried sick about you."

He stepped fully into the room. An undiscernible emotion flickered behind his eyes. He was never good at hiding his feelings. I looked at him closely.

"Hmm, is that why you dressed me up in these frilly clothes? I know this must have been your idea."

I reached down and shook the piece of skirt I held in my hand.

Thayer looked down and smiled, not skipping a beat before he answered.

"I just thought you would want to look like a princess waking up in her castle." He snickered at my flowing skirt.

The light fabric still twirled as I threw it out of my hand. It made me shudder to feel it against my leg.

"Well, now that you've had your laugh, would you mind getting me some real clothes?" I asked with one eyebrow raised so he knew this wasn't just a request.

"As Your Highness commands." He bowed low to the floor.

I slipped off my right shoe and threw it at him. He ducked behind the door and the shoe hit the wood instead of Thayer. The force of my throw finished shutting the door behind him. I turned back to Alec.

"You let him dress me up? How bad of a fight was this?" I accused Alec of not stopping the teasing in its tracks.

"I thought you looked cute in this little skirt," he moved his hand down the side of my leg where the skirt covered my skin.

"Mmm hmm, I bet." I gave him a quick wink. "You're going to pay for this later."

I pressed myself against him without breaking eye contact. I watched Alec's eyes light up as his hands snaked around me.

"I hope so," Alec whispered.

His hand slid slowly up my back as he pulled me closer. He finally pulled me in close enough to kiss me. I wrapped my arms around his neck and deepened his kiss. My body automatically responded to him. My hand reached up and moved through his perfect blond hair.

My body leaned in closer, and my breath quickened. A slow burn started in my stomach and grew until it nearly reached my face.

"You have no idea how good it feels to have you back," he said while his lips still touched mine.

Every word sent my heart soaring into the air.

The door opening interrupted the two of us. A small, pale woman stepped through the doorway and immediately locked her bright red eyes with me.

"I see someone finally woke up," she said.

I looked her up and down. My grip instinctively tightened on Alec. She looked familiar, in a way that made me think I had seen her in a nightmare, although I couldn't place where I had seen her before.

"Mara, this is Sage Trevan." Alec broke the silence. "She came to us while you were gone. Remarkable talent."

"It's nice to meet you." I extended my hand to her. "Alec has told me absolutely nothing about you."

She reached forward and took it. Her hand was warmer than I expected. She gave a fake smile to my smart remark.

"All right, I have your pants," Thayer announced as he came in the room. "Oh, there you are, Sage."

I stepped forward and took the small pile of clothes from Thayer's arm. I left him holding the shoes. I paused for a moment and waited for the rest of them to leave. Everyone remained in the room.

"What, you mean we can't watch?" Thayer spoke up first.

Alec lunged forward and smacked him on the arm. I looked directly at Thayer and scoffed. He laughed at me as he took a step back. I walked around Alec until his body blocked mine from Thayer and Sage's view and I dropped that awful skirt to the floor. I pulled the pants up my legs.

"Well, she's certainly still Mara," Alec remarked at the

skirt wrapped near his feet as he continued to face the others and be my changing screen.

Thayer laughed in agreement. "It's nice having her around."

Then he directed his next remark to Sage.

"How is that project coming along?" The tone of his voice changed back to serious.

"Exactly as planned," she responded confidently.

I could picture the smug look on her face without even seeing her. I finished pulling the shirt over my head and stepped out from behind Alec. My darker, tighter clothes felt better against my body. I left the slower skirt and stifling shirt laying in a pile on the floor. Thayer handed me my shoes and slapped Alec on the shoulder.

"Hear that, boss?" Thayer remarked toward Alec. "Good news, right?"

Alec turned and looked directly at me. His eyes took me in, from my face to my black sneakers.

"Excellent news," he said, smiling.

"I'm gonna to go find Nikki." Thayer rubbed his hands together and walked toward the old, wooden door.

"And Grae," Alec added.

"Yeah, of course. Didn't I say that?" Thayer smiled and winked in my direction as he left the room without another word.

I leaned against Alec with one hand and slipped my shoes on with the other. When I pulled the shoe over my heel, I let my foot fall to the floor. I shifted in my new clothes, allowing my body to adjust back to what I normally wore.

"He's a strange one." I nodded toward the door where he had left.

"No arguments there." Alec smiled.

"Where did we find him again?"

"That was Father, who spotted him and thought he would be a great asset one day." Alec mocked his father's voice. I smiled. "He was right, though. Thayer is a loyal friend."

"Loyal for sure, just not quite normal." I circled my finger around my ear so Alec would catch my jab.

He laughed and nodded.

"Did you need anything else?" Sage interrupted our banter with a question for Alec.

He paused for a moment and looked into my eyes carefully. I wondered what he thought he'd be able to see, not that I would let him in. He must have found what he was looking for because a crooked grin turned up the right corner of his perfect mouth.

"No, I think we're good," he responded to her while still looking at me.

The smile that followed made even me shiver.

CHAPTER
TWENTY-EIGHT

I opened the door from my room and stepped out into the hallway. They said I had been gone for days, but I didn't remember being anywhere else.

I walked around the corner silently and continued down the next hallway. The tall, textured walls and winding hallways felt like I was walking through a dream.

I hadn't done much yet, but I was already tired. I needed something to eat. I thought of the warm, coaxing energy that lay just outside the mansion's grounds. All I had to do was go and get it.

Temporarily distracted by my thoughts, I didn't notice when someone walked up behind me. As soon as I heard their steps, I whipped around and lunged. Even a newbie should learn not to sneak up on me.

Thayer's V-neck shirt balled in my hand as I slammed him against the wall before I noticed who it was I held.

"Ouch, Mara!"

"What are you doing here?" I hissed and tossed his shirt out of my hand. "You know you shouldn't sneak up on me like that."

His big, brown eyes looked up at me, and this feeling of forgiveness and kindness washed over me.

"I'm sorry," he mumbled.

The feeling inside me grew stronger. My heart burned for him. My hands softened at my sides like I would never hurt him. Even my face warmed when I looked at the precious, little Thayer Cade that stood in front of me.

I knew it was him. All I could think about was his innocent smile and how much I didn't want to hurt him.

"Can you forgive me?" He let a small smile slip, and I caught on to his game.

I relaxed into the feeling, instead of fighting it. His eyes lightened as he no longer had to put in as much effort. I stepped closer to him and put both of my hands on either of his shoulders. His eyes lit up.

"Of course," I answered him.

I leaned my face close and as his smile widened. My mouth brushed dangerously close to his and my hands moved to touch his shoulders. I moved my foot behind his. His smile fell from his face once he realized what I was doing.

Before he could say anything, I swept my foot under his and shoved him over. He would have fallen flat on his back had he not picked up on what I was doing. He spun around and caught himself on his hands in the plank position. He stopped his movement just before his face hit the floor, all of his glorious muscles flexing in his arms.

"You always fall for that." I chuckled.

"If you weren't so convincing it wouldn't be so hard to figure you out." He shoved himself off the floor and back to a standing position with utter ease.

I turned and walked the way I had originally wanted to go, toward the front door. Thayer followed.

"Where are you going?" he prodded.

"To get something to eat." I threw my response over my shoulder, not bothering to turn around.

"You mean someone, right?" he said as he skipped ahead and turned to face me.

I kept moving, forcing him to walk backward in order to keep eye contact.

"Depends." I shrugged my shoulders. "Anything good downstairs?"

Thayer paused instead of answering my question. I pulled my eyebrows together, wondering what was wrong. He stopped walking, which made me stop before I stepped right into him.

"Thayer?" I asked again.

"Nope, you'll have to go out." He answered my question too slowly.

I narrowed my eyes at his pause. His brown eyes flicked between mine. He was too nervous about something.

"Okay, I'll go out then." I tried to brush past him headed for the front door.

"Yeah. Let me just go get Alec." He held up his hand in the air to stop me.

We had just reached the end of the hallway where it opened up to the main courtyard. I came to a complete stop and stared at him.

What was going on?

"Why?" I asked him.

I looked deep into his eyes, hoping his face would tell me the answer. He looked around for a moment like he was hoping for someone else to step in.

"Thayer, look at me." I asked him nicely.

He turned his head to face me and, instead, directed his gaze to the floor. I had this feeling that if I looked into his eyes, I could find out what was going on. However, I couldn't read minds yet, so I was unsure why looking at him would be helpful. On instinct almost, I yanked his chin covered in smooth facial hair to force his eyes to meet mine.

Just as soon as I did, Alec walked around the corner.

"What's going on here?" Alec slowed his walk when he saw the struggle.

"Your puppy dog thinks I need an escort to go hunting." I said to Alec directly.

I noticed the few faces of people surrounding us turn to watch what was happening. A strange feeling came over me to tell me that something was off. The feeling settled in my stomach slowly. I shook it off and waited for Alec. He looked at Thayer for a long moment and then looked back at me.

"You don't need an escort," he scoffed, as if it was just as ridiculous as I thought it was. "He probably thought that I'd want to go with you because you did just recover from a massive injury, and we just wanted to make sure you didn't wander off again."

He smiled as he easily explained everything and put his arm around me.

Something was just slightly wrong. My skin puckered in goose bumps. I was about to say something, but then an unexpected feeling of appreciation came over me. The twist in the pit of my stomach melted away. I looked at Alec like he was trying to protect me because he loves me.

Alec glanced quickly at Thayer and then back at me.

"Fair enough," I said and relaxed my shoulders. The tension faded. "Well, let's get going then. I'm starving."

Alec's smile returned, and he turned me toward the front door. I started walking and held Alec's hand behind me in tow.

"You good, boss?" Thayer asked as we left.

"We're good, Thayer," Alec called over his shoulder. "Let's go have some fun, shall we? It's been a while since just the two of us went out." He slid his hand down my back and tucked his hand in my back pocket.

"Let's see if you can keep up," I challenged and started backing up, still facing him.

He pulled his hand out of my pocket and crouched in a ready stance. His fingers waved like he was getting his body ready to race. I raised my eyebrows to confirm that he accepted my challenge. His grin widened, and I saw a flash of triumph in his eyes already.

"That's my girl," he let out in a breath. His voice lit a fire inside of me, part competition and part desire.

Then we both took off to the outside world. I could feel him right on my heels as we ran.

My body felt stiff and achy. I was too low on energy. The Extractor must have taken more than I thought.

I shook off the thoughts. I may have been low on energy, but there was no way I was going to let him beat me. Plus, it didn't matter if I ran my reserve of energy to the lowest point. My replenishment was right up ahead.

I turned my focus to looking ahead and sensing where the warmest pockets of energy were coming from. I listened in close to hear the heartbeats of the unsuspecting humans. I smiled when I thought about how none of them knew I was coming. I was free and completely in control of what lay ahead.

My smile cracked across my face.

I eventually skidded to a stop just outside of a small town. We were about twenty miles away from the mansion. Alec halted behind me once he arrived two seconds later. I smiled and glanced over at him. He was breathing hard too.

"Did you do some training without me noticing?" he asked in between puffs of air.

I just shrugged my shoulders and reveled in my momentary victory. I did feel stronger, like I had been running for longer than my mind remembered. He stepped closer to me and put both of his hands around my waist from behind. His mouth brushed my ear.

"What do you feel?" he asked in a low whisper.

I paused, and his body pressed up against my back. Having him close sped up my already fast-paced heart rate. I took a breath and concentrated on the town in the distance. I closed my eyes and sensed a gang of people heading out to the river, moving fast. I could hear the roar of the engine from the side-by-side they were driving in.

Thrill-seeking teens, my favorite. My eyes snapped open and zeroed in on the direction of their pumping energies.

"I feel hungry," I said in a low growl so only Alec could hear.

I took off in my desired direction. Every step brought their warmth closer to me. The anticipation tingled all the way down to my toes. We came over the hill, and I locked the target in my sight. Four teenagers sat in the fast-moving vehicle, laughing and yelling at the driver to go faster. I dove down the hill and headed straight in front of their line of travel. Alec stayed on the hill watching the scene below.

I halted when I stood exactly in front of the vehicle. The passenger saw me and shouted at the driver to look out. I held my ground as I watched the vehicle swerve around me. The abrupt change in direction caused the vehicle to roll onto its side and come crashing into the soft sand.

After it had come sliding to a stop, I walked over to them. As I approached, they climbed out of the vehicle. Only the driver and back passenger were free when I arrived.

"You crazy, lady? Didn't you see us coming?" the driver exclaimed as he held his bleeding head wound.

The back passenger finished jumping out of the vehicle and turned back around to check his seat-mate. She was unconscious.

"Is that any way to talk to a lady?" I chided him.

I snapped forward and brushed the skin of his open neck. His body hit the ground, lifeless. The back passenger, who was previously looking down, was now staring straight at me.

"What did you do?" he asked in a tense, hushed voice.

He lifted his right arm and held it out to stop me from getting to him. His left arm dangled uselessly by his side. It must have broken. I looked into his scared brown eyes and tilted my head to the side.

"Are you hurt?" I asked kindly.

The look of confusion on his face could be seen from a mile away. His fear pumped even more adrenaline into his body, into his energy. I stepped toward him.

"Don't move," I gently commanded.

He obeyed. He stood still and waited until I was within breathing distance of him. The kid matched up to my height, but not nearly to my strength. He was breathing hard, and I could tell by his face this was worse than a horror movie. He had no control of the situation and no idea what to do. The feeling of sweet success filled in me.

The look he displayed was probably the mirror image of the ones my ancestors had long ago when they were experimented on. Humankind deserved to be knocked down a notch or two. I was just the messenger of their fate.

I looked at this poor teenager in my hand and focused on his eyes as the hot, throbbing energy screamed from him into me. His eyes drooped and, eventually, the only thing holding him upright was me. The last spurt of energy raced through to me, and I let him fall the rest of the way to the ground.

I circled my head around to stretch my newly rejuvenated muscles. I shook out my bare arms, and the energy from their systems melded into mine.

The combined total energy of those scared little boys would have been ample to keep me going for a while.

However, I was taught not to waste, and there were still two perfectly beating hearts in the vehicle just waiting for me.

I grabbed the side of the vehicle and pulled it over so it was standing on all four wheels again. The front passenger banged her head against the seat from the jolt of being flipped over again.

After being jostled, she shook her head out and looked up at me.

"What are you?" she asked me.

I took a step back as I looked at her. She wasn't scared of me. She was angry. She didn't struggle with the seatbelt that had locked up and kept her pinned. She didn't throw her hands in the air to stop me. I looked into her eyes and all I saw was hatred brimming.

I saw myself, except for one major difference. She was a human.

Sometimes I caught myself thinking they couldn't all be as terrible as we made them out to be. This was not one of those times. A life with the Shadows had taught me that they are all the same. If given the chance, they'd kill us because, in the end, their own inferiority terrifies them.

I walked up to her and ripped the seatbelt off of her. I grabbed her throat and hoisted her out of the vehicle and held her up to my face. Her feet dangled in the air.

"Haven't you heard the whispered stories? The monsters that come to steal your souls? Of course, you have. You humans just refuse to believe we even exist," I threatened her. "You think this kind of power should be exterminated or controlled, not appreciated. If you knew what I was capable of now, would you think I deserved to live?"

I actually wanted to hear her answer. I wanted to hear the lie seep through her teeth, saying that she would save me. That she would care about me.

"No."

I released my grip on her and she collapsed to the ground.

"No? You admit it then?" I stared down at her.

I was shocked at her honesty, considering I held her life in my hands. Most people groveled at this point. She made one final effort to look me in the eye.

"Not because of your power, but because of what you do with your power." She was coughing between words and rubbing her throat as she spoke. "You are heartless. You kill people. Why do you deserve to live?"

I looked in her eyes, and the anger melted away. She looked up at me like I was the one that needed help in this situation. If I didn't know better, I would say she looked like she cared about me. My eyes narrowed at her.

"You're good." I pointed a finger at her. "I almost believe you."

I leaned down to the ground and brushed my finger across her face. She slumped to the ground after a few seconds. I stood and shook off what just happened. I looked at the last girl in the back seat. She was still lying unconscious. I looked up at Alec, who had made his way down the hill.

"Did you want anything? She doesn't have much left," I called to him.

He shook his head. I looked at her and checked the pulse on her neck. It was faint. I laid my hand on her neck and felt the last bit of energy she had pulse into my hand. I don't know what it was that made a human's final energy sweeter than the rest.

I could feel all the power swirling inside me like a hurricane. I could lift a skyscraper I was so strong. I closed my eyes and enjoyed the high for a moment. Something inside me had awakened. It was like I had not been this alive in decades.

However long it had been, it felt so nice to be thrumming with life again. I walked around the vehicle and over to Alec. He stood just on the other side of the vehicle. He picked up the two boys and plunked them back down in their seats.

"How was it?" he asked. He walked around to the front of the vehicle as he talked. He reached into the engine and busted the gas line. "You looked like you were having a good time."

"I am having a great time. I feel alive and strong. I feel like myself, just better," I corrected his statement.

I shoved the vehicle back over to its side now that the deceased passengers were back in their seats.

"I'm so glad to hear you say that," he said, smiling. His eyes looked like they held more emotion and thought than just happiness for me. I couldn't quite put my finger on it.

"What's that face for?" I asked him.

He just reached over and pulled me close to him.

"I thought I was going to lose you back there. I'm glad things are back to normal, that you are back to normal again." He let out a breath of relief as he yanked me into his arms.

I melted into him as we kissed. I relished being held in his strong arms. My hands slowly moved down his waist. As they reached his belt line, I moved them around to the back, feeling his body underneath the fabric.

I reached into Alec's pocket and retrieved a lighter. I quickly sparked the flame and pulled away from him. He was smiling through his dark eyes.

I tossed the flame toward the open gas line dumping onto the ground. We looked at each other briefly before darting back up the hill. The engine erupted in flames as we neared the peak of the hill where we had started. I smiled looking down at our handiwork.

This was the life for me. All the energy, fun, and Alec I ever needed. I wanted this.

As I stood there with his arms around me, that feeling crept up on me again. That gut feeling that something was not quite right. I brushed it away.

What else could I want but this?

CHAPTER
TWENTY-NINE

"You're crazy if you think that's going to work," Thayer shouted.

Alec and I hadn't even walked through the doors yet, and we could already hear the clamor ahead. I made a face big enough so Alec could see. He smiled.

"Welcome home, right?" Alec chuckled as he opened the door. He stepped through, and I followed him. I looked to see what was going on, and as I did, the voices continued to argue.

"Just trust me," Grae explained sternly.

"You make a move on your own, and Alec will throw you out of here himself. This is too important to him." Thayer's voice hardened in his threat.

I paused just before I walked around the corner. Alec came up behind me.

"What's going on?" I whispered to him.

"You never know with these two and their egos." He shrugged his shoulders and sighed.

Thayer had the number-two spot locked in, but that didn't

stop him from making sure Grae would never be a candidate to replace him. Grae had the ambition to lead, while Thayer only wanted to follow. The power struggle commenced the day that Alec allowed Grae into the Shadows, and as far as anyone could see, it wouldn't end until one of them was gone.

I had my money on Thayer. Not only was I fiercely loyal to Thayer, but something about Grae had always rubbed me the wrong way. When it came time to dismiss him, I'd help Thayer toss his body out myself.

Alec didn't wait for them to finish the conversation. He just stepped around the corner and loudly announced his presence.

"All right, calm down. What seems to be the problem here?" At the sound of Alec's voice, the room quieted down the way it always did.

"Okay, just listen—" Grae began to explain. Thayer cut him off.

"No, it won't work yet, and you know it." His statement did not seem directed toward Grae but toward Alec.

Thayer's tone of voice finally softened as if it was someone he respected that he was now addressing. I shuddered at the thought of Grae ever thinking he could replace Alec. I would sooner see Nikki in charge than him.

"We can't know for sure—" Grae stopped talking as soon as he saw me walk around the corner. Alec turned around and invited me to come join him.

"I think we could put this fight to bed for now," Alec said and looked directly at Grae.

At Alec's command, Grae instantly shut his mouth and took a step down. I noticed Thayer's faint smile that he didn't even try to hide.

"Today is a cause for celebration. Mara is back home safe and sound," Alec announced and grabbed my hand.

He pulled it in the air like I just won a medal. Clapping erupted, and a few people came up and slapped me on the back.

"Thanks to you, Alec." I quieted them down. "Thank you for finding me and bringing me home."

I reached my hand up and touched his chin gently. My fingers felt his lips pull back into a smile.

"I was hoping you'd say that." His smile grew bigger.

He pulled me in the rest of the way and kissed me in front of everybody. They all cheered. My heart sped up at all the excitement. I finally pulled away from Alec and turned my attention back to the rest of the crowd.

"I think this calls for a party," I announced to everyone.

Excited gasps rippled across the crowd.

Thayer leaned down to Sage. She looked confused as she silently stared at everyone.

"Nobody throws a party like Mara does." Thayer couldn't hold back his excitement. He rubbed his hands together and bounced on his feet.

That night we danced, we sang, and we ate so much food. The music was loud, the lights were glamorous, and the food was exotic, both human and otherwise.

I had found a group of college tourists on a vacation nearby. It didn't take much convincing for them to want to follow a gorgeous woman to a party.

As soon as they arrived, I nominated Grae to be in charge of making their deaths look like an accident at the end of the night. I knew he would do anything I asked, and I didn't mind forcing him to work on the night we all had fun.

Once the party began, we set them loose among all the Shadows. Their poor little human brains had no idea what they had jumped into. Each of them looked like a lost puppy in a sea of the most beautiful people.

Tonight quickly became a party that impressed even me. I stood in the middle of the crowd that was bouncing with the sound of the music. This was one of my best parties yet. I felt any stress from today's events melt off me. Tonight, I was free. The high-energy exhilaration was flowing so strong you could almost taste it.

Around the room, my eyes met plenty of smiling faces. I spotted Nikki dancing with a human girl near the edge of the crowd.

The human appeared to be incoherent and happy despite the immense danger around her. I wondered how long Nikki would draw it out before she killed the human girl.

My eyes caught Thayer walking over to Nikki and the girl. His motive was apparent even through the dimly lit space. Also, it was Thayer.

Thayer turned the human girl around. Before Nikki could stop him, he took the girl's face in his hands and kissed her, his mouth almost completely covering hers. The bright energy from inside the girl instantly flowed from her lips to Thayer's. The girl fell to the floor and left Thayer to meet Nikki's disapproving gaze.

She punched his arm, and the piece of his shirt where her hand had touched the fabric shriveled and turned an inky black.

He narrowed his eyes, glancing at the blackened hole in his shirt. He immediately grabbed the shirt behind his neck and yanked it up over his exquisitely toned body.

She laughed as they both danced to the middle of the room. He dropped the remainder of his shirt on the floor.

The Whisperer of Death and the manipulating playboy. Nikki was gorgeous and Thayer had always been a sucker for a pretty face, but it was still so odd how good of friends those two had become over the years.

Alec came up out of the crowd and pulled me away. We dashed to the back of the courtyard behind the columns that held up the balcony. He held both of my hands in his.

"Well done, my love." He spoke loudly so his voice carried over the music.

"Thank you. It is a great party, if I do say so myself." I smiled.

He looked at me and reached up to brush some of my blond hair out of my eyes. He paused for a moment before he spoke.

"By the way," he leaned close to my ear, bushing his lips against me. "Happy birthday."

"Alec, stop it." I shoved him away lightly.

"What? It's March sixth. You didn't think I forgot, did you?" He smiled and pulled me closer to him, wrapping his hands around my back.

"You know it's not my actual birthday," I teased.

For as long as I could remember, Alec had always celebrated my birthday. He celebrated everything.

He remembered the night of our first kiss. Alec and I had flirted from the second our hormones told us the other gender was attractive. He was my first, and only, everything.

Charles, Alec's father, was still alive and had found out about it. Needless to say, he was not pleased with us at all. But that never stopped us. It only made us more clever. Looking back, it seemed like mere puppy love back then.

Alec praised the day of my first kill. It had taken years for Charles or Alec to convince me that killing a human was normal. Up until then, I had only ever left of my victims unconscious.

I never knew where that urge came from, only that I had never taken a life before. I remembered that moment quite vividly, even to this day.

I looked at Alec standing in front of me, no longer the teenager he was when he lost his father, or even the little boy when I had first met him. He was a strong, devious, and utterly striking man that I had pledged to follow to the ends of this world. Me and every other Shadow.

"March 6, 1813. The day we found you. The day your life started with us. Since we don't know your actual birthday, then I am going to celebrate this day." Alec ran his hand along my cheek, silencing any other protests.

"Careful now, someone might think you actually care about me." I smiled, my eyes never leaving his.

The music thrummed in the silence between us. His gaze softened when he looked deeper into my eyes. His mouth hesitated to ask something that was clearly weighing on his mind. His thick, perfectly shaped eyebrows lifted when he finally got the nerve to speak.

"Are you happy?" he asked me.

Three simple words. My eyebrows pulled together. The answer should have been obvious, especially to someone as perceptive as Alec.

I looked at the party beside us, the flashing lights, the familiar faces. I noted Thayer and Nikki trying to pull Sage into the throng. Fiona danced with two human boys, both of their distracted minds completely unaware of their quickly dropping companions. Marshall stood at the food table, shoving another treat in his mouth. Even Grae smiled as he bounced up and down with the crowd.

This was my home. It always had been.

"Of course," I responded, looking back to him.

He let his shoulders relax at the sound of my words. I eyed him cautiously.

"Then I have kept my promise." He brought his other hand up to my face.

He leaned forward just enough to brush a kiss on my lips. As soon as his warm skin touched mine, my breath halted. He pulled away, leaving me scrambling to remind myself to breathe.

"What are you talking about?" I asked him playfully.

"Nothing." He shook his head.

I pushed him away enough to see his expression. He just smiled at me, his eyes flashing in the lights. That smile of his had steered me through much of my life. After Charles was killed, it had been just Alec and me, taking on the world.

"You guys all right back here?" Nikki's voice interrupted us.

I looked over at her. She was wearing the tightest, blackest clothes in the entire room tonight. Her matching black hair hung in straight tresses all around her small shoulders.

"Yeah, we're fine," Alec answered easily.

"Good, because I need to borrow Mara from you." Nikki grabbed my hand and pulled me closer to her and away from Alec.

"Who said I was willing to share?" Alec challenged, taking my wrist in his hand.

Excitement flared inside of me at the thought of Alec fighting for my attention. I looked back at him and nodded.

I'll be back, I thought, and allowed him to hear inside of my mind. He dropped his hold on my wrist reluctantly.

"Great," Nikki cheered. "Thayer's starting a challenge, and you do not want to miss this."

I smiled at her. She tugged me through the crowd and to the front of the circle quickly forming around Thayer and Grae. They circled around each other, readying themselves to fight it out. Thayer, still shirtless, stood tall as he took easy and slow steps. Grae crouched low to the floor, never taking his eyes off Thayer.

"These two again?" I mumbled.

Thayer threw the first punch. Instead of moving out of the way, Grae froze in place, his eyes wide with fear. I looked back to Thayer, carefully concentrating his stare on Grae. Thayer had him locked in.

His punch cracked across Grae's jaw, and the crowd cheered. Grae stumbled back, shaking his head as his eyes finally returned to the normal, brooding anger they always had.

"I know, I know. It's sad because we all know Thayer is going to win," Nikki whispered to me, her voice barely audible above the music.

"I heard that," Grae growled as he spat blood from his mouth.

"You were supposed to." Thayer smiled at him, easily bouncing from his right foot to the left foot and back.

It was harmless fun. Someone would break it up before it ever turned nasty. If Shadows wanted to get any better at their skills, they had to go up against the best.

"So, how are you adjusting back to everything?" Nikki asked me without taking her eyes off the boys in the middle.

"What do you mean? It's not like I was gone for that long," I scoffed.

"Well, yeah. But Alec told me about the Extractor. That must have been terrifying." She quickly changed her question.

Grae focused on the floor beneath Thayer, changing the hard stone to a slick, watery surface. Thayer took a step and slipped immediately. His body crashed against the floor just as it turned back into stone.

The crowd cheered even louder.

"To be honest, I don't remember it." I shrugged, trying to avoid thinking back.

Part of me hoped I would never be able to find that

memory. I couldn't imagine looking into that person's eyes ever again.

"Anyway, I'm glad you're back." Nikki smiled over at me. "This place was pretty boring without you."

Grae took a moment of concentration to create a Shadow's dagger in his hand. He was not too talented at creating, so it took more energy than it should have. Thayer looked up from the ground to see the dark metal flicker in the flashing lights.

In order to end the game, one of them had to mark an X on the other. So far, Grae had the upper hand.

"Oh, I seriously doubt that." I stared at the two of them. "You knew I'd come back eventually. No matter what happens between me and Alec, you and I will always be friends."

"Aw, you really mean that." She touched a hand to her chest and overly faked her doe-eyed expression.

"Of course I do." I bumped her with my hip. She relaxed her hand and smiled. "You're the best friend I've ever had."

Something inside me gnawed at the sound of my statement. It felt wrong, felt like I was forgetting someone that I cared about more. I furrowed my brow as I thought through my mind, but nothing came up. No one else that I thought of as a better friend.

Then I looked down at Thayer standing to his feet in the middle of the enclosing circle. Everyone's eyes eagerly watched him.

"Well the best one that's not a crazy, testosterone-raging idiot," I finished.

That still wasn't the right answer, but I accepted it for now. Nikki laughed as she looked over to Thayer, still scrambling on his feet.

"I heard that!" Thayer shouted.

The metal barely missed grazing his arm as he moved. Grae didn't skip a breath before he turned and lunged for Thayer again.

"You were meant to," I repeated, cupping my hands around my mouth so he could definitely hear me.

Alec walked forward, standing on the opposite side of the circle, watching me and Nikki together. I winked at him before my eye caught Thayer staring directly at Grae. Another mistake.

Grae instantly stopped lunging for Thayer. He just stood there as his arms relaxed by his sides. His hand barely even held on to the dagger. Those darkest eyes looked like they were watching a rainbow being born, and a small smile formed on his face.

Thayer won again. He walked forward and took the dagger from Grae's hand. Grae didn't move at all, too happy to care about anything. Thayer twirled the dagger in his hand, taking a step back so he could get a clean shot. Then, he stopped and looked up at me.

"Care to do the honors?" Thayer asked as he flipped the dagger in his hand so the hilt faced me.

"You don't want to take the credit for yourself?" I said, stepping forward because I already knew his answer.

Thayer never stood in the limelight for too long. In his mind, the glory always belonged to Alec, or me, or Nikki. Anyone but himself.

I took the dagger from his hand, the metal still warm from his body heat. He walked around behind me and put his hands on either of my shoulders. His bare body pressed against my back as he leaned into my ear.

"I have been waiting a long time to see this again," Thayer whispered to me, looking at Grae with that stupid grin on his face.

I glanced over at Alec, his face tight as he watched Thayer touching me. I smiled at him and watched as his bravado melted in front of me. His mouth, in a thin line, changed to that crooked smile that made my toes tingle.

"Take him down, baby." Alec nodded his head to direct me toward Grae.

I turned my attention back to the man that everyone was still looking at. I could see the fight in his eyes as he tried to get Thayer out of his mind. Once Thayer had a hold on you, it was nearly impossible to get him to relinquish unless you distracted him. Grae clearly hadn't figured that out.

I walked forward, standing just arm's length from Grae. Without a second of hesitation, I shot the dagger forward and sliced a diagonal line from his shoulder to his abdomen. The pain finally struck his eyes as his trance broke from Thayer. I quickly lifted the dagger again and slashed another line, forming a bloody X on his chest.

The game was over.

Thayer turned to the crowd and raised his arms above his head. Their cheers erupted. Even the remaining humans shouted because they were too drunk to realize that this meant danger for them. Thayer rushed over to Sage and threw his arms around her, lifting her off the ground. The surprise in her bright red eyes was priceless. Grae slinked off into the corner of the room, dragging a human male behind him.

I smiled and looked back at Alec. He walked forward, stretching a hand out to me.

"Let's get back to this amazing party. I think I know the party planner, and she would not be pleased if she found us playing games instead of enjoying ourselves." Alec laughed as he threw his arm around me, and the crowd converged around us.

"Is that so?" I played along with him.

He turned to face me and grabbed both of my hands again. He danced to the music and pulled me into the middle of the dance floor. My eyes locked on his intoxicating stare.

The loud music pumped through our bodies. The people all around bumped into one another, laughing as they all danced. I looked around the room at my accomplishment, noticing all the smiles that matched my own.

I spotted Grae dragging another human out of the dance and into the empty hallway. The person's limp body flopped next to the rest of them. Seeing them piled up, something pulled at my mind, telling me this was wrong.

My gaze wandered back to Alec, his eyes zoned in on only me. I smiled instinctively. He never strayed away from looking directly at me. I was the only thing that mattered to him. For that moment, that was all I needed.

We swayed, and Alec sang along to the lyrics of the song. The sound of his beautiful voice and my dark laughter soared into the night.

I leaned my head back and took a deep breath, hoping to remember every single moment of bliss.

CHAPTER
THIRTY

The next morning, I was still walking off the haze from the party.

Alec had left me alone in his room to run to a decision meeting, muttering something about the creators causing problems again.

I hopped in the shower and watched all the water wash the colors of last night away. I stepped out and scanned my closet and all my familiar clothes. Even though I recognized everything in there, it felt like I was looking at them through new eyes.

A nostalgic feeling swept over me. I quickly got dressed and charged off for the day.

I walked through the hallway and headed to the main corridor. I wanted to see what the agenda was for today. Around the corner, I saw a group of destroyers hanging out around the stairs and a few stragglers training in the courtyard. Nikki sat above all of them.

After spending a while talking with them, I decided to move on to something more fun when I caught of a whisper across the dull roar of the courtyard.

"It's too soon for that."

I couldn't make out who that voice belonged to.

"Nothing is going to change between now and then." That voice was clearly Grae's.

This sounded like the conversation we had walked into yesterday. I walked through the courtyard and noticed another newbie who was directly in my way. He looked up at me as I approached and scurried to move out of my walkway.

How many people did Alec recruit? I didn't realize he was even looking for other people.

"I know we don't have it yet. But we do have—" Grae continued as I approached the room they were in. My eavesdropping was interrupted when I heard someone come up behind me.

This time I recognized the footsteps before I turned around.

"Again?" I scoffed as I turned around to see Thayer standing behind me.

I had walked all the way through the courtyard and moved down the hallway. He did not just happen to be there. He had a reason.

"Ears burning?" he asked me, trying to shift the blame on me.

"Yes, what's going on in there?" I nodded toward the room. Instead of avoiding my question like last time, he answered right away.

"A surprise. You wouldn't want to spoil it, would you?" Thayer asked calmly.

I raised one eyebrow to show him I was suspicious. His grin didn't falter as he stared back at me.

"I don't like surprises." I ended that conversation and turned to continue walking.

"Mara," he tutted as he reached out to grab my arm.

I looked down at his hand and then back up at him in

disbelief that he would hold me back from what I wanted. Thayer and I were friends, but he and I both knew that I was determined to a fault. If I wanted something, I wouldn't stop for anything or anyone.

"Don't think just because you are Alec's friend that I won't rip your arm off," I threatened him politely.

His eyes sparkled as he took another meaning to my statement. He stepped closer to me and kept his hold on my arm. I timed my breaths to make sure they stayed even. He moved forward until his body was only separated from mine by our arms.

"Oh, come on, Mara. You and I both know that I'm a little more than just Alec's friend." He lowered his voice.

"Mmm, is that right?" I asked him, matching his low tone.

He cracked a smile across his perfect face. I looked into his eyes, watching the excitement rise. Thayer was a notorious ladies' man, and he knew it too. That was his blind spot, which was right where I liked to hide. His hand slid down to my wrist, still holding me in place. I reached my hand up and put it on his arm, holding him in place as well.

The longer I looked into his eyes, the more I felt I wanted to know what he knew. Pictures flashed across my mind. Things that I had never seen before.

Alec held me in his arms. I laughed as I pulled him closer to me. Our eyes only saw each other. Thayer walked in, almost colliding into us. An awkward second later, he left the room.

Thayer raced me down the hillside to the mansion. His foot came out and tripped me. My body launched into the air and I took him down with me. We ended up on top of each other, laughing.

Alec leaned into Thayer, talking in a hushed tone. The words were too muffled to understand. Safe was the only word I saw. Alec nodded to Thayer and patted his back. A look of guilt flashed across Thayer's eyes.

These were not pictures I recognized. Because they were not coming from me. They were coming from him.

As soon as I realized what was happening, I snapped back to the present moment and gawked as Thayer's smile began to drop from his face.

"Did you just...?" Thayer started to ask me and then stopped because he didn't even want to hear himself form the question aloud.

"I just read your mind, I think," I confirmed what he was thinking. "How could I have...I've never done that before, have I? That didn't feel like the first time."

Scattered thoughts flooded my mind. It was so easy to get into his mind. I felt everything he had felt. I understood him, somehow. None of this made sense. I remembered wanting to see his eyes earlier because I thought then I could know what he was thinking.

I swear I saw Thayer mutter. *Not again.*

The pit in my stomach ached again. Something was wrong. There was nothing I could do to ignore it now.

"Mara, what are you thinking?" Thayer asked me. He still held my arm in his hand. I shot my hand toward the floor to release his hold on me. My arm broke free.

"I need to talk to Alec."

I sprinted to the door and burst into the room. The conversation immediately halted as soon as I threw the door open. The only thing I could hear was the lack of sound from everyone holding their breath.

"Mara, are you okay?" Alec was the first to speak up.

"No, I'm not okay." I rattled off the long list of things

that seemed wrong: "There are too many new people for me to have only been gone a few days. Everyone keeps asking me if I am 'okay' or following me around. And I just read his mind. I can't read minds, not yet anyway. I'm a Three, I've never done that before. What's going on? Either I was gone longer, or something... I don't know. Alec, explain."

I threw all of that out with one breath. You could hear a pin drop on a pillow in that room. Alec still looked shocked by everything I unloaded. Grae looked like he was going to burst if he didn't say something. Thayer held his breath so quietly I almost forgot he was there. The others in the room just looked at me and Alec.

"Mara, come here." Alec opened his arms to me.

"No, I don't want a pat on the head telling me that everything will be fine. I want answers." I finished and did not take another step forward.

"I want to give you those answers, but I also want to help you know that everything is fine. Maybe I can do both?" Alec continued in a calm tone.

He stood from his leaning position against the couch and walked over to me. Each step he took made me more worried that I wouldn't get a straight answer.

"Then start talking," I asked as I took a step back. He paused.

"It was longer than a few days, you are right about that," he answered my first question. "I didn't think the exact length of time was relevant when you first woke up. The important thing is that you made it back safe."

I slightly relaxed as I heard him talk. His voice had that effect on me.

"As far as reading minds, you did pick an easy one to start with. Thayer isn't exactly a safe bet when it comes to keeping information. If you batted your eyes enough, he'd tell you anything you wanted to know," Alec continued to explain.

I glanced over to Thayer, still standing upright in the corner of the room.

"Come on, we both know he's not wrong." Thayer shrugged and relaxed enough to lean against the doorway.

His brilliant smile deflected the tension for a moment. I laughed and even more stress left my body. Maybe I was worried for nothing.

"We are all checking on you because none of us have had a run-in with an Extractor and lived. You're kind of a hero around here. As if you weren't already before," he finished.

Alec always knew just what to say. I believed him. I wanted to believe him. He finished his walk over to me and put both of his hands on my face. I felt my love for him sweep over me. I leaned my head into one of his palms. The longer he looked at me, the more I thought that maybe I was overreacting a bit.

"Could you guys give us a minute?" Alec asked without looking away from me.

Most of the people began to move out of the room on his command. Thayer stayed and walked toward Alec until he was in my line of vision too. Grae stayed where he stood.

"What about downstairs?" Grae asked looking directly at Alec. I saw Alec's eyes harden as he kept his gaze on me. Thayer shot a glance at Grae.

"What's downstairs?" I asked, looking from Grae to Alec.

I remembered Thayer had told me to avoid downstairs earlier too. My suspicion crept back into my mind. The floating feeling of appreciation for Alec's honesty faded. I lifted my head up again and stiffened as I waited for the answer.

"You persistent son of a—" Thayer began to chastise Grae through clenched teeth. Alec cut him off.

"Thayer, that's not helping." Alec looked directly at Thayer, but it seemed like he was warning him.

Thayer backed off immediately and closed his mouth. His eyes looked over to Grae instead.

"Boss, we have to do something," Grae spoke up one last time. Alec turned slowly to face him. Before he spoke, I took over.

"Then do something." I stepped around Alec and walked toward Grae. "Tell me what's downstairs."

I stopped walking when I was within reaching distance from Grae. He took a step back into the wall. There was nowhere else for him to go. He took a glance at Alec for confirmation. I looked at Alec too. He just stood there and shrugged his shoulders. That was my cue.

"What is downstairs?" I asked Grae again, slower this time so he could understand even through his nervousness.

I reached my hand forward and pulled Grae's face around to look at me. His dark eyes looked like they were going to explode. He kept trying to glance at Alec.

"Alec's not going to save you now. You better just talk." I sauntered closer.

He stared into my eyes, and the words were right there on the tip of his tongue. I just needed him to spit them out. I moved, and Grae flinched, waiting for something painful to come.

I smiled at his unwarranted fear. I hadn't done anything to him yet.

"Mara, I will show you everything you need to know," Alec interrupted from the back corner of the room.

I didn't take my eyes off of Grae. He was still breathing hard in anticipation of something bad.

"Grae, if I were you, I would leave," Alec sternly urged him.

Obediently, I took my hand off of Grae, giving him one second to decide that he wanted to heed Alec's warning. Grae bowed his head to Alec and left the room.

"Oh, please, I could've taken him." I turned to Alec to see why he wouldn't let me continue.

"I know, and I appreciate the scare you gave him. I just think it's something you need to see for yourself instead of being told." His voice carried through the room even though the tone was not that loud.

"Why?" I told him instead of asking him.

"Because downstairs is the man who tried to take you away from us." He kept his eyes firmly fixed on mine.

"Take me away..." I took a moment to process what he was saying.

Alec waited until I understood what he meant.

Downstairs was the Extractor. I took a sharp breath in, knowing the man that was almost responsible for my death was sitting just a few floors away.

"There's one more thing, Mara. He thinks he's in love with you." Alec finished his explanation that left me with more questions than answers.

We walked down the stairs to the dungeons in silence. Alec reached back and held my hand. I followed him past most of the cells. Some were empty. Others had a person in there. I peered into each one, trying to guess which one would hold the Extractor.

I looked ahead with my eyes watching every move, every flicker of light, everything. My instinct told me something was wrong.

Then again, maybe that was just the fear talking.

"What do you mean in love with me?" I asked Alec, trying to distract myself.

"He loves you. He made that very clear when we showed

up to get you. I'm not sure how long he spent with you, or what happened, but I do know this. He thinks that you love him too," Alec continued to explain.

"Excuse me? He almost killed me," I protested.

"I know that. You know that. This is why I said this is something you just need to see for yourself," Alec said with a sigh.

He stopped in front of the door to the cell. I looked at him to confirm this was the right one. He nodded his head. I looked inside the window through the door and saw a man sitting in the corner of the room. He sat there holding his head in his hands. He looked helpless and sad. He didn't look particularly threatening, but maybe that was what made him even more dangerous.

He had two thick chains clamped on his wrists. The inside of the chains glowed with a faint white light. They were tech-enhanced and not just metal. I would have to ask about those later. I had never seen them before. For now, I looked back at Alec.

"Thank you for answering my questions. I'm glad that I can trust you," I said, nodding.

I put my hand on his shoulder. He leaned in and kissed my lips softly. He was different around me. He was more gentle and kind. He loved teasing and playing games with everyone. When it was just the two of us, he was sweeter. It made me feel special, like I had a power over him too.

"You can always trust me. Don't you forget it." He nuzzled my nose as he pulled the door open to the dank, secluded cell.

A giggle escaped my mouth as I walked through the door. I turned and looked forward and looked at the man in the corner. He had light brown hair and strong shoulders that hung down.

"What do you want?" the man groaned as he lifted his head up.

His green eyes fell on mine and froze. His mouth opened like he wanted to speak but didn't know where to start. Seconds of silence passed as I studied him. His eyes were a perfect shade of green, like sunlight shining through a leaf. Chills immediately brushed across my arms.

"Kate," he finally breathed.

He stood quickly, and his chains clanged along with his movement. I furrowed my eyebrows and looked at him. I didn't speak. Something about seeing him brought a strange feeling to my stomach. My memory could not place him, but my body reacted otherwise. He realized something was different about me, and he took a step forward gently.

"Do you know who I am?" he asked softly.

He lifted his hands like he was trying to calm me. His chains clattered as they lifted from the ground. I looked at him directly and tilted my head to the side.

I allowed a small smile to spread across my face and watched him light up. This was going to be too easy.

"Of course I do. How could I forget?" I said sweetly.

His smile shone brightly in the harshly lit room. He stepped toward me excitedly until his chains stopped him from moving farther. I waited for him to release that breath he had been holding in.

Once I saw his shoulders finally relax, I couldn't hold back anymore.

My smile fell.

"You're the Extractor who tried to kill me," I growled.

I felt my stomach turn over when I saw how hurt he was by my accusation. He made me nervous, for sure.

But I had never actually talked with an Extractor before. The man looked away from me and looked pointedly at Alec.

"What have you done?" the man shouted at him. I turned to see Alec's response. He leaned casually against the back wall and smiled.

"I didn't do anything. She is the same Mara she has always been."

He walked up to me and slipped his arm around the small of my back. He looked at me with his adoring blue eyes. Then he focused his stare back on the man.

"You're the one who tried to change that," Alec said.

The man yanked against his chains like he wanted to hurt Alec. I instinctively put my hand in front of him. As he pulled, the inside of the chains glowed brighter against his skin. I watched as the man stiffened and then slumped even more than he did before. The chains were taking energy from him. I stared at the metal bands clasping his wrists. I had never seen anything like that before.

"What are these?" the man asked Alec as he glared at him. His fists were still clenched, but he didn't move again.

"Aren't they fun?" Alec asked with a smile. I listened to hear his explanation as well. "A new recruit brought those in from one of the labs as her audition to be à Shadow. They created them to take energy from a Legend as they use it for their powers. If they never use their energy, then they are just metal chains, ones that even a Legend can't remove without a key."

"How did the recruit get them?" I asked.

A Legend walking out of a lab on their own would be impossible. But walking out with valuable technology was even less plausible.

"She used to work there and decided to come to the dark side," Alec answered with a playful smile. He glanced back at the man standing there. "Now we can keep threats like him away from us."

"Kate, he's lying to you. I would never do anything to

hurt you." He was breathing heavily from his struggle. "I love you."

"You were right," I muttered glancing back at Alec. Alec exaggerated a nod so I could see it from the corner of my eye.

"It's almost like he actually expects you to love him back," Alec muttered, as if the man were not standing right in front of us.

The man clenched his fists. Alec casually walked back to the door and leaned against the doorway.

"Kate, don't listen to him. I am telling you the truth. I love you, and you did love me," he began his plea.

I looked into his light eyes and couldn't see a reason to not believe him. He must be a good liar.

"Please, you have to remember. Remember our bench under the tree when I asked you endless questions. Remember Rachel, Cassie, Lisa, anyone that you cared about. Remember our first kiss on the porch. You were so nervous. I wanted to be with you so badly, and that was the first time I ever thought you felt the same way." His words became slower and more fervent as he kept talking.

"You honestly think words are going to convince me of anything?" I asked, an eyebrow raised, waiting to see if he could anchor his lies to something tangible.

It should have been an impossible challenge. His eyes sparked for a moment as he reached into his pocket, pulling out a simple, gold locket.

It dangled in the air harmlessly, but I still stepped back.

"I was going to give you this. It used to mean something to you. When I saw your drawing, I was devastated that everything I had with you wasn't real. Then I realized that I could either risk losing you or never really know if you and I were meant to be. I made my decision, and I brought this with me to show you that I wanted you to have everything. I wanted you to be happy," he confessed.

I glanced back at Alec. His expression seemed unfazed by the reveal. He looked straight ahead at the man, avoiding my gaze completely. I turned back to look at the shimmering locket swinging inches from my face.

"Because that's what you do when you really love someone." He looked deep into my eyes and tilted his head to the side.

I had seen that head tilt before. I looked at his face and scanned my memory for any kind of recognition. I searched for anything that looked like the gold necklace he held in his hand. My fingers twitched in excitement. My breath shuddered.

I found no memory to prove anything he said was true.

"I can't remember something that never happened. I don't know what you dreamed up for us, but it's not real." I leaned forward so he could almost touch me.

I looked him directly in the eyes. His face froze in torn confusion.

After the confusion melted away, the anger began to burn in his eyes. The man looked directly at Alec instead of me.

"I will kill you for this," the man uttered through clenched teeth.

He wrapped the necklace chain around his fingers. He stood firm, understanding that yanking on his chains would be worthless.

"If you touch him, I will tear you apart from the inside out." The threatening words burned through me.

I linked eyes with him long enough before he could realize what was going on. He had left his mind wide open. Getting in was like attacking a mere human. He instantly clutched his head in agony. The scream came next.

He fell to his knees as his scream overpowered the sound of his chains clanging with his sudden movement.

I thought after a few seconds, he would fight back. He didn't.

I released my hold on him and his body slumped into kneeling on all fours. The necklace around his hand gave a quiet tinkling sound as it hit the stone. He looked up at me wearily.

His eyes were still kind despite the ringing headache of an aftershock I was sure he was feeling. I almost saw an understanding smile.

"I know this isn't you." His voice was barely above a whisper.

He tried to keep his eyes on mine, but he couldn't after a few seconds. His head hung back down to face the ground. My mind tried to reconcile what I just saw with what I already knew.

"Let's go. There is nothing down here for me." I turned around and made my way to the door.

Alec watched my face carefully. I turned to shoot one last scowl at the man.

"I love you, Kate. No matter what." He spoke, yet he was no longer looking at me.

His head hung and his wearied eyes locked with the ground. If I didn't know otherwise, I would say that he looked like he still retained a flicker of hope.

Alec looked back at the man too and smiled like he had just won a fight.

We left the room, and I listened to the door bang shut behind us. Alec grabbed my arm and gently turned me around to look at his face. We were still visible to the man through the window in the door. He was watching us with pain evident in his expression.

"How are you doing?" Alec asked gently. His eyes searched mine.

"That was not what I expected it to be like." I spoke the truth. "He's just... It's a good thing you were there to get me away from him. I don't know what I would do without you."

My hand moved up to the side of his face. My fingers swirled in his hair behind his ear. He stared intently.

I glanced at the Extractor through the window and watched the jealousy spark in his eyes. Triumphantly, I moved my eyes back to Alec.

"Have I told you how much I love you?" I whispered to Alec and pulled his face closer to mine.

"Not for a long time." Alec grinned. I leaned in until his mouth was firmly pressed against mine.

Alec began to move his mouth along with my lips. I could tell that he was excited and trying to speed up the kiss. I followed willingly, forgetting about our audience in the cell. I wanted Alec to know that I still belonged to him, despite what I had just seen.

He broke the kiss, and before he was even far enough away from my face for my eyes to focus, I could see his gleaming smile. My stomach twisted in an excited tangle.

I leaned forward again, and this time I hugged him close to me.

Behind his back, I looked at the Extractor in the cell. He was standing now and trying not to watch, but was failing. I smiled and caught his eyes just before he left his head fall in defeat.

I wanted to see his pain but, instead, it was almost like he was graciously bowing out. Something about that still bothered me. He had to understand the doomed fate ahead of him. Yet he wasn't fighting to be freed.

It was almost like he didn't have a reason to leave yet.

CHAPTER
THIRTY-ONE

Kylan

I slowly stood back up from the floor. My head still rang with a mild pain, but the worst was gone.

I backed up so the chains gave me enough room to hold the necklace up to my face. It had almost worked, I could see it in her eyes. After a few minutes of alone time, the door creaked open again. It was Alec, with a smirk as wide as the doorway that blocked my exit.

"Clever move with the necklace," Alec said and nodded toward my hand, which still clutched the gold chain.

"How does she know about it?" I asked Alec, hoping his expression might give something away.

"What makes you think she does?" Alec fired back at me, trying to play this off.

His deflection told me this little locket was quite important to him. I twisted the chain in my fingers, watching his eyes focus on it.

"She showed me a sketched picture of this exact necklace. You want to tell me that's a coincidence?" I explained.

He ignored the question. So this necklace was not just important, but crucial.

"I should have known you had it all these years. Of course, Mother left it with you," Alec continued on. He still lingered in the doorway.

"What stopped you from coming to get it then?" I taunted him and dangled the necklace at arm's length. "You've had decades that you could have come and asked for it."

"The same thing that is stopping me now," Alec sneered. "You."

His eyes stayed trained on me instead of the swinging necklace I held in my hand. I gloated about my ability for the first time in so long.

"What's wrong? Scared?" I tried to entice him to jump forward for it.

"No, just wise." Alec backed off.

I knew he wouldn't reach for it. As impulsive as Alec was, he was not stupid. Judging by the way he still kept his distance from me, these special chains would not prevent me from taking energy.

He knew one touch was all I needed to drop him like a rock, and Kate would never have to know what I was capable of. I felt a twinge of guilt at the thought of continuing to keep this secret from her. If I had been honest from the beginning, we wouldn't even be in this place.

As soon as Alec knew that I hadn't told her, he knew that I would come quietly to the mansion.

Now, I was stuck, out of reach and out of options.

"Father was thrilled when he heard his second son was an Extractor. He was so proud of you, so excited to teach you how to hone your skill. I wish he could see the nothing you became," he said, still bitter from a decades-old feud.

"We only lived together for twenty-eight years, but

you haven't changed at all. I can see how bad you want this necklace and how bad you want her. What's your plan here? Maybe I could help," I asked him genuinely, hoping I could appeal to his brotherly side.

"I don't need you. I am going to leave and continue living my life with her while you sit here and grow weaker from a lack of energy. Eventually, I will come back down here to this cell and pry that necklace from your cold, dead hands." His eyes were the coldest I had ever seen them.

I saw no remorse in his face about the fact that he was going to watch his only brother die. Well, that was definitely a no to the brotherly appeal. One thing I did know was that Alec wasn't the same boy I left behind.

"Why her?" I asked Alec my real question.

He had obviously played with her memory, but I could see in his eyes that he did care for her. I knew how amazing she was and why anyone with a brain would fall for her. The only thing I needed to know was why he was fighting so hard for her.

"The only thing I have seen you fight this hard for was Dad's approval. Did you ever end up with that either?" I waited.

"He died before I got to ask him." Alec kept his gaze steady and his face blank.

He was never overtly emotional as a child, but time had made him cynical. The news was not surprising considering who Father was, but it still hurt. Then, I remembered.

"The Extractor..." I nodded slowly, finally understanding Kate's story of how her father-figure died.

That was Charles.

"Ironic, isn't it? The very thing that Father wanted you to become was what ended up taking his life." Alec smiled a weary smile, like he had been carrying this pain for a while.

"Maybe if he could have seen the future, he would have looked at you like the killer you are."

"I'm not that person anymore." I looked directly back at him and clenched my fists.

"Please." Alec waved a hand to dismiss my comment. "People don't change. I remember all those secret trips behind Mother's back. I can still picture that look on your face when you felt their final energy flow into you. Legend energy. It felt good, didn't it?"

"Stop," I talked over him. He finally stopped talking when he noticed he hit a nerve. "Things haven't been that way in a long time."

"Right, because you instantly turned good the day Mother yanked you away?" He raised his eyebrows, waiting for his answer.

I didn't say anything. Alec would know if I was lying. Any information I gave him would become fair game to be used against me.

"Don't tell me—did golden boy have a mean streak?" Alec almost laughed at me.

I still kept my silence. Memories I had long buried came flooding back. When Mother passed away, I was angry and alone. Scared faces of those I took it out on came flashing across my mind. I wasn't a Shadow, but I acted worse than one.

I was reckless and ruthless. The only thing that pulled me out was when I looked in a mirror and couldn't even recognize myself. I was so infused with energy it was almost bursting from my eyes.

But that was all I saw. No emotion, no smile, no future, no purpose. I was nothing.

When I finally hit rock bottom, there was nowhere else to run. That's when I decided to change things around.

Shortly after, I had met Derek. I never wanted anyone to feel that crushing loneliness that nearly drove me insane.

I allowed the past to stay buried. No one knew what I was capable of, not even my family.

"And I'm guessing your precious Kate doesn't know?" Alec looked at me with new interest, like he finally had the edge on me after all these years.

"You aren't exactly one to judge. You are probably the worst person I have ever met." I glared back at him, wanting to pull against my chains but understanding that would only drain my energy further.

"See, but I never lied about it. I have always been perfectly clear about who I am," he threw back at me.

"A monster? What has that gotten you other than a horde of followers compelled only by their fear of you and a girl that you brainwashed into falling for you?" My anger came bursting out with every word.

He deserved to know exactly what I thought of him and his sick lifestyle. Alec narrowed his eyes at me.

"Yet here I am, moments away from getting everything I want, and you are just out of reach of what you want. Must be torture, huh?" Alec grinned.

I looked into his eyes, and I couldn't see the brother that I knew all those years ago. I only saw the man he had become. He was heartless and cruel. The only true affection he showed was to my Kate. If I had ever hoped to get my brother back, that was long gone now. He was consumed with taking down the labs and keeping Kate with him, no matter what.

"And you need her for that?" I guided the conversation back to focus on him and why he needed Kate.

"Yes." Alec finally gave me a straight answer. "You have no idea what she means to me."

The way he talked about her gave me chills. I could tell, in some nauseating way, that he cared about her.

"Ripping away her memories is wrong, even for you." I couldn't look at him anymore.

"Well, you aren't exactly doing anything about it. You could have avoided all of this if you had told Kate what you were. You could have stopped this back in the forest. But you didn't because Kate would find out and you might lose her," Alec calmly taunted me.

The anger slowly boiled inside me. I clenched my fists to keep myself from losing it.

"Let me ask you this. Is it still worth it? She doesn't know about you, but you still lost her." His voice only made my guilt feel heavier.

"I didn't lose her. You stole her and forced her to become what you wanted. She clearly doesn't want anything to do with you. You had to block her memories just to get her to comply! Your master plan is being held together by her believing your lie," I almost growled at him.

I started putting the necklace back in my pocket. I may have had the locket, but he had the plan and the girl.

"From what I saw in her eyes just now, that won't hold together much longer. Looks like you have finally met your match," I said.

"But she doesn't know that. As long as she believes she is inferior to me, she will act like it. Then, what do I really have to fear?" Alec smiled as he saw me realize his point. "You and I both know the mind is a vastly powerful thing. She is only as strong as she thinks she is."

Unfortunately, he was right in that aspect. Kate was the only one who could free herself. As long as she believed Alec was stronger, she would never challenge him, and she couldn't understand her power until she did.

It was a perfect paradox.

I yanked against the chains again, willing them to shatter. In return, I felt more of my energy being pulled from my body.

I focused hard to even breathe. I hadn't felt so weak in a long time. That didn't stop the rage from boiling under my skin. If Alec stood a few inches closer, things would look much different.

That only made Alec smile more.

"Please, struggle all you want. That only makes my goal of wearing you down even easier." Alec looked at me one last time.

"Goodbye, brother." Alec nodded at me like he always nodded when he was done with a conversation.

The heavy door slammed shut behind him. I sank to the cold floor. The hate swelled inside of me so forcefully it almost blocked out the ache in my heart. I saw her. Her changed face, her blond hair, the cruelty in her eyes. She was still my Kate, but she looked nothing like the woman I remembered anymore.

We were both trapped, and I was determined to change that in any way I could.

THIRTY-TWO

I stared at the ceiling that night.

The familiar texture swirled in sparse patterns above me, leaning back in the oversized chair in my room. I tried to make shapes out of the raised parts as my mind wandered.

I couldn't stop going back to thinking about the Extractor downstairs. I knew he was perfectly harmless unless I touched him. He was no threat to me. Yet, I couldn't get him out of my head. I thought about that necklace he was holding.

Why did it look so familiar? I couldn't place it with a memory of mine.

What could be so important about a little locket anyway?

I tried to block the thoughts from my mind enough that I could move on. I focused on my breathing until the thoughts finally subsided. My mind unwillingly drifted off, and I felt my breathing slow as sleep enveloped me.

I stood in the middle of an old house. It was tiny and charming, especially for the early 1800s, but had little in it. I couldn't see out the window to look at where it was located. It was just me in this back room looking for a purpose to be here. I heard footsteps hurrying into my room. I could not quite see the face of the woman that walked in. I knew she was familiar to me and that I trusted her. She knelt down in front of me and reached for my hands.

"I don't know how much time we have, sweetheart, and I'm sorry that I have waited this long. I just wanted to make sure you were ready, but you are still so young." She brushed my face gently.

"This is something that was given to me by my mother, and now I am going to give it to you. She always told me that it was the key to a long, happy life. She was right." The woman touched the locket around her neck and began removing it as she spoke.

She now held the locket in her hand, closing her eyes and concentrating. The locket glowed faintly through the spaces in her fingers.

"I love you, more than you know." She handed the locket to me and kissed my forehead.

I felt her warm skin touch my small forehead. I remember feeling confused and scared, but when she held me I was safe. I only wanted to know what was going on, but by the look on her face, now was not the time to ask.

I heard a bang from the front of the house. The woman's head jerked around to face the sound. She stood slowly, and I watched as her hands clenched tight enough to force the blood out of her fingertips.

She walked out of the room, her steps creaking on the wooden floor, and left me alone in the corner.

My heart went out to her. I wanted her to come back and hug me and tell me that everything was going to be okay.

I heard scuffling in the other room, and I clutched the locket. As I did, I felt the warm feeling I had felt earlier when she held me. I scooted into the corner. I was lonely and scared, and I just wanted—

I jolted awake and gripped the seat under my hands.

I looked around until my mind worked out where I was. My breathing calmed, and I released the now-rippled fabric from my grasp. I ran my fingers through my hair to move it out of my face.

This didn't feel like a dream. It was too tangible. I saw the woman but couldn't see her face. I saw the cute, old house. I saw the necklace.

My conscious mind reviewed the dream, and as I thought about the necklace, it looked too familiar. I raked across my mind and realized it was the same locket I had seen the man downstairs holding.

The exact same locket.

If that was real, then it couldn't have been a dream. It almost felt like a memory.

I thought about the feeling the necklace had given me in the dream. I never had a mother, so I couldn't truly picture what that feeling could be like. But I remembered holding the necklace in my hand. I felt it. The warm, safe feeling fluttered through me.

I thought about what it would have actually felt like to have my mom holding me in her devoted arms. The thought spurred that warm feeling straight into my heart, where it melted.

I love you, more than you know. The phrase echoed in my mind. As it did, I felt stronger because of it. I sat up in my bed and looked forward, wondering. The longer I let the feeling build, the more I thought about the dream.

About my past.

Slowly, my past life that I stored in my memories expanded in my mind. My thumping heart continued to override what my logic was so strongly denying.

The mental wall came crashing down and everything came flooding back in. Memories came shooting through my consciousness. The information seemed freshly buried, and now it was rising to the surface.

I remembered my life as a Shadow. I remembered the fight with Alec. I could see myself leaving the mansion like I was watching the decision for the first time.

"Please. Catch me if you can."

"Let her go."

I looked further and pressed for my mind to give me more. I momentarily re-lived each persona I became after I left the Shadows. The memories made their way to the most recent transition.

I said goodbye to Tylee, the rough, dark-skinned, shorthaired woman before who loved the outdoors.

Each memory brought the emotions I felt after being that person. At last, I remembered being Kate and stepped into her shoes.

Now, I looked at Kate the sweet, new woman that existed as my reflection.

I could see the vision in my mind like I was watching a movie of Kate's life, of my life. The events unfolded before me as I slowly remembered.

"Ms. Martin, what a pleasure it is to finally meet you."

"Thank you, Mr. Lyle, I am excited to be here."

Finally, I saw a pair of welcoming green eyes flash across my mind, accompanied by a smile that I could not believe I had forgotten. Kylan.

"You know, I think you and I are going to get along."

"It's possible. Goodnight, Mr. Beck."

"Kylan." He corrected me.

"Kylan." I nodded.

"See you tomorrow, Kate."

I felt my love for him bursting through the seams of the vision. It encompassed everything. All these memories finally brought me to the most recent.

"I love you, Kate. No matter what."

He was here, and he loved me, despite finding out what I was.

My heart erupted with excitement as I thought of everything being on the table, and him still choosing me. He was mine, and I was his. I took a moment to catch my breath and sort through all the memories that had all presented almost simultaneously.

I shot out of the chair. The love of my life was downstairs in a cell. I ran through scenarios of how we could escape. I decided if I was going to do something, it would have to be soon. I spent the next few minutes listening carefully to the few traffic patterns happening during this time of night. I wanted to plan the route with as much detail as possible.

After what seemed like far too long, I decided that it was now or never and cracked open the door to my bedroom. I took the first step out of the room and let out a breath of air. I was confident this was going to work. I had to be.

I tensed my muscles and carefully walked down to the dungeons below.

I tiptoed down the hallway and made it all the way to the stone stairs leading down to the dungeons. I carefully laid each foot on the next step so as not to make a sound. I was grateful that as Mara, my main shoe choice was a sneaker, silent and sturdy.

Once I reached the bottom floor, I stopped and listened again.

It was all clear.

I stepped carefully down the hallway, already sensing Kylan was near. My heart pumped faster, and I could feel the blood rushing through my body. Not only was I about to see him, I was about to save him. I smiled.

For a moment, my concentration lapsed, and that was when it all started.

CHAPTER
THIRTY-THREE

"Where are you headed?" someone said behind me.

I almost jumped out of my own skin. I flipped around to a defensive stance and my eyes snapped up to see who was there.

Grae stood behind me, his dark skin blending in too well with the dim lights of the dungeon. I narrowed my eyes at him, just like Mara would have. After all, to him, nothing had changed.

"I could ask you the same thing, creep. I could've hurt you," I insulted instead of answering his question.

I was shocked by the words as I said them. It made me realize what a brash personality I had as Mara.

"But you didn't." He stared at me, his eyes wondering too many questions.

I kicked myself for no longer having the knee-jerk reaction to hurt people who threatened me.

"No, you lucked out this time," I said.

I wanted him to try and contradict me aloud. I wanted to hear what he was thinking from his own mouth, even if I already knew his suspicion.

I kept walking forward to the next cell. I looked inside,

ANGIE DAY

and a young boy lay in the corner of the room. My shoulders weighed down with guilt. I didn't want to do this.

Mara would have been thrilled by the chance to hurt another human. Kate appreciated humans, even loved some of them. Kate had learned that they are not all alike, and most of them are not bad at all.

Unfortunately, I couldn't be Kate right now. I yanked open the door and looked back toward Grae.

"Haven't you ever heard of a midnight snack?" The words slithered out of my mouth too naturally.

The boy stirred as he heard the door open. He sat bolt upright as soon as he saw me. I walked toward him and bent down so I was almost eye level with him.

"Who are you? What do you want?" he asked, tears pooling in his eyes.

He blinked furiously to hold them back. He almost choked on his own words. This kid was terrified. He must have been brought here without any kind of explanation. I imagined that horror for him. Waking up in a new place with nothing and no one that was familiar.

I could see bags under his eyes and his lips were chapped. He had been here for a while. My heart ached for him.

"You all do ask the same questions," I muttered to the boy, my voice void of any emotion. It was easier than choking back the hurt.

I moved my hand so it was over his hand that lay flat on the cold floor. His eyes narrowed as he tried to figure out what I meant by that.

"Please just let me go," he begged, looking directly at me.

"I can't do that." I tried to smile and somehow let him know I didn't want to hurt him.

I knew he couldn't possibly believe me, but I couldn't blame him for that.

"Everything is going to be okay, you'll see." I nodded as my smile slowly fell from my face.

I began to leech the energy from where my hand touched his hand. His eyes widened in surprise, and then they slowly fell until they closed.

He slumped on the ground. I could sense the small amount of energy in his body. It was enough to keep him going, but not enough to keep him awake. A night's sleep should allow him to recover.

I felt a lump in my throat as I looked at his uncomfortable position. I wanted to adjust him so he could sleep better, but Grae was watching me. I couldn't touch the kid now.

The new energy coursing through my veins sharpened my vision and strengthened my muscles. I stood up and felt the warmth radiate from me. I turned to face Grae.

"Looks like you left a little behind?" Grae questioned as he watched the kid's chest continue to rise and fall. I turned around and looked at the kid behind me for the last time.

"Looks like it." I shrugged my shoulders and looked back at Grae. "Oh well. Then he can sleep it off and be ready again for tomorrow. Plus, I'm not going to bend all the way back down there just to pick up the scraps. It's not worth the stretch."

I didn't need to look at him to know that Grae was narrowing his eyes at me. He knew exactly what I thought of him, and nothing had changed in the past few decades. Slashing an X through his chest the other night should have proven that.

The new energy swirled around inside of me. I truly didn't want to hurt this kid. Even looking in his eyes broke my heart but with the extra energy, I could now do this.

I left the door to the cell open behind me. Grae followed me out. I paused and took a deep breath. All at once, I spun around kicked Grae square in the chest. He slammed back into the side of the wall. I had left the door open just enough that he missed hitting the metal and creating a loud sound for everyone in the mansion to hear.

I crouched down. Instead of waiting for him to gain his stance, I reached for him.

I grabbed him by the neck and closed my hands around his throat. His breathing immediately stopped. I pulled him back up to a standing position, holding him just slightly off the ground. If this was going to work, Grae couldn't scream to alert the others.

His hands shot up to grab mine. He was still spinning from having the wind knocked out of him. He looked directly at me.

"I knew it," he croaked out. "Alec's plan failed."

"Then why did you push me to find out?" I questioned him.

"We had to know if you were committed before—" he cut off his words mid-sentence, still struggling to speak.

He twisted in my hands, glaring at me as he changed his train of thought.

"Maybe you weren't worth all the hype to begin with," he sneered and brought his hand down from my hand and reached for his pocket.

A dagger flashed in his hand. I recognized the shape of the knife instantly. An image of the same dagger was engraved on both of our arms. My eyes widened.

"This isn't a game, Grae," I snarled at him, warning him to drop the knife.

"No, it's not," he answered, gripping the dagger even tighter in his hand.

Now I knew what it was like to stand on the opposite side of that dagger.

He shoved the knife forward before I could dodge it completely. He sliced through my shirt and grazed my side. The pain burned into my body. Grae drew his hand back and before I could suck in a breath, a hand shot forward and grabbed onto Grae's wrist.

I ignored the trickle of blood coming from my sliced skin. Instead, I watched, intensely focused, as the unthinkable happened.

Energy swirled from Grae's body into the hand that had grabbed him. The bright yellow light was impossible to mistake.

I was petrified where I stood, not even daring to breathe.

I hadn't seen anyone take energy from a Legend since Charles was killed. Overcoming my daze, I spun my head to look at who was doing this. My eyes met a pair of familiar, green eyes looking back at me.

Kylan.

Grae began to weaken in the knees, and he fell to the ground when I freed my hold on his neck. I just stared at Kylan standing right behind me. My eyes filled with shock as I took a staggering step away from him.

"Alec was telling the truth about one thing." Kylan stepped back to give me my space. He stood to his full height, and I could see the new energy glowing in his eyes.

"How did you get out?" I asked quickly, still not daring to move.

"Some idiot walked by my cell swinging the key a little too closely. Shadows are too arrogant for their own good. I caught hold of him, and now he is asleep in my cell. I was just waiting for the right time to leave, then I heard your voice," Kylan explained calmly, not wanting to startle me.

It was so good to hear his voice again, and this time

through ears that knew him. The calm feeling melted some of my fear.

"You really are an Extractor?" I edged closer to him.

"Destroying cells. You asked me earlier what I couldn't do. I have the other Four Levels besides that one," he said, finally honest. "That was one of the reasons my mother took me away from this place. She knew the monster I would become if I stayed here. Alec never forgave my betrayal."

"He never forgave mine either. I thought I was the first person to ever walk away." I laughed a bit, feeling more tension release from my muscles.

I was reminded of my appalling past that he had accepted. Maybe I could do the same for him.

"No, you're not that special," Kylan joked easily as if we weren't standing in a dungeon in hostile territory.

His eyes sparkled with a renewed hope. I had realized how much I needed to see it. All my muscles relaxed now as I looked up at his confident eyes.

"I guess not." I smiled at him.

Kylan reached into his pocket and pulled out the necklace he had shown me earlier.

"This was a necklace that my father gave to my mother when they were still together. I'm not sure how you found out about it, but I knew I had seen it before. When I saw that you had it, I thought..." he struggled for words.

"You thought they sent me to get it from you," I finished for him, now understanding his reaction to seeing the sketch in my house.

"I decided to trust you. It took me a few hours to even find it. I was going to give it to you in the forest before..."

He didn't pursue that sentence. Instead, he handed me the infamous locket.

I turned it over a few times. It was made of soft gold with a delicate chain. I moved my fingers to open it.

"You can't open it." Kylan stopped me from trying as he unclasped the chain to place it around my neck. "My mom tried for a long time, but it's sealed shut. Nothing opens the locket."

"Why?" I asked.

He shrugged his shoulders. I kept looking at him as he moved his hands around my neck to fasten the necklace on me. I tried not to shudder when his skin touched mine. Having an Extractor, even Kylan, this close was unnerving.

"I'm sorry." Kylan pulled his hands away. "I know this changes things. I should've told you sooner."

I looked up at his perfect green eyes as I straightened the necklace on my neck. I closed my eyes. I coaxed my cells to change their shape to the form I most wanted to be. I felt my hair, skin, and entire look changing back. I opened my eyes and saw my reflection in Kylan's eyes.

"You're still you. I'm still me." I smiled at him.

The person who stood by me and cared about me despite my past. Despite everything, he still wanted me.

"Kate." He put his hands on either side of my new face and kissed me gently.

My heart flew through the roof when his lips touched mine. A flurry of hope brushed through my entire body. My hands held on to him like he was the one thing keeping me from falling apart. Everything around me faded as my breath mingled with his.

We were going to make it out of here, alive.

"Mara." Alec's voice echoed through the hall behind us.

CHAPTER
THIRTY-FOUR

I spun around and stood defensively in front of Kylan, not that he needed my protection.

Alec stood, looking at us with jealousy raging in his eyes. Thayer stood directly behind him with the same expression. Both of them were witnessing a major loss.

"It's over, Alec," I spat at him. "Your plan didn't work."

Alec moved closer to us, undeterred. He stepped over Grae's sleeping body slumped against the wall. He focused all of his attention on us.

"You know, Mother swore she didn't know where it was," he continued to speak. "She is a better liar than I thought."

"Don't talk about her like that." Kylan clenched his teeth, and his knuckles turned white.

"Simmer down. That's not the point of the story." Alec interrupted Kylan's anger like he wasn't staring at a death threat. Instead, he just kept on talking.

"This locket belonged to Lydia Hayes, the first Legend. She sealed it so that only her posterity could open it. She wrote in her journal about this locket and said it held the key to all her power, how it would be the thing that might save us all. This locket was thought to be a myth, but it was instead a well-kept secret."

"Why would this locket be so important to you then? You need Lydia's son or daughter to open it. She never had any children." I tried to connect the dots.

It was widely known in Legend culture that Lydia escaped the lab after she was created. She was the strongest to ever exist, the only Level Five. The scientists never repeated their mistake of giving one person all the power again. When she left and freed the others, she lived and died alone.

But Alec wouldn't risk everything for something he knew wouldn't work anyway. I narrowed my eyes at him, watching his every movement.

"So the legend says." Alec kept his eyes trained on the locket.

He looked at it like it was the answer to his prayer.

"Enough with your ambiguity. Just let us go. You can't keep us down here forever," Kylan spoke up and took a step toward him.

"I know," he admitted. His shoulders seemed a little more slumped than usual.

Was he actually giving up? That was before I saw the fire ignite in his eyes. My shoulders fell.

"But that doesn't mean I can't try," he finished and lunged forward.

Thayer and he both leaped into action at the same time. Kylan stepped around me and grabbed Alec by the shirt just as Alec snatched the necklace from off my neck. The delicate chain snapped against me.

Thayer wrapped his arms around my waist and tackled me to the floor.

"Don't do this, Alec! I'll kill you!" Kylan shouted as he tossed Alec against the wall.

"You won't." Alec shoved back hard against Kylan and threw him against the opposite wall. "I know you. You're weak. Even now, when your own life is in danger, you still can't."

Alec threw a punch across Kylan's face. His head snapped to the side, as I heard a bone shift under Alec's fist. Kylan staggered back before turning his calculating eyes on Alec.

"Maybe not for my own life. But for her, I could." Kylan lunged forward again and reached for Alec. Alec dodged his grasp and kicked his legs out from under him.

I struggled against Thayer's arms but knew that his strength was something I could not match. I thought about how it feels to take energy from a human and how convenient it would be to be able to use that and take Thayer down.

I could end all of this right now.

I focused on Thayer's hands that held my arms from swinging at him and wished that I could rip the energy from him but settled for clawing my hands at any piece of skin I could grab. I watched the others as Kylan spun around and grabbed Alec by both of his upper arms.

Alec smiled and looked at me, watching every move. That's why he wasn't afraid of Kylan in the forest. I didn't know about Kylan's power yet, which made Alec safe in front of his brother for the first time.

"You're out of luck, brother. She knows." Kylan's own smile grew as Alec's immediately turned ice cold.

His ace up the sleeve was gone. The bright energy began flowing from Alec's arms into Kylan's hands. The insane amount of energy running in Alec's body was probably more than Kylan had tasted in decades. The glow of pleasure shined in his bright green eyes as he held on. Eventually, Alec could not hold himself up anymore, and Kylan let him drop to the stone floor. Now it was Alec kneeling in front of Kylan.

At the same time, I noticed out of the corner of my eyes that Thayer's hands were glowing. I felt the energy rushing into my system.

Alec was staring at me with the same look. I watched the shock on Alec's face diminish as his energy sapped away. His face fell even more when he saw the energy flowing around my own arms.

If human energy was enticing, then Legend energy was out of this world. Compared to this, taking a human's energy sounded like settling for stale bread. It would do the trick, but it was not nearly what would satisfy.

Every cell in my body seemed to shatter to make room for this new energy. I couldn't think a coherent thought long enough to breathe or move.

All I could do was feel.

Alec's hands hit the floor as he gawked at me with wide eyes.

"I'm too late." Alec's words came out forced as he struggled to keep his eyes open.

Despite his lack of energy, his hand still clasped the locket.

Thayer had finally relinquished his hold on me and staggered back.

I stared in fear at my free hands. I felt his strong energy crazing through me. He leaned against a wall, sliding to the floor. He must barely have any energy remaining in his body. It was smart of him to let go when he did.

"Kate, how is that possible?" Kylan looked at me, just as

confused as me. "I thought that was the one Level you didn't have?"

"It is," I breathed.

I looked down at my body and then back at Thayer's weak frame behind me. I looked up at Alec to explain. "I would have to be a Level Five, and that is not possible."

"It is possible. Unlikely, but possible." Alec said, breathing hard from a lack of energy.

"This is what you were hiding from me all those years," I commanded him now. "Why? How?"

"Contrary to popular belief, Lydia Hayes did have one daughter..." Alec stopped talking to set the locket on the floor and shove it forward.

"You."

The locket skipped across the stones and stopped promptly near my feet.

I picked it up from the ground and tugged at the centered clasp. I watched as the locket glowed momentarily in my hand and the clasp released with a faint click.

It was true.

Before I finished opening the locket, I returned my gaze to Alec.

"We needed you to realize your full potential, but before we could hand this power to you, we needed to know you would stay, and we needed the locket. We couldn't take on the main lab in Louisiana without it. You remember what happened the last time we tried that," Alec explained in a breathy voice from his sitting position on the floor. He was still too weak to stand.

"How did you know I was her daughter?" I asked him frankly.

All the stories about her were wrong. The look on Alec's face told me that he knew something I didn't. At this point, I was quite used to that look coming from him.

"I was there the night she died." Alec's shameful eyes lowered.

"How did she die?" I asked.

My voice cut through the silent air in front of me. My mind was reeling. I had a mom. I had a mother. All this time...

"She was killed," Kylan spoke in place of Alec. "The last straw for my mom was when she heard of my father and his 'team' killing a Legend. Up until then, they had only murdered humans. That was Lydia?" Kylan looked at Alec now too.

I could see in his eyes that he already knew the answer. So did I.

My eyes darted from Kylan back to Alec. "You killed my mother."

"I was there that night Father found Lydia's home. My job was to find you, and he was going to take care of the rest. We had only heard rumors about a possible child of Lydia's. Once I saw you huddled in the corner there, I told him we had found you. I still remember her scream when she knew that there was nothing she could do to protect you anymore." Alec's eyes closed.

For the first time, it almost looked like he felt guilty.

"If she was the most powerful Legend, how could you have killed her?" I questioned further, still clutching the locket in my hand.

"She was protecting you. She couldn't take us all without her full focus. We knew that," Alec spoke slowly so I could follow.

He reached his hand back to the wall behind him. He winced and pressed with all of his strength to give him enough leverage to stand. He held close to the wall for support, his breathing ragged.

I looked down at the locket in my hand. The soft gold tempted me to unlock its contents. Years of searching and here it finally was, sitting helplessly in my hand.

How could a trinket so small hold all that it is told to keep?

I scowled at Alec's anxious eyes. There was nothing I could do to hold back my anger.

"All of those years...All of this was so you could carry out your vengeance on the humans?" I stared at Alec, hoping there was some other motive that I couldn't see. He couldn't be this heartless.

But he was raised that way. Alec was just a product of what Charles made him. I hissed at the memory of the man I thought was a father to me. Alec's gaze broke away from mine. It was all the answer I needed.

"I had a mother...I had...You stole everything from me! You actually let me believe that I was in love with you." I screamed at him.

Then I whispered my last question, "How can you live with yourself?" I honestly wanted an answer to that one.

"I wasn't supposed to fall for you. It was just supposed to be business. After Father died, I couldn't stop myself. I just...I needed everything you offered. You and I were perfect for each other." He stumbled and for the first time was out of words. "That...that part wasn't a lie. I truly loved you."

"That's not love, Alec."

His muscles clenched at my rejection. Now that I knew everything, I could decide for myself how I truly felt about him. This was his one chance to know what it would be like if I knew everything.

"Please don't go," he gasped, almost completely out of breath.

He stumbled forward a few more steps before falling on his knees, directly in front of me. He grimaced in pain as he hit the floor.

"You don't actually expect me to stay after all that," I challenged.

"Please, at least open the locket. I have waited decades for this day. You have no idea," he asked, reaching for it instead of me.

"You're right." Kylan said, "She couldn't know what this must be like for you. Everything you ever wanted is right in front of you, and yet someone is taking it away. Must be torture, huh?"

Alec's head bowed gently to the floor. He knew what he was asking of me. Yet, he couldn't help himself. He had been groomed since birth to be the monster he was now. Nothing could change that. I bent down gently to his level and caught his eyes with mine.

"When you love someone, you want them to be happy, right?" I reiterated my words from earlier. "Let me be crystal clear about this. I loved you, Alec. You were everything I ever wanted."

His eyes looked suspicious at first. I waited patiently with an understanding smile masking my face. I waited until I saw it.

Hope.

I saw a flash of excitement in his eyes that meant he was expecting to get what he wanted even though he had lost. That was the moment.

"Thanks to you, those feelings are gone." I stood and turned away from him.

"You know where to find me, if you need me." Alec's voice somehow still had pride in it.

I spun around and looked him dead in the eye. His offer was sincere, although more of a threat, meaning that I would need him someday.

"I won't need you. I never did," I promised.

Only Alec could still show strength while kneeling on the floor.

I stood proudly and walked with Kylan to the stairs leading away from the dungeons and into the rest of the mansion. A small part of me wondered if I ever would see this place again.

We walked past every Shadow who had heard the commotion downstairs. I looked into the eyes of the people who not only betrayed me once, but twice. I had no idea how many of them knew who I actually was. Maybe Alec never told them.

Kylan followed behind me as we walked past the courtyard. Before I could turn down the main hallway to get to the front door, Nikki stood in my way.

"You knew, didn't you?" I asked her.

She didn't lower her gaze or step aside.

She just looked at me with growing contempt in her eyes. She crossed her arms in front of her chest.

"You can still choose to stay," she offered, a glimmer of hope in her eyes. "If you walk out that door now, we are done."

She looked straight at me with her piercing brown eyes. I felt Kylan's hand touch my shoulder. I appreciated the support. The person before me was someone I had called a friend for the majority of our lives.

But all of that was over.

"No. We were done the second you sided with Alec instead of me." I glared at her.

Her eyes widened, surprised that I would actually

choose to leave this mansion, to leave her. She took a breath in and narrowed her eyes at me. Nikki stepped to the side, allowing me to walk toward the exit that I had been dreaming about.

This was the last time I planned to set foot in this place. The last time I left too quickly to care. While the mansion held many bad memories, it was my home at one time.

I would always remember these walls.

Kylan yanked on the thick door in front of him. The door swung widely at his beckon. I stepped through from the cold, stone floor to the fresh, soft earth. The sun peeked through the trees, and the cool air breezed across my face.

I took my first breath of freedom.

No running, or hiding, or deceiving ahead. I was truly free this time. Alec could find me if he wanted to, but it would all be pointless now. I reached my hand out to Kylan and he wrapped his fingers around mine.

"You're a free woman now," Kylan remarked gently. His eyes glowed with pride as he looked at me. I could feel his love and admiration radiating from him. "Where would you like to go first?"

I looked back at Kylan's bright green eyes. His warm, inviting smile would be there every day from here on out. Thoughts of exotic places and fun adventures flashed through my head.

However, there was one constant in all of them. Kylan. I could go anywhere and do anything, yet at this moment, my heart didn't yearn to be unleashed the way I thought it would. I wanted something I hadn't wanted in a long time.

After all my searching, I found it.

I had a long road ahead of me with new questions and answers to find. In that respect, not much had changed. The one thing that was different this time was that I was no longer alone.

I had Kylan, and he had me. Together, there was nothing we couldn't do. So, I answered his question with the truest honesty I had expressed since I met Kylan.

"Let's go home."

THE END

TO THE READER:

Writing this book has been a dream and I am thrilled to share this story with you. I could not be a published author without readers like you that want to pick up a book. In the age of the internet, I know there are plenty of options out there for entertainment. I want to thank you for your support in reading this book. You have no idea how much it means to me. If you completed this book, then I want to dare to ask you for one more thing. Leave a review. Whether you liked it or hated it, I want to hear about it. The best way to support this book or get your thoughts across about the story is to leave a review on a website like Goodreads or Amazon. I would love to hear from you!

Again, thank you so much for taking a chance on this book. There is so much more of this story to be told. Hopefully you can join me on this journey.

ACKNOWLEDGEMENTS

Publishing is a long process and a unique journey that I never imagined myself taking. When I was little, I wanted to be a mom more than anything. Along the way, I found writing. I realized that I loved building stories and creating characters and worlds.

However, this journey was not taken alone. I had so many family and friends help me. Professionals put time and effort into this work along with me. I don't know where to start in thanking people, but let me try.

To my husband: You were the person that saw the very first version of this book. You changed my perspective on writing. Your support was crucial at the early stages. I needed you to be there for me, and you were. You let me take a chance on publishing this book and it has paid off. Please know that I love you and I am thrilled to have you by my side for any other books in the future.

To my mom: I cannot thank you enough. You helped me grow up and learn to reach for my dreams. Dad taught me about hard work and you taught me how to find the happy things in life. Thank you for holding my hand when I needed it and pushing me forward when I needed that.

To my family: You guys are the best. All of you were so helpful in giving me feedback on the story and making sure that I knew I had talent. I leaned on you so much growing up and as I learned more about myself. You were always there when I needed you, and publishing this book was no different. I appreciate your help, support, bolstering, and never-ending love.

To Sam Ryals: I don't know where to begin with you. You came into my life and turned everything around. You made college an amazing experience. You have been a huge source of support in every part of my life, but especially with this book. Your opinion mattered to me and you were willing to read this story over and over again. Thank you for all your time and all your support. Before I met you, I didn't know how much I needed you in my life. Thank you for being you.

To Suzanne Johnson and my other editors: Thank you for all the editing work you did on this book. Your insights and direction were so helpful. I appreciate what you've done for me and everything I've learned from you in the publishing process. Without you, this book would not be anywhere close to the marvelous level that it is now. Thank you so much.

To Sarah Hansen: The cover you designed was beautiful. Truly amazing. You took all my thoughts and ideas and captured what I wanted for this story. Thank you for everything you did to make my book a reality.

To my betareaders: Sharing my story to begin with was incredibly hard. I was nervous beyond belief and you guys made me realize that publishing this book could be real. You were the start of everything. Thank you.

ABOUT THE AUTHOR

Angie Day found her love of writing while in college where she studied psychology and eventually went on to a master's degree. She noticed the need for romantic and fantastic adult stories that were still wholesome and clean. So, she took matters into her own hands with her debut series. When she's not devouring the next book, she is spending time outdoors with her husband.

To follow along with her journey, find her on social media or check out her website.

www.angiedayauthor.com
@angiedayauthor

DON'T MISS
THE NEXT BOOK IN THE
LEGENDS & SHADOWS SAGA

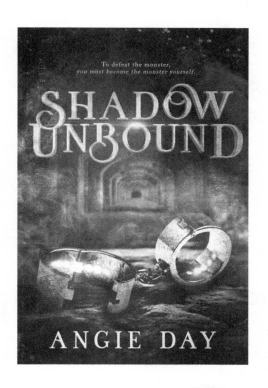